FINDING LEXIE

SEAL Team Hawaii, Book 2

SUSAN STOKER

CHAPTER ONE

Pierce "Midas" Cagle crept along the vast desert, all his attention on his targets. He and his SEAL team had been dropped by helicopter about three miles back, well away from where two hostages were being held. Their objective was to rescue the American and Danish hostages and kill or capture the kidnappers.

This would've been a fairly routine mission for Midas and his team, except for one thing.

He knew one of the hostages.

Midas had gone to high school with Lexie Greene. He hadn't seen or talked to her in almost fifteen years, but that didn't mean he hadn't immediately remembered who she was when he'd read her name.

Lexie had begun attending his high school their senior year. Midas might not have exchanged more than two words with her except for the fact that they'd been paired together for an assignment in English class. She'd been funny, friendly, and smart. Much to Midas's surprise, since she'd normally kept to herself and rarely met anyone's eyes.

Midas, in contrast, had been outgoing and popular. He was the captain of the swim team and a state champion in the sport as well. And the ladies liked him, so he'd never had to work too hard to find someone to date.

After graduating, Midas had gone his own way, joining the Navy and becoming a SEAL, and he hadn't thought twice about the shy girl he'd once known. Until he'd read the report about the hostages in the Somali desert.

Since realizing Lexie was the girl he'd known in high school, Midas had almost obsessively watched the videos the kidnappers had taken of her and Dagmar Brander, an auditor for Food For All, the international aid organization Lexie also worked for.

She and Dagmar had been walking out of the Food For All building in Galkayo, a town near the border of Somalia and Ethiopia, when they were thrown in the back of a truck and driven into the desert.

That was three months ago, and the kidnappers were demanding ten million dollars for the safe return of Dag and Lexie. At first it had been five, but when the money had quickly been raised by Dagmar's brother, the kidnappers decided no—it was five million for *each* hostage.

Lexie and Dagmar had languished in the desert for months while negotiations continued.

But word had come down that Dagmar wasn't well. He had heart problems, and in the last video, Lexie begged that the money be paid, as she believed her boss had experienced a stroke.

After hearing that, the United States and Denmark had agreed it was time to act. The SEALs were moving in with a Danish Jaeger Corps team. They were Denmark's elite special forces, and their assistance was welcome.

Intel had said there were ten to fifteen men guarding the hostages in the desert, and satellite photos had given Midas and the other men the general layout of the crude camp. There were a few scraggy trees, which Lexie and Dagmar spent most of their time under. They didn't seem to be tied up or otherwise restrained...because honestly, where were they going to go? It was at least ten miles to any kind of outpost, and even farther to get back to Galkayo.

Midas looked over at Mustang, who was indicating that he and Aleck were going to head to the right. Nodding in agreement, Midas pointed to the left and then to Pid. Mustang gestured to Jag and Slate and swirled his finger in the air.

The command to spread out and surround the camp was their agreed upon plan. The Danish special forces would do the same, staying back a bit farther, making sure none of the kidnappers managed to slip by the SEALs.

For the first time in ages...maybe ever...Midas was nervous about a mission. He knew it was because of his personal connection to the hostage.

He was also curious about Lexie after reading her file. She'd been working for Food For All for the last fourteen years. She'd traveled all over the world, lived in a dozen different countries...and yet, she somehow still had an innocent look about her in the videos. What she must have seen in some of the poorest parts of the world apparently hadn't made her jaded or hard. Not like Midas felt his experiences had done to him.

It was ridiculous to think she was the exact same girl he'd known in high school, but still, looking at her photo in the report and seeing her on the videos the kidnappers had recorded, Midas had a feeling she hadn't changed much. The thought of her being hurt or killed in the next twenty minutes was abhorrent.

He also wondered if she'd remember him.

It wasn't likely.

Most of the time the people they rescued were strangers. Names on a piece of paper. Unfortunate men and women who'd gotten embroiled in dangerous situations, often through no fault of their own. But personally knowing a kidnapping victim was new for him. He'd been trained to focus on the job at hand and block everything else out. But he couldn't stop thinking about the Lexie he'd known years ago.

How she'd blushed shyly when he'd complimented her on having good ideas for their project.

How she used to scrunch up her nose when she was thinking extra hard.

How she'd stopped to help a boy pick up stuff he'd dropped in the hall one morning.

How Lexie had paid for a girl's lunch when she didn't have enough money, and then had to put back the sandwich she'd been planning on eating herself, since she was short the necessary cash.

The fact that Lexie worked for an international aid organization was proof that the kind girl he'd known was now a thoughtful and giving woman. And Midas wanted to make sure such a person lived to see another day.

His resolve hardening, he returned his attention back to the task at hand. Lexie and Dagmar had suffered enough. It was time to get them out of the desert and to safety.

* * *

Elizabeth Lexie Greene lay on her back under what she considered "her" tree and stared up at the stars. It was amazing how bright they were without any light pollution getting in the way. The desert was pitch dark when the moon wasn't full, like tonight. Their kidnappers had lanterns and flashlights, but it was late, and most of the men guarding them were asleep.

There was a fire over by the men's two trucks, but it had mostly burned down to embers. Dagmar snored lightly a few feet away, and Lexie turned to look in his direction. She couldn't see more than a vague outline of his body on the ground, but she was reassured by the fact she could hear him breathing.

More than once she'd thought that he might be dying. He'd most definitely had a stroke at some point, as his words were slurred now and his left side was weaker than it had been. She hadn't known the man very well before they were kidnapped. She'd been in Galkayo almost six months before Dagmar had arrived to do a review of processes and to make sure everything was running up to Food For All's standards.

She was fairly used to the inspections. After years of working for the organization, Lexie was well aware that the board regularly sent in auditors to review the various operations around the world. Dagmar had been there for just a week, and they were heading out to inspect one of the organization's gardens in a nearby neighborhood when they were snatched off the street.

It was the scariest thing Lexie had ever experienced. One second she was enthusiastically telling Dagmar about everything they'd done to help the locals and how well the garden was working out, and the next, she was thrown into the back of a truck and looking down the barrel of a rifle.

The first few weeks had been the worst. Trying to get used to living in the open desert, trying not to say or do anything that would get her beaten, and hoping against hope they'd be released.

But after hearing how much the kidnappers were asking for ransom, Lexie was slowly beginning to resign herself to the fact that it was likely she wouldn't make it out of the desert alive. Dagmar might be able to convince their captors to let him go. He had money. Lots of it. And his twin brother had been doing everything in his power to get him released.

But Lexie? She was expendable. She was one of thousands of Food For All employees. And she had no family to speak of. No one was going to pay five million dollars for her. No way in hell.

She was shocked when the original ransom amount had been raised within days by Dagmar's brother, but instead of letting them go, the kidnappers had gotten greedy. They'd changed the terms of their release, demanding five million for *each* of them—and declaring that neither would be freed until the entire ten million had been handed over. They'd obviously been confident that if five million could be raised so quickly, another five million would be easy.

They were wrong.

Lexie felt guilty as hell that she and Dag were both still in the desert after his brother had raised the original ransom. Especially considering Dagmar's health. He needed to see a doctor. Needed a hospital. And instead, they were lying on the hard, sandy ground with only a dying tree above their heads to protect them from the elements, praying something would happen to make their kidnappers finally set them free.

A noise in the distance caught Lexie's attention.

Normally, she wouldn't have thought twice about odd noises, but she'd been in the desert long enough to know what was ordinary and what wasn't. She lifted her head and stared in the direction where she thought the noise had come from, but because of the darkness, she couldn't see much of anything.

Then suddenly, all hell broke loose.

What seemed like dozens of men began yelling all at once. Telling everyone to stay down. To put their hands in the air.

She even heard someone calling out *her* name, telling her and Dagmar to stay where they were.

"Oh my God," she breathed.

It was hard to believe this was happening. She'd dreamed about being rescued just about every night since she'd been taken, but never actually thought it would happen. Since Dagmar was somewhat powerful in his country, her only hope had been that the Danish government might send someone to their aid.

But the voices she heard were definitely speaking English.

"What?" Dagmar asked, startled awake by all the commotion going on around them.

"Stay down!" Lexie whispered loudly, sidling over to where he was lying nearby. "I think we're being rescued!" she told him excitedly.

"Please, God, let it be true," Dagmar whispered.

Over the last three months, Dagmar had become more and more depressed. He wasn't used to roughing it in any way, shape, or form. And being sick hadn't helped. At first he'd been optimistic, sure they'd be released within days. But with each week that went by, his attitude had changed for the worse. Lexie could hardly be upset with him for becoming despondent; she'd had her share of bad days. And it wasn't his fault he'd been born rich, never having to struggle for anything in his life.

As their kidnappers awoke amid all the shouting, they didn't do as they were ordered. Instead of putting their hands up and surrendering, they immediately grabbed the automatic rifles they kept by their sides day and night. They fired indiscriminately into the darkness around the camp.

Lexie squealed and buried her head in her arms and tried to make herself as small as possible. The sound of gunfire was loud in the otherwise quiet desert, and all she could think about was how much it would hurt to be shot. She wanted to curl up into a ball, but figured it was better to stay flat.

The sound of gunshots echoed in the desert, sounding loud in the quiet of the night. The kidnappers were yelling at each other and trying to figure out who was shooting at them, and from where. Lexie's heart was beating a million miles an hour. She was terrified that at any second, one of the kidnappers would haul her or Dagmar up and use them as human shields to try to escape.

She couldn't tell the difference between the bad guys' and good guys' bullets, had no idea if she and Dag were about to be rescued or if their kidnappers would win the battle. If that happened, they wouldn't be happy about the ambush...would maybe even kill her and Dag.

She knew she was breathing too hard but couldn't calm herself. She kept her eyes squeezed shut as the sounds of gunfire slowly tapered off. She could hear men yelling to each other in English, and prayed that was a good sign.

"Lexie?" a voice called out.

Lexie slowly lifted her head. She winced as a beam of light nearly blinded her. She squeezed her eyes shut.

"Sorry," the deep voice said from much closer. "Are you all right?"

Lexie lifted her head once more but made no move to get up. She was so used to having to get permission to do anything, she didn't even consider sitting up or standing. Even when the person talking to her wasn't yelling and didn't sound pissed off.

She couldn't make out the features of the man standing above her, but she could see he was wearing a desert camouflage uniform. He had on a vest with all sorts of gadgets attached to it. Lexie's neck hurt from craning to look up at him, but again, she wasn't going to move until she was given permission.

"Lexie? Were you hit?"

That's right. He'd asked her a question. "No. I mean, I don't think so," she said softly.

"Can you sit up?" the man asked.

Lexie nodded, even though she wasn't sure she could. She'd never been as scared in her life as she'd been in the last few minutes. But not one to shy away from doing something difficult, Lexie did her best to shift so she was on her knees, sitting on her heels.

"How are they?" another man asked as he walked over to them.

"Lex is good. Not sure about Dagmar."

Dagmar!

Lexie quickly turned toward him and saw he was laboriously rolling onto his back and blinking rapidly. His right hand was massaging his left chest, which wasn't a good sign.

"Shit," the second man swore, then turned his head and whistled. Before she knew what was happening, three more men had approached their little tree and were crouching next to Dagmar. She could hear them talking to Dag in Danish... but he wasn't answering.

"Come on, Lex, let's get you out of the way," said the man who'd first approached her, reaching down and putting a hand under her elbow. She let him help her stand, leaning on him as he walked them a little bit away from where she'd been peacefully watching the stars a short time ago.

"Are you really all right?" the man asked.

Lexie glanced up—and realized for the first time how tall the man was. She'd never really felt all that short; at five-seven, she was a fairly average height for a woman, but this guy towered over her. "You're really tall," she blurted, and immediately scrunched her nose at her inane statement.

But the soldier merely chuckled. "I am. Six-four. It's a pain in the ass being tall when trying to sneak up on someone. I don't exactly blend into my surroundings."

Lexie wished she could see better. There was something about the man that seemed...familiar. But that was crazy. They were in the middle of an African desert. There was no way she knew this guy. "I don't know," she said. "No one in camp saw you or your friends until you yelled at them."

"True. It's good to see you again."

Lexie frowned. "I'm sorry, do we know each other?"

"Sorry. Yeah, we did at one time. I'm Pierce Cagle. We went to the same high school our senior year."

Lexie blinked in surprise. Talk about a blast from the past.

Even if it wasn't dark, and she wasn't in the middle of the desert, she didn't think she'd have recognized him. This wasn't the halls of their old high school, and he was the last person she'd ever expected to see again. Especially on the other side of the world.

"Midas!" one of the other men called out. "Chopper'll be here in five!"

The man in front of her gave his teammate a chin lift, then looked back down at her.

"You still go by that nickname?" she asked. There were so many things she should be asking right about now, but that was the question that popped out. She remembered the kids at school called him Midas because of all the gold medals he'd won when he was on the swim team.

He chuckled, actually looking a little sheepish. "Yeah. My mom thought she'd be funny and send me a package when I was in boot camp, addressed to me by my nickname. It stuck."

"Too bad there's no water around here for you to show off your swimming skills," Lexie mused inanely, then immediately regretted it. She was such a dork. Always had been.

But amazingly, Midas just grinned. "Got plenty of that back in Hawaii where I'm stationed."

"You're in Hawaii? Really? I've always wanted to live there," Lexie said.

Midas reached for her elbow again and pulled her out of the way of the three men who were carrying Dagmar.

"I can walk," he complained weakly.

"Yes, sir," someone said in a Danish accent. "But why walk when we can carry you just as easily?"

"Where are we going?" Dagmar asked.

"The best option would be to go straight to the ship waiting off the coast of Somalia," one of the other soldiers said. "But your brother paid for a doctor to be flown to Galkayo. He's been there for a month, waiting for you to be released. Your brother was adamant that you go to the hospital there as soon as you were rescued, to be checked over. Especially after he heard you weren't doing well."

"Perfect," Dagmar said. "Yes, that's better. I want to see my doctor. Not some stranger who doesn't know my history. I'm sure Magnus knew the moment I started feeling poorly. Twin connection and all..." he explained.

Lexie knew all about Magnus and Dagmar's connection. He'd talked about it several times over the last few months. She would've preferred to go straight to the ship, but then again, if she was as sick as Dag, and had someone who cared enough to send a doctor just in case she was released, she'd probably want to see them as well.

"Are you okay to walk?" Midas asked her.

Lexie nodded. "Yeah."

He stared at her for a long moment.

"What?" she asked.

He shrugged. "You're just really...calm."

"I'm not really," she countered. "Inside, I'm a mess. My legs feel like jelly and I'm having a hard time believing this is real. I've had dreams like this, you know. Where we were rescued. But I always woke up and was still here, under that tree, trying not to get fried to a crisp in the sun."

"It's real," he told her.

The whirring of a helicopter sounded in the distance, and Lexie turned to look in that direction, even though it was still dark out and she couldn't see much. She glanced back at Midas. "Are they all dead?"

He didn't pretend not to know what she was talking about. "Yes. We had hoped to capture at least one of them to interrogate, but that didn't happen."

Lexie swallowed hard. When she and Dag had first been taken, she'd tried to *not* hate their kidnappers. She remembered hearing one talk about his family...about his newborn daughter. And how another was the sole support for his elderly parents.

Her kidnappers were human, and many times circumstances drove people's actions. Poverty, hunger, and feeling hopeless were all too common in the places she'd lived over the years.

But as time went by, and especially after they'd doubled the ransom amount, she'd had more difficulty feeling even a small bit of empathy for the men. Desperate or not, nothing gave them the right to hold her and Dag against their will and terrorize them for months.

"It bothers you, doesn't it?" Midas asked.

Lexie shrugged and let Midas lead her away from the patch of sand she'd called home for the last few months and deeper into the desert. "They weren't exactly nice, but they didn't hurt me. Didn't rape me."

"They just held you against your will, belittled you, and made you feel as if you were worthless."

Lexie stumbled, but Midas made sure she didn't fall. "How did you know that?" she asked quietly.

"I know the type," Midas said dryly. "When they got the first five million, they could've let you both go. Instead, they got greedy. Probably told you that it was *your* fault you weren't already free. That if you were a better employee, if you were more important, the other five mil would've already been paid. Even made it seem as if it was your fault that *they* were greedy assholes who wanted more money."

Lexie kept her eyes on the ground as they walked across the sand, toward where she guessed the helicopter would be landing to pick them up.

Midas wasn't wrong. She'd been thrilled when the ransom was raised so quickly, had thought they'd be released. When they were informed that the price on their heads had increased, Dagmar had been *furious*. He'd lost his cool for the first time, lashing out, demanding that they let *him* go at least, since his family was the one who'd raised the five million.

Their captors just laughed at him.

And Lexie *had* felt terrible. Because he wasn't wrong. It was her fault he was still stuck in the desert.

"Don't," Midas said.

"Don't what?"

"Don't let them get into your head. It didn't matter where the money came from or how much it was. Once they got *anything* for their demands, it was only going to make them want more."

Lexie supposed that was true. But she still felt guilty.

"When the chopper arrives, close your eyes so sand doesn't get in them," Midas ordered.

"How will I be able to get to it if I can't see?" Lexie asked.

"I've got you."

The longing those three words invoked was immediate and intense...and surprising.

She'd always been a loner. Perfectly happy moving from place to place, country to country, all on her own. She didn't have close friends or family. Hadn't had a serious boyfriend in years. She liked being single. Liked being able to travel the world.

But after what she'd been through in the last three months, Lexie fully understood just *how* alone she was in the world. Her dad hadn't been the best father, and he was gone now. They'd moved around too much when she was growing up to build any close friendships. She hadn't gone to college, and the people she'd met through Food For All were great, but they were busy moving around and helping others, just like she was. And she was fine with that.

Therefore, over the years, she'd forgotten what it felt like to lean on someone.

Maybe she'd *never* known the feeling.

But those three words coming from Midas made her long to experience it.

"Lex?" he asked.

"Sorry, yeah, I heard you," she told him quickly, doing her

13

best to throw off her melancholy. As soon as she got a shower —and drank a dozen huge glasses of cold water—she'd feel more like herself. "But if I trip over sand, I'm gonna be mad at you."

Midas chuckled. "I seem to remember you being very even keeled. Have you ever been mad at someone in your life?"

Lexie was amazed all over again that this man remembered anything about her. He'd impressed her in high school. He was popular back then, but he hadn't been an asshole about it. He'd never looked down on other kids and he'd stuck up for them when they were being bullied. He was friendly...and had even mostly hid his disappointment when he'd been paired with her for a project.

She shrugged. "Being mad doesn't really help the situation."

"True."

It was shocking how one second they were standing in the dark desert, chatting about nothing in particular, and the next it was like they were engulfed in a wind tunnel. A helicopter appeared as if out of nowhere, its rotors sending sand flying in all directions.

Lexie immediately closed her eyes against the onslaught and couldn't help but lean into Midas. She felt his arm go around her back as she huddled closer to try to keep from being pummeled by the sharp grains of sand. She had no idea how he was able to see, but when she felt him move forward, she didn't hesitate to shuffle alongside him.

"Hold your hand up," Midas said loudly in her ear after a minute or so.

Keeping her eyes squeezed shut, Lexie did as he ordered. Immediately, she felt her hand being grabbed by someone else. Before she could adjust, she felt as if she were flying through the air—and then the sand was gone.

She squinted her eyes open and saw that she was inside the chopper, and Midas was climbing in behind her.

A man dressed exactly like Midas pointed to the other side of the helicopter, and Lexie immediately went to where he'd indicated. She slid to her butt and watched as Dagmar was loaded and half a dozen other soldiers climbed onboard.

Someone handed her a headset and she slipped it over her ears, sighing in relief at the immediate silence.

Midas came over to sit next to her, and he adjusted the mouthpiece closer to her lips. "Can you hear me?"

Lexie nodded.

He smiled at her. "Good."

She wanted to ask where they were going and what would happen next, but suddenly she was incredibly exhausted. The adrenaline that had coursed through her veins when the shooting had started was waning and she was finding it hard to keep her eyes open.

When Midas put his arm around her shoulders and tugged her closer, she went willingly. Her head landed on his shoulder and she sighed. She heard the soldiers talking to each other through the headphones. They were concerned about Dagmar's condition and were discussing the stop they were going to make in Galkayo.

But Lexie only vaguely listened. Once the door to the chopper closed and she felt the huge machine lift off, it was as if her body and mind completely shut down.

She was safe. Her kidnappers were dead. Nothing else mattered.

* * *

Abshir Farah watched from his hiding spot about a half mile away, teeming with frustration, as the two helicopters rose into the night sky. He'd left the camp to hunt at just the right moment. He knew without a doubt that his friends and comrades were dead. He'd heard the shots and came running to assist, but by the time he'd gotten close to camp, it was obvious the soldiers had already killed everyone.

They'd waited too long to get rid of their captives. They should've taken the five million dollars and released them. But instead, his comrades had insisted they could get more.

Anger filled Abshir. He *needed* that money. His family was starving. Living in filth. He'd been counting on the cash to get them out of the slums and into a proper home. His wife was pregnant with their sixth child, and there was no way he'd be able to feed one more person without that money.

But maybe there was still a chance to get their captives back...

The helicopters were headed toward Galkayo. If he was lucky—and he was obviously lucky, since he was still alive right now and not lying dead in the sand with his friends—they'd go back to where it all started.

He'd heard the rumors that the Danish man's family had flown in his personal doctor. There was only one hospital in town, and if they took him there, perhaps Abshir and some of the others could get him back. And this time, they'd take the five million dollars.

It was worth a shot.

Abshir knew time wasn't on his side. He needed to get to camp and see if one of the trucks was still working. He had no idea if the soldiers had disabled the vehicles or not. If possible, he would go back to town and tell the others what had happened. They'd want to avenge their friends, and his dead comrades' families wouldn't be happy that foreigners had come into their country and killed their loved ones.

Yes, with luck, they'd have both the man and woman back in their grasp, and this time they'd be smarter about their demands. Smarter about where they hid. Maybe they could beat on the woman a bit and see if they couldn't get the

American government to pony up some money for her as well as get the five mil for the man.

They had a second chance to salvage this operation, but Abshir had to work quickly. Spread the word about what had happened.

Deep down, he knew what he was doing was wrong. But his world was every man for himself. And Abshir needed money to feed his family. If that five million disappeared, they were all screwed.

CHAPTER TWO

Midas wasn't happy. He and his team had originally expected to fly to a US Navy ship stationed in the gulf, but they'd learned at the start of the mission that the Danish special forces team had been instructed to go to Galkayo and bring Dagmar to the hospital.

Apparently, Magnus Brander had enough money for the government to give in to his demands to take his brother back to the town he'd been kidnapped from, so he could see his personal physician. Then, and only then, would he consent for Dagmar to be flown elsewhere...with his doctor in tow, of course.

On the helicopter, he and his team briefly discussed taking Lexie to the US ship and leaving Dagmar in the care of his own countrymen, but Lexie had become visibly upset for the first time upon hearing that plan. In light of all that she'd had been through, and because they were worried about her mental health just as much as they were her physical well-being, Mustang decided they'd continue with the previously altered plan to accompany the Danish soldiers, and Dagmar, to the hospital.

Dagmar's physician would be allowed to do a short exam,

Lexie could be seen by a doctor at the same time, then they'd get the hell out of there. It would still be difficult for Lexie to say goodbye to the man she'd been held captive with for months, but hopefully after she'd had a little more time to process that they were safe at last, she'd be a bit calmer about leaving.

The situation wasn't ideal, but the SEALs were used to having to pivot at the last minute. Besides, Dagmar *did* need immediate medical assistance.

The decision made, Lexie had quickly passed out against his shoulder, and no matter how loud the others spoke through the headset, she didn't seem to flinch.

He marveled that she looked the same as she had in high school. Well, not exactly. She'd matured, of course, but she had the same curly brown hair that seemed to have a mind of its own. Even now, dirty from months in the desert, the strands seemed to be alive, curling around some of the equipment hanging on his vest. She'd used a piece of twine she'd probably found out in the desert to hold back the shoulder-length locks, but it wasn't enough to completely tame it.

Midas remembered being fascinated with her hair back in high school, when they were working on their English project. She was constantly shoving it back behind her ears, but inevitably it would fall forward again, annoying her. Back then, she'd smelled like peaches, and he had no idea if it was her shampoo or lotion or what, but he'd associated the sweet fruit with her for months after he'd last seen her. She didn't smell like peaches now, of course, but that didn't mean his brain didn't recall the memory.

Her hazel eyes were just as he remembered, as well. They'd had an uncanny way of somehow seeing through his bullshit. There was one day when he'd been upset over something—he didn't remember what—and when she'd asked how he was doing, he'd lied and said he was fine. She'd studied him silently, then gently pushed for him to confide in her.

SUSAN STOKER

Aside from his parents, she may have been the *only* person in his youth who'd ever bothered to see beyond the cheerful jock he'd always tried to project.

She was about half a foot shorter than he was, and even though Midas hated to admit it, he hadn't missed the way she'd filled out since high school. Even after being in the desert for months, she was still curvy in all the right places. He hadn't been able to take his gaze off her ass as she'd climbed into the chopper. He felt like a total dick for ogling her in the middle of an op, though it didn't diminish his appreciation.

But more than her hair or her looks, Midas was impressed with her attitude. Over the years, he'd observed just about every kind of reaction from the people they'd rescued. Some were scared to death, others were hysterical and couldn't be calmed down, and then there were the hostages who were pissed that they hadn't been rescued faster. But Lexie fell into a category all her own. She'd stayed calm. Was obviously scared but hadn't let it paralyze her. She was worried about Dagmar, and smart enough to let the SEALs do their job.

It was safe to say Midas was intrigued. Lexie Greene had grown up to be what seemed like an amazing woman.

She shifted against him, and Midas tightened his grip on her as the chopper began to slow. They'd have to land a bit outside the town. Aleck and Pid, along with two of the Danish soldiers, would secure transportation while the rest of the group stayed with the helicopter and the freed hostages.

The situation wasn't ideal, to say the least. The sun was rising, which meant the residents would be waking up. While this part of the country wasn't as openly hostile toward Western soldiers, no one wanted to push their luck. Hence the reluctance to return to the town.

"Has anyone notified my physician that I'm here?" Dagmar asked as the chopper lowered toward the ground.

Midas frowned slightly. The man had remained awake

throughout the flight, talking about what he'd endured in the desert. Not once had he asked about Lexie. Or if anyone had been hurt in the extraction.

He wasn't overly impressed with Dagmar so far, sick or not.

"We'll do that when we land," Slate reassured him in a curt tone.

It seemed as if his teammates shared Midas's thoughts on the man.

"She okay?" Jag asked, motioning to Lexie with his head. She was deadweight against Midas, which didn't bother him in the least. He wondered when she'd last had a good night's sleep. He bet it was before she was taken.

Midas nodded, not wanting to say much through the headphones with everyone listening.

It wasn't until the chopper jolted as it landed that Lexie stirred. She lifted her head and looked around in confusion. Midas helped her remove the headphones after he and everyone else did the same.

He watched as she recalled where she was and what had happened. She turned and met his gaze, wrinkled her nose in apology. "Sorry I fell asleep on you," she said in a low, husky voice.

A strand of her hair had become tangled in the webbing of his vest, and Midas reached up to free it at the same time Lexie did. Their fingers brushed against each other...and what felt like a jolt of electricity shot up Midas's arm.

It was obvious she'd felt something similar, as her eyes widened and she immediately dropped her hand. "Sorry," she said again.

"Nothing to be sorry about," he told her. "I seem to remember your hair having a mind of its own in school too."

She huffed out a laugh. "I've seriously thought about cutting it all off a time or two. It's a pain in my ass."

Midas looked at her in horror.

She rolled her eyes at his reaction. "It's just hair. It would grow back. Besides, right now, it's gross. If I'd had the chance, I would've chopped it off out in the desert."

Midas knew that probably would've made her feel better physically, and maybe mentally too, but he couldn't help but be relieved she hadn't done it.

"Stay alert," Aleck warned everyone as he and Pid jumped out of the chopper. "We haven't had a chance to take the temperature of the town. We'll be back as soon as possible."

"Take the temperature?" Lexie asked as she looked at Midas.

"See how the citizens feel about Westerners," Jag answered.

Lexie glanced his way and nodded. "I think, like in a lot of places, there are those who hate all things American and Western, but for the most part, I've found people here are gracious and welcoming."

Midas smiled, as did his friends. They might be gracious and welcoming to someone like her, someone who was there to provide assistance and who was as nonthreatening as she was. But it was a whole different thing when it came to soldiers.

"Let's hope that's true," Mustang muttered.

"You don't believe me," Lexie responded, sitting up straighter.

"It's not that we don't believe you," Mustang said. "But you *were* kidnapped here. Those rose-colored glasses of yours might make it difficult for you to see the people who aren't pleased to have Westerners in their town."

"I'm not an idiot," Lexie said in a controlled tone, while still somehow conveying her irritation. "There are assholes everywhere. All you have to do is look at the news to see that. Back home, people are also killing each other. Abusing children. Holding people for ransom. Somalia, and Africa in general, isn't any more dangerous than walking down the street in some of the neighborhoods where I grew up."

Midas couldn't help but agree. She had a point. A damn good one.

Mustang nodded. "Right."

"Seriously," she insisted. "I've met some of the most generous people here. Families who have nothing, but still offer to share the last scoop of beans in their pantry. They're a proud people, and I think all they want is to be treated with respect and to live a comfortable life. Not an extravagant one, but a life where they aren't constantly worried about where their next meal is coming from."

Midas remembered Lexie as being a bit submissive. She'd always been quiet, never really said much. But listening to her defend the people she'd met in Galkayo made him see her in another light. She was clearly passionate, and she stood up for what she thought was right. She'd definitely found something that she loved to do, and it showed.

She reminded him of a mama bear defending her cubs. It was impressive.

"Easy, I wasn't trying to offend you or the Somali people," Mustang said with a smile.

Midas felt her muscles relax. "Sorry," she said with another adorable scrunch of her nose. "I'm protective of the people I work with. Just because someone doesn't have much money doesn't make them less worthy or a threat."

"We're trained to see everyone as a threat," Jag commented.

Lexie faced him. "That's kind of sad," she said quietly.

It was. But it had kept them alive, so Midas didn't mind. He knew he was somewhat jaded. He didn't trust easily, except for the men on his team. He tended to see trouble around every corner. In contrast, Lexie was the opposite. She trusted first, and probably found out the hard way when someone wasn't as genuine as they appeared.

It made him want to protect her from all the assholes in the world.

Which was ridiculous, as she was a mission. Nothing more.

Sure, things had worked out for Mustang and Elodie—a woman his teammate had fallen for on a previous mission—but that had been a fluke. A miracle. Once Dagmar saw his physician and they made it to the Navy ship safely, he'd never see Lexie again. She intrigued him, but in a few hours, she'd be just a memory once again.

The wait for Aleck, Pid, and the Jaeger Corps members seemed to take forever. By the time they returned, the sun was creeping higher in the sky and the heat was starting to make the inside of the chopper uncomfortable.

The fact that they'd been rescued seemed to finally be sinking in for Lexie. She didn't seem as shell-shocked as she had earlier. And the panic she'd felt when she'd learned she and Dag might be separated seemed to have dissipated. Though it was obvious Dagmar wasn't doing well, and she continued to watch him, a worried expression on her face.

The rumble of two trucks arriving was a welcome sound, and Midas helped to get Dagmar ready for transporting. Lexie hung back, not getting in the way and pitching in where she could.

When they'd gotten Dagmar settled in the back of a truck, Midas motioned to Lexie.

She immediately came toward him.

"Sit there," he told her, indicating a spot in the back of the truck, away from the tailgate.

Without complaint, she climbed up and scooted down the bench-style seats until she was tucked into a back corner. Nodding in satisfaction, Midas turned to Mustang—only to find his friend smirking at him.

"What?" he asked quietly before following Lexie inside.

"Nothing. Just noticing that you've got her completely protected, don't you?"

"Don't start with me," Midas grumbled.

"What?" Mustang echoed not so innocently.

Deciding to ignore his friend's teasing, Midas hopped into the back of the truck and sat close to Lexie. Putting her in the back made sense. He and Mustang would be between her and the tailgate...and anyone who might want to hurt them.

Driving through town had him on high alert. None of them would ever forget what happened in Mogadishu. And while Galkayo wasn't nearly as big as the capital city, he'd never forgive himself if Lexie had been saved from a kidnapping, only to be killed after returning to the town she seemed to love.

Midas kept his eyes peeled for trouble as the trucks rumbled toward the hospital. It was a two-story concrete building in the middle of Galkayo. There was no emergency room, per se, just a large open space that was already packed with people. Slate and Jag carried the gurney holding Dagmar, and they were immediately led down a hall to a private room.

Midas gestured for Lexie to follow him, but she shook her head and walked toward the check-in desk instead.

"What are you doing?" he asked, coming up behind her.

"I'm not going to come in here and butt in front of all these people," she protested.

"Lexie, you were kidnapped," Midas said in exasperation. "You're dehydrated, filthy, and need to be seen *now*, not a few hours from now."

She straightened her shoulders and, once again, her nose wrinkled before she spoke. "And everyone else has been waiting for who knows how long. I'm okay, Midas. Yeah, I'm thirsty and would kill for a shower, but that doesn't mean my needs are more important than anyone else's."

"We're going to leave as soon as Dagmar gets looked at and you've had a chance to say goodbye," Midas said. "And since we're here, you're going to at least get a cursory exam before we leave."

"I think we both know that Dagmar isn't doing well. He might even need surgery. I don't know if that's possible here, but he's not going to be leaving in the next hour," Lexie insisted. "We've got time."

Midas sighed. She was right, but that didn't mean he liked it. "Have you always been this stubborn?" he asked.

She smiled then, and it literally lit up her face. "No. I think you bring it out in me."

Midas chuckled. She was lying through her teeth, and they both knew it. "Fine. Put your name on the list. But I'm sticking by your side until we leave."

Her smile turned into a frown. "Why?"

"Why what?"

"I'm perfectly fine here," she said. "Look at all the people around. No one's gonna come in, grab me, and drag me out."

"You're right, they aren't," Midas told her. "Because I'll be next to you the whole time, making sure of it."

Lexie stared up at him for a long moment before finally nodding. "Okay."

"Okay," Midas echoed.

She got herself on the list and explained why she was there. As expected, the lady said the wait would be lengthy because of the number of people ahead of her. But Lexie merely nodded.

They headed to a corner with two empty seats and she settled into the uncomfortable chair without complaint. The woman sitting next to her had a toddler, and Lexie immediately turned to the little boy and began to engage him in conversation.

Midas watched her with a mixture of surprise and awe. The woman had just been rescued from a damn kidnapping and here she was, sitting in a crowded waiting room, playing with a kid. She was the most genuine and exasperating woman he'd ever met. She should be demanding something to eat and drink. Insisting that she be seen so she could change clothes and shower. But instead, she seemed perfectly content to put everyone else first.

Her naivete was a bit worrisome. It was charming at times, but more importantly, it was dangerous to her safety.

An hour later, Midas was done.

He could see Lexie's energy was fading, even though she was doing her best to pretend she was fine. When Pid walked through the lobby on one of his rounds, Midas motioned to him to get Lexie seen. He didn't care if that meant they pushed ahead of the others waiting.

Twenty minutes later, Lexie's name was called and Midas helped her stand. She wobbled a bit, and he scowled.

"I'm fine," she said. "I just moved too fast."

He didn't bother to respond. They both knew that wasn't the case. She was at the end of her rope, and he was done pretending everything was fine when it wasn't.

He kept a steadying hand on her arm as they made their way through the waiting room toward the hallway where Dagmar had disappeared a while ago. Midas hadn't heard anything about the other man's condition, but he knew his teammates were keeping on top of the situation. Mustang and one of the Jaeger Corps were keeping their eyes on him, while the other men on both teams patrolled the area and the hospital for trouble.

A nurse led them to a stairwell, and Midas heard Lexie groan under her breath. He wanted to pick her up and carry her but had a feeling that would only cause her embarrassment. So he shifted his grip so his arm was around her waist and did his best to support her as much as possible as they climbed up the one flight to the second floor. The nurse ushered them into a small room halfway down a hallway.

The woman did her best to hide her distaste, but it came through loud and clear when she said, "There's a small shower in the bathroom, if you want to get clean. There's also tooth-brushes and toothpaste in there."

Lexie didn't take offense. In fact, she seemed to perk up a bit. "Oh my God, brushing my teeth sounds awesome! And I'd love a shower. Oh, but I don't have anything to put on afterward."

The nurse looked Lexie up and down and said, "I'll grab a pair of scrubs for you."

"Thank you so much."

The nurse left, and Lexie turned to Midas with a huge smile on her face. "Oh my God, I'm so excited!"

Midas could see that she truly was. It took so little to make this woman happy.

The nurse returned with a pair of scrubs and a bag of saline, obviously anticipating the doctor's orders. She handed the clothes to Lexie and put the IV fluids on the counter nearby. "Take your time," she said. "It might be a bit until the doctor can see you." Then she turned and left.

Midas wanted to demand that the doctor make Lexie a priority, but he knew she'd be upset if he fussed. At least she was in a room now. It was something.

Lexie gave him a small smile and gestured to the bath-room. "I'll just go and...you know. You don't have to wait in here for me. I'm sure you have some sort of," she gestured with her arm, "super-soldier thing to do."

Midas chuckled. "Super-soldier thing?"

Lexie shrugged. "Yeah."

"I already told you, I'll be sticking by your side until we're safely on that ship."

"No one's gonna come in here and grab me," she protested.

"You're right. Because as I told you before, I'm going to be here, making sure."

"Fine. But if I sing off-key while in the shower, I don't want to hear any comments." Then she spun and headed for the tiny bathroom. Midas had caught a glimpse of it when he'd entered the room. The shower wasn't much more than a spigot coming out of the wall. No stall. No curtain. But he supposed Lexie wouldn't care. A shower was a shower.

While she was busy getting clean, Midas checked in with his team. Aleck reported that they were still waiting for test results on Dagmar and things looked normal around the hospital.

Relieved, Midas paced the room, trying to work out some of his nervous energy. The op in the desert had gone off without a hitch. They'd extracted the hostages and, other than making the unplanned stop back in town, everything was going smoothly.

He didn't know why he couldn't shake his uneasy feeling.

Twenty minutes later, and about ten minutes before he thought he'd see her, Lexie opened the door to the bathroom. Her hair was wet, but still just as curly as when it had been dry. The scrubs she wore were a bit big on her, but she still looked one hundred percent better now that she was clean.

"I needed that," she admitted.

"It's amazing how a long hot shower can make you feel better," Midas said, doing his best to vanquish abrupt thoughts of Lexie naked in the shower. They were wrong as hell and completely inappropriate. He was on a mission; he needed to remember that.

"Hot?" she echoed, scrunching her nose.

Midas winced. "Cold, huh?"

"Yeah, but honestly, it didn't matter. I've never been so happy to see toothpaste and soap in my life. My hair'll need actual shampoo to make it manageable, but I'm thrilled with what I got."

"Come on. Come sit," Midas said.

Lexie sat on the examination table in the middle of the room and sighed in relief.

"Lie down," Midas ordered.

As proof of how tired she was, Lexie didn't protest. She did as ordered and shifted until she was lying on the padded table. There was no pillow, but that didn't seem to faze her.

Looking around, Midas made a split-second decision. He might get in trouble for it, but fuck it. Lexie had waited long enough. He rummaged through some drawers until he found what he needed.

He ripped open an antiseptic pad and reached for Lexie's arm.

"What are you doing?" she asked, pulling her arm back and holding it against her belly.

"Starting an IV," Midas said without hesitation.

"But...you aren't a doctor," Lexie protested.

Midas couldn't stop the chuckle from rumbling up his throat. "I'm a SEAL," he countered. "I can put in an IV without too much issue."

"I don't want you to get in trouble."

Midas merely shook his head. He wanted to get this done, but he needed her acquiescence. He looked her in the eyes and said, "Do you trust me?"

Something inside him sparked to life when she didn't even hesitate before saying, "Yes."

"You're dehydrated, Lex. You need fluids. The one bottle of water you drank while we were waiting isn't enough. An IV will be quicker and will make you feel better in no time. Hopefully Dagmar's doctor will finish up quickly and we can get you both back on the chopper and out to the Navy ship. But until we know what Dagmar's condition is, we have no idea what the next few hours will bring. Let me help you."

She bit on her lower lip for a moment before she nodded. "Okay."

Midas studied her. "You have a hard time accepting help," he said matter-of-factly.

"I like being the helper, not the helpee," she said with a shrug. "Besides, I let you rescue me from the desert, didn't I?"

Midas laughed. "True. Come on, hold out your arm."

She did, and he vaguely noted that Lexie didn't look away as he prepped her arm for the needle.

"Not squeamish?" he asked.

"No. I've seen more than my fair share of grotesque things."

"Like?" Midas asked, wanting to keep her talking. He wasn't sure how difficult it would be to get the IV started. If she was too dehydrated, it might be tough to find a vein.

"Kids with wounds that had maggots in them. Babies with bellies so distended from starvation it looked as if they'd just swallowed a cantaloupe. Women who'd been beaten by their husband so badly, their eyes swelled shut. Men whose feet were so blistered they were covered in blood and pus...and yet they still put on ill-fitting shoes and walked ten miles to try to find work so they could get money for their family."

Her words were unemotional and flat, but Midas had a feeling that was a protective mechanism.

Thankfully, the needle slid into place in her arm without difficulty and, after he'd hooked up the saline and hung it on a pole by the bed, he sat on the edge by her hip.

Lexie looked down at her arm, up at the bag of saline, then into his eyes. "Wow, that was impressive."

"Told you I knew how to put in an IV," he said a little smugly.

"So you did."

"Still so calm," he said, shaking his head.

Lexie shrugged, and Midas put a hand beside her opposite hip and leaned a bit closer. She didn't take her gaze from his.

"I can't figure you out," he said quietly. "I have so many questions. And I also can't help but want to know all your secrets, and figure out what's going on behind those beautiful hazel eyes of yours."

CHAPTER THREE

Lexie blinked as she stared up at Midas. He really didn't want to know what she was thinking right about how. He'd probably be appalled. Or at the very least, shocked to know that she was wondering if his lips tasted as good as they looked.

It was incredibly inappropriate. But Lexie had just made it through three nightmarish months as a hostage. She was allowed to have a few improper thoughts.

Pierce Cagle had always been good-looking. Tall, broad shoulders, slender, funny, great smile, and a good personality to match. When she'd met him in high school, it was so obvious he was out of her league. She was the new kid who'd faded into the woodwork. He was Midas, the golden child of the pool and their entire school. She'd never heard anyone say anything bad about him. He'd even still been friendly with his few ex-girlfriends.

When she'd been assigned to work with him on an English project, she'd been scared to death. But in the end, those couple of weeks had been enough for her to develop an intense crush. Of course, she hadn't done anything about it, and he wouldn't have given her a second glance. But even after they'd graduated, and she'd taken her first assignment with Food For All, she'd thought about him now and then. Wondered where he was and what he'd done with his life.

Then, out of the blue, he was back.

It was an odd thing, to have a man you used to know and crush on show up to rescue you...and to find out he was still just as amazing as you'd thought he was a decade and a half ago.

And he wanted to know *her* secrets? She had none.

She couldn't help but glance down at his left hand, which was resting on his thigh. No ring. But then again, that didn't mean much, as she supposed even if he was married, he wouldn't wear a ring while on a mission.

"What?" he asked.

Damn. He was too observant. She remembered that about him too.

"Nothing."

"Lex...what?" he insisted, leaning even closer.

"I just was wondering if you were married."

He looked surprised at the question. "No. I'm not."

"Oh." Lexie wasn't sure what else to say. The man leaning over her had definitely changed *physically* since high school. He was more muscular. Not as lean. It was hard to tell exactly, while he was wearing his uniform and all that gear strapped to his chest, but it looked like he still had the same broad shoulders he'd had back in the day, though his thighs and butt had filled out.

And yes, she'd noticed. How could she not? She wasn't dead, and Midas was a hell of a good-looking man.

When he chuckled, her gaze whipped back up to his.

Shit, had she been staring at his legs? Or worse, *between* his legs?

Knowing she was probably turning bright red, Lexie did her best to hide her embarrassment. "Right, okay... I was just...um...wondering if this detour would make someone wonder when you'd be back home or something."

Lexie had no idea what she was saying, but she had to at least try to explain why she was checking him out and wanting to know if he was married.

"When we go on missions, we can't talk about where we're going or how long we'll be gone," Midas said. "National security and all that."

"That makes sense. Although I'd think that would be hard on you."

"Hard on *me*?" Midas asked, his brows furrowing. "Don't you mean hard on my nonexistent wife?"

"Well, sure. I mean, it would suck not knowing where you were or what you were doing, but I can imagine that it would be just as stressful on you. Wondering what your *wife* was doing, if she was all right, if the toilet was overflowing, if the yard was being mowed...you know, that sort of thing..." Her voice trailed off at the end and she felt stupid. "Never mind. I'm obviously delirious."

Midas shook his head. Had he leaned even closer?

He had. Holy shit. It took everything in her not to reach up and pull his head down to hers. She wasn't normally a very sexual person, but now that she was safe, clean, and feeling much better, she couldn't seem to help her crazy thoughts.

"Mustang is married," he said softly.

"He is?"

"Yeah. He met Elodie on a mission. Not too far from here, actually. She was on a cargo ship that was taken over by pirates."

"Oh my!" Lexie exclaimed. "She's okay?"

"Yeah. Anyway, she ended up in Hawaii and they started dating. Some other shit happened, but they're good. They got married...and you're right, Mustang *does* worry about her. I think it's just part of who we are. We solve problems. We know too much of the dark side of life, and knowing he isn't there if something goes wrong eats at him. Elodie can take care of herself, and she's got people who look out for her when we aren't there, but it's not the same."

"Elodie. That's an unusual name."

Midas nodded, but Lexie saw his gaze flick down to her lips, and she couldn't help but lick them.

He leaned even closer, and just when Lexie was sure he was going to kiss her, the door opened and a dark-skinned man wearing a long white coat entered the small exam room.

Midas stood and backed away from the table, but he didn't go too far. He stayed near her feet, as if ready to protect her if the doctor did anything he didn't like. Lexie wanted to protest, to tell him he was being ridiculous, but after being on her own for what seemed like her entire life, she couldn't deny she liked having him there.

"It is so good to see you, Lexie Greene," the doctor said with a smile. "All of us here at the hospital have been worried about you."

"Thank you," Lexie told him, overwhelmed.

"When you were taken, we feared for you," the doctor went on. "We were not sure you'd return."

Lexie scrunched her nose and nodded. "Me either."

The doctor glanced at Midas, then looked back at her. "Somalis are good people. Not all of us want to harm Westerners."

"I know," she told him. "I've been here long enough to see that for myself."

The doctor nodded, then said, "You look good. Better than your friend."

"How is he? I was afraid he'd had a stroke. He started slurring his words and he seemed weak on his left side," Lexie said.

The doctor nodded, but said, "I am sorry, I cannot offer particular details about other patients."

"I understand," Lexie said immediately.

The doctor glanced at Midas once more. "I need to examine my patient," he said.

Midas crossed his arms over his chest. "I'm not leaving. My mission is to return Miss Greene safe and sound, and I'm not letting her out of my sight until I complete that mission."

Lexie's heart dropped just slightly at the knowledge that she was just his "mission." It was a good reminder, though, that Midas was doing a job. He hadn't come to Africa because of her specifically, but because he'd been ordered to.

She was suddenly very glad she hadn't completely embarrassed herself by kissing him. God, that would've been mortifying.

"Lexie?" the doctor asked. "Does he have your permission to stay?"

She nodded. "Yes."

"I'm assuming this is your handiwork?" the doctor asked, picking up Lexie's arm to study the IV line Midas had inserted.

"Yes."

The doctor examined the needle and nodded. "It looks good." Then he continued his examination, asking about what had happened when she was in captivity and how she felt.

Lexie wasn't embarrassed to answer his questions. She hadn't done anything wrong, and while she hadn't enjoyed what had happened to her, she knew things could've been a lot worse.

After twenty minutes of poking and prodding and questions, the doctor stepped back. "You're dehydrated, sunburned, and you've got sand flea bites all over, but I suspect none of that is a surprise. I don't see anything that is immediately life threatening, but I recommend you check with a doctor when you get back to the United States and have a full blood panel done. While you look good, and were very lucky, you could still have underlying issues that aren't obvious from a physical exam. You're sure you weren't sexually assaulted?"

Lexie shook her head. "I wasn't."

She saw the doctor's gaze flick to Midas once more, before he met her eyes again. "I can have a female nurse come in to talk to you if you prefer."

"Honestly, they didn't touch me like that. I swear."

The doctor still looked skeptical, but nodded. "All right."

"How much longer do you think Dagmar Brander will be here?" Midas asked.

"I am not sure. His physician insisted on bloodwork and our lab is working on analyzing that now. He...he is a very sick man."

Midas nodded. "Can Lexie stay here until he's discharged?"

"Of course," the doctor said. "She needs fluids. I'll have another bag brought in for when that one is gone."

Lexie supposed she should be irritated that Midas and the doctor were talking over her and not to her, but she was so exhausted, she couldn't keep her eyes open. The examination table was the most comfortable thing she'd lain on in months and the air conditioning in the building felt heavenly.

She jerked when a hand landed on her shoulder and her eyes popped open.

"I apologize. I did not mean to startle you," the doctor said. "The best thing you can do is rest. I hope what happened doesn't turn you off from our country forever."

"No," Lexie answered. "I definitely want to come back someday."

The older man smiled at her, shook Midas's hand, then turned and left the small room.

Lexie expected to feel awkward, being alone again with Midas after all the questions the doctor had asked about her health, but she was just too tired to work up the energy to be embarrassed.

"Close your eyes," Midas said gently.

"That would be rude," Lexie said, but her eyes shut anyway.

He chuckled. "It's fine. I'm gonna go check with my team, but I'll be back."

"Thought you weren't going to leave my side," Lexie mumbled.

She heard Midas snort out a laugh. "I won't be gone more than a few minutes. I'm going to ask one of the nurses to step in here while I'm gone. Besides, you're gonna be out of it in thirty seconds."

"Am not," she protested weakly, not even sure why she was disagreeing with him.

She thought she felt a hand brush against her hair, but decided she must be delirious. Why would Midas be touching her so gently? She was a stranger to him...even if they had known each other once upon a time.

"Sleep, Lex. When Dagmar gets the okay to leave, we're gonna have another loud, uncomfortable helicopter trip to the Navy ship."

Lexie nodded, and was just on the verge of losing consciousness when her eyes popped open.

She was surprised to see Midas standing very close to the edge of the bed, staring down at her. She thought he'd left, or at least would've been halfway out the door. "Midas?"

"Yeah, Lex?"

"If things get crazy later and I forget...thanks for finding me. I mean, I know it's your job and everything, but still. Thanks."

"This has been one of the most enlightening missions I've been on in a very long time," he said enigmatically. "I'll be back soon. You'll feel better once all that fluid is in you."

Lexie nodded. She wanted to ask him why rescuing hostages was enlightening. She'd assumed that, as a SEAL, he did this kind of thing all the time.

Too tired to think about it any longer, Lexie closed her eyes and slept.

CHAPTER FOUR

Midas forced himself to walk out of Lexie's room and down the hall. The woman had him tied in knots for reasons he couldn't begin to understand. She was shy, generous, funny, and so damn trusting it was almost scary. He had no idea how she wasn't jaded and disillusioned from working in some of the poorest areas of the world.

It wasn't until she was talking to the doctor that he fully realized she didn't really blame her kidnappers for holding her hostage. She honestly believed they were simply desperate men doing desperate things for money.

Midas shook his head in disbelief. Lexie held little or no ill will toward the men who would've killed her without a second thought if he and his team, and the Danish special forces soldiers, hadn't surprised them.

But he couldn't deny that her...*goodness*, called to him on a level he hadn't experienced before. He knew next to nothing about the woman Lexie had become; hell, he didn't know much about the teenager she'd been all those years ago. But that didn't seem to matter. She intrigued him, and he was feeling extra protective of her.

Midas ran into Slate in the hall on the first floor and got

an update on Dagmar. As Lexie's doctor had said, he wasn't doing well. He was hanging in there, but seemed to be getting weaker and weaker rather than stronger, now that he was finally getting medical attention.

"We shouldn't stay here too long," Midas warned.

"I know. I want to be gone yesterday," Slate agreed. "And so does Mustang. He's been talking to the doctors about when we can move him. He needs advanced cardio care, which he won't get here. So the longer we linger, the more damage could be done to his heart."

"What's the holdup then?"

"His brother is working on chartering a jet to fly him straight back to Denmark. But apparently there's a lot of red tape involved, not to mention the question of whether Dagmar is strong enough to even make the flight."

"That's a good thing, though, right?" Midas asked. "The brother obviously has enough money to get Dagmar home sooner rather than later."

Slate shrugged. "I think so, but so far the doctors haven't agreed to release him. And we've been asked to help the Jaeger Corps provide security from here to the airport. It wouldn't do for him to get kidnapped again right when he's about to fly out of here. So until the doctors, Dagmar's brother, and the Danish government figure out their next steps, we're in a holding pattern. And you know how much I love *that*. How's Lexie?"

Midas wasn't thrilled about waiting around any longer than they had to, but he couldn't deny he was relieved Lexie was getting some much needed medical attention. "Good. Dehydrated, but overall she was lucky. She's sleeping upstairs while we're waiting on our next move."

"You okay?" Slate asked.

"Yeah, why?"

"You just seemed...extraordinarily concerned about Lexie."

"I know her," he admitted.

"*What?*"

"I know her. We went to high school together."

"Why didn't you say anything before?" Slate asked, flabbergasted.

"It wouldn't have changed anything. I mean, I haven't seen her since graduation. It's not like we were friends or anything." Midas did his best to keep his words nonchalant. But he should've known his teammate would pick up on his conflicted feelings.

"But there's something there, isn't there? It's why you insisted on being the one to watch over her while we're here," Slate pressed.

"I just... She's gotten under my skin," Midas finally said. "I don't know why."

"I'm probably not the person to be having this conversation with, as the last serious relationship I had was...oh, that's right...never. But after watching Mustang and Elodie dance around each other, and how stressed out he was when he didn't hear from her after we left that cargo ship, all I can say is, make sure you get her contact info. And give her yours."

"I'm not Mustang," Midas insisted.

"You aren't. And Lexie isn't Elodie. But I know you, Midas. If she's gotten to you, you'll need to figure out why. And you can't do that if you don't communicate with her."

"I'm sure it's just the situation. And the fact that I know her," Midas argued, not believing his own words. "And as soon as we land on that Navy ship, we'll be separated and that will be that. This isn't exactly the time or place to try to get to know each other. A few hours, tops, and she'll be just another mission."

"I don't know why you're trying so hard to dismiss her, but no one can force you to get to know her if you're determined not to. Though, you know as well as I do that things happen for a reason. We've been through too much shit and seen too many damn miracles for this to be a coincidence."

Midas pressed his lips together. Slate was right. They'd even talked about this exact thing, coincidence, more than once. What were the odds he'd be sent in to rescue someone he'd known in his youth? Slim to none.

"What can it hurt to get her email?" Slate asked. "I don't know if she has a phone, but if she does, exchange numbers as well."

"She works for an international aid organization," Midas protested. "It's bad enough that my job takes me all over the world, but it's not like I can move to Africa to be with her *if* we click," he argued, doing his best to talk himself out of getting in any deeper with the intriguing woman upstairs.

"Excuses," Slate said unsympathetically. "If she's the one for you, she's the one for you. You'll figure out a way to make it work."

"Fuck, you're annoying," Midas told his friend. "I can't wait until you meet someone and come up with all sorts of reasons why you can't be with her."

"That's highly unlikely. I'm a grump who sees the worst in humanity. And unlike you, I'm cool with keeping things casual with a woman I'm seeing. I'm not looking for some deep connection and wanting to immediately move a chick in with me and get married."

"You meet the right woman, you might change your mind," Midas said.

"Don't get your hopes up," Slate told him.

"Hey guys," Jag said as he walked toward them. "I've been trying to get you on our radios for a few minutes."

"Dammit! These things a piece of shit," Slate said, shaking his head and tapping the receiver in his ear. "I knew we should've brought the longer-range radios."

"Too late now," Jag said.

"What's up?" Midas asked.

"Looks like we've got about an hour before we'll be heading out," Jag said. "Dagmar's physician finally gave the green light to move him."

"We going to the ship?" Midas asked. "Or the airstrip?"

"The airstrip," Jag said. "Magnus Brander finally got his way, and he's paying a shitload of money to get his brother out of here. The helo will pick us up there and take us to the ship, then we'll head home shortly thereafter. How's Lexie?"

"She's good. Sleeping upstairs in an examination room. I'll wake her up in about forty-five minutes and we'll meet you guys down here so we can head out. Any issues from the locals?"

"Not so far," Jag said. "Pid and Aleck are keeping their eye on the neighborhood. I think we got Dagmar and Lexie inside before most people realized we were here."

"I'm assuming not all the kidnappers were at camp," Slate added. "We had intel that there were around eighteen people coming and going from the desert. We only took out about a dozen. We need to keep our wits about us until we go wheels up."

Midas and Jag both nodded.

"Yeah, that's why Aleck and Pid are keeping watch," Jag said.

Feeling uneasy about Lexie being left on her own, Midas said, "I'm headed back upstairs. Let me know if the timetable gets moved. The sooner we're out of here, the better I'll feel."

"Same," Slate said.

Midas didn't even tease his friend about his legendary impatience. Right about now, he was one hundred percent in tune with Slate. He gave his friends a chin lift and headed for the stairs.

He slipped into Lexie's room, nodded at the nurse as she left, and was relieved to see Lexie right where he'd left her. She'd turned onto her side and the arm with the IV was hanging over the edge of the table. Her hair was mostly dry now, and even more out of control than it had been when he'd first seen her in the desert.

Midas smiled. He had no idea why he found her hair so fascinating. Maybe because it was wild and crazy, and she was anything but. It was an odd dichotomy.

He pulled a chair closer to the bed, putting himself between Lexie and the door, and stared at the woman on the table as she slept.

What was it about her that drew him so unexpectedly? It made no sense. He didn't even really know her. But what he'd learned since seeing her lying on a thin pallet in the desert was enough for him to want to know more.

He gave some thought to how they might continue to get reacquainted, but everything his mind came up with seemed flimsy. He had no idea what she was planning to do once they got to the US Navy ship. He assumed she'd fly back to the States until Food For All assigned her another post. Midas didn't know nearly enough about the organization to guess how many locations they might have around the world. Would Lexie head back to Africa? South America? The Caribbean? There were so many people who needed assistance, she could literally be sent anywhere.

And he'd be in Hawaii, where he was stationed. Paradise. Of course, there were people who were in need there too, but he didn't imagine Hawaii was on Food For All's short list for sending people to help.

Sighing, Midas shook his head. He couldn't think of how in the world he and Lexie would ever be able to have a real relationship...not that he had any idea she'd even be interested.

Although...he'd seen the way she'd studied him earlier.

He couldn't believe he'd been about to kiss her. Talk about inappropriate.

No, it wasn't smart to keep in touch with Lexie after they got out of here. It was too complicated. He still had quite a few years in the Navy and he couldn't imagine, after years of traveling around the world, that Lexie would want to settle down in one place. She'd be bored in a week.

Feeling depressed over a relationship that was ending before it had even started, Midas closed his eyes and scooted down in the chair so he could rest his head on the back. He crossed his feet at the ankles and did his best to turn off his mind.

A loud bang jerked Midas out of his catnap fifteen minutes later.

He bolted upright in the chair and cocked his head, trying to figure out what it was that had woken him.

When a second boom quickly sounded, Midas moved. He jumped to his feet and was by Lexie's side in a heartbeat.

"Lex? Wake up!" he said in a low, urgent tone.

Her eyes immediately popped open and she stared up at him. "What's wrong?"

Midas was about to pull her to her feet when he saw the IV sticking out of her arm. He swore. "Stay still for a second," he ordered.

Lexie nodded without hesitation. He had a moment to be grateful that she wasn't asking him a million questions as he reached for the IV he'd put in not too long ago. She hadn't gotten as much of the saline solution into her body as he would've liked, but it couldn't be helped. He quickly slid the needle out of her arm and pressed hard on the small puncture wound with his thumb, even as he was pulling her into a sitting position.

He could hear yelling now. It was muffled, coming from somewhere within the hospital. He didn't know how much time they had, but he guessed it wasn't much.

"We need to get out of here," he told Lexie.

She nodded. "Okay."

Fuck, Midas was impressed. She wasn't panicking. He

could see she was scared—her eyes had dilated and she was breathing a bit too fast—but she was holding it together.

He picked up her hand and pressed it over the small wound on her inner arm. "It'll stop bleeding soon, but for now, keep pressure on it."

Lexie nodded as he took her free hand and headed for the door. He listened for a moment, then eased it open a crack. Hearing men yelling from the stairway, he immediately closed it again. Without a word, he towed Lexie toward the window.

"Midas?"

"Something's wrong," he said, stating the obvious. "I haven't heard from my team, but I'm guessing the missing kidnappers figured out where you and Dagmar were taken, and they aren't happy."

"Do you think they're okay?" she asked.

"The kidnappers?" Midas asked in confusion as he concentrated on opening the window and formulating an escape plan.

"No. Your friends. And Dagmar."

"They're fine," Midas told her. In actuality, he had no idea what was happening downstairs in the hospital. He wasn't getting any intel through his radio, but he didn't have time to worry about it. He needed to get Lexie out and away from whoever was currently taking over the hospital. And he figured he had about three minutes, tops, before the men in the stairwell opened the exam room door in the search for their missing hostages.

Looking out the window, Midas was relieved to see a gutter downspout right outside the window. He turned to Lexie. "I'll go first. All you need to do is stand on the small ledge outside the window, shimmy over to the gutter and then slide down. Okay?"

Lexie peered around him out the window, then looked back at him with huge hazel eyes. "Are you crazy?" she asked.

"No. I'll be at the bottom to catch you and to slow your descent."

"Midas, that's not a fireman's pole or anything. It's a freaking gutter. There's nothing to hold on to!"

Midas took her head in his hands and tilted her face up to his. "You can do this, Lex. You *have* to do this. I don't know who those men are, yelling in the stairwell, but I'm assuming by the blasts I heard that they aren't here to pass out lollipops and spread good cheer. Yes, I've got a rifle, but I don't have unlimited ammo. We have to get out of there. I will *not* let them get their hands on you again. Understand?"

She swallowed hard, took a deep breath, then nodded.

"Okay?" he asked, trying not to be impatient, even though he knew every second counted. They needed to be out of here by the time the men in the hallway got to this room.

"Okay. I've always wanted to try pole dancing. This is kinda like that."

It wasn't, but he didn't contradict her or laugh at her joke. "Watch me, then do exactly what I do. We've got this."

She nodded, and Midas didn't waste any more time. He hated leaving her in the room, but they couldn't go out the window at the same time. He regretted that they were on the second floor, but at least if either of them fell, it wouldn't kill them.

Ducking, Midas threw one leg over the windowsill and stepped out. The ledge was only about three inches wide, but that was enough space for him to quickly inch along and grab the gutter.

"Now, Lex. Come on," he urged as he did his best to brace his boots against the slippery metal downspout.

He waited until Lexie was on the windowsill before letting gravity do its thing. He slid downward quickly, in a semi-controlled manner, until his feet hit the ground.

Immediately looking up, he saw Lexie doing her best to cling to the gutter. He mentally swore when he saw her bare feet. Fuck. She'd only had on a pair of flip-flops when they'd rescued her from the desert, but those would have been better than nothing right about now. He hadn't even thought about grabbing them for her; he was too concerned about getting her out of the room.

It couldn't be helped now. He'd find something for her feet later. First things first.

"Do it," he called out in a loud whisper. The hair on the back of Midas's neck was sticking straight up and he felt like a sitting duck. The exam room faced an alley, which at the moment was empty, but he knew it wouldn't be for long. He and Lexie needed to get the hell out of there and find some cover.

Amazingly, Lexie's bare feet were actually a good thing. Her skin helped her cling to the gutter, making her descent painfully slow. When she was within reach, Midas reached up and snatched her off the side of the building. He wanted to carry her—oh, how he hated to put her clean bare feet down in the dirt of the alley—but he needed his hands free to protect them both as they fled.

"Good?" he asked.

Lexie nodded.

Without another word, Midas hooked her fingers in the waistband of his pants and headed down the alley, away from the front of the hospital. Any second, he expected to hear someone yelling at them from one of the windows on the second floor, but miraculously, they made it to the end of the alley undetected.

But they didn't exactly blend in. Two white people, in a predominantly black neighborhood, stood out like a sore thumb. And the fact that he was dressed in desert fatigues and had a rifle slung over his shoulder didn't exactly help matters either. Everyone they passed would be able to remember them easily, and tell anyone who might be hunting for them which direction they'd gone.

"This is two, anyone got ears?" Midas said into the mic of the radio as he and Lexie made their way deeper into the neighborhood around the hospital.

Silence greeted him. Shit.

They'd known these radios weren't top of the line before they'd left the States, but no one had expected them to completely go tits up in the middle of the op. Midas wasn't too worried. His team wouldn't leave without him and Lexie, and they'd talked enough about backup plans to their backup plans to know what to do, but he hated feeling cut off from his friends.

Midas split his attention between where they were going and Lexie. The streets and alleys they were winding through were dirt covered, but that didn't mean there wasn't broken glass and other things that could cut her feet. He also hated that she hadn't gotten as much of the IV into her system as he'd hoped. Fuck, the woman had just been held hostage for months, and now they were on the run from who knew what.

But Midas was sure that if they'd stayed in that hospital room, they'd both probably be dead. Those blasts he'd heard were explosions. And when he'd looked down the alley after descending the gutter, he'd seen smoke rising from the front of the building.

He prayed his team was all right, but his mission was Lexie. Rescuing her had been the objective from the beginning, and nothing had changed.

Midas stopped at the end of another alley and peered around the corner, only to swear under his breath and turn back the way they came.

"What? What did you see?" Lexie asked as she followed him.

"Nothing good," he said grimly.

He'd seen half a dozen men coming down the street toward the alley. All six held semi-automatic rifles and didn't look happy. There was more and more yelling coming from all around them, as well. It sounded like the men were riling up their neighbors. He had no way to know for sure if these were allies of the kidnappers, but Midas had no desire to face off against a bunch of armed men, for any reason.

He frowned as he tried to think of where to go, but the number of shouting voices around them seemed to be increasing by the minute.

This wasn't good. Not good at all. The last thing they needed was to be cornered. Midas couldn't help but think about Mogadishu once more. The visions of what mob mentality had done to the special forces men and pilots who'd been trapped in the city flashed through his mind.

As he rushed Lexie down another narrow alley, a door suddenly opened, and Midas came to an abrupt stop. He felt Lexie run into his back, but held his ground as he stared at the dark-skinned woman who'd opened the door.

He and the woman locked gazes for what seemed like an eternity before Lexie peeked out from behind him and said, "Astur?"

"Lexie?" the woman asked.

Before Midas could stop her, Lexie had rushed around him and was hugging the woman. "Oh my gosh! It's so good to see you!"

The woman's gaze flicked back to Midas's and then down the alley, when they heard more men yelling.

Without a word, Astur grabbed Lexie's arm and pulled her toward the door she'd come out of.

Midas wasn't about to let the women out of his sight, and he followed close behind. He didn't mind going inside, it would hide them from the growing mob in the streets— including the armed men he was more and more certain were hunting for Lexie—but he had no idea if they were jumping out of the pan and into the fire.

The door shut behind them, and Midas realized they were in the back room of some sort of store.

"Trouble you in," Astur said to Lexie.

She scrunched her nose and nodded.

"Hide. Here," Astur said.

"We don't want to get you in trouble," Lexie said immediately. "If we can cut through your store and out the front, we'll be fine."

"No fine," Astur said with a shake of her head. "More men. Look for Americans. Heard them."

"Shit," Lexie swore. She looked up at Midas. "What are we going to do? Maybe you should just go. They're looking for me, not you. You can get back to your team and..." Her voice trailed off.

It didn't matter what she was going to say. He wasn't leaving her. No way in hell. "I'm not leaving," he said sternly.

"Hide here," Astur repeated. "I work at store. No one think you here."

Midas studied her. He had no idea who this woman was. But he didn't see any malice in her eyes. If anything, he saw concern. Not for him, but for Lexie. That didn't surprise him.

She moved, pushing Lexie to the side and crouching down by the door they'd just entered. She tugged at the boards near their feet until a small space was revealed. It was some sort of storage space, most likely, and Midas could see a few stray cans and some flat cardboard boxes at the bottom, lying in the dirt.

"You hide here," Astur said, standing and pointing into the hole.

Lexie looked up at him again, and Midas hated the uncertainty on her face. He wasn't so sure about this either. He didn't know this Astur woman; for all he knew, she was working with the men looking for them and the second they were in the hole, she'd go outside and lead the group straight to them.

More yelling sounded outside the shop in the alleyway,

and Lexie's eyes got wide. "I don't think we'll both fit in there," she whispered.

"We'll fit," Midas said, making a decision. It would be tight, that was for sure. He wasn't exactly small, and as the tallest man on the team, this was the least ideal situation for him to be in. But if it meant keeping Lexie safe, he'd do whatever it took.

He stepped down into the hole, which was only about three feet deep. He sat on his ass in the dirt and moved his rifle around to his right side. He scooted over as far as he could to the right and gestured for Lexie to join him.

She looked even more skeptical, now that he was inside the hole.

"It looks like a coffin," she told him with a frown on her face.

"Lexie, there's no time," Midas warned her as the voices outside grew closer.

"Shit," she muttered. Then she turned toward the woman who'd led them into the store and gave her another hug. "Thank you, Astur."

"You help Astur and children. We help you," she said as she returned Lexie's hug. Then she gently pushed Lexie away and gestured to the hole impatiently.

Taking a deep breath, Lexie gingerly stepped into the hole and lay down against Midas. She wiggled a bit, trying to get comfortable, and before she'd even stopped moving, Astur had replaced the boards, making dust fall on top of them. A light in the back room shone through the cracks in the floor, giving them just enough dim illumination to see each other.

She hadn't dropped the last board over their hiding place a second too soon, as the door to the alley flew open with a crash.

Midas tensed and curled his finger around the trigger of his rifle. This was it. Astur could easily give them up right here and now, and if the men had weapons of their own—and if they were smart—they'd shoot first and ask questions later.

But no shots were fired. What sounded like several men stomped into the back room of the store and began speaking in Somali. Midas had no idea what was being said, but Astur didn't seem afraid to speak her mind. Their voices raised and, at one point, Astur stomped her foot. At least, he thought it was her. In outrage? In anger? In frustration? Midas didn't know, but he was as tense as he'd ever been. He could feel every breath Lexie took, as she was literally plastered against him.

Her head was resting on his shoulder, one arm tucked against her side, and thus *his* side, with the other flung across his lower belly. He could feel her gripping the edge of his tactical vest and their legs were tangled together.

It could've been five minutes or fifteen, but after a very tense wait, with more foot stomping and more yelling, the men finally left the small room, heading back into the alley from where they'd come.

Silence greeted their departure, and even Astur left the back room, presumably heading to the front of the store.

"Holy shit," Lexie whispered.

"Shhhh," Midas warned in a barely there tone.

He felt her nod against him and, one by one, her muscles began to relax.

Then they lay there in that cramped hole under the floor for what seemed like hours.

The heat rose, and Midas's legs started to cramp. Still, neither he nor Lexie moved. He'd been trained to stay in one position for hours, but Lexie hadn't. And she still wasn't one hundred percent after her ordeal. Midas had been impressed with her before, but with each minute that ticked by, his admiration rose.

The back door had opened twice more, and each time, Astur went head-to-head with whoever had entered, until they eventually left. Midas was aware that they were one cough, one sneeze away from discovery, and he prayed the dirt falling through the cracks didn't set either one of them off.

Before long, the shouts and yelling from the alley stopped and silence filled their hiding spot and the back room of the store. When Midas was fairly confident it would be safe to speak in hushed tones, he whispered, "You okay?"

"Yeah. You?"

"Peachy. This must be how sardines feel in a can."

He felt more than heard Lexie's snort of laughter against his shoulder. Then she said, "How can I be laughing? There's nothing remotely humorous about this situation."

"Embrace the suck," Midas said.

"Pardon?"

"Embrace the suck," he repeated. "It's something we said back in SEAL training. It means the situation is bad, but deal with it. Accept the shitty but unavoidable situation, in order to move on."

"I'm not sure that's very inspirational," Lexie said. "What else you got?"

"The only easy day was yesterday?" he joked.

Surprisingly, Midas was enjoying this. Probably because Lexie wasn't freaking out or hysterical. This was the kind of conversation he'd have with one of his teammates in a similar situation.

"Yeah, no. Because yesterday wasn't easy," Lexie said in unequivocal terms. "Try again."

Midas chuckled softly. "How about...you're amazing. And there's no one I'd rather be in this situation with than you."

"Right," she said with a small shake of her head. "And I've got an ocean-view house in Kansas to sell you."

"Seriously, you think I'd want Mustang in here with me like this?"

It was Lexie's turn to laugh softly now. "Um...that might

be a little uncomfortable. I mean, it can't be fun to have *me* in here with you. We don't exactly fit."

"I'd say we fit perfectly," Midas said before thinking twice about his words.

"I guess it's a good thing I was able to shower. You wouldn't be as happy with me practically lying on you like this if I still smelled like I did. Three months is a long time to go without soap."

Midas did something then that he'd been wanting to do since he saw her lying on that examination table. He turned his head and buried his nose in her hair. It didn't exactly smell like sunshine and roses, but the strands were soft against his face.

"Are you smelling me?" she asked in confusion.

"Just breathing," he retorted. "And your hair is in the way."

"You're weird," she told him.

Midas smiled. He was. But at the moment, he didn't care. His fingers relaxed from their grip on the rifle for the first time and he reached up and ran a hand over her hair, smoothing it away from her face.

This wasn't the time or place to think about how much he liked the feel of Lexie in his arms. He felt relatively safe at the moment, but he wasn't about to creep out of their hiding spot until nightfall, hopefully after whoever was searching for them gave up, so they had quite a few hours to go.

His conversation with Slate came back to him, about how there were no coincidences. Midas had resigned himself to the fact that he didn't have time to get to know Lexie before they went their separate ways. Well, the universe had basically just laughed in his face as if to say, "You want time? I'll give you time."

And he wanted to know everything about her.

"Tell me about Astur," he said, asking the first thing that came to mind. "How'd you know you could trust her?"

CHAPTER FIVE

Lexie felt like a terrible human being. Here she was, hiding for her life, and she was enjoying being plastered up against Midas. If someone had told her high school self that she'd one day be in the position she was in right now, she would've laughed in their face.

But she couldn't deny that she wasn't hating the feel of his hard body under hers. Was amused that he'd smelled her hair. And loved the tender feel of his hand running over her head, smoothing her crazy curls away from her face. It helped that their hiding space wasn't pitch dark. Astur had left the light on in the small back room of the shop, and the rays of light peeking through the cracks in the floor was just enough so Lexie didn't feel as if she was buried alive.

She was still scared out of her mind and didn't feel all that great. She was hungry and thirsty, but she didn't want to risk moving from their hiding spot. The men weren't trying to find her to give her a goodbye party. They sounded pissed that she'd escaped.

Kicking herself for not asking Midas or any of this team-mates how many people they'd killed at the desert camp, she realized now that there had to be at least one person who'd escaped. Who'd seen what happened and had spread the word.

She, more than most people, knew what the ransom money meant for the kidnappers. She didn't agree with the way they were trying to get money to survive, but on one level, she understood it. Desperate people would do desperate things, especially if they had a family.

And she'd met some very desperate people in her years working for Food For All. Particularly here in Somalia. Maslow's Hierarchy of Needs was a real thing. Most people didn't think much about their basic needs, because they were easily met. But Lexie had known more than her share of people over the years who weren't getting those basic needs met. Food, water, shelter, sleep, clothing. Beyond those, everything else was secondary.

"Lex?" Midas prompted.

She realized with a start that he'd asked her a question. "Sorry. I met Astur when I first got here about six months ago. Food For All provides its workers with housing, but all the rooms in their main building were taken, so I was given a small house about two blocks away. I was kind of glad. I like living among the locals. Anyway, about a week after I'd arrived, I'd just left the food pantry when Astur walked up with her three kids. Hodan, her daughter, is around five; Cumar, her middle son, is nine; and Shermake, her oldest son, is sixteen. They were in pretty bad shape. They were dirty, their clothes were torn, and Hodan was the only one who had shoes on. Astur didn't speak much English, but I understood that she was looking for food for her kids."

Lexie hated remembering this, but she knew Astur and her family were among many who were hungry and homeless in the world. "I turned back around to go get them some food, but my supervisor at the time was closing up the building and told me no, that we were closed and it was against regulations to give away any food or clothing after hours. That pissed me off. I mean, Food For All's entire mission is to provide food for freaking all. I had heard bad things about the supervisor before I'd arrived in the country, but dismissed the talk as gossip.

"Anyway, Astur was upset, but she took Hodan and Cumar by the hands and walked away. And while I wasn't happy, I didn't want to piss off my boss in my first week, so I didn't say anything. I walked home and when I got to my street, I saw Astur and her kids again. They had settled under an awning of a business across from my small house. So... I invited them in."

"Jesus, Lex," Midas said with a shake of his head.

"I know, I know...but you should've seen them, Midas. They needed someone to give a shit about them. And at that moment, I was the only one around. So I convinced them to come inside, and I made a simple and quick meal for everyone. When I started rearranging the furniture, pushing it back so I could make a pallet on the floor, Astur began crying. It took everything I had to convince her to stay, and they spent the night in my living room. In the morning, they had a small breakfast, then they left. But that night, I saw them on the street again, and invited them in a second time.

"This happened every day for about a month. Shermake, the oldest boy, was the most proficient in English, and we practiced every night. They were all very quiet and respectful, and every morning they'd head off to wherever they went to spend the day. I started to enjoy the company, so I was happy when they were waiting near my place when I got home from work."

"You were giving them free food and a place to stay, why wouldn't they keep coming back?" Midas said dryly.

"But they were giving *me* just as much," Lexie insisted. "I was in a new country, trying to figure out all the customs and stuff, and Shermake was a great help. Astur took me to a farmers market one weekend, and it was fascinating to see the interaction between her and the vendors. She was as fierce a negotiator as I've ever seen. And yes, I was paying for the food, but if she was truly just mooching off me, she wouldn't have cared about getting the best deal."

"It looks like she got herself figured out, since she's working here in this store," Midas noted.

"Shermake told me that their father had gone to Ethiopia to earn money for the family. He'd been gone longer than they'd planned, and Astur ran out of money. She lost their small hut and had no choice but to live on the streets with her kids. Yuusuf eventually came back and had been very lucky. He'd earned enough money to rent them another place, and Astur decided she wanted to help earn money for their family so they never had to be homeless again."

Midas didn't say anything, and Lexie tilted her head back, trying to see his expression. She didn't have enough room to maneuver any farther, but she could see the outline of his face. His jaw was tight, and she thought she even saw a muscle ticking there.

"What?" she whispered.

He dipped his chin and turned his head a bit, and their gazes met. "You've always been concerned about others," he said.

Lexie shrugged. She used to feel embarrassed about wanting to take care of other people, but after making it her career, she'd ceased to care what others thought. "So many others have it worse than I ever did. It feels good to help."

There was a moment of silence before Midas asked, "You had it bad?"

Lexie didn't respond, not sure what to say. She didn't want this man to pity her. She was fine. She'd survived and was satisfied with where she was in her life.

"When I joined the Navy, I was so naïve," Midas said. "I grew up with loving parents and two great siblings. Karen was a pain in my ass, but I would've killed anyone who tried to hurt her. I guess that's what older brothers do for their little sisters. Max was always trying to be like me. He even joined the swim team, and the little shit broke one of my records."

Lexie smiled. She didn't know a lot about Midas, they weren't really friends in high school, so she drank in each and every bit of information she discovered about him.

"My parents were happy, treated us kids like we were the most important things in their lives, and we always had awesome Christmases with a ton of presents. When I asked for all the trendy clothes, they usually bought them for me. I had lots of friends and didn't really have to work all that hard in school for good grades. I was spoiled, I can admit that now, though my folks did a good job of trying to make sure we appreciated what we had. But when I joined the Navy...all of a sudden, I was nothing. Just another grunt who'd been a big fish in a small pond in his hometown, and then I was this tiny little minnow in a huge ocean. It was definitely a shock."

"I'm sure you didn't stay a small fish for long," Lexie commented.

He chuckled softly, and she felt the rumble in his chest against her own since they were pressed together. If she'd been in this hole in the floor with anyone else, Lexie would've been extremely uncomfortable. But something about Midas made her relax.

"I learned really fast that it didn't matter where we all came from. If we were going to make it through boot camp, and then SEAL training, we all had to work together."

"Embrace the suck," Lexie said with a smile.

"Exactly. Over the years, I've seen a lot of shit. People acting like assholes toward each other. Disrespecting their children, their wives, their neighbors. Fighting over something they probably didn't even understand. Have you seen the movie *World War Z*?"

Lexie blinked at the change in topic.

"I have a point," Midas said.

"That's the movie with Brad Pitt and the zombies, right?" she asked.

Midas nodded. "Yeah. Anyway, there's a part when they're running from the zombies in Jerusalem, and Pitt's character looks back and sees a boy in the mayhem, crouched down in the middle of the street with his hands over his head. All the zombies go around him without even looking twice at the boy, even though they're biting everyone else. You're kind of like that kid."

Lexie scrunched her nose and frowned. "In what way?"

"Everyone else around you is fighting and clawing for something. Food. Power. Money. And then there's you. A calm light in the darkness. Giving out smiles and food. Making friends in the most hostile territory. It's like the dark can't touch you."

"Um, I think you're forgetting that I was kidnapped and taken hostage," Lexie said dryly.

"No, I'm not. You were kidnapped, and that sucked. But they didn't touch you. And trust me, that is a fucking *miracle* as far as I'm concerned. Most hostages aren't so lucky. They kept you reasonably healthy and alive."

"They wanted money," Lexie felt obligated to mention. "If they killed me, that would've cut their ransom in half."

She felt him shrug.

"All I'm saying is that I'm realizing you've always been that way. You went out of your way to befriend the socially awkward kids at school. You gave up your own lunch money to buy someone else a sandwich. You volunteered to be in a group with the kids no one else wanted to work with. You're a good person, Lexie. And while it completely freaks me out that you've probably been inviting complete strangers into your home and feeding them for years, it's obvious you love what you're doing."

After a long moment of silence, Lexie blurted, "I joined Food For All to get away from my father."

She felt every muscle under her go taut.

"Explain," Midas bit out.

"He didn't hit me, but he wasn't very nice," Lexie admitted for the first time ever. She'd never talked about her dad to anyone. Partly because she hadn't been very close to any of her coworkers. She wasn't around any of them long enough. Between her switching locations frequently, and them doing the same, it was a part of life to meet someone one day and have them be gone the next. But something about lying in the dark with Midas, and the fact that he knew her from so long ago, made opening up not as difficult as she might've expected.

"He was never sure what to do with a daughter. He was also an alcoholic, always being fired from jobs for showing up drunk. We didn't have big fancy Christmases. I think the last time we had a tree was when I was in elementary school. When he got drunk, the last thing he thought about was making dinner for me."

"Where was your mom?" Midas asked.

"Gone. She left when I was little. I barely remember her. She and my dad fought all the time. My memories are of yelling and me hiding in my room when they went at it. Anyway, we moved around a lot, which was why I ended up in Portland my senior year." Thinking about that year, and when she'd met Midas for the first time, made her think about how difficult school had been for her. "I'm not stupid," she said a little fiercer than she intended.

"I never said you were..." Midas told her, sounding confused.

She felt his fingers lightly stroking the arm that was around his belly. She didn't know when he'd started doing so, but she couldn't deny that it felt amazing...comforting.

"Sorry. That came out of left field. I was thinking about school and how hard it was for me. My grades weren't great. I just...I'm dyslexic. And because we moved so much, and my dad was too concerned about getting money for his booze, he never bothered to get me tested. School was hell. Letters were all jumbled on the page for me and I did my best to hide how lost I was most of the time. I don't blame the teachers for not catching on, I cheated on tests a lot." She shrugged. "And there was always someone smarter, or dumber, than me for them to concentrate on. I fell through the cracks."

"Shit, Lex—" Midas began.

But she interrupted him. "No, it's fine. My dad didn't help, laughing at me and calling me stupid when I'd bring home my report card. And I'm *not* looking for sympathy, but I can remember just about every time someone was nice to me when I was growing up, since it happened so rarely.

"There was this girl, her name was Renee, and we were in fourth grade together, I think. We were at recess and she asked if I wanted to play with her. It was the first time anyone had ever asked me that. We played on the swings and ran around together at recess for the rest of the year. I was so happy. The next year, she was in a different class and she got new friends, but I'm still grateful for that year.

"Then at one of my junior high schools, a boy noticed that I was sitting by myself at lunch, without eating, and he bought me a cookie. I could go on, but... I'm sure you get it. When you're invisible and someone finally sees you, and does something nice, it sticks with you.

"And I'm not telling you this to make you feel guilty about your own upbringing, or anything you've done in the past. I'm just trying to explain why I am the way I am. Though not very clearly," she admitted, chuckling lightly. "To most people, including my own father, I was invisible. I *see* the invisible, Midas. They call to me, and I can't help but be nice to them. To try to help them. It gives me such satisfaction, and I hope that maybe, just maybe, someday they'll remember when someone did something nice for them, and they'll pass it along. The world needs more nice and less hate."

"Yes, it does," Midas agreed.

"And while I'm thinking about it, thank you for not pitching a fit when Mrs. Allen stuck you with me for that project."

"Lex," Midas began, but she talked over him again.

"No, I'm serious. I know I was the last person you wanted to work with. You had your eye on Candace, and she was certainly pissed she wasn't paired up with you. But you still smiled at me, and you didn't make me feel as if I was a burden."

"You worked your ass off on that project," Midas said. "And had some damn good ideas."

She shrugged. "I'm sure you could've gotten an A if you were with someone else. I wasn't much help in typing up the paper."

"Hey, I was pleased as hell with that B we got. I enjoyed talking with you, Lexie. I'm just sorry I was so clueless about your situation."

"Don't be," she told him. "There was no way for you to know, and I certainly wasn't going to tell you anything about it and make you feel sorry for me. Besides, you're one of those good memories I was talking about a second ago. School sucked for me. But because of you, I can look back at my senior year and have at least a few good memories."

Midas hadn't relaxed under her. If anything, he seemed to be more tense now than he was earlier. Lexie hadn't meant to upset him.

"You still talk to your dad?" he asked after a moment.

"No. He died a few years ago. Cirrhosis of the liver."

"Good."

The single word was said with a venom that Lexie hadn't heard from Midas in the hours since he'd been by her side.

"He didn't deserve you. I understand more about why you are the way you are, and why you do what you do now. No father should tell their child he or she is stupid. And you said you weren't abused, but you absolutely were, Lex. I'm sorry that happened, but you got the last laugh. I hope he died a painful and lonely death and is looking down on you now, regretting every damn harsh word he said to you."

"Midas," Lexie protested, but he kept going.

"The fact that Astur didn't hesitate to help you doesn't surprise me in the least. You're a shining light of goodness in an otherwise dark and difficult life. You were there for her and her children when she needed kindness the most. Don't change, Lex. Ever. The world needs more people like you. You balance out people like me."

Lexie shook her head. "No, Midas, you're a good man."

He chuckled, but it wasn't a happy sound. "You don't know me."

"Okay, fair point, but I don't know anyone who would've done for me what you've done. You stayed by my side, didn't wait for the doctor to put in that IV so I could get some fluids. You didn't leave me when things went sideways, even though we both know you could've gotten away a lot faster without me hanging off you. You trusted me when I said Astur would help us, and you didn't complain or hesitate to climb in this hole with me. In case it's escaped your notice, this would've been a lot more comfortable without me in here with you."

"And that's another thing that makes me so pissed off on your behalf," Midas retorted. "The fact that you don't know anyone who would've done the decent thing to help you is ridiculous."

She shook her head, not sure how to make Midas understand. "I'm not like the Candaces of the world," she told him. "People don't bend over backward to open doors for me, to buy me lunch, or go out of their way to get to know me. But don't feel sorry for me. I'm okay with that. I've learned to enjoy being by myself. I can do what I want, live where I want, and if I want to spend my paycheck on a needy family who lives down the street, I can do so without having to worry about what someone might think."

"I'll say it again, the world needs more Lexies in it than Candaces."

His words felt good. But she had a feeling he was probably just saying that because of the situation.

"You don't believe me," Midas said with uncanny insight.

"I believe that you mean that right now, in this situation, yes," she said diplomatically.

She felt him shake his head. "I wish your dad was still alive. I would've liked to pay him a visit and tell him what an idiot he was."

Lexie laughed. She couldn't help it.

"What?" he asked.

"My dad wouldn't care. He never cared what people thought about him."

"My parents would love you," Midas told her.

Lexie jolted slightly. "What? No."

"They would," he insisted. "They're always telling me I don't smile enough. They complain that I'm not nice enough to people. I mean, I'm not an asshole, but I don't go out of my way to befriend people, and my job has made me cynical and a little untrusting. You? You're nice to *everyone*. They'd love you."

Lexie didn't know what to say to that. She shifted in Midas's arms and winced when a bead of sweat rolled down her temple. The scrubs she had on felt damp from the heat and sweat, and the shower she'd taken recently felt as if it was forever ago.

"You okay?" Midas asked.

"Just hot. But that's better than shot or re-kidnapped," she said quickly.

"Always looking on the bright side of things," Midas said lightly.

"It doesn't help to be negative all the time," she told him. "All that does is make the situation seem worse."

"True."

"I mean, there could be bugs in this hole," she said, then felt Midas shiver under her.

"I hate bugs," he said.

Lexie couldn't help but laugh. "The big bad SEAL hates bugs?" she asked.

"Yup. I'll take snakes and alligators, and even bats over bugs."

"Bugs in general don't bother me," Lexie admitted. "They're actually kind of fascinating. But I can't stand cockroaches. Those things give me the creeps."

"How're your feet?" Midas asked after a minute or two.

Lexie let out a sigh.

"What?"

"You change subjects faster than anyone I've ever met. One second we're talking about bugs, then you're asking about my feet."

"I'll give you a little insight into my mind," he said. "We were talking about bugs, which got me to thinking about the sand flea bites you have from the desert. Which led me to thinking about the hospital and how happy you looked after your shower. And then I started thinking about how much I liked your hair. It seems to have a mind of its own. Then I recalled how happy you were to have the scrubs to put on, when a lot of people would be upset they didn't have their own clothes. Which made me remember how smooth your skin was when I put in the IV, and finally, your skin made me think about your feet without shoes as we escaped from the hospital. I can't sit up and examine them myself right now because, well, neither of us can move even an inch in this coffin-like space, so I decided to at least ask how your feet felt."

"Um...wow. Okay. That actually made sense. They're okay.

I haven't worn shoes in a long time. I mean, I had flip-flops, but they were cheap and hurt my feet. So I went without them most of the time. My soles are tough, and honestly, I was more concerned about getting away from the people who were willing to set off explosives in a freaking hospital than about my feet."

"Right. I'll look at them when we get out of here."

"When we get out of here, we'll probably need to get to your team. There won't be time to have a sit-down and put a bandage on my booboos," she told him.

"So you admit that you're hurt? Where? What hurts? Maybe we can wiggle around to—"

"I'm *fine*, Midas, seriously. And we can't wiggle anywhere."

He sighed. After a moment, he said, "You called me Midas."

Getting used to his abrupt change of topics, and secretly finding it cute as hell, Lexie just went with it. "It's what your friends all call you. Do you not like it?"

"Elodie calls Mustang by his name, Scott."

Lexie wasn't sure what his point was. "Would you rather I call you Pierce?" she asked.

He shrugged. "I want you to call me what *you* want to call me. I have to admit it would be weird to hear my real name, though. I know it doesn't faze Mustang to hear his name, but the only people who call me Pierce are my parents and brother and sister."

"I know teachers all called you Pierce, but it's hard for me to think of you that way. I guess it's because I've seen you in SEAL mode. And a SEAL named Pierce just doesn't seem to fit."

He chuckled. "Your first name isn't Lexie, but that's what you go by," he said. "There a reason?"

"My mom chose the name Elizabeth. When she left, my dad decided he hated that name and told me in no uncertain terms that he was going to call me Lexie, and that I should get used to that name instead. I was too young to really understand or care. And when I did get old enough to understand... I agreed with him. So I kept Lexie."

"It's a pretty name. Unique."

Shit. This man was killing her. She knew she was probably reading more into the situation than she should, but they'd definitely been through some intense moments in the last half a day, which made her feel even closer to him than she might've otherwise. "So what happens next?" she asked.

"We wait," he said immediately.

"No, I mean, after we get out of here and meet up with your team and leave Galkayo?"

He shook his head. "There's that positivity you have going on again," he muttered.

"What? You'd rather me lie here and believe someone will find us, kill you, and drag me off into the desert again to ask for a ransom they'll probably never get, so eventually they'll get tired of having to feed me and bring me water and they'll either sell me off to someone else to use and abuse or just kill me outright, leaving my body in the desert to be picked off by flesh-eating birds and sand fleas?"

"Good God, woman. No! Shit."

"I tend to be positive, but that doesn't mean I can't be negative," she told him.

"Obviously. So, right, *when* we get out of this hole, meet back up with my team, and get the hell out of here, we'll do what we'd planned all along. Fly to the Navy ship. You'll get some food, be looked over by another doctor, then arrangements will be made to get you back to the States. Food For All will be contacted, and I'm assuming they'll be thrilled that you're all right, and they'll arrange for you to go back to the States to recover from your ordeal. You have a home base?"

Lexie sighed. At no point in Midas's description of what was ahead of them did he mention keeping in touch. She kind of expected that. She was a job for him. But it still stung a bit. "Not really. I mean, I guess Oregon is as much a home base as anywhere. When I got my first overseas assignment, I didn't have much in the way of furniture. I left most of my stuff—you know, extra clothes, books, knick-knacks, things like that—at my dad's house. The landlord basically got rid of everything after he died. I never really missed any of the stuff I left with my dad though. I've collected some things over the years, but Food For All packs up and moves my belongings when I switch locations, kind of like the military does when service members go to a different post."

Midas nodded. "Makes sense."

When he didn't say anything else, Lexie closed her eyes. She didn't know what she'd expected him to say. That he wanted her to move to Hawaii? That was ridiculous.

"Do you think it would be all right for me to close my eyes for a while?" she asked, doing her best to keep any emotion from leaking into her voice.

"Sure. It's probably a good idea. I don't know how long we'll be down here. It's probably smart for us to lay low until the sun goes down. Then we can head out under the cover of darkness. You going to be okay without something to eat for that long? I'm kicking myself for not making sure you got something in the hospital."

"I'm fine." And she was. Because of her time in the desert, she was used to going long stretches without food. And the water she drank and the fluids she'd gotten before having to escape the hospital would be enough to keep her going until nightfall.

"Then go ahead and sleep," Midas said.

"I'm not too heavy against you? I could probably move off you a bit," she offered, kind of hoping he'd agree. She desperately needed space from this man. He'd gotten under her skin, and she had an awful feeling it was going to break her heart when he left her on the Navy ship.

"Too heavy? Not a chance, Lex. Stay. I like having you here."

Shit. No one had ever made her feel as safe and special as he did. Could a thirty-three-year-old woman have a crush?

Yes, she decided. Definitely.

Without another word, Lexie closed her eyes. The man under her smelled like sweat and gun oil and leather, but for some reason, it didn't bother her. Probably because she knew she was also sweaty and not so fresh at the moment. But she much preferred Midas's scent than that of someone who wore too much cologne and smelled like processed perfumes.

"Midas?" she whispered.

"Yeah?"

"Thanks for coming to get me."

She could've sworn she felt him kiss the top of her head, but figured it was just wishful thinking.

"Thank you for being the strong and positive woman you are. This really would've sucked if you did nothing but bitch and complain about the accommodations."

Lexie smiled, though she was having a hard time staying positive all of a sudden.

She'd feel better when she woke up. When she was tired, negative thoughts seemed to sneak into her brain a little easier. By nightfall, she'd have a better handle on her emotions.

Also, sleeping would give her a respite from falling any harder for the man under her.

The last thing she felt before she succumbed to the lure of exhaustion was Midas's fingers lightly stroking her arm.

CHAPTER SIX

Midas stared at the boards inches from his head. He didn't know how long Lexie had been asleep against him, but he figured it was several hours.

He couldn't sleep. He was too hyper alert to the movements above them. People came and went from the back door inches from their hiding spot, and he kept his right hand on the rifle at his side.

He had no idea what his team was doing, but he figured they were hunkered down somewhere waiting for the sun to fall below the horizon, just as he was. He had no concerns that they'd leave without him. A SEAL never left a SEAL behind. Ever. They'd wait as long as it took for him to come out of hiding.

Midas also wondered what had happened back at the hospital. He hoped Dagmar had been able to be extracted without any complications.

As they had all day, his thoughts turned to the woman lying practically on top of him. He'd been right when he'd thought this mission was unlike any other. Not only was it the first in which he personally knew one of the hostages...

but he was feeling things for Lexie that he'd never felt for anyone he'd saved before.

He'd *hated* hearing about her difficult childhood. How she could be so good, so kind, after being treated the way she had was beyond him. But she was. The way Astur greeted her was proof that it wasn't an exaggeration either. She'd saved that woman's life, and probably her kids' lives too, taken them in without asking for anything in return. And Astur was clearly grateful.

He'd never met anyone as unselfish as Lexie. She worried about others before being concerned about herself.

A part of him wanted to shake her and tell her that she needed to look out for herself first, but he suspected that if he did, she'd just smile up at him, pat his hand, and tell him she'd be fine.

He'd never met a woman like her. And he ached to get to know her even better. He wanted to discover all her secrets. All her likes and dislikes. The favorite places she'd worked. Her hopes and dreams.

When she'd asked what came next, he'd laid it out as unemotionally as possible—but what he *hadn't* told her was how much he wanted to keep in touch.

Nothing about his situation had changed. He'd have to go back to Hawaii and his job with the Navy would continue. He wasn't a fan of long-distance relationships, but he ached to know what Lexie's next steps were.

So while he hadn't mentioned it earlier, he planned to stay involved in her life, if she was open to that. He wanted to talk to her on the phone, to email, or even write a damn hand-written letter if he had to. She'd definitely piqued his interest, and he wasn't ready to just let her walk away as if they hadn't spent some of the most intense hours of their lives together.

Lexie stirred against him, and Midas waited to see if she'd completely wake up this time or if she'd fall back asleep, as she'd done several times before. Midas wasn't the kind of person to enjoy sitting or lying around. He'd always been a morning person, eager to get up and start his day. He didn't watch much TV and, if given the choice, would always rather go for a walk or run or swim, than hang around doing nothing.

But surprisingly, he was perfectly content to lie there and hold Lexie as she slept. Yes, he had no choice at the moment but to stay where he was, but he had a feeling sleeping in on a lazy Sunday with her back home would feel just as amazing.

That should've freaked him out. Instead it just made him sad...because he was fairly sure that would never happen. He just couldn't see how to get from hiding out with Lexie in a hole under a Somali shop to having her in his arms in his comfortable bed on Oahu.

"Damn," Lexie whispered huskily as she woke.

"What?" Midas asked in alarm, his mind already making preparations to get out of this hole and get her some help for whatever was wrong.

"I hoped it had all been a dream," she said.

Midas relaxed a fraction. "If it's any consolation, things have been quiet for a while now. In another hour or so, I think we can get out of here and go find my team."

She nodded. "I didn't mean to sleep so long."

"You needed it."

"Were you able to sleep at all?" she asked.

"I rested," Midas told her. There was no way he was going to let down his guard enough to sleep. Not when that could mean Lexie being hurt or kidnapped again. She was his mission...but she was also much more than that. Things were personal for him now.

Lexie shifted against him again. There wasn't enough room for her to maneuver much more than that.

"You okay?" he asked.

"Just stiff," she replied.

Midas felt her flex her feet one at a time, which made him

think about her lack of shoes once more. It bothered him on a visceral level that she was barefoot. He should've taken care of her better. The thought of her having to walk around Galkayo without shoes was repugnant.

"What?" Lexie asked.

Midas jerked in surprise. "What, *what?*" he asked.

"You got tense. What's wrong?"

Midas wasn't surprised she was as in tune with him as she was. Then again, they were lying together like lovers, so it was hard to hide any physical reaction. "I was just thinking about your lack of shoes," he admitted. "I feel awful about it."

"Why?" she asked. "It's not like you had a chance to find any for me. And neither of us expected we'd have to crawl out the window like we did. Besides, being barefoot isn't anything most of the locals haven't experienced at one point in their lives."

"True. But I'm responsible for you. I should've anticipated something going wrong. I was too lax."

"You are *not* responsible for me," Lexie retorted heatedly. "I mean, okay, sure, in the eyes of the government, you're responsible for getting me to the ship. But I'm an adult, Midas. I'm perfectly able to make my own decisions about my life. And I doubt you've got the psychic ability to know what everyone around us is going to do every second of the day. I'm more than grateful to you and your team for freeing me and Dagmar, but that doesn't mean I'm an empty-headed damsel in distress. If I started screaming right now and brought all the bad guys running, would you be responsible for what happened to me next? Or if I insisted I needed to stop and go shopping on our way out of here, would you be responsible for whatever happened as a result?

"Shit happens, Midas. We can either deal with it as it comes, or freak out and have a meltdown. I haven't had the luxury of being able to have a meltdown in my life. I've had to brush myself off and keep going. And I'm not about to stop now. Unless you tell me you're some sort of seer and know what's going to happen in the future, you need to quit beating yourself up for things you can't control."

God. She was magnificent.

She was level-headed and passionate and so far from being a spoiled diva, it wasn't even funny. He wasn't offended by her outburst. Yes, her argument was a bit over the top, and he hadn't thought his comment would set her off like it had. But it certainly didn't turn him off. He liked that she wasn't afraid to speak her mind.

Midas had never given much thought to the kind of woman he wanted in the long term—but this was it. *She* was it. He wanted a strong and pragmatic partner, someone who could function when he was deployed.

He apparently didn't respond fast enough for her, because she asked, "Are you pissed at me? I'm sorry. Now that I've thought for two seconds about what you said, and I realize I kind of overreacted. I can also admit I don't know what I'd do if you weren't here. I'd have no clue what to do next... other than going back to the Food For All building, which I'm guessing wouldn't be in my best interest right now. I'm not saying I'm not scared, because I am. But if I let my fears overwhelm me, things could get even worse."

"I'm not upset, and I agree. And I never saw you as a damsel in distress," Midas said. "From the moment I saw your name on the reports and realized that I knew you, this mission ceased to be like any other for me. I appreciate and admire how you've conducted yourself so far, Lex. You've been amazing. I just... I don't like the thought of you being in a disadvantaged position. I could carry you if I needed to, though it would be harder for me to protect us both. But you not having shoes means that you could get hurt, and I can't do a damn thing about it. *That's* what bothers me about you being barefoot. It makes you more vulnerable. That's all."

He felt Lexie take a deep breath, then nod against him.

"I'm sorry. I'm always cranky when I first wake up. You know what I miss most?"

"What?"

"Coffee. The good kind. The kind that's way too sweet and doesn't really even taste like coffee. The kind where you take a sip and your taste buds wake up and take notice. That first swallow, it's like heaven."

Midas chuckled. "I like it black."

"Gross."

His smile widened. Then he sobered. "What are your plans after we get you to safety?" he couldn't help but ask. He knew his way of changing subjects irritated people. They were just talking about coffee, and suddenly he was turning the conversation in a more serious direction. But now he was thinking about her sitting on his back deck, watching the sunrise, sipping a cup of way-too-sweet coffee and smiling about it.

He knew the odds of that ever happening were slim to none. And he couldn't help but wonder where she would go when they got out of Somalia. Would she go back to the States? Take another assignment immediately? If she took time off, it didn't sound as if she had any family or close friends to hang out with until she was ready to start work again.

But instead of asking him how the hell he'd gotten from coffee to her future, he felt her shrug against him. "I don't know."

The short answer didn't make him feel any better.

"I need to talk to my coordinator at Food For All, see what my options are. For all I know, I don't have a job anymore."

"That's bullshit," Midas said angrily. "It's not like you were gallivanting around the city causing trouble when you were taken. You were with one of the head honchos and were outside their headquarters. If you don't have a job, you should sue."

Lexie patted his stomach as if trying to calm him down. "I was just saying it's a possibility. I don't really think they'd fire me because I was kidnapped."

"They better not," Midas growled.

"The thing is, I like what I do," Lexie said. "I like helping others get back on their feet. It's so satisfying to see the men, women, and families I work with be able to make it on their own. To not need Food For All anymore. I'd like to keep doing what I'm doing...but I think I'm ready to choose my assignments a little more carefully."

Midas closed his eyes in relief. "Good," he said.

He felt more than saw her looking at him. "You'll go back to Hawaii, huh?"

"Yeah," Midas said as he opened his eyes and saw the same damn boards above his face that he'd been staring at for hours. He tucked his chin and looked down at Lexie. Her hair was in disarray around her face and he could feel some of the strands sticking to the stubble on his face. "Any chance Food For All operates in Honolulu?"

The question came out without thought, and he desperately wished he could see the look in Lexie's eyes.

"I don't know. But I would think so. I mean, they're in a lot of the big cities in the States. New York, Chicago, Detroit, Orlando, Houston, LA... I would think Hawaii has its share of homeless and hungry families."

"It does," Midas confirmed.

They stared at each other, neither saying anything. Midas wanted to tell her how much he'd love it if she came to Hawaii, but wasn't sure how she'd take it. Yes, they'd known each other in what seemed like another lifetime, but they were both very different people than they'd been back in high school. And Lexie seemed to be content with her job. And she was good at it. She could help the needy in Hawaii, but would she want to settle in one place after all the exotic locations she'd lived and worked?

He wanted to ask, but instead, Midas kissed her forehead gently. He let his lips linger on her skin, wanting more, but *not* wanting to take advantage of the situation.

He felt Lexie's hand on his stomach move. It skimmed up his chest, brushing over his Kevlar vest and the various tools that were attached to it, and then her fingers were on his cheek.

"Lex?" he whispered.

She didn't respond verbally, but he felt her shift against him. Her chin lifted and then their mouths were only inches apart.

God. He wanted to kiss her. Wanted it more than anything he'd ever wanted in his life. It was as if his soul was crying out to taste her. To make her his.

That was crazy. They were still in danger. He was a SEAL who lived in Hawaii, and she was a hostage he'd rescued.

But she was so much more than that.

Lexie licked her lips, then moved her head closer.

Their lips brushed against each other lightly. Once. Twice.

Midas growled. He hated not having more room. Hated not being able to touch her the way he longed to. With her hand still on his face, Midas licked against her bottom lip, asking permission for entry.

She gave it immediately, but instead of waiting for him to make the first move, her tongue pushed into his mouth.

Midas smiled even as he kissed Lexie back.

She kissed as she did everything else...with enthusiasm and damn the consequences. Their kiss was more emotional than passionate, but it was no less life altering for Midas.

After a minute or so of the best, most intensely emotional kiss he'd ever had in his life, he felt Lexie pull back. She stared at him as her thumb brushed back and forth over his cheek. He wasn't sure she was even aware she was doing it.

Midas ached to touch her, as well. To cup the back of her head, tangle his fingers in her untamed hair and devour her. But all he could do was meet her gaze and make sure she knew how much he admired her and wanted to keep in touch.

He took a breath to say the words, when the back door opened and someone entered the store.

And just like that, the mood shifted. Midas's hand tightened on his rifle and all his attention was on the footsteps above them. But instead of continuing into the store, they stopped. Scraping sounded on the wood, and Midas tensed further.

He felt even more protective over the woman in his arms now. No one was going to take her from him. No way in hell.

One of the boards above them shifted a fraction, then whoever had moved it stepped back.

"It's okay. Safe," a deep voice said from above.

Midas didn't move. And when Lexie shifted against him as if to push the boards back, he shook his head sharply. She settled back down.

"Lexie? It's Shermake."

"Shermake?" she asked, loud enough for the person to hear.

Midas pressed his lips together in frustration. He remembered that Shermake was the name of Astur's oldest son, but he had no way of knowing if it was really him above them. If he was on their side or the side of the kidnappers.

But he had no choice now, the person in the store obviously knew they were there, so he needed to act.

In one swift movement, he sprang upward. He knew he'd jostled Lexie way too hard, but it couldn't be helped. He'd rather her be bruised than dead.

The boards above them flew out of the way as he exited the small space under the floor. Midas's muscles protested after being in one position for so long, but he ignored the insignificant pain. He pointed his rifle at the young man in the small back room as he stood.

Shermake immediately raised his hands, showing he was unarmed.

Looking around, Midas saw that he'd come into the store alone, but that didn't mean there weren't others outside waiting to ambush them.

"Friend!" the boy said quickly.

Midas felt more than saw Lexie coming up to her knees at his feet, and he said, "Stay down, Lex."

"Shermake?" she asked again, ignoring his warning.

Then she stood all the way up and sat on the edge of the hole.

"It is me," the boy said with a small smile for Lexie.

She tugged on Midas's pants. "It's okay, Midas. I know him. He's Astur's son. We're good."

Midas couldn't be completely sure of that, but he did lower his rifle so it wasn't pointed straight at the kid.

"Don't—" Midas said, but it was too late. Lexie had already climbed out of the hole they'd been in for hours, taking the few steps to reach Shermake. Then they were embracing as if they were long lost friends, separated for years.

"You've gotten so tall!" Lexie said with a small laugh.

"And you short," Shermake retorted.

Midas did the math and realized the kid in front of him was less a boy than he was a man. He was probably closer to seventeen now, and around here, that meant he had way more responsibilities than a kid the same age in the United States. He was a few inches taller than Lexie, would probably be over six feet tall when he finished growing. He had on a black T-shirt, brown shorts that went to his knees, and a tattered pair of sneakers on his feet. His hair was cut short...and he was looking at Lexie as if he worshiped the ground she walked on.

It was that look that made Midas relax. He saw nothing but worry for her in the boy's expression.

"What are you doing here?" Lexie asked.

Shermake looked down at her as if she was crazy. "Helping you," he said. "Mother said you were here. Had to wait for dark. So happy you okay. Sorry my people steal you."

"It wasn't your fault. Your English has gotten really good," Lexie praised.

"I be practicing," Shermake said. "Come, we go. I know where American and Denmark soldiers are."

"And Dagmar?" Lexie asked. "The man who was kidnapped with me?"

Shermake shook his head. "I know not."

"Wait," Midas said, not quite ready to fully trust this young man yet. "I'm sorry, but I don't know you. How do we know we can trust you?"

"Midas," Lexie protested, but he didn't take his gaze from Shermake's.

"You trust me," he said. "I know men who watch for Lexie. They not good. Lazy. No want to work for money. Abshir Farah. He was in desert. Not killed. Came back here to tell story about desert fight and get friends to try to take Lexie again. Want money. I can get you back to friends. Trust me."

Midas pressed his lips together. It was always a possibility that they hadn't killed all the kidnappers, but it was surprising how fast this Abshir person had gotten back to Galkayo and gathered the troops. He and his team had made an error in coming back. They should've gone straight to the ship. But the Jaeger Corps had talked them into agreeing to Magnus's plan. Money talked, and it was obvious the Brander family had some serious power to be able to influence the special forces the way Magnus had.

"I swear on my family life, Lexie is safe with me," Shermake said in a low, earnest tone.

Midas finally nodded. He still didn't one hundred percent trust the kid, but it would be preferable to have a guide through the streets of Galkayo. Especially if he knew where his team was holed up.

He held out a hand to Lexie and something within him settled when she immediately came to his side.

"Stay next to me at all times," he ordered. "If I go too fast, tell me. If you're in pain, tell me so I can help you."

"Okay, Midas. I will."

"I mean it. We have no idea what or who is waiting for us outside this door. My objective has always been to get you out of here safe and sound. Doesn't matter that we aren't in the desert anymore, my goal is the same."

"I understand," she said solemnly.

Midas couldn't help adding, "And after that," he gestured to the hole in the floor with his head, "I'm even more determined to make sure you get out of here without a fucking scratch."

Lexie licked her lips, as if remembering what had happened right before Shermake interrupted them. She nodded.

Midas reached out and tucked a lock of hair behind her ear. It was plastered to her head on one side, the side that had been pressed against his shoulder. He could see sweat marks at her neck and underarms. She was a hot mess...and he'd never been more attracted to a woman in his life.

A noise behind them caught Midas's attention, and he looked over Lexie's shoulder to see Shermake sitting on the floor, untying his shoes.

He took both off then stood and held the sneakers out to Lexie. "You wear on feet."

Lexie looked confused. "What?"

"Your feet. Wear," Shermake repeated.

"He's giving you his shoes," Midas explained.

Lexie shook her head and took a step back, running into

Midas. "No, I'm not taking your shoes," she said stubbornly.

"Yes. Take," Shermake said just as stubbornly.

Midas reached for the shoes and nodded at the boy. "Put them on, Lex."

"No. Midas, you don't understand. When I met him months ago, he had not one pair of shoes. He was barefoot, as were his brother and sister. I'm not taking his shoes. I can't."

"You are," Midas said, kneeling at her feet and holding one of the sneakers.

"I get another pair. Big box of shoes come from France. Lots of shoes for all. I get more. You need. My feet are tough. Street no bother me. You *need*." Shermake looked extremely concerned.

"Shit," Lexie said under her breath. "He'll be offended if I *don't* take them."

"Exactly. Now come on, I don't know about you, but I'm ready to get out of here," Midas told her. He was touched the boy had offered his shoes to Lexie. It would absolve one of his many worries when it came to sneaking through the city streets. Not having to worry about Lexie stepping on glass and slicing up her feet would make him feel much better. He just hoped the boy didn't suffer that fate.

She put one hand on his shoulder to keep her balance as she lifted a foot. Midas slipped the shoe on and quickly tied it as tightly as he could. Once the second sneaker was on, she turned to Shermake. She hugged him once more. "Thank you so much."

"They fit?"

Midas knew they didn't. They were too big, but she smiled up at him and nodded anyway. "They're perfect," she told him.

"We no need shoes," the teenager said. "We need education. Teach us how to *make* shoes, and we no need charity. Teach us how to make clothes, and we no need second-hand

American ones. Teach us how to make electricity, do math, make water last, and Somali people grow stronger."

Lexie squeezed his arm. "I know. I do."

"We would not need to take people for money if we had ways to make it for ourselves," Shermake said.

Midas nodded. He understood. What was the saying? Give a man a fish and he can feed his family. *Teach* a man to fish, and he can feed a village.

Shermake shook his head as if clearing it, then he knelt near the hole Midas and Lexie had been in all day and placed the boards back to the way they were before, concealing the hiding spot. "We go now," he said.

Midas took Lexie's hand and tucked it into the waistband of his pants once more. "Be careful," he told her, nodding down at her feet. "Don't trip."

"I won't," she said.

Then the three of them slipped out the back door and headed into the alley behind the store. It wasn't as dark as Midas would've liked it, but the sun was definitely below the horizon. In thirty minutes or so it would be pitch black, and hopefully he and Lexie would be back with his team by then.

Shermake moved confidently down the alley and Midas followed more cautiously. He was ninety-nine percent sure the teenager wouldn't betray them, but he wasn't willing to risk Lexie's life by letting down his guard.

They exited onto a street and immediately entered another alley. Then another. And so it went. Shermake kept to the narrow alleyways of the town, staying in the shadows. He didn't hesitate when deciding which way to turn, and Midas was quickly lost. They cut through some pretty sketchy areas, but the few people they saw didn't even glance their way.

Within twenty minutes, they'd arrived at a part of town that was obviously more prosperous than where they'd come from. Shermake crouched down in yet another alley and

Midas did the same, ever aware of Lexie sticking right by his side.

"You go alone now," Shermake said. "Cross road there, go right until brown house, take left and you will see soldiers."

Midas nodded. "Thank you."

"Did for Lexie."

"I know," Midas said. He wasn't offended in the least. Lexie had a way of gaining loyalty from everyone around her.

"I'll never forget you," Lexie said as she shifted around Midas to give the boy one more hug.

They all stood as Shermake said, "I never forget you too."

Lexie pulled back and kept her hands on the teenager's shoulders. "Keep studying. Your English is good, but it can be better." She smiled to let him know she was teasing him. "You are going to do great things, Shermake. I know it. Tell Hodan and Cumar I'm sorry I missed them. Take care of your mom."

"I will," Shermake said. "Go now. Be safe."

Lexie nodded.

Midas reached into one of the pockets in his vest and pulled out some Somali shillings. He and his team made it a point to always carry some local currency, just in case. It had come in handy more than once in past missions.

The exchange rate of shillings to dollars was ridiculous, so much so that Midas wasn't too surprised that Lexie and Dagmar's kidnappers were so desperate to get them back. A thousand shillings was less than two American dollars. The highest denomination of shilling was one thousand, and he pulled out twenty of them, all he had on him, and held them out to Shermake.

The boy's eyes widened, and he took a step back, shaking his head.

"Take it," Midas told him. "I wish it was more, but it's all I have on me."

"I no help for money," the teenager said stubbornly.

"I know," Midas said. And he did. "But please, let me help

you. I'm indebted to you, and will do what I can to help you and your family in the future, but for now, it would please me if you took this."

It was less than forty dollars, but he had a feeling for Shermake and his family, it was a fortune. The poverty rate in the country was estimated at sixty-nine percent, meaning that many people made less than two dollars a day.

Midas didn't know how he was going to make good on his promise to help Shermake's family, but he'd figure it out. He could never fully repay Astur and Shermake for what they'd done for Lexie. And himself by extension.

The boy finally nodded and took the money, stuffing it into a pocket in his pants. Then he turned without another word and headed back the way they'd come.

"Shit, now I'm crying," Lexie said with a small sniff.

Midas wanted to comfort her, but he needed to get her to safety. "Cry and walk," he said gently.

"You're a good man, Pierce Cagle," she said as she once more grabbed hold of his waistband.

"Just a thankful one," he returned. "He could've led us straight to the people who were looking for you."

"He wouldn't do that. He's watched his family struggle and hates that he can't help more. He's a good kid."

"Even good kids can get led astray by the prospect of money," Midas said.

"I know."

She didn't say anything else, and Midas didn't press his point. They walked to the end of the alley and when Midas peered out into the street, it was empty. He quickly followed Shermake's directions and within five minutes, he saw the best sight he'd seen in hours.

Five shapes appeared out of the shadows. Shapes Midas recognized.

"About time you decided to join us," Aleck joked.

"Shit, Midas, you been taking a nap somewhere or what?" Pid asked.

"Fucking radios, we need to trash these and get new ones," Slate complained.

"You two all right?" Mustang asked.

"Jesus, what did you do to her, Midas? She looks like she's been through the wringer," Slate said.

"You should see the other guy," Lexie deadpanned.

Everyone chuckled, and the tension in the air lessened tenfold.

Midas was relieved that she didn't get offended by Slate's comment. So far she'd taken literally everything in stride, and it was amazing, really. But no matter how well Lexie seemed to be holding up, she'd most likely crash at some point. She'd been through hell, and while she was coping remarkably well, he had a feeling when she had a moment to herself, to reflect on all that had happened, she'd crumble.

"We getting out of here or what? Where'd you and the Jaeger Corps stash Dagmar? Let's get them and get the fuck out of here already," Midas said.

Silence fell—and Midas mentally swore.

"What? Did they already leave?" Lexie asked, looking at everyone in confusion.

For the first time since they'd left the hospital, Midas put the strap of his rifle around his head and arm, resting the weapon on his back. He didn't need to keep it at the ready, his team would protect both him and Lexie.

He put his arm around Lexie and pulled her into his side even as Mustang broke the news. "He didn't make it. I'm so sorry, Lexie."

"What?" she asked in a shocked whisper.

"When the explosives went off at the hospital, he had a massive heart attack. He didn't make it."

"No," she whispered, shaking her head. "He was okay. I mean, I knew he was sick, but he was talking. He was *fine*."

"He had a stroke in the desert, like you guessed. His heart was too weak to take any more stress. When the kidnappers found out he was dead, and that you'd slipped through their fingers, they ran off to hunt you down. The Jaeger Corps left a few hours ago with his body. They're heading to Italy, and then on to Denmark," Mustang said.

Lexie's chin dropped to her chest and she sighed deeply. She stood with her arms at her sides as Midas hugged her against him. "Lex?" he asked.

"I'm okay," she said softly. "I just can't imagine what his brother will think. I guess they were really close. It sucks that he was actually rescued, only to die before he could get home."

"I'm sure Magnus Brander would appreciate your condolences once we get you somewhere safe," Jag said.

"Yeah," Lexie said with a nod, but Midas could tell she was lost in her own head.

"Come on," he said. "Let's get the hell out of here, yeah?"

"Fine by me," Pid said.

"Just been waiting on you," Slate said with a small smirk.

Midas knew his friends were teasing. It was obvious they'd been worried.

"How'd you find us, anyway?" Mustang asked.

"A friend of Lexie's led the way," Midas told them. He explained Shermake's and his mother's role in their escape. Then said, "I'd like to repay them when we get home."

"I'm sure Baker will be happy to help track them down," Aleck said. "All he'll need is their names and other details that you can remember, and it'll be done."

"Who's Baker?" Lexie asked.

"A guy back home in Hawaii who gets stuff done," Jag said.

"Wow, that was vague," Lexie complained.

"He's hard to explain," Mustang told her as they walked. "He's a former SEAL, a hard-core surfer dude, and a bit like a mainframe computer. He knows everyone, can find any information about anyone, and is grumpy as fuck."

"He sounds fascinating. Is he as good-looking as you guys?" Lexie asked.

"You think we're good-looking?" Jag asked, exaggeratingly puffing out his chest.

"Well, you're all looking a bit rough. Especially him," Lexie said, gesturing with her head to Slate.

His friends chuckled. She was grieving for Dagmar, that was obvious, but she was still doing her best to be friendly to his team.

"Did I ever formally introduce you to everyone?" Midas asked.

"No. But it's not like we really had the time," Lexie said.

"True. So, that's Aleck. His last name is Smart, so you know why his nickname is Aleck," Midas said quietly as they walked. He assumed they were headed for the LZ for the chopper that he hoped was on its way to pick them up. They'd have to board quickly, just in case the kidnappers tried one last time to prevent Lexie from leaving the country.

"So are you really a smart aleck, or did you just get stuck with that moniker?" Lexie asked.

"Oh, I one hundred percent live up to my nickname," Aleck said with a smile.

"Next to him is Pid; his first name is Stuart," Midas said.

Lexie groaned. "Jeez, you guys need better nicknames."

"Then there's Jag, whose name is Jagger."

"Ah, that's better," Lexie said with a smile in his direction.

"The impatient one is Slate—whose last name is Stone—and Mustang is our team leader."

"The one married to Elodie, right?" Lexie asked.

"You heard about my wife?" Mustang asked.

She nodded. "We had a bit of time to kill today," she said.

"You and Elodie have something in common. I met her in

the Middle East too. Of course, she was on a ship and not on land, but still."

"She sounds pretty amazing," Lexie said.

"She is," Mustang said simply.

"And she makes a hell of a hamburger," Aleck added.

Lexie groaned. "Let's not talk about food, okay?" she asked.

Midas made a mental note that getting food for Lex was his top priority.

They walked for another five minutes, the team making small talk with Lexie. Midas knew they were trying to distract her from what was going to be an incredibly dangerous few minutes as soon as the chopper was incoming.

They arrived at the outskirts of the neighborhood they'd been walking in and Midas stared out at a large expanse of desert. It was fascinating how the town simply ended and the desert started. There were literally no lights in front of them, only sand as far as the eye could see...which wasn't very far at the moment, since it was dark.

"Can she run in those huge sneakers?" Pid asked Midas.

"I can run," Lexie answered for herself.

"Sorry, didn't mean to talk over you."

"It's okay. I know I'm just the chick you were sent in to rescue, and I'm no Navy SEAL, but I'm not helpless either," Lexie told him.

"I'm guessing there's a story behind those shoes," Jag said. "As far as I know, you weren't wearing them when we rescued you from the desert."

"Nope. Shermake gave them to me," Lexie said.

"Yeah, Baker will definitely want to help," Slate said, understanding how important a gesture it was that the teenager had given up his shoes.

"You all ready?" Mustang asked.

Everyone nodded.

"Ready for what?" Lexie whispered to Midas.

"To run. When that chopper approaches, everyone in town's gonna know. And the people who don't want you to leave will try to get here as fast as they can," he told her.

"Then it's a good thing they can't run faster than the helicopter can fly, isn't it?" Lexie asked.

Midas heard his teammates chuckling, but he couldn't take his eyes off Lexie. She looked incredibly sad, but now she also had a determined gleam in her eye. She also still looked as if she'd been through hell and back, but it was now somehow part of her charm. "Definitely," Midas agreed. "Stay by my side," he told her. "Mustang and Aleck will take point, we'll go after them, and Pid, Jag, and Slate will have our backs. When we get to the chopper, just hold up your arms and Mustang and Aleck will help you inside. Crawl away from the door as soon as you get inside. Okay?"

"Okay," she said immediately. "And I've already done this once, remember? Piece of cake."

Her voice wobbled a little, but she lifted her chin as if daring him to comment on it.

There was no way Midas was going to say a damn word. He'd be worried if she wasn't a little scared of what was about to happen. But Midas had the utmost trust in the Night Stalker helicopter pilots. They were badass in their own right and could fly in the worse of conditions. As long as they could get inside the chopper, they were good to go.

"Incoming," Mustang said.

Midas heard the rotor blades of the helicopter as it flew fast and low toward the LZ.

Within seconds, sand flew in all directions and Midas felt Lexie duck her head against his chest as she did her best to protect her face. He took her hand in his and leaned down. "On the count of three, run like hell. Keep your eyes closed. I won't let you fall."

She nodded, and his belly clenched with the amount of trust she was literally putting in the palm of his hand.

"One, two, *three*," he counted, then took off running, Lexie at his side.

The sand hurt his face but he ignored it. Getting to safety was more important than a little discomfort right about now. He watched as Mustang and Aleck leaped into the opening of the chopper and immediately turned with their arms outstretched.

Midas positioned Lexie at the door and shouted, "Arms up, Lex."

She immediately complied and disappeared inside the helicopter. Midas leaped in behind her and was quickly followed by the rest of his teammates. Within seconds, he felt the chopper lurch, then they were in the air once more.

Everyone was tense for several minutes as they flew fast back toward the desert—and hopefully away from anyone who might want to try to shoot them down.

But their exit from Galkayo was uneventful. As the lights from the Somali town got smaller and smaller, Midas breathed out a sigh of relief. He turned to Lexie and gave her a thumb's up. They hadn't paused to put on headphones, so they couldn't talk, but it didn't seem to matter. She beamed at him and returned his thumb's up.

Yeah, it was safe to say Lexie Greene was officially under his skin. And Midas had no idea how he was going to be able to give her up.

CHAPTER SEVEN

Lexie did her best to put on a positive and happy face for the SEALs. She was certainly thankful to be out of danger of being re-kidnapped, but her future was still so uncertain. Not to mention, she was completely out of her depth. She didn't know much about the military, and being deposited on a US Navy ship was so far out of her comfort zone, it wasn't even funny.

More than that, she knew that her time with Midas was coming to an end. He'd go back to Hawaii with his team, and she'd be on her own once more.

For the first time ever, Lexie wasn't happy with her solitary lifestyle. When she'd first joined Food For All, she'd been thrilled to get away from her dad and his snide remarks and his constant belittling comments. She'd enjoyed living by herself and not having to answer to anyone. But now she understood she literally had no one who would be worried about her. No one to know or care if she disappeared off the face of the Earth.

Being kidnapped had brought home just how alone she truly was. And it sucked.

She loved the closeness Midas seemed to have with his

friends, and hearing about Mustang and his wife made a visceral longing rise up within her. She wanted that closeness but had no idea how to get it. With friends or with a man.

And it sucked even more that she felt such a connection with Midas. She wanted to think he felt it too. That kiss they'd shared had literally rocked her world. But they hadn't had time to talk about what it meant...if it meant anything at all. It could've just been the situation.

Midas had given her a set of noise-canceling headphones to wear in the helicopter, but they weren't connected to the rest, so she had no idea what the others were talking about. Midas tapped her on the shoulder and pointed out the small window, and she sat up straighter to look outside and caught a glimpse of a huge Navy ship. It was dark outside, but the lights on the ship were like a welcoming beacon. The chopper turned and began to drop elevation, and Lexie steeled herself.

This was it. They'd land, and she'd have to say goodbye to Midas.

She wasn't ready.

But ready or not, the helicopter slowed as it descended to the deck of the ship.

Lexie started badly when Midas put his hand on her thigh. They still couldn't talk because of the noise, but when she looked over at him, he smiled and nodded.

It was a little pathetic how much that simple touch meant. Lexie wasn't a touchy-feely person. How could she be when she'd been single for so long? But after spending the day plastered against Midas, she was beginning to see why people craved human touch so much.

The chopper landed without much fuss and Lexie winced at the bright lights shining inside the interior through the open door. Midas helped her take off the headphones, then Slate and Jag held out their hands, assisting her to climb out of the machine.

A woman was there to greet her. "On behalf of the *USS Nimitz* and all her crew, welcome home, Lexie," she said.

"Um...thanks," Lexie mumbled.

"I've been ordered to bring you straight to the infirmary so you can be looked over. Don't worry, you're safe now."

Lexie nodded. She'd expected to wait for Midas and his team to exit the helicopter, but the woman gestured in front of her and said, "After you."

Without a choice, Lexie headed in the direction the woman had indicated. She looked back to see if Midas was coming too, but saw he was preoccupied talking with his team and the other Naval officials who had greeted the chopper. He didn't even look over as she walked away.

Lexie felt off-kilter and nervous, now that Midas wasn't with her. It was stupid. This was an American ship and the woman escorting her to the infirmary was gracious and nice. But she'd hoped to at least get to say goodbye to Midas. To thank him again. To tell him...

She wasn't sure what she wanted to say.

Her escort held open a thick steel door and Lexie stepped over the threshold. She winced as it clanged shut behind them. The sound was loud and final.

That was that. Midas would head back to Hawaii with his team and she'd...

She wasn't sure what she would do next.

Once inside the ship, the woman stepped in front of her and led Lexie down several staircases and hallways until she was hopelessly lost. There was no way she'd be able to find her way back up to the deck...not without a lot of help.

As she walked, the woman chattered about nothing in particular, pointing out things like where the enlisted and officers ate, and the break rooms. Everyone they encountered nodded respectfully as they passed, but the farther they got from the chopper, and the SEALs, the more self-conscious Lexie became. She knew she looked rough. Her hair was probably sticking up in its usual unruly way, her scrubs were filthy from sweat and dirt, and she wore Shermake's too-big sneakers on her feet. All the sailors she passed were dressed in immaculately pressed uniforms.

Finally, they arrived at a door bearing a big red cross. They entered the infirmary and her escort gestured to a table toward the back of the room. The room was empty except for them, and for some reason that made Lexie feel even *more* self-conscious. She'd never been comfortable being the center of attention.

"Go ahead and sit there," the woman said. "The doctor's been notified that you're here, so I'm sure he'll be arriving soon."

"I don't want to be a bother," Lexie said.

The woman's brows furrowed as if she was confused. "A bother?" she asked.

"Yeah. If the doctor was sleeping or something, I could've waited until the morning to see him. All I need is a place to sleep."

The sailor shook her head. "Lexie, you were a hostage. You need to be seen right away. Besides, it's his job."

"Right. Sorry," Lexie said, feeling as if she'd been chastised for some reason.

"There's a gown over there you can change into," the woman said, pointing over to a stack of plastic-wrapped garments. "I'm just going to step out while you change. It really is good to see you. We were all pulling for you."

Then she nodded and turned and left the room.

Lexie didn't move. She didn't want to change her clothes. She felt vulnerable enough as it was. She wasn't going to be practically naked when she met the doctor for the first time.

Shivering as the chilly temperature of the room began to register, Lexie lifted her feet and put them on the edge of the table she was sitting on. She knew she was probably contaminating the clean paper under her, but she didn't care. She wrapped her arms around her legs and sighed.

Why being here felt scarier than anything else she'd done in the last twenty-four hours, Lexie didn't know. Maybe because she was surrounded by strangers and had no idea what would happen next. It wasn't a good feeling. How would she get off this ship? Where would she go? Did she still have a job with Food For All?

She didn't like feeling so out of control of her own life.

Lexie rested her cheek on her updrawn knees. Suddenly, she was exhausted. She'd been running on pure adrenaline and bravado since the SEALs had attacked the camp out in the desert. Yes, she'd gotten some sleep in the hole with Midas, but that seemed like a lifetime ago.

Her muscles hurt, her heart hurt for Dagmar, and she was sad that she hadn't gotten to say goodbye to Midas or his friends. She knew they probably rescued people all the time, so she wasn't anything special to them, but this was the first time *she'd* been rescued. And she would've felt a lot better if she'd at least gotten to say thank you.

Not sure how much time had passed, Lexie jerked when the door to the infirmary opened once more. A man who looked way too young to be a doctor entered. He smiled at her and said, "Lexie Greene?"

She nodded.

"I'm Doctor Chow. I understand you've been a POW for a few months, is that right?"

Lexie was annoyed. It was stupid, but she couldn't believe this guy didn't already know.

Then, she immediately felt bad. How egocentric was she? Thinking everyone would automatically know who she was and what she'd been through.

"Yes," she said. "But I feel pretty good, all things considered."

He was carrying what looked like an iPad, which he lifted

and begin to tap. He looked up at her after a short period of time and frowned. "You haven't changed into a gown."

"No," she said. "I feel more comfortable in what I'm wearing." And she did.

The doctor nodded, as if reading more into what she'd said. "You're safe here," he told her. "No one will hurt you."

"I know," Lexie said. Then it dawned on her what he meant. "I wasn't raped," she said.

He nodded again, but it was clear he didn't believe her.

Lexie wanted to cry. She didn't want to be here. "I wasn't," she insisted. "I'm tired. And hungry. And thirsty. I'm sore from hiding out all day in a hole under a floor of a shop in Galkayo. I'm cold because I'm not used to the air conditioning. But I'm honestly surprised at how good I feel. I just need a shower, some clean clothes, and a place to sleep." It felt good to stand up for herself.

But the doctor's next words wiped away her confidence.

"How about you let me do a complete workup and figure out what you need?"

Lexie sighed. She knew the man was just doing his job. She nodded. What else could she do?

* * *

Midas was annoyed. After they'd landed on the aircraft carrier, he'd been momentarily preoccupied talking with the Night Stalkers who'd picked them up, and when he'd turned around to escort Lexie to the infirmary, she was gone.

Mustang informed him that she'd already been led away. Then he and the rest of the team had to debrief about the mission. He'd had to explain what he'd done at the hospital, and where he and Lexie had hidden out all day. He'd listened as the rest of his team reported about Dagmar's death and what they'd done to avoid the groups of men looking for Lexie and Dagmar.

The digital meeting with their commander back in Hawaii had gone on for three hours. Once everything had been recorded and reported and their superior officers were satisfied for the time being, Midas and the rest of the team were dismissed.

They had a few hours to get some sleep, then right after first light, they were being flown to South Korea before heading back to Hawaii. Midas was exhausted, but there was no way he'd be able to sleep without seeing how Lexie was doing.

He was sure she was fine. She was probably sleeping anyway, but leaving without talking to her seemed...wrong. It felt as if they had unfinished business. After all, they'd been interrupted right after that amazing kiss, and he hadn't even had a chance to let her know he wanted to keep in touch.

"You going to find Lexie?" Mustang asked in the narrow hallway outside the conference room they'd been in for the last few hours. The other guys had already left to hit the showers and to catch some z's.

"Yes," he said, a little more forcefully than he'd meant to.

"Easy," Mustang said. "I was just asking."

"Sorry. I know."

"Things were pretty intense there for a while, huh?" Mustang asked.

Midas nodded. "She was amazing though. Didn't panic. Even when we had to go out the window of the hospital, she didn't even flinch. She ran through the streets with me without shoes on, Mustang. And not once did she complain about it."

"She doesn't seem like the complaining type," his friend said. "It's damn lucky you two ran into that woman she knew."

"Yeah. But here's the thing, if it wasn't her, I'm convinced it would've been someone else. She doesn't have a mean bone in her body and is generous to a fault."

Mustang tilted his head. "It sounds as if she's more than a mission to you."

"I think she is," Midas admitted out loud for the first time. Then he shook his head. "But there's no way this is gonna work out."

Mustang laughed. Actually threw his head back and laughed at him.

Midas glared at his friend. "You're an asshole," he said, frowning.

"I'm sorry," Mustang said, not sounding sorry at all. "But you're standing there saying it's impossible for anything to work out with the woman you rescued, to a man who recently married a woman he rescued while on a mission halfway across the world from where he lives."

Midas pressed his lips together. His friend's comment was convoluted, but he'd made his point.

Mustang went on. "Look. I know how you feel, okay? Out of everyone on the team, I *know*. You know how crazy I was when we got back to Hawaii and I was waiting to hear from Elodie. I drove you all nuts. But there was something about her that was different than anyone else I'd met. The odds of us making it were slim to none, but I'm standing in front of you a very happily married man, madly in love with his wife, telling you not to give up. I've never seen you this worked up about a woman, Midas. Don't let her be your biggest regret. A relationship with her might not be easy, but it could also be the best thing that's ever happened to you."

"I just don't know how it can work out."

"I didn't either. All I knew was that it sucked that I had to leave Elodie on that ship," Mustang said. "You just gotta trust that if you and her are meant to be, it'll work out."

"Well, that was vague as shit," Midas complained.

Mustang chuckled. "Sorry. Go find her, Midas. Tell her flat out that you want to keep in touch. See where things go from there."

"Thanks," Midas said.

Mustang clapped him on the shoulder and nodded. "For the record? I like her. I obviously don't know her as well as you do, but I can see the appeal."

His friend's approval meant a lot to Midas. It wouldn't've stopped him from keeping in touch with her regardless, but it felt a hell of a lot better to know Mustang approved.

Midas knew he should probably shower before he tracked down Lex, but he was too impatient to see her. To find out what the doctor had said. To make sure she was good. It took a bit to find the infirmary because he wasn't familiar with the ship, but after a few wrong turns, and asking some of the sailors who were out and about even at this time of night, he found it. Midas had no idea if she would still be there, but it was a place to start.

He pushed open the door and looked around the room. There were several examination tables, as well as twin-size cots along the back wall, for those patients who needed extra monitoring. His eyes immediately zeroed in on the only cot in the back that was occupied.

Midas walked toward it, eager to talk to Lexie.

But when he got his first glimpse of her, his stomach dropped.

She was lying on her side, and he could literally see the blanket over her vibrating because she was shaking so hard.

"What the fuck?" he muttered. Midas went to his knees beside the low bed and put his hand on Lexie's shoulder. "Lex?" he asked.

She rolled over—and Midas mentally kicked himself in the ass. Her face was red and blotchy from crying, her eyes were swollen and, even as he watched, more tears spilled over her lids.

Without a word, he got up and gently scooted her over, climbing onto the small twin mattress with her.

"Midas? What are you—"

"Move over," he said, interrupting her.

She did as he asked, although the tiny amount of space left on the mattress wasn't going to be enough. So Midas switched to a position he knew would work. He lifted Lexie and rolled to his back, tucking her against him in the same position they'd been in for most of the day. It was hard to believe they'd been in that hole only hours ago.

Instead of protesting, Lexie snuggled into him and turned her face against his shoulder. Her arm went across his chest, and this time he could feel everything. Without his Kevlar vest and all his battle accoutrement, she felt even better against him.

"You're so warm," she said softly.

Midas shifted so he could pull the blanket she'd been using up and over her shoulders. "They always keep the infirmary cold, I don't know why," he told her.

"It's fine. It's just, after spending all that time in the hot desert, I think my body's all out of whack."

It was good to hear her talking somewhat normally, but Midas was still kicking himself for not being there when her adrenaline finally wore off and she broke.

"Are you all right? What did the doctor say? Why are you still in the same scrubs you've been wearing all day? And are you seriously still wearing Shermake's shoes?" Midas asked, feeling the sneakers against his calves as she curled around him.

"He said I was dehydrated," Lexie answered, irritation easy to hear in her tone. "He got annoyed with me when I wouldn't change. He was condescending and made me feel as if somehow getting kidnapped was my fault. I got the impression he was hoping I was all banged up or shot or something, and when all he could find wrong was that I was hungry, dirty, and thirsty, he was disappointed."

Midas's irritation rose tenfold. But he did his best to keep his voice calm as he spoke. "I'm guessing life on an aircraft carrier isn't always the most exciting for the ship's doctor. I'm sorry he made you feel that way."

She shrugged but didn't comment. Eventually her shaking subsided, and Midas felt her sigh against him.

"Midas?"

"Yeah, Lex?"

"What are you doing here?"

"You think I was gonna leave without saying goodbye?" he asked.

She shrugged again. "I don't know anything about how the military works. I figured you and your friends might leave right away."

"No. We had to debrief," he told her. "After we landed, I was talking to the guys who flew us out, and then I turned around and you were gone."

"I was gonna say something, but you were busy...and the woman who greeted me seemed anxious to get me inside," Lexie said.

"I'm sorry," he said.

She shook her head. "No, it's fine."

"You eat?"

"Yeah. The doctor called someone and they brought me something."

"Something?" Midas questioned.

"Yeah, don't ask me what it was. Some kind of meat in a heavy sauce. Honestly, I was so hungry I would've eaten anything."

"You get your sweet coffee?" he asked.

She snorted. "No. Two bags of IV fluids and two bottles of water."

"To be fair, that was probably better for you."

"I know."

"You know there's a shower in here," he said gently.

"It's stupid, but the more the doctor tried to convince me to change, the more nervous it made me. I don't have *anything*, Midas. Nothing. No clothes. No shoes. Not even underwear. And if they take these scrubs away..." Her voice trailed off.

Midas got it. He did. "It's okay," he said.

"It's not. I'm being ridiculous. I mean, these scrubs aren't even really mine. I've only had them less than a day. They're dirty and sweaty...but they're literally all I have."

Midas's heart ached.

"And I'm not giving up Shermake's shoes. He gave them to me when they were probably the only pair he had. Yeah, he can get another from whatever charity organization is giving them out, but still."

"It's okay," he assured her again, running a hand over her hair. It was just as unruly as the last time they'd lain together, but this time his hands were free and he had room to touch her. His fingers tangled in the thick strands, and he couldn't help but smile.

"If you're not careful, you'll lose your hand," she told him.

She'd stopped crying, which Midas was grateful for. He hated to think of her lying alone in this room, cold, uneasy, and upset. "I'll risk it," he told her.

Several minutes went by in silence. Midas felt content just to hold her and stroke her hair gently.

Lexie broke the silence by asking, "I know why *I'm* still in my dirty, smelly clothes, but why are you?"

He chuckled. "We went to debrief and just got out a bit ago. I wanted to make sure you were settled and all right, so I came straight here."

She got up on one elbow and looked at him with an incredulous expression. There was a light on across the room, more than enough to see each other.

"What?" he asked.

"When do you leave?"

"In a few hours."

She fell back down on him with a sigh. "There's a shower in here you could use," she said, echoing his words.

"I know. But I'm comfortable where I am at the moment."

"Midas?"

"Right here."

"I'm gonna miss you," she admitted softly.

Midas closed his eyes in relief. God, this woman was so much braver than he was at the moment. He hadn't wanted to pressure her. To talk about what would come next for them, if anything. "Me too."

"You're gonna miss you too?" she teased.

"Smart-ass. You been taking lessons from Aleck? No, I'm gonna miss *you*."

"But not me smushing you when you're trying to sleep," she quipped.

"I actually like this. A lot," he told her. "You think you might want to keep in touch when we leave?" Midas blurted. He winced at how abrupt the question was, but he couldn't take it back now. He held his breath, waiting for her response.

She picked up her head once more to look at him. "Seriously?"

"Yes?" It came out more a question than a statement.

"I'd love to," she said with a smile.

"Phew," he said with exaggeration.

"I have to warn you though, I dictate my emails and texts, because you know...dyslexia, and there are usually typos."

"Don't care," Midas said immediately.

"You might when you can't understand what I'm saying," she warned.

"If I don't understand, I'll tell you. But you're underestimating my ability. I'm a big bad SEAL, you know."

She laughed as she lay back down once more.

"I've never felt this way before," he admitted.

"What way?" she asked.

"Connected. Concerned. Excited to get to know someone better. Frustrated that I have to leave in a few hours. Worried about what's next for you."

Lexie didn't immediately respond.

"Lex? Too much?" he asked.

"No," she said, shaking her head. "I just... I feel the same, but I was just wondering if it was because of the circumstances. I mean, I told you I wasn't a damsel in distress, but what if I am? What if I'm feeling so connected to you because you rescued me?"

Midas couldn't help but feel disappointed at the idea. Though he understood. He did. "I can't tell you how to feel," he said. "But you have to understand that I've been involved in the rescue of more people than I can count. And I've never skipped a shower, a meal, and a nap to make sure they're all right. I've always let the doctors do their thing and moved on.

"You've gotten under my skin, Lex. Maybe it's because I knew you in high school. I don't know. But I'm not willing to just let this go. I've never seen Mustang as happy or content as he is right now. And if it worked out for him and Elodie, why can't it work out for me too?"

He'd probably said too much, but this was important, and he knew it. He had a feeling if he left without making sure Lexie understood this wasn't casual for him, he'd never see her again.

"I have no idea what's next for me," she said softly. "Seriously, no clue what happens next. Where I'm going, how I'm getting back to the States, *if* I'm going back to the States. I need to talk to my boss at Food For All and see if I even have a job. I'm scared to death, and before you came in here, I was feeling sorry for myself and having a pity party. But I like you, Midas. I always have, even back when we were teenagers. And now that I know you a little better...yeah, I definitely want to keep in touch."

"Good," he said firmly. "I'll give you my phone number, email, and address. Feel free to call me whenever you want, and write or text. And you're gonna land on your feet, I know it. The authorities on the ship are working on figuring out how to get you somewhere safe, and they'll help you get in touch with the Food For All people. Don't worry about all that. You're in good hands here on the ship."

She nodded against him. "Okay. I'll give you my email too."

"Okay," he echoed.

It felt as if a ton of bricks had been lifted off his shoulders. She wanted to stay in touch. It didn't answer the question of where things would go for them, but it was a start.

His eyes began to get heavy as he lay with Lexie against him. He'd set his watch alarm so he knew he wouldn't oversleep, and that, along with the woman in his arms being safe and the knowledge that they'd be communicating after he left, was enough to finally make him let down his guard.

Midas fell into a deep sleep, more restful than any he'd gotten since he'd learned that Lexie Greene, a girl he used to know, had been kidnapped.

* * *

Midas's watch vibrated what seemed like minutes later, but had actually been three hours. Regretfully, he slipped out from under Lexie and headed for the small bathroom in the infirmary. He saw his duffle bag sitting inside the door to the room and smiled. Thank God for Mustang. He showered and changed into clean clothes before returning to Lexie's side.

She'd turned onto her side after he left and was clutching the pillow to her chest. Midas covered her with the blanket that had slipped off her shoulders and couldn't resist leaning in close and kissing her forehead.

Her eyes opened, and she stared at him for a second before turning onto her back. "It's time?" she asked.

"Unfortunately, yes."

"Be safe," she told him.

"Always."

"You showered," she said.

"Yeah, I didn't think the guys would appreciate my stinkiness on the long flights home. Not to mention everyone else."

"You being clean makes me realize how dirty I am," she said with a wrinkle of her nose.

"I left you some clothes in the bathroom," Midas told her. She blinked. "You did?"

"Yeah. They'll be too big," he warned. "You and I aren't exactly the same size. But I figured you might not mind the too-big T-shirt. You'll have to roll the sweatpants, but they should make do until you can find something that fits better. They do have a commissary on the ship, so you can get something in your size."

"Thank you," she whispered.

"I also left two pairs of socks and a small bag. You can put your shoes and things in it so no one mistakenly throws them away."

"Shit, you're gonna make me cry," Lexie said, as she lifted to a sitting position.

"Don't do that," Midas pleaded.

They stared at each other for a long moment.

Midas wasn't sure who made the first move, but suddenly they were both leaning toward each other. Then their lips met. Unlike when they'd kissed in Galkayo, this kiss didn't start out slow and easy. It was passionate and almost desperate from the get-go.

Midas had the use of his hands this time, and he palmed the back of Lexie's head, holding her in place as he devoured her. She gave as good as she got, moaning in the back of her throat and clutching the front of his shirt as they kissed. He hadn't shaved yet, and he was aware that his stubble was probably irritating her, but he couldn't stop.

Their tongues dueled; he nipped her bottom lip, and she did the same. He tilted his head one way, then the other, all while holding her still for his assault on her lips.

Midas was hard as a pike, and he wanted nothing more than to push Lexie back on the bed and show her how much she was beginning to mean to him. But this wasn't the time or the place. Anyone could walk in, and the last thing Midas would ever do was put Lexie in a position to be embarrassed.

He pulled back, but kept his hand on her head. He brought his other hand up and cupped her cheek. They were both breathing hard and he could see her pupils were dilated. Her cheeks were flushed, her lips were plump from their kiss. She was fucking gorgeous, and Midas hated to have to leave her.

"Wow," she whispered.

"This isn't goodbye," he said, a little harsher than he'd meant.

She nodded.

"I mean it," he warned. "The second you get off this ship, I want you to get a phone. Even one of those throwaway ones. I need to be able to talk to you. Find out where you are, what's going on."

"I'm sure Food For All can help me get one," Lexie said.

"Good."

He rested his forehead against hers and slowly untangled his hand from her hair. It was as if even her hair wanted to hold on to him, because it took a few seconds to free himself from the curly mass. "You've got this," he said softly. "You're amazing, Lexie. Things will work out. I know it."

He didn't know if he was talking about things between them working out, or her life in general, but it didn't matter. He was well aware that Lexie didn't need him. She was perfectly fine on her own. But he was beginning to think that *he* needed *her*. She made him want things he'd never even thought about before. Having a family. Doing more than merely existing between missions.

"I'll let you know when we get back to Hawaii."

She nodded.

Midas pulled back and sighed. It was time for him to go. "No goodbyes," he said again.

She nodded.

"See you later," he said softly.

"See you," she echoed.

Midas stood and walked backward toward the door, not wanting to turn his back on her. He gripped the handle, took a deep breath, then pushed the door open before finally turning around to step out.

Each step down the hall was painful, but he vowed this wouldn't be the last time he saw her. Somehow, someway, he'd see Lexie again and prove that the connection they felt was real. And not just a matter of circumstance.

* * *

Magnus Brander sat in a leather chair in his office staring straight ahead at nothing, in disbelief. He had no idea how this had happened. It was bad enough that his brother, his twin, had been kidnapped, but not once had Magnus ever thought he wouldn't get through the ordeal.

Some people scoffed at the notion that twins had some sort of higher-level connection, but in his and Dagmar's case, it was absolutely true. When they were babies, they'd had their own language. They'd babbled for hours and had been able to understand each other perfectly.

When they were in grade school, they'd pitched a fit if they weren't allowed to be in the same classes, on the same teams, or to do the same activities. Then they were rowdy adolescents, playing the normal tricks twins played on teachers and friends when they were teenagers.

And throughout it all, they were connected on a visceral level.

When Dagmar fell off his bike and broke his arm, Magnus felt it. When Magnus was in a car accident in his twenties, Dagmar had been the first person to call him, having known something was wrong.

So when Dagmar had been kidnapped while visiting one of the Food For All outposts, Magnus had sensed it immediately.

He'd done everything in his power to free his twin, even personally putting up the ransom amount that had been demanded.

But it wasn't enough.

The bastards had reneged on their agreement and doubled the amount.

There was no way Magnus would have paid for some American woman he didn't even know. And the more he'd learned about this Lexie Greene person, the more adamant he became. She didn't even have a college education, for God's sake! She was a nobody. *Had* nobody. Why should he—or Food For All, for that matter—pay for her release? Employees like her were a dime a dozen.

Dagmar was smart. And talented. And worth something.

And Magnus had just gotten word that his brother was dead. But he didn't need to be officially informed.

He'd already known his other half was gone. It was as if the moment it happened, part of his soul had been destroyed.

An emptiness sat in his chest where Dagmar's presence had resided. No one who wasn't a twin would understand.

Magnus was numb.

Yet deep down, a flicker of emotion was building...

Determination to make the person responsible for his brother's death pay.

As far as he was concerned, there was only one person on his radar.

Lexie fucking Greene.

If it hadn't been for her, Dagmar would've been released when the kidnappers were notified that the five million had been raised. But because of Lexie, they'd gotten greedy. Had decided to hold out for more.

Magnus didn't care that some people would think he was being crazy. He knew he wasn't. Lexie was the reason his best friend, the other half of his soul, was *dead*.

She was a fucking nobody! If she'd been worthy or important enough for someone to pony up the ransom for her, his brother would still be alive! *She* was the reason the kidnappers hadn't let his brother go.

And she'd regret being the one to live while his brother had died. Magnus didn't know how, or when, but he'd make it happen.

Lexie Greene needed to die. She might as well have held a gun to Dagmar's head and pulled the trigger. This was her fault. *All her fault*.

CHAPTER EIGHT

Lexie scanned the crowd as she walked toward the baggage carousels in the Honolulu International Airport. It had been one month, two days, and eighteen hours since she'd last seen Midas.

The first thing she'd done when she'd landed in Germany after being flown there by Food For All, and after talking to one of their relocation specialists, was get a cell phone. She'd sent Midas an email letting him know she now had a phone, and he'd responded literally within ten minutes.

They'd talked either via text, email, or phone calls every day since, while she'd spent time in Germany resting, regrouping, and replacing her wardrobe. It had been her choice to stay for so long. She'd had a lot of thinking to do about her future.

She had to give it to Food For All, they'd gone out of their way to help her transition back to the States. They'd paid for her hotel in Germany, as well, and given her all the time she needed to process what she'd been through and what she wanted to do next. Even though she'd only been held captive for three months, it felt like the entire world had passed her by in that time. It was silly really, not that much had changed, but acclimating to being able to do what she wanted, whenever she wanted, was tougher than she'd thought it would be after her rescue.

She'd also been allowed to choose her next assignment. She could go literally anywhere in the world where Food For All had a presence. Usually, she had to choose assignments based on what was available and according to seniority. Even though she'd been working for the organization for a decade and a half, there were plenty of people above her in the food chain, so she'd never gotten the most choice locations.

When she was presented with the list of every Food For All location, there was only one that really appealed.

It was crazy. Was she really going to choose to go to Hawaii because of a man?

Yes. Absolutely.

Lexie couldn't get the time she'd spent with Midas out of her head. While she one hundred percent wouldn't wish what she'd been through on anyone, she couldn't help but remember how attentive Midas had been during her visit to the Galkayo hospital. He'd been concerned enough not to wait for the doctor to put in her IV. She'd felt safe when they were hiding from the men hunting her. She'd never had anyone be so protective of her before. And while she knew part of that was because she was a mission, that wasn't the only reason.

And his kisses were like nothing she'd ever known. She wasn't inexperienced, but she'd felt like a virgin when he'd kissed her. Simply because she'd never felt with anyone the way she did when his lips touched hers.

She'd also chosen Honolulu because the giddy feelings inside her hadn't subsided since she'd said goodbye to Midas on that ship. They'd only gotten more intense. He sent her funny memes, was super sweet in his texts, and sent long, rambling emails about what he did each day. He definitely wasn't acting like a man who was only interested in sex. She'd met more than her fair share of men like that. And none had tried to get to know her like Midas was.

She wanted, and deserved, a good man. One who went out of his way to make her happy. In return, she'd do the same. And so far, nothing had made her think Midas wasn't that man.

She'd been super nervous when she'd called to tell him that she had the option of going to Honolulu. If he didn't think it was a good idea, then she'd choose her second choice, Paris. She'd never been to France, and figured it was a place she needed to experience at least once in her life.

But the second she'd mentioned to Midas that she was considering Hawaii, he'd sounded like a kid on Christmas morning. He was so excited, telling her without hesitation that he would absolutely love it if she came to Honolulu.

So here she was.

Lexie felt like a teenager with her first crush. Every time her phone vibrated or dinged with a message, she smiled like a loon. She'd given Midas her travel schedule but didn't expect him to meet her at the airport. She'd planned on going to the small studio apartment Food For All had procured for her and sleeping for twelve hours straight. Then she'd clean herself up and see if Midas wanted to meet.

But the second she entered the baggage area of the airport, she saw him.

And he was even more good-looking than she'd remembered.

Midas was standing in the middle of the walkway, not caring that travelers had to steer their luggage around him. He was tall enough to see over most people, and his piercing eyes met hers as she walked toward him.

He wore a pair of jeans that seemed to be molded to his muscular frame. He looked as if he'd been born to wear the Hawaiian shirt he had on, as well. The large blue hibiscus flowers adorning the cotton shirt brought out the color in his eyes. On his feet were a pair of flip-flops. The entire ensemble, along with his tanned skin, made him look like he belonged here in this Hawaiian paradise.

He was also intimidating like this. In the desert, when he was wearing his uniform, a Kevlar vest, night-vision goggles, boots, and covered in dirt like she'd been, she didn't feel as self-conscious, for some reason. But seeing him now, all six feet, four inches of extremely handsome man, stopped her in her tracks.

He was on the move before Lexie realized that she'd stopped walking, then he was there in front of her. Without hesitation, he pulled her into a huge bear hug.

And just like that, all Lexie's insecurities vanished.

She fit against him perfectly, just as she had back in Somalia. Sure, they were standing now, and not lying in a tiny little hole in the ground or a small twin-size hospital bed, but the feeling was the same.

"Welcome to Hawaii," he said as he pulled back, not taking his arms from around her.

"Thanks," she whispered.

"You look..." His voice trailed off as if he was searching for the right word.

"Tired? Rumpled? Like one of the homeless people I serve?" she asked with a scrunch of her nose. She'd dressed in comfort for the very long flights to Hawaii. The elastic-waisted cotton pants and thin long-sleeve blouse weren't exactly the height of fashion. But they were comfortable, which was her goal.

"Fucking beautiful," Midas said as his eyes roamed from the top of her head, all the way down her body. His hand brushed up her arm and he fingered a lock of her out-of-control brown hair. She'd done her best to tame it before she'd left Germany, but after so many hours of traveling, and sleeping in uncomfortable airplane seats, she was sure it was just as crazy looking as it had been when she'd first met him.

Lexie's belly clenched as he simply stared at her. The look in his eyes told her all she needed to know. That he was just as glad to see her as she was him. Some of the anxiety over whether or not she was doing the right thing in coming here dissipated. If Midas was playing her, he was an absolute master. But she honestly didn't think so. It was refreshing to know a man so open about his feelings.

Then slowly, as if waiting for her to rebuff him—which definitely wasn't happening—Midas bent his head toward hers. Lexie went up on her tiptoes and met him halfway. Their kiss was tender and sweet, and way too short for her liking. But all the sparks she'd felt a month ago were still there.

"I got you something," Midas said, letting go of her reluctantly and bending to pick up the paper bag at his feet. Lexie hadn't even noticed him holding the bag earlier; she'd been too busy ogling his body.

He pulled out the most amazing-smelling lei and smiled at her. "May I?" he asked.

Lexie didn't know why she was blushing, but she could feel the heat on her cheeks. She nodded and dipped her chin as he brought the necklace of flowers up and over her head.

The second the flowers settled over her shoulders, she was surrounded by the smell of plumeria.

She ducked her head and buried her nose in the petals, then smiled up at him. "I love it. Thank you."

"Of course," Midas told her, then gently pulled her hair out of the lei. The petals were chilly against her neck, but it was the feel of his fingers against her skin that made her break out in goose bumps

"Your stuff should be on carousel three," he said, reaching for her with one hand, and her small carry-on suitcase with the other.

Lexie couldn't stop smiling as they walked through the airport side-by-side. It was silly, but she'd never been met at the airport before. She'd always gathered her own bags and made her way to the taxi line to go to whatever accommodations Food For All had made for her. She could get used to this. Very used to it.

And that made Lexie a bit nervous. It would be beyond painful if things with her and Midas didn't work out. She knew he would set a high bar for any future boyfriends she might have. He already had with his emails and phone calls, meeting her at the airport, the lei.

Shit, maybe this wasn't the best idea after all.

"I know you're probably exhausted, so I put off the guys and their big 'welcome to Hawaii' party they've planned for you."

Lexie blinked. "What?"

"They're excited that you're here. Not as happy as I am, but close. So they planned a barbeque on the beach to welcome you to town. Aleck's condo complex has a great private beach and grills we can use. And Elodie agreed to cook for us, not that it was hard to convince her. It's gonna be this weekend instead, on Saturday afternoon. Is that okay? If not, we can reschedule. I told them you'd have to check in with your bosses here and see what your schedule is like."

Lexie's mind was spinning. "Um...wow. Okay."

"What's wrong? Is it too much? The guys can be a bit... enthusiastic sometimes. And we tend to come up with any excuse to get together during our downtime. If you don't want to—"

"I do," she reassured him quickly. "It's just that I've never had a welcome party before."

Midas smiled down at her. "I'm glad I can be your first."

Shit, that sounded so dirty coming from his mouth, but Lexie merely smirked.

"Ha. Sorry. That sounded perverted," he said as they approached the baggage carousel. He let go of her suitcase and pulled her into him again. Lexie landed against his chest with a small *oof*. He grinned. "I can't believe you're here."

"Me either," she said as she rested her hands on his chest.

His grin faded as he got serious. "I'm so damn thankful though. This isn't casual for me. I know it's fast, but I haven't been able to stop thinking about you since I left that ship. I've loved every conversation we've had, and I've lived for your messages and emails. You're different, Lexie. I don't know why, but you are."

She swallowed hard. How he knew she needed reassuring, she had no idea. But then again, maybe he didn't, and was just as nervous as she was about this. But she appreciated him not beating around the bush and saying exactly what he was thinking. It was refreshing, and she hoped it boded well for their relationship.

"Same for me. I was nervous about what I was going to do after Somalia. Without you and the lady from Food For All, who basically held my hand as far as telling me what would happen next and helping me with the media, I'm not sure what I would've done."

"You would've figured it out, I have no doubt," Midas told her. "And the few interviews you did were perfect. You did an amazing job in condemning the kidnappers, while still bringing to light the plight of the less fortunate around the world. Your organization should be very proud of you."

Lexie shrugged self-consciously. "You were there. You saw how desperately the people want to provide for their families and live a life without constantly having to worry about corruption, where their next meal is coming from or having a roof over their heads. I don't agree with kidnapping for profit, but I understand it."

"Well, there will be no kidnappings here in paradise," Midas said firmly.

"Good," Lexie said.

They stood there staring at each other for a long moment, ignoring the hubbub of people chattering around them.

"Mustang was right," Midas said after a moment.

"About what?"

"He said if things were going to work out, they'd work out."

Lexie scrunched her nose. "Um...that sounds like a vague saying people put inside fortune cookies."

Midas laughed, and Lexie could only stare up at him. He was so damn good-looking, even more when he laughed. And she was in his arms. Damn, she felt like the luckiest woman in the world.

"That's basically what I told him. But, here you are."

She could've said something about how there was no guar- antee things would work out between them. Relationships were hard work, and they might find out that they weren't as compatible as they'd hoped. While she loved talking to Midas and they seemed to click, in a few months, things could be very different. But she'd never regret taking a chance and coming to Hawaii. If a relationship with Midas didn't work out, it would gut her, but she'd be okay. She was in Hawaii, she was doing a job she loved, and she didn't need a man to be happy, she'd already proven that.

But she couldn't deny that having Midas by her side felt pretty damn good.

The suitcases began to appear on the conveyor belt, and Midas turned her in his arms so her back was against his chest, his hands draped around her waist. She pointed out her suitcase and he hefted it off the belt without even a grunt. Lexie was impressed; she knew firsthand how heavy that sucker was. She'd had to pay a fee in Germany because it was overweight.

She grabbed the handle of her carry-on as Midas pulled the heavy suitcase toward the exit. He once again took her hand in his and smiled down at her before heading out the door.

Lexie inhaled deeply, loving the smell of the tropical air. She couldn't believe she was really here. In Hawaii. Yes, she'd picked this assignment because Midas lived here, but she couldn't deny she was excited to experience everything the island of Oahu had to offer. Hiking, swimming, boogie boarding, snorkeling, sightseeing, going to a luau...she wanted to do it all.

"You look happy," Midas remarked as they approached his vehicle.

Lexie simply stared at the Ford Mustang convertible Midas was putting her suitcase into.

"Is this yours?" she asked.

"Nope. I just decided it looked cool and wondered if your suitcase would fit in the back seat," he said with a straight face.

Lexie turned her startled gaze to him.

He laughed. "Yes, of course it's mine. I know it's a little over the top, but when I first arrived here, I couldn't imagine not having a convertible. Got a good deal on this since it's a few years old."

"It's...holy shit, Midas, it's perfect."

His grin widened. "I take it you like it."

"Like it? I *love* it!"

He took her carry-on from her and added it to the suitcase in the back. "You got something to tie your hair with? I love your hair when it's all out of control, but I'm thinking you might not be as happy when we get to your place and you have to try to get a brush through it."

Lexie nodded. She usually had a hair tie handy. She dug in her crossbody purse and came out with an old fashioned fabric scrunchie. She knew it was so '80s, but she didn't care. They worked best with her hair since it was so thick.

She quickly twisted her locks into a messy bun at the nape

of her neck and wrapped the material around it. "Ready," she declared happily.

"Come on, let me show you my island," he said, opening the passenger door.

"*Your* island?" Lexie teased as she sat down. "I didn't know you owned the whole thing."

He chuckled as he headed around to the driver's side. He got in and put an arm on the back of the seat behind her. "Lex?"

"Yeah?" she asked.

"I'm gonna do everything I can to make sure you don't regret coming here." He looked completely serious.

"I'm not going to regret it, no matter what," she said.

"I'm so damn happy you're here," he said, before leaning toward her.

Once again, Lexie met him halfway. She could get used to kissing this man whenever she wanted.

This time, their kiss was long, slow, and deep. Lexie was breathing hard when Midas pulled back. He lifted his hand and ran his thumb over her bottom lip sensually, smiling at her gently before reaching for the ignition.

As they navigated the parking garage and headed toward the interstate, Lexie tried to figure out what was so different about Midas than anyone else she'd dated. Maybe it was the way he was totally keyed into her when they were together. He wasn't looking around to see who else was nearby. He wasn't lost in his head, thinking about something or someone else. He was focused on *her*, and what she was saying and doing.

It was a little intimidating, but extremely flattering at the same time.

Maybe that was because he was larger than life. Not only tall, but muscular and obviously able to deal with anyone who might want to say or do anything rude. Maybe it was because she'd known him as a teenager and they had that as a base for what they were feeling now. Maybe it was simply a matter of intense chemistry and sexual attraction.

Whatever it was that connected them, Lexie wasn't going to question it.

She couldn't stop smiling as they headed toward downtown Honolulu. The wind whipped around her head and face, the sun beat down on them, and even though she was tired from traveling, Lexie felt buzzed.

Together, they figured out how to get to the building where her small studio apartment was located downtown. It wasn't anything special to look at, and the area around the building wasn't the best part of town, but Lexie had lived in worse. Much worse. Nothing could disappoint her right now.

They checked in with the building manager and, after he'd looked at her identification and she signed some paperwork, he gave her a key to her new place. Midas came up with her to check it out. She was on the twentieth floor and luckily not too near the elevator. Lexie eagerly unlocked the door and stepped inside.

The décor was probably from the seventies, and there was a slight mildew smell in the air, but she wasn't too concerned. The kitchen was to the immediate left when they walked in. There was a small sink, a microwave, a two-burner stove top and what looked like a tiny oven. A small refrigerator was against the wall and a bar long enough to seat two people comfortably separated the kitchen area from the rest of the small space. There was what looked like a double-size bed in the middle of the living area, a small dresser against the far wall, a tiny desk, and that was about it.

But Lexie didn't care about any of that. She immediately went to the window and threw back the curtains, eager to see the view.

For a second, she just stared at what she saw. Then she chuckled. And that turned into a giggle. Then she was flat-out laughing.

"Um...wow," Midas said as he came up next to her.

Lexie was laughing too hard to respond immediately. She looked out the window again, and instead of the ocean in the distance, or even the mountains from the interior of the island, all she saw was the building next to hers. Her room was right across from another apartment in that building.

Where an elderly man was walking around his living room in nothing but a pair of tighty-whities.

She immediately shut the curtains and turned to Midas. He was staring at her with a mixture of amusement and pity.

Lexie got herself under control and shrugged. "Well, the view isn't what I'd hoped, but I'm still here in Hawaii," she told him.

"Always optimistic, aren't you?"

"How can I be anything but?" she asked seriously. "I'm healthy, I have a roof over my head, a job, and I'm in freaking *Hawaii*. If I want to see the beach, I can get there in minutes. And...you're here," she finished shyly.

"I am," he agreed, stepping toward her.

Lexie's heart rate increased as she stared up at Midas.

He reached for the scrunchie she'd put in her hair and gently pulled it out, being careful not to pull on her hair. Then he fluffed the curls and smiled. "Fuck, I love your hair," he muttered before leaning down and kissing her. But instead of the long make-out session that Lexie craved, he ended the kiss all too soon.

"I'm gonna head out. You probably want to unpack, and I know you're tired. I'll call you later, if that's all right."

Lexie nodded eagerly. "Yes, it's more than all right," she told him. "I'll check in with my new boss and see what my schedule will be like so I can let you know about Saturday."

"Sounds good. What do you want to do first, now that you're in Hawaii?" Midas asked.

"Eat a shave ice," she said immediately

Midas laughed, and the sound echoed throughout the

small space. "Out of everything you can do, *that's* what you pick?"

"Well...yeah. I've heard they're awesome."

"They're overrated," Midas countered. "But if that's what you want, that's what we'll do."

"Thanks," she said, overwhelmed with this man's generosity.

"I'm looking forward to showing you around," he told her. Then he leaned down, kissed her forehead sweetly, and headed for the door. Before he left, he turned and said, "First things first, we'll go shopping for some blinds that'll still let in some light, but won't allow anyone to see in. Okay?"

"Okay," Lexie agreed.

The door shut behind Midas with a small click, and Lexie realized that she was still smiling like a crazy person.

Every time she came to a new city or country, she was apprehensive about everything. This was the first time she didn't feel that apprehension as sharply. And Lexie knew it was because of Midas.

She was looking forward to spending more time with him and seeing his friends again. She'd liked them from the little she'd spoken to them, and she couldn't deny she was interested in meeting Elodie. It was a bit intimidating, thinking about how strong the other woman was. She'd been through some pretty harrowing stuff, and on top of everything, she was apparently a renowned chef. Lexie had barely graduated high school, and she didn't have any skills she could boast about. But after everything she'd heard about Mustang's wife, she hoped they might still be friends.

Lexie headed for her suitcases that had been left by the door. She should go to the grocery store she'd seen outside her apartment building, but for the moment, she needed a nap more than she wanted to eat. She'd unpack, take a shower, then a long nap. Then she could begin her life here in Hawaii.

Her phone vibrated with a text before she reached her suitcase and she pulled it out of her pocket.

Smiling, she read the text that Midas had just sent.

Midas: I'm very glad you're here. Welcome to Hawaii.

Lexie knew she had another huge, sappy grin on her face, but she couldn't help it. She brought the phone up to her lips to dictate a return message.

Lexie: Thanks. Me too. Thanks for picking me up at the airport.

    Midas: Anytime, Lex. Anytime. Get some sleep. Talk to you soon.

Just as she was about to put her phone down on the counter, she noticed that she had an email message she'd missed earlier. It had probably come through when she was on one of her flights. It was from Magnus Brander.

She'd emailed the man a couple of times, wanting to offer her condolences. She hated that she hadn't been able to get to Denmark for Dagmar's funeral.

Ms. Greene,

Thank you for your correspondence. You are correct, I miss my brother fiercely. It has taken me this long to be able to answer messages. As you were one of the last people to see him, I would very much like to talk to you. To find out more about your time in the desert. I will be in touch.

Sincerely,

Magnus Brander

She was relieved Magnus had emailed her. She'd gladly talk to him about his brother. Dagmar didn't deserve what happened to him, and it was still hard to believe he was gone.

Making a mental note to reply to the email later, Lexie put her phone on the small kitchen counter and grabbed her suitcase. It was still hard to believe she was in Hawaii, in the same city as Midas. Life was definitely looking up.

CHAPTER NINE

"Stop pacing, man. Jeez, you're making *me* nervous," Aleck complained.

Midas frowned at his friend. "I'm not nervous."

"Whatever," Aleck said with a roll of his eyes.

"Okay, fine. I'm a little nervous, but it's just because Lexie wouldn't let me pick her up. She said she wanted to learn the bus system, so she'd meet me here," Midas finished.

It had been three days since Lexie had arrived in Hawaii. He'd talked to her every day, and seen her the first two. This would be the third day, and he was anxious to be with her again.

Lexie was...fun. Not like jump-up-and-down, bring-atten-tion-to-herself fun, but Midas found that when he was with her, he smiled all the time. He loved watching her experience what Hawaii had to offer for the first time. He was also making a mental list of all the things he wanted to show her.

But today, she was coming over to Aleck's condo complex and they were having a cookout with the rest of the team and Elodie. Lexie had told him she was excited to meet the other woman, but also nervous. He was one hundred percent sure she had nothing to worry about. Elodie was just as anxious to meet her. He had no doubt the two women would get along great.

Everyone was outside in one of the pavilions near the beach. Elodie was already hovering near the grill, making sure Mustang and Pid didn't "mess up" the burgers. She was very particular and protective of her food, which Midas thought was hilarious. The team loved to tease her by pretending they were going to do something outrageous when they cooked, just to see if they could rile her up. It worked every time.

At one time, Midas had thought having Elodie hanging around with them would change the dynamics of the team, but that hadn't happened. She'd become a natural addition to their group, and he could only hope the same happened with Lexie.

He wasn't ready to pop the question or anything, but there wasn't a doubt in Midas's mind that he wanted a long-term relationship with Lexie. He felt comfortable around her, as if they truly had known each other for years. She made him laugh, turned him on, and he wanted to spend every free second of his time with her. The latter was the biggest clue that she was different from any other woman he'd gone out with.

He'd even told his mom about Lexie just the other night. She'd called to check in and see how he was doing, and Midas hadn't thought twice about telling her all about the woman from high school he'd reconnected with.

He'd blabbered on for twenty minutes straight before his mom had finally burst out laughing.

"What?" Midas had asked.

"I've never heard you talk about someone like this before," his mom replied.

"Like what?"

"Nonstop. As if she can do no wrong."

It wasn't as if Midas didn't think Lexie had faults. He knew she did. As did he. But he wasn't all that concerned about them. Her good qualities would far outweigh whatever negatives he might discover over the next few weeks and months.

Of course, his mom was thrilled for him and said she couldn't wait to meet Lexie. Midas had no idea when that would happen, as his parents were in Portland and he was over here in Hawaii, but they did make the effort to come visit him every now and then. It wasn't as if vacationing in Hawaii was a hardship. And if they could combine a trip to see their son with a romantic getaway, all the better.

His phone vibrated in his hand and Midas immediately looked at it.

Lexie: I just got off the bus. I'm headed your way.

"Lex is here," he told his friends. "I'll be back."

Everyone nodded, and Midas took off at a jog. He headed through the condo lobby and exited out the front doors. To his right, he spotted Lexie, and he started in her direction.

She had her hair tied back in a low ponytail today and wore a pair of tan shorts and a tank top with a large pineapple in the middle of it. She was smiling at him, and she literally seemed to glow.

The second he got within arm's reach, he acted without thinking. He pulled her close and kissed her. He literally couldn't resist.

She melted into him, holding on to the front of his shirt with both hands.

Every time he touched her, kissed her, she seemed to sink further into his heart.

"Hey," he said after forcing himself to lift his head.

"Hi," she returned.

"Any issues with the bus?"

"Nope. The public transportation system here is really good. Did you know I can take the bus all the way around the island?"

"Yeah, but it would take twice as long than if you let me drive you around," he said.

Lexie smiled up at him.

"Anything new happen since I talked to you last night?"

She chuckled. "What, you think I might've won the lottery or something in the few hours since we last chatted?"

"I never know with you. You might've gone out to take a walk and ended up saving the governor's life or something, and been invited to the mansion and now you're BFFs with his wife."

Lexie rolled her eyes. "Whatever. I did go down to the grocery store last night after we talked."

Midas frowned at her. "It was late," he stated.

"I know, but I wanted to bring something today."

"I told you not to worry about it."

"I know what you said, but it's just not in me to show up with nothing. I got stuff to make some cookies."

"Cookies?" Midas asked, looking down at the bag she was carrying.

"Yes."

"What kind?"

She tilted her head and smiled up at him. "You like cookies?" she asked, instead of answering his question.

"Of *course* I like cookies," he told her.

"I'm just asking, because it doesn't seem to me as if you eat anything that's bad for you," Lexie said, patting his flat stomach.

Midas grabbed her hand and brought it up to his mouth, kissing the palm before placing it on his chest, keeping his hand on top of hers. "I eat junk food," he said. "I just exercise a lot to work it off. Now what kind of cookies did you make?"

"If I say oatmeal raisin, are you going to be disappointed?"

"Hell no. Why would you ask that?"

"Some people hate raisins."

"Not me. Is that what you made?"

"No. I mean, I like any kind of baked good. You already know all about my sweet tooth. But I decided to make my favorite, pumpkin spice with cinnamon cream cheese frosting."

Midas's mouth watered. "Can I have one?" he asked, reaching for her bag.

Lexie laughed and twisted out of his reach. "No, they're for dessert."

Midas pouted, making Lexie laugh even harder. "Wow, is that a pathetic look," she told him.

"I didn't know you could cook," he said, turning her toward the building.

"Believe me, I'm not an expert by any means. But this recipe is super easy."

"Well, I know they're gonna be a hit. The guys are suckers for home-baked goods."

"I hope they like them. I know not everyone is a fan of pumpkin spiced anything. I would've tried to make something Hawaiian, but I haven't had time to research it."

"They'll love them," Midas reassured her. "And you've been busy at work since you've gotten here."

"I have. But I really do love the people I work with," she said.

Midas listened fondly as she rambled on about the people she'd met at Food For All. The building the organization worked out of was only a couple blocks from her apartment building, and she'd spent the last two days getting the lay of the land at her new job. She'd met the other full-time men and women who worked there, some of the part-timers and volunteers, and had definitely jumped in with both feet as far as the people who came for food and assistance were concerned.

She'd told him last night about a woman who'd come by inquiring about free food for her and her husband, who were living on the streets. They usually earned enough to get food by panhandling, but they'd both been laid low by the flu recently and hadn't had the energy to sit out in the sun, begging for spare change from tourists. So they were rundown, sick, and hungry. Lexie had packed up food for them and had walked with the woman back to where her husband was resting.

On one hand, Midas hated how often Lexie put herself in danger, but on the other, he was so damn proud of her. She saw people that most of humanity did their best to ignore. She saw them as the human beings they were and treated them with respect.

He held open the door to the condo complex and followed Lexie inside.

"Wow," she exclaimed, looking around at the opulent interior of the building.

"Yeah, it's a little over the top. We give Aleck shit about it all the time."

"How in the world can he afford to live here on a military salary? Unless I'm totally confused and you guys are making a lot more than I think you are."

Midas chuckled. "We aren't. I can assure you of that. Aleck's loaded. Well, his parents are. They're in real estate, and they bought the penthouse in this place and kind of insisted Aleck live here. He's working on paying them back for it, but they aren't being very gracious about taking his money."

"Oh, wow, the penthouse?" she asked.

"Yup."

"I never would've guessed," Lexie said.

"Yeah, he's completely down-to-earth," Midas said. "But I have to say, we sure do love coming here for our get-togethers. Wait until you see his balcony, the view is amazing."

"Not like what I see when I open my curtains, huh?" Lexie teased.

It was Midas's turn to wrinkle his nose. "Um. No."

She giggled as Midas held open the door on the other end of the lobby that led out to the grassy area behind the condo complex, where the pavilions and grills were located.

As natural as breathing, Midas reached for her hand as they walked toward his team.

Slate was the first to see them. "Thank God," he said, loud enough for everyone to hear. "Now we can eat."

"Remember, he's the impatient one," Midas told Lexie as they approached.

"Wow, everyone looks so different with clothes on," she mused.

Midas bit back a laugh.

"Oh shit, I didn't mean it that way," she said almost immediately. "I meant with *real* clothes on. You know, like shorts and T-shirts, not the uniforms they were wearing when I last saw them."

"I knew what you meant," Midas said, amused.

"Jeez, I'm totally gonna say something else to embarrass myself, I know it."

"Naw," Midas told her. "You're good. Besides, I'm sure one of the guys will say something stupid before too long, so no worries."

"Good to see you again!" Aleck told Lexie as they entered the pavilion.

"Yeah, you don't look quite as much like something the cat dragged in," Pid agreed.

Jag smacked his friend on the back of his head. "That was rude, asshole," he said.

"Told you," Midas murmured to Lexie. He was glad to see she was smiling and not at all offended by Jag's sincere, if awkward, statement.

"Hey," Slate said with a jerk of his chin.

Mustang walked over to them with a smile. "I'm thrilled that you were able to work it out to come to Oahu. When my men are happy, I'm happy. And believe me, Midas is fucking thrilled."

"Scott, you probably shouldn't swear when you first meet someone," Elodie scolded.

"I'm not meeting her for the first time," Mustang protested. "Besides, Midas *is* fucking thrilled. He's been in a much better mood since she arrived."

"Mustang," Midas warned, seeing the blush that crossed Lexie's face.

"All right, sorry. I'm just saying...it's very nice that you're here," he told Lexie.

"Thanks, I'm glad to be here," Lexie said politely.

"And I'm Elodie," Mustang's better half said, holding her hand out. "Scott told me all about what happened to you. Okay, not all of it, because he can't legally do that, but he told me enough. It's crazy that we both had a run-in with Somalis."

"Not all people from Somalia are bad," Lexie said immediately. "I met some amazing men and women there."

"Oh, I know, I didn't mean to imply differently," Elodie said with a small frown.

"It's just that poverty is so rampant over there. Most people don't have the opportunities that we have here in the States, or in other countries. Fathers and mothers have to feed their families, and they'll do whatever it takes to be able to do that."

"I understand. I do," Elodie insisted. "Shoot, now you must think I'm a horrible person. I'm not, I swear."

Midas saw Mustang frown and take a step closer to his wife, as if to protect her.

"No! I don't think that at all," Lexie said, her brow furrowing in consternation. "*I'm* the one who's sorry. I tend to go on and on about things I'm passionate about and don't

take into account the connotations of what I'm saying. I
don't condone what the pirates did to your cargo ship, or the
men who kidnapped me and Dagmar, not in the least."

"Whew," Elodie said, pretending to wipe sweat from her
brow. "For a second, I thought I'd really put my foot in it."

"No, not at all," Lexie said.

"Good. Now, if our guard dogs will stand down, we can
head over to the grill and make sure Slate isn't squishing the
hamburgers. I've told him a hundred times not to do that, but
he literally can't seem to help himself."

Lexie smiled, and Midas relaxed.

Mustang stepped away from Elodie as well, and Midas let
out a small whoosh of relief. Never in a million years would
he have thought he'd go toe-to-toe with one of his teammates, but when it came to Lexie, he realized he absolutely
would. Though, he should've known Lexie wouldn't let things
get to that point. She was kind from the tips of her unruly
hair down to her toes. She'd do whatever it took to smooth
things over, just as she'd done here.

"Don't let Slate sneak a cookie," Midas warned as Lexie
headed for the grill with Elodie.

"Cookies?" Mustang asked. "What kind?"

"Pumpkin spice," Lexie told him.

"I think you should let me take those for you. I'll just put
them on the table with the other food," Mustang said slyly.

"Don't do it," Midas told her. "He's worse than Aleck
when it comes to dessert."

Elodie laughed. "I swear, you guys act like you've never
eaten before. I seem to remember there being a plate of
chocolate-dipped raspberries twenty minutes ago, and now
it's completely empty. You didn't even save any for poor
Lexie."

Mustang went over to his wife and pulled her into his
embrace. "You can't blame us. You're just too good of a cook,"
he said.

"Flatterer," Elodie complained half-heartedly.

Midas caught Lexie's eye and smiled at her. She didn't seem uneasy, and he'd suspected she'd get along with everyone just fine. That was just her way. She accepted people exactly as they were.

Elodie pulled out of her husband's embrace and hooked her arm with Lexie's. "Come on, we'll guard your cookies from the hungry jackals and make sure Slate isn't messing up the burgers at the same time."

Aleck appeared at Midas's side, and he pulled his gaze from Lexie long enough to look over at his friend. "What?" he asked when Aleck didn't say anything.

"Nothing. I like her."

It wasn't as if Midas needed his friends' approval, but it sure meant a hell of a lot that he had it. "Thanks. Me too."

"Yeah, that's obvious. But..." His voice trailed off.

"What?" Midas asked again.

"It's just been...fast," Aleck finished with a shrug.

"It has. But we're not getting married tomorrow," Midas told him. "I like her. A lot. We're still getting to know each other. But I'll tell you this, she's unlike anyone I've ever dated before. Just wait, someday you're gonna meet a woman who completely knocks you off your feet, and I'm gonna remind you of this conversation and your skepticism."

Aleck shrugged. "Just because you and Mustang have found great women, doesn't mean the rest of us will."

"True, but sometimes when we least expect it, the exact right person falls out of the sky and into your lap."

Aleck burst into laughter. "A take on the song 'It's Raining Men', huh?"

"I wasn't being literal, asshole," Midas said, slugging his friend on the shoulder.

"Seriously, happy for you, man," Aleck continued. "I just don't want you to get hurt."

"I appreciate it. I have no idea where things will end up

with Lexie and me, but I have a good feeling about it. Besides, if things go sideways, I know you'll have my back."

"Fuck yeah, I will," Aleck said.

"Come on, those burgers have to be done. I'm starved."

Midas headed for the grill with Aleck, observing as Pid laughed at something Lexie said. He wasn't surprised in the least that she fit in so well. He imagined that she could be plunked down in the middle of a primitive cannibalistic tribe smack dab in the Amazon rainforest and within an hour, she'd be best friends with the chief's wife and children and welcomed with open arms. A little dramatic, maybe...but no less true.

* * *

Lexie felt like pinching herself. It was two hours after she'd arrived, and she'd had the most delicious hamburger she'd ever eaten, everyone had raved over her cookies and devoured them, and they were now in the freaking penthouse apartment at the condo complex, watching an afternoon storm roll in from the ocean.

Aleck's penthouse was everything she imagined it would be and more. It was classy and expensive looking, but also somehow comfortable. Maybe it was the pillows and blankets strewn across the furniture. Or the books sitting haphazardly on the bookshelves. Or the dirty dishes in the sink in the kitchen. It looked lived in. Not like a showplace where you were afraid to touch anything.

She was currently sitting on the balcony with Elodie. The guys were doing something inside, Lexie had no idea what, and she was happy for the chance to talk to Elodie one on one. She guessed that maybe Mustang and Midas had urged the others to give them some space, and she was grateful.

"This is so amazing," Lexie said.

"Isn't it? The first time I came up here, I had major balcony envy," Elodie said without a trace of jealousy.

"I think this balcony alone is bigger than my studio apartment," Lexie agreed. "And when I open my curtains, I get an up close and personal view of the old guy in the building next to mine, who likes to walk around in his underwear."

"Seriously?"

"Unfortunately."

Elodie giggled. "Holy shit! The same thing happened to me before I moved in with Scott. But at least Midas has a good view."

"I wouldn't know," Lexie said.

Elodie looked over at her in surprise. "Really?"

"Really. I mean, I haven't even been here a week yet."

"I knew that, but you and Midas just seem so...close. I just assumed you'd been over to his place."

Lexie knew she was blushing, but she wasn't sure why. "We're still getting to know each other."

"You guys went to high school together, right?" Elodie asked.

"Well, sort of. I moved to Portland my senior year. We were in a few classes together, but didn't really know each other."

"That's not the impression I got from Scott."

"I mean, we knew each other, but we didn't hang out or anything. He was the swim captain, state champion, and was popular with the girls. I was...me. We did get put together for a project once though."

"And?"

"And what?" Lexie asked.

"Did you fall madly in love with him and have been mourning his absence ever since?" Elodie asked with a gleam in her eye.

Lexie could only laugh. "No. I mean, I might have thought about him here and there, but he was pretty much just a good memory. But don't tell him I said that, it might hurt his fragile ego."

Elodie chuckled. "Yeah, none of the guys are hurting when it comes to self-esteem, are they?" she asked.

"No. But then again, they're all good-looking, honorable, and freaking Navy SEALs."

"True."

"But seriously, it sucked always being the new kid in school. I never really had any close friends because by the time I got there, they'd already formed their cliques. I was always an outsider, which wasn't so bad once I got used to it. Midas was super popular, and everyone knew he was joining the Navy when he graduated. I'm lucky to have even graduated at all," Lexie said.

"Really? Why? Or...was that rude? Sorry. I'm not very good at this girl-talk thing," Elodie said, seeming a little self-conscious.

"No, it's not rude at all. I brought it up. And I'm loving getting to know you. Most of the time when I get a new assignment in a new city, I'm on my own. It was nice to be invited today. Anyway, I have dyslexia, and it was undiagnosed when I was in school."

"What? Why? That makes no sense," Elodie said, obviously irritated on her behalf.

It felt good to have someone else on her side. "Like I said, we moved around a lot, and I guess I just slipped through the cracks. It didn't help that my dad always told me I was just stupid. I think some of that seeped into my psyche and I believed him."

"What a jerk," Elodie exclaimed.

"Yeah, he definitely wasn't going to win dad of the year," Lexie said. "But he did the best he could."

"He still around?" Elodie asked.

"No. He died a few years ago."

"Hmmmm."

Lexie couldn't help but snort a laugh.

"What?" Elodie asked.

"Your reaction was much more...subdued than Midas's."

"I can imagine," Elodie said. "He's a lot like Scott. Protective and with a nasty temper when it comes to people messing with me."

"You guys haven't been together all that long, right?" Lexie asked, hoping she wasn't being too nosey.

"Not really. But because of everything that happened, we clicked really quickly. I guess danger has a way of doing that."

"Yeah," Lexie agreed.

Elodie smiled at her. "That's right, you would know all about that, huh? Are you really okay after what happened to you? I read some news articles about what happened, and it sounds awful. I mean, it wasn't exactly a walk in the park to be on a ship that was taken over by pirates, but everything was over really fast compared to your ordeal."

"It wasn't fun," Lexie said. "But mostly it was boring."

"Boring?" Elodie echoed in surprise.

"Yeah, besides the actual kidnapping part. That was scary as hell, I can admit. But once we got into the desert, we pretty much just sat around, being ignored most of the time. And after Dagmar had the stroke, we did even less. Before that, we tried to at least walk around and get some exercise... watched at all times, of course. But afterward, I sat with him in the shade and tried to keep his spirits up.

"The worst part was not knowing what was coming. We could've been there for months to come, or negotiations might've wrapped up and we could've been released. I didn't honestly think anyone would come in like Midas and his team did, though. That was completely unexpected."

"So, the kidnappers just ignored you?"

"Well, not exactly. They liked to taunt us and tell us that no one was going to pay the ransom and we'd end up dead... things like that."

"Wow, I'm sorry. That sounds horrible."

Lexie shrugged. She'd worked really hard over the last month to put the ordeal behind her. She didn't mind talking about it with Elodie because she was honestly trying to understand, not pump her for juicy info she could put in a news article to get more clicks.

"Can I ask something without sounding like I'm judging?" Elodie asked.

"Of course."

"So, after you were rescued, you guys all went back to the town you were taken from, right?"

"Yeah."

"Why? I mean, that makes no sense. Why didn't you get the hell out of the country and go straight to the US ship?"

Lexie sighed. "Of course, hindsight being what it is, we should've. But Dagmar's brother has a lot of power in Denmark, and he pulled some strings and probably threw a bunch of money around, and he flew Dagmar's personal physician to Galkayo. The Danish special forces were pretty much ordered to bring him to town to be looked over before being transported to the ship."

"Oh."

Yeah. It sucked that Dagmar had survived three months in the desert, and a stroke, only to die because of an ambush at the hospital when sympathizers—and maybe even some of the kidnappers who hadn't been in the desert when the camp was raided—had tried to retrieve him so they could get the ransom money. "I've been emailing back and forth with Magnus, and he feels horrible about what happened."

"You have?" Midas asked from behind them.

Lexie turned around and saw Midas, Mustang, and Aleck standing at the door to the balcony. She hadn't even heard it open. "Yeah."

"I didn't know that," Midas returned as he came toward

her. "Scoot forward," he said, and without thought, Lexie did just that.

He sat behind her on the lounge chair, then pulled her back against him, so she was essentially using him as a backrest. He handed her a cup of coffee, and with one look, she could tell he'd made it just how she liked it. With a ton of sugar and milk and a dash of actual coffee.

Relaxing against him, Lexie continued, "I sent him a note right after I got to Germany, as well as the day after Dagmar's funeral. I wanted him to know how sorry I was about what happened. It took him a while, but I finally did hear back. He's hurting, and desperate for any scrap of information he can get about his brother's last moments and about our time in the desert."

"Hmmm."

"What does that mean?" Lexie asked, craning her neck to look at the man behind her.

"Easy, Lex. Nothing. It's just interesting, that's all."

"Do you guys believe in the twin connection thing?" Elodie asked Mustang and Aleck. Her husband had lifted her and plopped her on his lap in her chair, and Aleck was in a third chair, leaning back against the wall as he stared out at the ocean and the quickly passing rain storm.

"I'm not a twin, but if someone said they could feel what their brother or sister felt, I'd have to believe them," Mustang said.

"Same," Aleck agreed. "Although it would be weird. I mean, can you imagine being Magnus and feeling his brother have a stroke, or his fear when he was kidnapped, or when his heart finally gave out in the hospital from stress?"

"I think that's why Magnus wants to talk to me," Lexie said. "He wants to understand what happened."

"I have to say it," Midas added quietly. "If he hadn't insisted on us stopping in Galkayo, Dagmar may not have died."

Silence met his statement.

Lexie couldn't argue or disagree, because he was probably right. "It still sucks," she said after a minute. "It's not fair to judge on what we should or shouldn't have done after we know the ending. I mean, we could go back and say that we shouldn't have walked out of the Food For All building at the exact time we did. If we'd only stayed an extra ten minutes, maybe we wouldn't have been taken."

"Not true," Slate said, joining them on the balcony. Jag and Pid were at his heels, as well. "I think they'd targeted Dagmar for sure. He was a bigwig in the organization. And having a woman always helps the cause. Makes people more desperate to rescue her."

"Seriously? That's stupid," Lexie fumed.

"Stupid or not, it's a fact," Jag said with a shrug, leaning against the wall next to Aleck. "If they'd been able to nab a kid, it would've been even better."

Lexie sighed. "Why are people so cruel? I just don't get it."

Midas stroked her arm as she took a sip of her coffee. "Good versus evil," he said softly. "It's the way of the world."

"Well, it sucks," Lexie said with a pout.

"Agreed. But you're doing your part to help those less fortunate," Pid said. "How's that going?"

It was the right thing to ask. Lexie loved talking about the men, women, and children she worked with. "It's interesting how every city I've worked in has different needs. I mean, hunger and needing shelter is always a constant, but here in Hawaii, there are fewer entire families that are homeless, and more mentally ill men and women than I've seen in other places."

"Yeah, it's a problem," Aleck agreed.

"You're being careful though, right?" Midas asked.

"Of course. And they're not as scary as you think," Lexie told him.

"Um...okay, if you say so," Midas replied, obviously not believing her in the least.

"They aren't," she insisted.

"Holy crap, look!" Elodie cut in, the awe easy to hear in her voice.

Looking to where she was pointing, Lexie gasped. There were two perfect rainbows arching over the ocean right in front of them. "Oh my God, it's beautiful," she whispered.

"Eh. Wait two minutes and the tourists will be back on the beach, screaming their fool heads off and ruining it," Aleck said cynically.

"Seriously?" Lexie said.

"Yup."

"No, I mean, you're seriously going to sit there and not admit those rainbows are freaking amazing?" Lexie asked.

"Yup," Aleck said with a smile.

"You're spoiled," Elodie declared.

"Totally," Lexie agreed.

"Hate to not be on my bro's side, but they're kind of right," Slate said with a smirk.

"Maybe we should switch apartments," Lexie mused. "Let him look at my naked neighbor for a while, that should make him appreciate this amazing view more."

"Is she *female* and naked?" Aleck asked. "I might take you up on that, if she is."

"No. Think Homer Simpson in his underwear, scratching his butt, then picking up whatever he's eating for dinner."

"Ewwwww," Elodie drawled.

"Disgusting," Pid agreed.

"Yup." Lexie laughed.

"Oh, wow, look how stupendous those rainbows are," Aleck drawled.

Everyone laughed.

Lexie felt Midas rest his chin on her shoulder, and she glanced over at him. "Comfy?" she asked.

"Extremely," he agreed.

So was she. Sitting back and giving him more of her weight, it was still hard for Lexie to believe she was in Hawaii, in a penthouse, on a huge balcony with an amazing view, oohing and ahhing over a double rainbow with people who were quickly becoming special to her. How was this her life? Sometimes it was hard to even remember the long days and nights in the desert.

"Happy?" Midas asked as the others started a conversation about what they wanted to do next weekend. He'd already told her the team did their best to hang out together at least once a week outside of work. It kept their relationships solid, and based on more than just military shit.

"So much, it's kind of scary," Lexie told him honestly.

"You want to come over to my place tomorrow?" he asked. "I could take you down to Waikiki so you can check it out."

"I'd love to."

"I'm picking you up, though," he said sternly.

Lexie laughed. "Okay."

"Lex?"

"Yeah?"

"Thank you."

"For what?"

"For being here. I know you had your choice of assignments, and it means the world that you chose Hawaii."

This wasn't the time or place to get mushy, but she'd make sure Midas knew it hadn't even been a question. She'd felt something with him. Maybe it had been fast-tracked because of what they'd been through together, but being here truly felt like the right decision.

"You're welcome," she said softly. She deserved this. Deserved to be happy. And she most definitely was.

Midas kissed her temple, then sat back. She squeezed the arm he had around her waist and turned her attention back to the rainbows, which were now dissipating. She prayed that their connection would be more substantial than the fleeting beauty of the sun meeting the rain.

* * *

Magnus ignored the phone that was ringing on the desk in front of him. He knew he should answer it. It was probably his assistant, who would beg him to look at some spreadsheet or email. But how could he concentrate on work when all he felt was a huge gaping hole in his chest?

He physically felt the severed connection from Dagmar. Doctors would scoff at him. His friends wouldn't understand. But Magnus knew what he felt. Part of himself was gone forever, had died in that hospital along with his brother.

He'd *felt* Dagmar die. Had felt his terror, his pain, his anger.

And it was the anger that was beginning to fester within Magnus now. He knew why his brother had been angry in those last moments. He was outraged that he was about to die when he should've been safely back home in Denmark.

It wasn't a secret that Magnus had personally collected the money the kidnappers wanted. Dagmar would have known, would've expected it of him. But when they'd unexpectedly doubled it, demanding five million for each hostage, that had been Dagmar's death sentence.

It should've been that bitch! The woman no one was willing to pay for.

She should've been the one to die, not his smart, talented, outgoing brother.

And as Magnus read the email in front of him, he was even more sure of that fact.

Magnus,

Your brother wasn't happy when we learned that we wouldn't be set free. We'd heard our kidnappers talking about the ransom. They said that since the five million had been raised so quickly, it wouldn't be a big deal for five million more to be raised. Dagmar tried to tell them it would be a good-will gesture for them to release one of us, but they just laughed.

He knew you'd done all you could for him. He loved you so much. Talked about how the two of you could always feel each other. More than once, he said he was worried about you, that you weren't doing well. But he also knew you were doing all you could to free him. Even when he had a stroke, he said you'd know and would do what you could to help him.

You were lucky to have him as a brother.

~Lexie

Yeah, he was lucky all right. And if it wasn't for her, he'd *still* have his brother.

Magnus never understood his brother's charitable streak. He was much happier staying at home in Denmark and enjoying life's little pleasures. He wasn't married, preferring to pay for a woman's company when he wanted it, then kicking her ass out in the morning. He liked his expensive cigars, quality cognac, and silk sheets. Beggars annoyed him. As did those who tried to convince him they didn't deserve their shitty situations. If they were smarter, had fewer fucking babies, and worked a little harder, they wouldn't be homeless and needing a handout from *him*.

But Dagmar had been easier to sucker. He'd gone to a charity dinner one night, held by Food For All, and they'd convinced him to invest a shit ton of money in their organization.

Since Dagmar had never married either, Magnus was his only heir. And even though his net worth had doubled with his brother's death, the only thing Magnus cared about was learning as much as he could about the organization that had contributed to his brother's death.

He wanted to know how it operated, who was in charge, who decided where their employees worked and lived, and how much everyone was paid.

Magnus clicked on a folder on his computer labeled *Elizabeth Lexie Greene*. He needed to know *everything* about his enemy...and a good starting place was her employment file with Food For All.

He'd already contacted the organization and let them know he wanted to take over where his brother had left off. That he wanted to be an auditor like Dagmar had been. He knew they'd say yes; they wanted the money he'd dangled in front of them like a carrot too much to deny him.

He smiled for what seemed like the first time in a month.

Yes, Ms. Greene would pay for Dagmar's death if it was the last thing she did. But first, he wanted to make her suffer. Wanted her to be stressed out. Worried. Scared. Just like his brother was before taking his last breath. She'd experience *everything* Dagmar had felt before she died. That would be his final gift to his brother.

CHAPTER TEN

Lexie was excited about today. Yes, she wanted to experience the famous Waikiki Beach, but she was also looking forward to spending more time with Midas. The longer she spent talking to him and hanging out, the harder she fell.

She knew she was already a goner, and it had only been a few days. But everything she learned about the man made her respect and like him all the more. Sure, he was a Navy SEAL, and that alone would garner her admiration, but he was so much more than that. He was generous, and polite, and obviously a great friend to his teammates. Elodie had told her that he was super protective of her—as was the rest of the team—simply because she was Mustang's wife. He wasn't afraid to make fun of himself, and he was obviously a hard worker.

He ran every morning, then worked on the Naval base, but still found time to chat and message her throughout the day. He seemed genuinely interested in her work and how her day was going. They always found something to talk about, and she never felt as if he was asking about her job just because he thought it was expected.

Yes, it was safe to say Pierce Cagle was a good man. And

that scared the shit out of Lexie. She didn't want to let him down. Wanted to be worthy of him, and that was one thing she'd had a hard time with all her life. Her dad certainly hadn't made her feel as if she was worthy of his, or anyone's, attention.

Being with Midas made her happy, sure, but it also made her yearn for a long-term relationship. She wasn't quite sure if he felt the same.

Consciously putting her worries aside, Lexie vowed to enjoy the day. It was Sunday and she had the day off, and she was going to get to see more of the island.

Her phone rang and, seeing it was Midas, Lexie answered it on the second ring. "Hi," she said cheerfully

"Hi back," Midas said. "You sound happy."

"I am," she gushed. "I have the day off, it's a beautiful day, and I get to spend it with you." She spoke without thinking, and for a second, when Midas didn't immediately respond, she wondered if she'd been too enthusiastic.

But then he said, "Couldn't have said it better myself. You ready?"

"Yeah."

"Good. I'll be pulling in front of your building in about three minutes."

"I'll be there," Lexie assured him.

"Lex?"

"Yeah?"

"I'm looking forward to today. To spending time with you."

Lexie swallowed hard. She hadn't expected Midas to get so serious this early in the morning. "Me too," she said.

"Good. See you soon."

"Soon," she echoed and clicked off the phone. She spun and grabbed her purse, putting the strap over her head and arm and headed for the door.

Three minutes later, she walked outside and saw Midas's

convertible waiting for her at the curb. He climbed out and came around to her side of the car.

"Hi," she said.

"Hey," he replied, leaning down.

It seemed like the most natural thing in the world to go up on her tiptoes and put a hand on his chest to balance herself. The kiss was short and sweet. Midas smelled like soap and coffee. She licked her lips, tasting him there.

He groaned.

Lexie couldn't help but smile. She'd never felt particularly sexy in her life. She was just who she was. But around Midas, her feminine side preened and she couldn't help but lick her lips again.

This time, Midas smiled and lifted his hand to smooth her hair behind her ear. "Hair tie?" he asked.

Lexie had purposely left her hair down, simply because she knew Midas wouldn't be able to keep his hands to himself. Whenever he was around her, his hands seemed to gravitate to her curls. She'd never liked anyone playing with her hair in the past, but she craved Midas's touch. She reached into her purse and pulled out a scrunchie with a small grin.

"May I?" he asked, nodding to the material in her hand.

"You want to put my hair up?" she asked.

"Oh, yeah."

His answer seemed odd, but it made Lexie's belly clench. She nodded, handed him the hair tie, then turned her back to him.

Goose bumps broke out on her arms as she felt Midas's fingers lightly combing through her curly strands as he gathered them into a ponytail. He was taking his time, and Lexie knew she'd stand there in the middle of the sidewalk for as long as it took him to finish. Why having his hands in her hair felt so intimate, she didn't know. No one had ever done this for her before. Not her mom that she could remember, and certainly not her father.

Lexie closed her eyes and felt her nipples tighten as Midas continued to stroke her hair. He expertly wrapped the scrunchie around the locks several times, and gave her one last stroke before putting his hands on her shoulders and leaning down.

"Thank you," he said huskily into her ear.

His warm breath brushed her skin, making Lexie long to grab his hand, tow him up to her room, throw him down on her bed and have her wicked way with him. Never in her life had she been this turned on, and he hadn't done anything but touch her hair.

She was a goner.

Lexie opened her eyes and started to turn around to... She wasn't sure *what* she planned to do. But right that second, a homeless man walked by and nearly sideswiped her with the oversized bag he was carrying on his shoulder.

Luckily, Midas already had his hands on her, easily pulling her back against him and out of the way, preventing her from being smacked in the face by the man's belongings.

"What the fuck?" Midas said under his breath, but Lexie recognized the man and had already taken a step toward him.

"Good morning, Theo," she said gently. He was one of the regulars at the Food For All building. He was fairly tall at six feet or so, and lanky, with longish brown hair. Most of the time it was unkempt and greasy, making him seem a little scarier somehow; it looked as if it had been quite a while since he'd had a shower. She guessed him to be in his mid-forties. He was also...intense. Had a habit of staring at people, not seeming to know, or care, that he was making them uncomfortable.

Some of that was probably because Theo wasn't in his right mind. He mumbled under his breath a lot, and Lexie didn't know the details of his mental illness, but the few times she'd seen him, he didn't seem to even know where he was.

She couldn't help but worry about him. She was concerned about *all* the people she met. It made her job stressful, but she had a driving need to do everything in her power to help those who visited Food For All.

Theo mumbled something under his breath, then turned to meet her gaze. It was one of the first times he'd looked directly at her, and for some reason it startled Lexie, making her take a step back reflexively.

"You shouldn't be here," he said quite clearly.

"Oh," Lexie said, not sure how to respond.

"She's allowed to stand on the sidewalk," Midas said, shifting her so he was mostly in front of her.

"Food building, not this one," Theo replied, then lowered his head to stare at the crack in the sidewalk at his feet.

Putting her hand on Midas's back, she leaned around him and said, "I'm not working today, but Jack and Natalie should be there. They'll get you some breakfast," she told him.

"Don't like waffles," Theo said robotically.

"There's lots of other things you can have," Lexie soothed.

Theo then muttered something else and shuffled down the sidewalk toward the Food For All building without another word.

Lexie felt more than heard Midas sigh in relief.

"He's harmless," she said.

"You've known him, what, three days?" Midas asked. "You have no idea what he's capable of."

"I don't know what *you're* capable of either," Lexie retorted a little more forcefully than she'd intended. "But you don't see me being an asshole to you or crossing the street when you're approaching, do you?"

Midas ran a hand through his hair. "I'm sorry," he apologized immediately.

Lexie sighed. "No, *I'm* sorry. I have a tendency to be protective of the people I serve at work."

"I'm protective too," Midas replied. "It's who I am. I doubt I'll ever be one hundred percent comfortable with you interacting with people like him."

"What? People who are hungry and just want something to eat?" she fired back.

Midas didn't rise to the bait. "No. Mentally ill. They're unpredictable, and no matter how well you know someone, he could turn on you in a heartbeat."

Lexie knew he was right. She'd seen it firsthand a time or two throughout the years. But that didn't mean she had to like it. And you didn't have to be mentally ill to turn on someone. So-called "normal" people did it every day.

"I would never hurt you. Ever," Midas said softly, as if he could read her mind. His blue eyes were piercing in their intensity as he stared at her.

Lexie sighed. "I know. I just...there's no good solution for people like Theo. He needs assistance, obviously, but there's no one to facilitate getting him that help. He has no money, so it's not like he can pay for meds or a doctor, anyway. Bringing back the insane asylums of old isn't the solution. They were horribly abusive and did more harm than good. But letting Theo and those like him simply wander the streets to fend for themselves isn't the answer either. Neither is arresting him. The prison system is no place for someone with a mental illness. Sometimes I'm the only friendly face they see all day. People are cruel, Midas, and I do what I can to mitigate that."

He turned abruptly, pulling her against his chest. It startled Lexie, but she melted into him as she rested her forehead on his shoulder.

"You're right, of course you are. But the thought of someone hurting you literally makes me ill. If I could, I'd put you in a bubble so nothing and no one could ever lay a finger on you."

Lexie couldn't help but giggle.

"What?" he asked, pulling back a bit so he could see her face.

"I'm just picturing me walking down the street in a giant hamster ball."

Midas grinned.

"I know you think I'm naïve," she told him seriously. "But I'm not. I'm always cautious when I'm at work. When our clients are obviously having a bad day, I keep my distance. Believe it or not, today is a very good day for Theo. I mean, I don't know him all that well yet, but I've seen him several times and he actually had a conversation with me just now. He hasn't done that with many people."

"That was a conversation?" Midas asked.

Lexie didn't read any sarcasm in his tone, so she nodded. "Yeah."

"Okay, Lex. But please, promise me you'll be careful. I just found you, I don't want to lose you."

Lexie felt *that* all the way down to her toes. "Okay," she said softly.

"Your hair all right? Is the tie tight enough?"

"It's perfect," Lexie told him. "Should I be jealous about how you learned to do that?"

He chuckled. "I watched my sister do it all the time growing up. And I was a swimmer who was around lots of chicks who were constantly putting their hair up. I've never actually done it before, so I wasn't sure if I did it right."

"You did," Lexie reassured him, and just like that, she was turned on once again.

Midas's eyes flicked down to her chest, and Lexie refused to squirm. She was a grown-ass woman, and if she found her... boyfriend—she supposed she could call Midas that, even though she'd just gotten to town—hot, it was perfectly fine.

She wouldn't be here if she hadn't felt a connection with him, and from how much they'd talked since she'd arrived, she felt confident in calling him that...at least in her mind.

Midas snaked one hand up her spine and palmed the back of her head, and the other tipped her chin up. "You look beautiful today," he said softly.

An asteroid could've landed right next to them and Lexie didn't think she would've noticed. She only had eyes for the man in front of her. "Thanks. You look nice yourself."

He grinned. "I can't wait to take you out for real. I'll have to beat men away with a stick. You in a dress, high heels, that amazing hair done up? Shit, I'll be lucky to make it through the night without embarrassing myself." He inched forward, and Lexie could feel his erection against her belly.

She couldn't help but feel thrilled by Midas's words and actions.

"Please," she scoffed. "You're hot as hell in your uniform, I can't imagine what you'll be like all dressed up. It'll be *me* trying to keep women from throwing themselves at you and slipping you their phone numbers."

Midas grinned. "Not happening," he said. "Your number is the only one I want. And women can throw themselves at me, but my hands will already be full with you."

His words were cheesy as hell, but Lexie felt all fluttery inside anyway.

Midas lowered his head once more, but before he could kiss her, a loud honk scared the hell out of her. Lexie jerked in his arms, and Midas tightened his hold. "Easy, Lex."

"Move it, asshole!" a man yelled from the large SUV behind Midas's convertible.

"I guess we're going," Midas said.

"Guess so," Lexie agreed.

He took hold of her hand and walked her to the car, holding the door open and closing it once she was settled inside. Then he jogged around his car, flipped off the impatient jerk behind him, and climbed into the driver's seat. "I thought I'd take you the long way to Waikiki, if that's okay. Let you see a bit more of the island. It's still early, and it's Sunday, so the traffic shouldn't be too bad."

"Sounds good to me." Lexie didn't care where they went, as long as she got to spend time with Midas.

"Great. We'll head up 61 to Waimanalo, past Makapu'u Point, Hanauma Bay, cut over to Kahala Avenue so we can go past Diamond Head and the zoo before finding a place to park at the far end of Waikiki, then we can walk the whole thing. Sound good?"

"Midas, I have no idea where any of what you just said is. So I'm just gonna sit here, soaking up the wind, sun, and company, and enjoy being in Hawaii."

Midas pulled away from her building, ignoring the man behind them, continuing to berate him for being so damn slow to move, and smiled at her. He reached for a take-out coffee cup in the holder between them and handed it to her. "Figured you could use a pick-me-up this morning."

Lexie took the cup and saw that he'd gotten her the exact coffee she liked. Damn, this man. He was one of a kind, and it was hard to believe he was with *her*. "Thanks," she said as she took a sip.

"Good?" he asked.

"Perfect."

The self-satisfied smile on his face didn't bother Lexie in the least. He *had* done good. She was definitely impressed.

As they headed for the interstate, Midas gave her a running commentary about the buildings they were passing and pointed out things of interest. He might not be a native, but he obviously knew his way around the island, and some of its history. Lexie sighed with contentment as she tried to look at everything at once.

* * *

Three hours later, Midas still couldn't keep his eyes from Lexie. They were walking hand-in-hand down Waikiki's busy shopping street. They'd taken the path along the sand and beach itself on their way down, and now they were lazily walking back toward where he'd parked. They passed high-end store after high-end store, though Lexie didn't seem inclined to shop.

He wouldn't really have cared if she did, though that wasn't really his thing, and it didn't seem to be hers either. Not that he thought a woman who'd lived in some of the poorest places in the world would be addicted to shopping, but it was a relief nevertheless.

They'd talked nonstop all morning, yet Midas craved to know more about her. She was friendly to anyone they passed, smiling at everyone.

She'd even stopped to help a mother who was obviously at the end of her rope. She'd had a toddler in a stroller who was screaming, and her son, probably around six or seven years old, had a bloody nose that she was trying to get under control. Lexie entertained the baby while ordering Midas to run into a fast food restaurant nearby to get more napkins for the poor mother. By the time he got back, it seemed as if Lexie and the woman were best friends. He never would've guessed they'd just met each other.

The only place she wanted to stop at was ABC Stores, the knickknack shop full of kitschy, cheap Hawaiian souvenirs. She ended up buying a tie-dye shirt that said Honolulu on it, a pair of plastic flip-flops, a bag of Maui onion potato chips, a towel with an image of a sunset, a hula girl that was supposed to be put on a dashboard, some Chapstick, and a pen that had sea turtles all over it.

She grinned like a little kid when she exited the store, and Midas couldn't help but be caught up in her good mood. "You know most of that crap is made in China, right?" he asked.

"Don't care," she said, her smile not dimming in the least. "Now hush, don't ruin my Hawaii high."

"Your Hawaii high?" Midas echoed with a chuckle.

"Yup."

He took the bag from her and intertwined their fingers with his other hand. They walked on for a bit and when they neared his car, he asked, "You still want to come hang out at my place?"

She turned to look at him and immediately nodded. "Yes."

Midas smiled. Why it had been so hard to ask that question, he didn't know. Well...yes, he did. It was because he was afraid she'd change her mind. He wanted her undivided attention. While he loved how friendly and outgoing she was, he couldn't help but be selfish and want all that unbridled positive energy aimed at him.

He got her settled into the passenger seat and went around to get in the driver's side. Lexie was digging into the bag from the ABC Stores—and she pulled out the hula girl in triumph.

"No," he said as sternly as he could.

"Yes," she countered.

Midas simply shook his head. He knew he wasn't going to insist she leave the gaudy hula girl in the box. If it made her happy to put it on his dashboard, he'd let her.

Lexie peeled off the sticker on the bottom of the thing and Midas tried not to grimace as she pressed the dancing doll onto his dashboard. That adhesive was going to be impossible to get off, but again, after seeing Lexie's delighted expression, he didn't have the heart to bitch about it.

"Look, Midas! It's awesome!"

He simply shook his head and started the engine. The doll shook her hips to and fro as he pulled out onto the street, and Lexie's giggle shot straight through him. Fuck, he was going to get so much shit from the guys. But he didn't even care. Seeing Lexie so happy and carefree was worth the ribbing.

He couldn't help but remember the moment he'd seen Lexie in the desert, scared out of her mind, disheveled, but determined to not be a liability. Then when they'd hunkered down in that hole in the shop, she'd been worried about what was going to happen next. He much preferred to see her this way. Lighthearted and happy. He had a feeling it didn't take much to please this woman, and he made a mental vow to do what he could to make her life fun and carefree.

His place wasn't anywhere near as impressive as Aleck's—not that any of the other guys' were either—but he'd made it as comfortable as he could. They passed the airport and went by the joint base Pearl Harbor-Hickam, where he worked. He wanted to take Lexie to the Pearl Harbor Memorial at some point, but today, he headed toward Barbers Point, where his small house was located.

He'd lucked out when he'd first come to the island and was able to take over another SEAL's lease. The man was being moved stateside and was happy to not only hand it over to a fellow SEAL, but to not lose any money on his lease at the same time. There were two small bedrooms, a combination dining and living area, a functional kitchen, but it was the yard that was the biggest draw for Midas.

He couldn't quite see the ocean from his place, but he could hear the waves and smell the ocean air. And the mango and guava trees in his backyard were a major plus. He'd spent quite a bit of time building a deck with a cover and picking out the most comfortable deck chairs he could find. He'd even built a bar on one side of the deck, complete with a mini-fridge and sink. It wasn't perfect, but he was proud of the fact he'd built it all himself.

He pulled into the driveway and hopped out to open the garage door. He'd learned never to underestimate the Hawaiian weather. It might be completely sunny without a cloud in the sky now, but in an hour it could be pouring. Midas pulled into the one-car garage and waited for Lexie to come around to his side. He held out his hand and she immediately took it.

"Ready?"

She scrunched her nose. "For what? Do you have a protective pet ostrich or something that's gonna try to peck out my eyes when we go inside?"

Midas laughed. "No. But I have to warn you, I don't have a huge balcony like Aleck."

Lexie shrugged. "So?"

"Right." He turned to open the door to the house, but Lexie stopped him with a hand on his arm.

"I don't care what your place looks like, Midas. Seriously. You've seen my tiny little closet of an apartment. Besides, I'm not with you because of where you live or what material possessions you might have."

"Why are you?" The question just popped out, and Midas wished he could call it back the second the words left his lips.

She grinned. It was a sexy and mischievous smile. "Because of your hot body, of course," she teased.

"Yeah?" Midas asked, wrapping an arm around her waist and lifting her off her feet.

Lexie shrieked with laughter and braced her hands on his shoulders. "Of course. Why else?"

"Well, I was hoping my large...personality had something to do with it."

She threw back her head and laughed some more, and Midas couldn't take his eyes off her. She was so beautiful. And it was more than her looks. Her joy for life couldn't be contained. Her spirit was much like her curly hair, unruly and wild.

She got herself under control and peered at him. "You gonna put me down?" she asked.

"Nope," Midas informed her as he easily held her against his body and turned the doorknob.

"A girl could get used to this," she said with a laugh as he carried her into his house. There was a small entryway just off the garage door, but the entire house could be seen at a glance as soon as he stepped into the living area.

The door to his bedroom was open, and Midas was relieved that he'd remembered to make his bed that morning. The second bedroom door was shut, because it was full of junk he'd acquired over the years. A set of weights, a bicycle, a bookcase full of military thrillers, and other odds and ends.

Lexie wiggled against him, and Midas reluctantly leaned over and set her feet on the floor. She put the plastic bag from the ABC Stores on a table as she passed it and headed into the kitchen. Turning in a circle, she examined the four-burner stove, the white fridge that was probably twenty years old, the toaster, blender, air fryer, and coffee maker on the counter, and the cracked tile on the countertop before she met his gaze.

"I like it," she said.

Midas burst out laughing.

"What?" she asked, her brows furrowing.

"Lex, this kitchen's older than I am. Nothing matches, there's no extra space on the counter, there's no dishwasher and there's absolutely nothing special about it."

She shook her head. "You're wrong. It's lived in. I can picture you here in the mornings drinking your coffee, thinking about the upcoming day. It doesn't matter that nothing matches, all that matters is that it works."

"Come here," Midas ordered, holding out his hand. He needed to kiss her. Now.

She smiled slyly at him. "Why?"

He couldn't help but grin. "Because I want to kiss you," he admitted.

"Oh. Okay," she said and started for him. When she got

within reach, he pulled her into him, careful not to hurt her, and bent his head.

Then he kissed her as he'd been longing to all day.

Every minute he spent with this woman, she snuck deeper and deeper under his skin. She had a way of looking at the world that he never would, if she wasn't by his side. She admired the kids in the ocean learning to surf, laughed at the antics of crabs in the sand, and watched with rapt admiration the dancers hired to entertain the crowds in the open-air mall. She made everything seem new and shiny, while Midas was more often jaded and skeptical of the motives of the people around him.

She made him a better person, simply by being herself.

If he'd thought Lexie might let him be in charge of their kiss, he was wrong. She pulled on his hair and tilted her head to a better angle, pushing her tongue deeper into his mouth. Smiling, Midas let her do as she pleased. Her eagerness and enthusiasm turned him on even more.

But as much as he wanted to back Lexie into his room and strip her naked and make long, slow love to her, he didn't want her to think that's why he'd invited her to his house. He pulled back, and he loved the small smile on her face and the way she sighed against his lips.

"Thirsty?" he asked gently.

She nodded.

"Water? Lemonade? Coffee? Tea?"

"Water's fine. Thanks."

Midas kissed her on the forehead and headed for a cabinet. He got down a plastic cup, opened the freezer and put some ice cubes into it, then filled it from a container in the fridge. He walked back to her and she took it with a small smile.

"No bottled water?" she asked.

Midas shrugged. "It's not good for the environment," he told her.

Her smile widened. "No, it's not."

They stared at each other for a moment before Midas mentally shook himself. He was seconds away from hauling her into his bedroom after all, and he knew he needed to distract himself. "Come on, the kitchen and living area aren't terribly exciting, but I know you'll love my yard."

He put his hand on her back and guided her to the sliding glass door that led outside. He opened it and waited with bated breath to see her reaction. This was his pride and joy, something he loved.

"Holy crap, Midas. This is..." Her voice trailed off as she gazed around the area.

The fruit trees were lined up near the fence and there was a small patch of grass in the middle of the area. They stood in the shade of the deck, and the breeze that constantly blew off the ocean felt cool against his face.

She walked across the yard to the trees and reached up to touch a mango. Then she did the same to the guava tree. She turned and studied the wooden deck he'd built, then walked back toward him. Lexie put her cup down on the small table between the two deck chairs and gingerly lowered herself onto a cushion. The chair reclined as she leaned back, and she smiled up at him.

Midas returned the grin and pushed the footstool closer so she could put her feet up.

She sighed in contentment. "Just so you know... I'm never leaving."

He chuckled and sat on the other chair. He had four more chairs just like these in the second bedroom in his house, for when the rest of the team came over. But he supposed he needed to find a couple more since Elodie was now in the picture...and of course for Lexie.

"Seriously, this is...it's better than Aleck's balcony," Lexie said.

Midas snorted. "Right."

"It is," she insisted. "I mean, I'll admit that the double rainbow was pretty impressive, but this feels more intimate. We're right here next to the grass, I can hear the wind blowing through the trees, and if I get hungry, I can literally go and pick a fresh mango. And this deck...it's..." Her voice trailed off.

Midas looked over at her...and saw Lexie pressing her lips together as if trying to keep her composure. "Lex?" he asked in alarm.

She waved a hand. "I'm good," she said in a wavering voice. "It's just that, whenever I'd dream about having a house of my own, this was the kind of yard I wanted. Nothing huge, because it's a pain in the ass to mow, but with trees, and a covered deck just like this one. Somewhere I could relax without having to worry about the sun baking me, or a place I could bring a blanket out to a chair and simply enjoy the sounds of nature. It's perfect, Midas," she said sincerely, turning her head to look at him.

He wanted to scoop her up and hold her, but Midas forced himself to stay still. "Thanks. This is my favorite place in the world. After a hard mission, I'll come home and sit out here for hours, grounding myself and getting my equilibrium back. It's private, so I don't have to worry about anyone interrupting me, and even if it's raining, I can still sit here and enjoy it."

Lexie nodded. "You're lucky, Midas."

He was. He knew that. Even more so to be sharing his space with her.

The rest of the afternoon went by way too quickly. Midas and Lexie talked about everything from politics, to the pros and cons of tourists in Hawaii, to his job...what he could tell her, at least. They talked about Food For All, and Midas learned that Lexie had gotten a couple more emails from Magnus Brander. The man was taking more interest in Food For All and wanted to pick up where his brother had left off.

Midas told her more about Baker Rawlins, the reclusive former SEAL who lived up at the North Shore, and who'd helped reassure Mustang and Elodie that she truly was safe from the New York mobster who'd forced her to go on the run in the first place.

Of course, that comment had led to many questions about Baker, and just when Midas was about to get a complex that she seemed more intrigued about the other man than she was with him, she stood up and stepped over to his chair.

"May I?" she asked, gesturing to his lap with her head.

Midas held out his arms. "I thought you'd never ask."

Lexie settled into his arms without fanfare, squirming and burrowing until she was comfortable. Midas had never been so thankful to have chairs that reclined than he was right that moment.

"I have to say, you're much more comfortable to lie against without all the stuff on your vest."

He chuckled. "You say that now, but you didn't seem to have any trouble falling asleep on me in that hole."

"True," she said with a small sigh. "It's so hard to believe that it wasn't that long ago," she said softly.

Midas reached up and pulled the tie out of her hair, something he'd been aching to do all afternoon. He smoothed the locks away from her face, then ran his hand over them again and again. He petted her hair absently and felt her sigh of contentment against his neck.

"I wonder how Astur is doing."

"At risk of making you fall for Baker and not me, I talked to him about Astur and her family," Midas said.

Lexie lifted her head and stared at him. "You did?"

"Yeah. I promised Shermake I'd do what I could for them, so Baker is working on something for me."

"What?"

"I want to sponsor Shermake, Cumar, and Hodan if they want to go to a university. East Africa University has a campus there in Galkayo. They specialize in computer science and engineering. There are also a few health science programs too. But if they aren't interested in those, they can go to Puntland State University, also in Galkayo, or they can choose to go to a residential program at Mogadishu University."

Lexie's eyes were huge in her face at that point.

"Breathe, Lex, before you pass out," Midas said, mildly concerned.

"You...why...oh my gosh, Midas!"

"I owe Shermake and his mother *everything*. They gave you a place to hide until I could get you out of there."

"They gave you a place to hide too," she told him, collapsing back onto him.

"No. Astur didn't give a shit about me," he said. "If she'd run into just me in that alley, she would've gone back inside her shop without a second thought."

Lexie didn't comment, which made Midas sigh. She knew he was right.

"I got to thinking about what Shermake said. About wanting to learn to do things for himself, to provide for his family and his countrymen without having to rely on charity. And while I can't save the world, I thought maybe I could help Shermake become the best man he could be, so he could in turn do some good for the world."

"Shit, now I'm crying," Lexie said with a huge sniff.

"Don't cry," Midas soothed as he cupped the back of her head and held her against him. He loved how her hair latched onto his fingers as if it had a mind of its own. "I don't know what Baker's been able to find out for me yet. First, he has to find Shermake and his family. I don't even know their last name. Then he has to talk to the universities and find out what the process is for providing a scholarship. Then set up a trust for the kids so the money will continue to grow and be enough when the younger ones are ready to go to college.

And if they decide they don't want to attend, the money is still theirs to do what they want with."

Midas felt Lexie wipe her face on his shirt, and he chuckled. "Did you just rub snot on me?" he teased.

"No," she mumbled. Then, "Maybe."

Fuck, he loved this woman.

Whoa. Love... Was that even possible after such a short period of time?

Yeah, it totally was.

"Knock yourself out. My shirt'll wash," he told her.

She sniffed for a few minutes, but eventually Lexie lifted her head once more. Her face was blotchy and her eyes were red, but Midas had still never seen anything as precious in his life.

"No one's ever done something like that for me before," she said softly.

"You're worth it," he said simply.

"Now I'm gonna have to find a way to pay you and this Baker character back," she said.

All sorts of dirty things sprang to Midas's mind, but he kept them to himself.

As if she could see into his head, Lexie rolled her eyes. "Why are guys always so perverted?" she asked somewhat rhetorically.

"Hey, I'm holding a beautiful woman, one I admire greatly, and one who I just spent a wonderful day with. You can't blame me," Midas told her.

"Seriously, Midas. Thank you. You have no idea how much that will change those kids' lives. And probably their parents' too."

"I never would've thought about it if it wasn't for you," he said honestly. "You make me want to be a better person."

She smiled at him. Then said, "I have to get up. Blow my nose. And you probably have things you need to do."

He did, but Midas shook his head anyway.

"I had an amazing day," Lexie said. "Thank you for taking me around."

"Of course. And someday we'll stop at all those places we saw on our way to Waikiki."

Her eyes lit up. "I'd like that."

"Good." As much as Midas wanted to keep Lexie right where she was, he knew she had stuff to do too. He sat up, taking her with him, and helped her stand. Then he grabbed her empty cup and they headed inside. He pointed out the bathroom and put her cup in the sink.

Midas had a busy week ahead of him. A new threat was immerging in Papua New Guinea that they were keeping their eyes on, and they had several intense training sessions planned for the week. As much as he wanted to spend every waking minute with Lexie, he had responsibilities, as did she.

He knew she'd be working long hours at Food For All to continue to learn how everything operated. She wanted to get to know her fellow coworkers better and make sure they knew she was willing to do her part. Not to mention, the two mobile events that Food For All had planned for the week. They'd be setting up in Ala Moana Regional Park, which was notorious for its homeless population, as well as heading over to Kapi'olani Regional Park near Diamond Head to pass out free food. Lexie had organized both, determined to work hard not only for the organization, but for the people she served as well.

When Lexie exited the bathroom, Midas simply stared at her for a moment.

"What?" she asked, self-consciously running a hand over her hair.

"Nothing," he said with a shake of his head, moving toward her. "I'm just so glad we got to spend the day together."

"Me too," she agreed. "I really do love your house."

"Good. Because I hope you'll be wanting to spend more time here with me."

"If that was an invitation, I accept," she said a little shyly.

"It was. And good. Come on. We can stop and grab some dinner before I get you back to your place."

"Sounds awesome," she said.

"There's a place called Thelma's not too far from here. We can get something to go and it should still be warm by the time I get you home."

"Thanks," she said.

"Anything for you," Midas said, meaning it. He placed his palm on her cheek and rubbed his thumb back and forth over her smooth skin. "You good now?"

She nodded.

"May I kiss you again?"

"I'd be upset if you didn't," she said honestly.

Midas grinned, and was still smiling as his lips met hers.

It was more than a couple minutes later when he finally took a deep breath and stepped back from her. One hand had slipped under her shirt, and she had one of her own down the back of his pants. He still didn't want to rush her, but Midas had a feeling it would be sooner rather than later before they ended up in bed.

He couldn't wait. He had no doubt making love with Lexie would completely blow his mind. He felt anything but casual about their relationship, and once he was inside her, that would be it for him. He knew it.

He couldn't read the emotion swirling in her eyes, but was comforted by the fact that she was as reluctant to leave as he was for her to go.

"Come on, Cinderella. Let's get you home."

She scrunched her nose in that way he loved so damn much. "I'm not sure that fairy tale fits me," she complained.

"If the shoe fits," Midas quipped.

She groaned as she grabbed her purse and bag, and they headed for the garage.

This time, Midas let her put her own hair up; if he touched her once more, he really would drag her into his bedroom.

The stop at Thelma's didn't take long and way before he was ready, he was pulling up in front of her building once more. He jogged around the car to open her door and kissed her on the forehead. "Have a good night," he told her.

"You too."

"Call me later?" he asked, not able to resist.

Lexie nodded.

"See you soon," he said, refusing to say goodbye.

"Later," she responded.

Midas watched until she was safely inside the doors to her building before heading back to his car. As he drove to his house, he remembered the smile of contentment on Lexie's face as they drove, and as her hair did its best to escape its confines.

He was head over heels for her. With not one ounce of regret. Lexie was the best thing to happen to him. Midas now knew exactly how Mustang felt when he was with Elodie.

Somehow, the world just seemed like a better place when he was with her. He didn't deserve her, but he was going to do whatever it took to make sure she never realized that.

CHAPTER ELEVEN

Three weeks later, Lexie knew she'd never find another man like Midas. They'd talked every day, and he'd started coming over and picking her up from work each evening and taking her back to his place for dinner. She loved spending time with him. He always made her feel valued. He listened to her as she talked about her day and the people she worked with. She'd never felt as close to anyone as she did Midas.

They'd hung out with his team the previous two weekends as well. Lexie was starting to get to know the other guys better, and wasn't surprised they were as wonderful as Midas. He wouldn't want to hang out with them if they were assholes.

And she'd found a fast friend in Elodie. She'd called to ask her a question about salvaging a cake she was making because she didn't have oil and was feeling too lazy to go to the store. Elodie had suggested applesauce and, amazingly, Lexie had some on hand. Then they'd talked for another hour as Lexie baked.

Moving to Hawaii had been the best decision she'd ever made, and Lexie couldn't be happier.

It was Friday, and she had a few more hours to get

through but was already looking forward to the weekend and spending it with Midas. She was content with how their relationship was progressing, although she wouldn't complain if he invited her to spend the night.

Thinking about having sex with Midas made her shift a little self-consciously. The man was impossible to resist, not that she wanted to. She was aching to sleep with him, in fact. But he was being chivalrous. He'd said he didn't want to rush her because she was important to him, wanted to make sure she knew he wasn't with her simply to get off.

Which was very sweet and all, but it had been a long time since Lexie had been with a man, and she was more than ready. If making out with Midas got her all hot and bothered, she couldn't imagine what actually seeing him naked and having him touch her all over would do.

Lexie was packing boxes in the back pantry at Food For All when her phone vibrated. Looking down, she saw it was an incoming phone call from an unknown number. Frowning, she answered.

"Hello?"

"Is this Lexie Greene?" the man on the other end asked.

"Yes, who is this?"

"This is Magnus Brander."

For a second, Lexie had no idea who that was. Then it clicked. "Oh! Hi. Is something wrong?"

"No, no, no. I'm sorry, I didn't mean to concern you," Magnus said. "Is this a bad time?"

Lexie had no idea why Dagmar's brother was calling her, though she wasn't sure she believed him when he said nothing was wrong. They'd exchanged several emails over the last few weeks. They had started out formal, with Lexie expressing her condolences, and had evolved to become more friendly and chatty.

It was a surprise, actually. Lexie hadn't expected to make

friends with Magnus, but with every email, she let down her guard a bit more.

"No, this is fine. I'm just packing some lunches for the team to take to the streets tomorrow."

"Ah, yes, the mobile food pantry. It is a good idea. It was yours, yes?"

Lexie shrugged. "Yeah. How are you doing? Are you okay?" she asked, still trying to figure out the reason for Magnus's call. It wasn't that she didn't want to talk to him, it was just unusual, and she wanted to make sure he was all right. He'd asked her for details of his brother's last moments alive, and every time he emailed, he'd pressed for more and more information about what happened in the desert, and specifically, what she and Dagmar had talked about.

Lexie had done her best to tell him what she could remember, even though she worried about him. Obsessing over his twin's death wasn't healthy...but she tried to remind herself that everyone mourned differently, and the fact that the men were twins was a whole 'nother level of pain she'd never understand.

"I am fine," Magnus said. "I'm sure you are wondering why I am calling."

"Well, yes. I mean, I don't mind, not at all, but..." Her voice trailed off. She'd given Magnus her number a few emails ago, when he'd seemed especially down about Dagmar's death.

"You know that Dagmar was very involved with Food For All," Magnus said.

Lexie nodded even though he couldn't see her. "Yeah, he was one of only a handful of auditors who traveled around to the various outposts and reported back to the board." She'd been intimidated by the fact she was responsible for showing Dagmar around Galkayo, explaining the programs they'd put in place to help the less fortunate residents. She'd been honest about the shortcomings of their programs and how they were working to improve them. Then, of course, they'd been kidnapped, and they were no longer employee and boss.

"Yes. I have thought about it a lot, and decided I want to honor my brother by stepping into his place," Magnus said.

"I think that's great," she told him.

"Yes. I am pleased. And because of the special circumstances, I asked if I could come to Hawaii as my first assignment."

Lexie smiled. "You're coming here?" she asked.

"Yes. If that is all right."

"Of course it is," Lexie assured.

"You have been so kind, so helpful and understanding, I wanted to meet you in person. To thank you for being there for my brother."

"Oh, Magnus. I'm so looking forward to meeting you in person too. When will you be here?"

"There is more paperwork to be done, but I believe the board said I should be able to leave in a month or so."

"That's great!"

"Yes. And while I will be observing the Food For All facility and making notes on the employees, I would like to spend some time with you as well. To talk about my brother, of course."

"Sure. And maybe you'd like to meet my boyfriend? He was actually in Somalia too. He briefly met Dagmar."

"Oh?" Magnus said.

"Uh-huh. Although, shoot...maybe I wasn't supposed to mention that," she mused, scrunching her nose in contrition.

"It is okay. I won't tell," Magnus said.

"Thanks. But anyway, he's heard a lot about both you and Dagmar, and I'm sure he'd be happy to sit down with us."

"This is good. I would like to know as much about my brother's time in Somalia as possible...I miss him."

Lexie frowned. "I'm sure you do. I really am sorry, Magnus."

"Yes. Anyway, I didn't want it to be a surprise when I showed up. Wouldn't want you to keel over in shock when you saw me. After all, Dagmar and I are...were...twins."

"I appreciate the head's up. Do I need to tell Natalie that you're coming?"

"Natalie?" Magnus asked.

"Oh, I guess you haven't gotten a list of all the employees yet. She's the manager of Food For All here."

"The board is supposed to notify her," Magnus said. "They will send out a memo, but you know how sometimes those things fall through the cracks. Then again, it is my understanding that Dagmar sometimes did surprise inspections, so maybe it would be better if you didn't say anything. I wouldn't want my first assignment for Food For All to be compromised, and if the board knew we were talking, it might be considered bad form."

"I understand." She didn't want to do or say anything that might get Magnus in trouble. She'd never met or talked to the people on the board of Food For All. The organization was based out of the United Kingdom, and the men and women in charge had a reputation for being very strict and by the book. Still, she was grateful that she'd been hired all those years ago, and that they were letting a grieving man step into his brother's shoes.

"Thank you," Magnus said. "You are busy, so I will let you get back to work. You've been there since early this morning, yes?"

"Yeah," Lexie confirmed. She'd shared her general schedule in an email a while ago. He'd been curious as to how she spent her time and what it was she did, and she'd been happy to tell him. Because she lived near the facility, she had no problem going in early to get the coffee started, and to do whatever else needed to be done before they opened the doors for breakfast.

"I hope you aren't working too hard," Magnus said.

Lexie chuckled. "I'm not. I love what I do and helping others isn't a hardship. And this weekend, Midas is taking me to the Dole Pineapple Plantation. They have a maze, which I'm super excited to try out."

"Midas is the man who knew Dagmar?"

"Yes."

"I hope he treats you well."

"He does," Lexie reassured Magnus. The more they talked, the more comfortable she became. What happened to Dagmar was tragic and horrific. If she gained a friend in his brother as a result, it would make her feel a little better.

"It sounds as if you are happy," Magnus said.

"I am."

"Good. I will let you go now. Do you mind if I call again?"

"Not at all. Call anytime."

"Thank you. I will be in touch soon and will update you on the progress as to when I will arrive."

"I'm looking forward to it."

"As am I," Magnus said. "Goodbye."

"Bye."

Lexie clicked off the phone and stuck it back in her pocket.

Seconds later, Ashlyn, one of the other full-time employees, entered the pantry and asked, "You okay? I thought I heard you talking."

"I'm fine," Lexie said, happy the other woman had bothered to check on her. "I was on the phone."

"Your man?" Ashlyn asked with a smile.

"No." Lexie grinned. "A friend," she said, remembering that she was supposed to keep Magnus's arrival on the down low.

"Cool. Anyway, Natalie sent me in to see if you could come out and help walk the room with Pika. It's crazy crowded, as it is on most Friday afternoons, and people seem restless. You're so good with everyone that she thought it might be best for you to mingle."

"Oh, of course. I'm happy to. I'm not done here though," Lexie said.

"No worries. Jack and I will finish packing up the lunches after you leave. You're leaving early today, right?"

"I can stay if I need to," Lexie told her.

"No, no, no, that's not why I asked," Ashlyn said with another smile. "You've been the first one here since you got the job, and it's been a relief for me, since I'm not a morning person. Jack is able to get his kids on the bus now, and Pika likes to surf in the mornings, so you're doing us all a favor. We have no problem with you heading out early."

"Whew," Lexie said, pantomiming wiping her brow. She put down the paper bags she'd been opening to make it easier to stuff them and smiled at Ash.

"Seriously, you're doing an amazing job and we're glad to have you."

"Thanks."

"You doing anything fun this weekend?" Ash asked as they headed for the main room. It was where everyone gathered to eat, to get out of the heat for a while, and simply to chat with others. It got pretty crowded at times, and as Ash hinted, because of the stress the people they served were under, scuffles sometimes broke out. The staff did their best to mitigate that, and to calm everyone down when tempers got out of control.

"Midas is taking me to the Dole Pineapple Plantation so I can try out the maze."

Ash rolled her eyes. "Seriously, girl. That's for tourists."

"Well, I *am* still a tourist," Lexie said with a laugh.

"If you want something else fun to do, let me know and I'll see what I can come up with. Better yet, ask Pika. He was born and raised here. He'll know what all the cool kids do."

"Thanks. I'm sure Midas and his friends have some ideas

of other things that aren't as crowded and touristy too, but so far, I'm loving everything I've seen and done."

They walked into the main room, and Lexie could see immediately why Natalie had asked her to come out and help. It seemed even more crowded than usual...and there was an odd feel to the atmosphere. She couldn't put her finger on it, but she nodded at her boss across the room, not missing the look of relief on Natalie's face that she and Ashlyn had returned.

Lexie then looked over at Jack and Pika, who were passing out lunch boxes to those who wanted them. Each cardboard box had an apple, a small bag of chips, carrots, and a ham and cheese sandwich. They weren't extravagant, but the food was always welcome.

For the next forty minutes, Lexie went from person to person, making small talk. Some seemed eager to chat and others completely ignored her, but she did her best to make everyone feel welcome.

Theo was there, sitting in his usual spot by himself against a far wall. His gaze constantly scanned the room as if he was looking for something, or someone. Lexie headed in his direction.

"Hello, Theo. It's good to see you today. How are you?"

He grunted in response.

"It's hot out today, isn't it? I mean, it's Hawaii, so it's always warm, but I think today is hotter than normal. Maybe that's why so many people are here, huh?"

"People. Lots of people."

"Yeah, I know. Did you get something to eat? I can go and grab you an apple or sandwich if you want one."

"I ate a sandwich."

"Good. That's great. Is there anything I can do for you?"

Theo looked up her then, and Lexie had to force herself not to take a step back. He had a look in his eyes that made her nervous. She wasn't sure why. Maybe just because all his attention was focused on her.

"You're pretty," he said. "I like your hair."

"Um...thanks," Lexie replied, running a hand over her hair self-consciously. She'd tied it back in a ponytail this morning, like usual, and she could feel that it was extra crazy because of the heat and humidity.

"You should be careful," Theo said. "There are crazy people here."

Lexie nodded, knowing he was referring to himself as much as he was others. He knew he was different. "But everyone's still a human being," she said quietly. "Just because they don't think the same as everyone else doesn't mean they aren't valuable."

Theo's head tilted and he stared at her without blinking. Lexie had no idea what was going on in his head, and she could admit that he made her nervous. She hated that, because she prided herself on not judging people, but his piercing gaze definitely made her apprehensive.

"Well, if you don't need anything, I'm gonna talk to some of the others."

Theo didn't respond, and after she'd walked away and spoken to a few people nearby, she happened to glance back him. He was still watching her with an intense stare.

A group of four men entered the facility then and captured Lexie's attention. She hadn't seen them before, but that wasn't too surprising. She was still new and still meeting the regulars who came to get assistance.

Jack went up to the men and greeted them, pointing toward a table near where she was standing. There were two women already sitting at the table, but they got up when the men approached.

"Welcome to Food For All. Can I get you something to eat?" Lexie asked politely.

"Fuck off," one of the men muttered under his breath as

he shoved a chair out from under the table with a foot and collapsed into it.

"I'd like something to eat," another man said with a leer as his gaze ran up and down her body.

For the first time, Lexie felt *very* uncomfortable. Generally, the men and women, and even kids, who came for assistance were respectful and almost embarrassed about being there at all. But these men seemed eager to cause problems.

And also for the first time, Lexie did something she never did. She walked away without attempting to help the group any more. She didn't know why they were here, but it didn't look like it was to get food or apply for state assistance.

Natalie had obviously seen the men acting in a less-than-respectful manner, because Lexie saw her motion to Jack and Pika to intervene.

Lexie continued around the room, saying hello and smiling to others as she passed. She felt her phone vibrate once more in her pocket, and she pulled it out, needing a break. Backing up against a wall so she could keep an eye on the room, she smiled when she saw it was Midas calling.

"Hi."

"Hey, beautiful. I thought I'd check in to make sure you were still going to be able to get off work at three."

"Yup. Wait, where are you? What's that in the background?"

Midas chuckled. "I'm on a boat headed back to base. We had a training exercise off shore today. I think the driver's got a hot date, because he's going damn fast. You're hearing the waves hitting the bottom of the boat."

"Oh, wow. Okay. Did it go well?"

"The training? Yeah. Of course. How's your day been?"

"Interesting. Magnus called me today."

"He did? You're still emailing him, right?" Midas asked.

"Yeah. He said he's gonna be in Hawaii in about a month and wanted to let me know."

"He's coming here?"

"Yes. Since he's getting involved with Food For All and taking over for Dagmar. He'll be doing site visits and stuff. He requested that this be his first assignment because he said he wanted to meet me in person."

Midas didn't say anything for a long moment.

"Midas? Are you still there?"

"I'm here."

"What's wrong?" Lexie asked.

"I think I'm jealous," he said.

Lexie's mouth fell open in disbelief. "Seriously?"

"Well, yeah. I mean, you've been emailing him fairly regular, and now he's going out of his way to visit you."

"Midas, he's way older than me. I mean, like, by at least twenty years. And trust me, I'm not interested in him in *that* way. He's like an older brother, or even a father figure. I feel bad for him because he's really missing Dagmar. He's having a hard time getting over his death. I think he feels a connection to me since we were together so long in that desert. That's all it is. You have nothing to be jealous about. Jeez."

"Okay."

She wasn't sure if he was *really* okay with what she'd said or not, so she continued trying to convince him. She wasn't upset that he was uneasy about Magnus's place in her life. Some men got jealous—and turned mean as a result. Overbearing and abusive. But she had no doubt Midas wouldn't be that way. However, she could imagine him pouting on whatever boat he was on, and she wanted to reassure him.

Her voice lowered so no one nearby would overhear. "Besides, the only guy I think about late at night when I'm in bed is you."

"Yeah?" he asked.

Encouraged, she went on. "Yeah. I swear just looking at you makes me hot."

"Shit, Lex," he swore. "You're killing me here."

"For the record... I know that you aren't dating me for sex. You've made that more than clear. You've driven me everywhere, put up with me sticking that hula doll on your dash, taken me to every touristy thing I've asked you to, even that luau last weekend. And you're going to get lost in that maze at the Dole place with me, even though I'm sure it's not how you want to spend your time."

"I'll be with *you*, so it's exactly how I want to spend my time."

Gah. He was so damn sweet. "Right, anyway, all I'm saying is that I get it. And I appreciate it. But... I want more."

"More? You want me to take you somewhere else? Just say the word and we'll go," Midas assured her.

"I want you to take me to bed," Lexie blurted. She thought she heard a choking noise on the other end of the line. "Midas?" She had second thoughts about being so blunt.

"Jeez, Lex. Have mercy."

She grinned. "I just want to make sure you know you have nothing to be jealous about. You're the only guy I want."

"Good," he growled.

He said something else, but Lexie's attention was suddenly focused on movement across the room. "Hang on," she said tensely.

"What's going on?" he asked, any tenderness gone from his voice, as if he'd flicked a switch.

"I don't know... Oh, shoot! Theo's in a fight."

"The same guy we saw on the street the a few weeks ago?"

"Yeah."

A few women screamed, and suddenly there seemed to be a stampede away from the side of the room where the fight was happening.

"Lexie?" she heard Midas ask, but then a woman tripped

over a bag someone had placed at their feet while they were at a table and smacked right into Lexie. Her phone went flying out of her hand and landed on the floor a few feet away.

More people screamed, and now it seemed as if everyone was yelling. Lexie grabbed the woman who'd run into her. "You okay?"

She nodded but immediately turned and headed for the exit, along with many of the other people who'd been in the room.

It was complete chaos for a minute or two as half the room did their best to disappear out the front doors at the same time, the other half yelling. Some were encouraging the fight, others were trying to stop it. Lexie tried to calm the few kids who were there and keep people from pushing others over and trampling them as they tried to get to the door.

Looking around, Lexie saw her phone had been kicked under a nearby table, and she scrambled on her hands and knees to grab it. "Midas?" she yelled a little hysterically when she brought it up to her ear.

"What the *fuck* is going on?" Midas barked, sounding a bit hysterical himself.

"It's okay," she said.

"Seriously, talk to me right now," Midas ordered. "What's happening?"

"Theo got in a fight," she said.

"Damn him," Midas muttered.

"No, it wasn't his fault. I mean, I'm not one hundred percent sure if it was or not, but I'm guessing it was the other guys who came in. They weren't very nice."

"What does *that* mean? Dammit, Lexie, you need to start explaining. Pid's on the phone with the cops right now. They need to know what they're about to walk into."

"He's on the phone with the police?" Lexie asked,

confused. "But you guys are on a boat in the middle of the ocean."

"Exactly. Which means I can't get to you as fast as I'd like. So the next best thing is sending in the police. Now tell me what's happening so I can tell Pid, and he can tell the officers."

"Oh, well... I think things are good now. Most of the people here left when the fight got nasty. Jack and Pika have two of the guys who were being assholes in headlocks, Ashlyn is talking to Theo and—oh shit."

"Oh shit, what?" Midas asked impatiently.

"Natalie got her shotgun out. She keeps it back in her office. She's keeping the other two guys from doing anything stupid. I need to go help!"

"No! You need to stay right where you are, hopefully well out of range of that shotgun or some asshole's fists."

"I'm okay, Midas. It's fine. Natalie's got the situation under control. I'll call you when everyone's calmed down."

"No, Lex, don't—"

But she'd already clicked the off button. She felt guilty about hanging up on Midas, but she really did need to help her coworkers and not hide under a table, completely useless.

She scooted out and walked to the other side of the room, heading for Ashlyn.

"Is he all right?"

"He'll have a hell of a black eye, but damn, I had no idea Theo could fight like that," Ash said.

Lexie looked at Theo—and this time she *did* take a step back when she saw the look on his face.

He. Was. *Pissed.*

At her? She couldn't tell. The amount of anger emanating from the man was scary as hell. Despite that, she couldn't take her eyes from his, and they stared at each other for a long moment.

A noise at the door broke the weird connection she and

Theo seemed to have and when Lexie turned to look at the entrance, she saw half a dozen police officers headed her way with their guns drawn. Without thought, she lifted her hands in the air, letting them know she was unarmed.

She saw Theo mimic her out of the corner of her eye, but the policemen and women didn't seem concerned about them. All their attention was on Natalie.

"Drop the weapon!"

"Put the gun down!"

Several seconds went by in confused chaos as the officers ordered Natalie to disarm, while she and Jack tried to make sure the cops knew what the hell had happened.

Thirty minutes later, Lexie was sitting at a table watching an officer talk to Natalie, another taking notes as Pika explained what had happened, and a third and fourth attempting to talk to Theo, who was sitting on the floor against the wall staring straight ahead, not talking at all. The four men who it seemed had started the altercation had been taken away to the police station. From what Lexie understood, three had active warrants and the fourth man tried to deck one of the cops, so he was arrested on the spot as well.

She'd already given her statement to an officer when the front door burst open once more.

The officers all turned to face whatever the new threat was, their hands on their weapons, but all Lexie could do was sigh in relief.

She had no idea how in the world Midas and his team had gotten downtown so quickly, especially if they'd been on a boat in the middle of the ocean somewhere, but she was so damn happy to see them, she immediately began to shake.

Midas took in the room, and the second he saw her sitting at the table, he headed in her direction. Mustang reassured the officers that they were from the Naval base as Midas hauled her up out of the chair and into his arms.

He buried his head in the crook of her neck and squeezed her almost to the point of pain.

"Ease up, Midas," Aleck said. "You're squishing her."

Lexie felt his arms loosen a fraction, but he didn't let go of her for several moments. Then he eased back, but only far enough so he could meet her gaze. "Are you all right?"

"I'm fine," she said, running her hands up and down his arms soothingly.

"Fuck," he muttered.

"Sit," Aleck ordered. "Before you fall down."

"I'm not gonna fall down," Midas told his friend, turning his head to glare at him.

"Just making sure. I mean, I don't think you even breathed the entire trip here."

"How did you guys get here so fast?" Lexie asked.

"Fast? Shit, it took forever," Midas said.

Aleck shook his head. "We told the guy driving the zodiac that if he got us to port in seven minutes or less, we'd give him a hundred bucks. Money talks."

"But then you still had to get here from the base," Lexie said in confusion.

"Yup. The Naval police gave us an escort," Aleck said.

"Oh, man. I'm sorry, Midas. I shouldn't have hung up on you. If I'd explained, no one would've had to go to so much trouble. I'll pay back whoever paid the money to the boat guy."

"Like hell you will," Aleck said under his breath at the same time Midas spoke.

"You *shouldn't* have hung up on me," Midas agreed, shaking her a bit. "Do you know the hell I went through, wondering what the fuck was going on here? If you were hurt?"

"I told you I wasn't," Lexie explained.

"No, you didn't. Lex, all I knew was that there was yelling and screaming, then you said there was a fight and Natalie was armed. Someone could've overpowered her and taken the shotgun and hurt you or the others. Shit…" he said, closing his eyes. "I've never been so damn scared in my life."

And just like that, Lexie felt terrible. She hadn't meant to scare Midas, didn't know the man was even capable of being frightened. But looking at him now, it was obvious he'd been completely freaked out. She put her hand on his cheek. "I'm okay," she said softly.

Out of the corner of her eye, she saw Aleck back away and give them some privacy.

"There we were, having a hell of an eye-opening conversation, giving me all sorts of ideas, then the next thing I know, there's screaming and you aren't on the other end of the phone anymore. Then you come back and say everything's fine, except you sound hysterical and Natalie has a shotgun and you hang up on me! I swear to God, Lex, I just aged about thirty years. Please, I'm begging you, never do that again. My heart can't take it."

"I won't," Lexie said immediately. And she meant it too. She'd never had someone as worried about her as Midas apparently was. She truly hadn't thought much about hanging up. But if the roles were reversed? If she'd been talking to him and realized something bad was happening around him and he'd hung up on her? She wouldn't be happy. He was letting her off way easier than he should've. She knew it, and vowed to be a better girlfriend in the future.

"Careful," Pid said from nearby.

Midas looked at his teammate, then wrapped an arm around Lexie's waist and pulled her out of the way of the two policemen leading Theo toward the doors.

"Oh, you aren't arresting him, are you?" Lexie asked, frowning.

"No. We're just taking him to the hospital to be looked over. He doesn't seem to be in his right mind," one of the officers said.

Theo looked at her, then locked eyes with Midas. "You should take better care of her," he said in a low grumble.

"Excuse me?" Midas said.

Lexie could feel the angry vibes coming off him.

"It's her fault," Theo said. "You should watch her carefully."

Midas growled. Honest-to-God growled, deep in his throat, and Lexie was alarmed enough to move so she was between him and Theo.

"Easy, man," Mustang said, putting a hand on Midas's biceps.

The cops quickly led Theo away, and Midas said, "What the fuck was that?"

"He's not in his right mind," Mustang said. "You can't take anything he says to heart."

"That sounded like a threat to me," Midas told his friend. "And he blamed her for whatever happened here. You said you weren't anywhere near them when the fight started, right?" Midas said.

Lexie ignored the slight tone of accusation in his tone. He was stressed, and she couldn't really blame him. She wasn't too happy with what Theo had said herself. She'd gone out of her way to be nice to the man, and she had to admit that he made her nervous.

"Right," she told Midas and the rest of the team, who were now gathered around them. "I talked a bit to Theo, small talk, then came over here when you called."

"The cops mentioned one of the four men who were here said something about you," Slate added, speaking up for the first time. "Then claimed Theo jumped him for no reason. They hadn't even said two words to him when he attacked."

"Will he get in trouble?" Lexie asked, concerned about the mentally handicapped man now.

Midas sighed and shook his head.

"What?" Lexie asked.

"You. The man all but threatened you, and you're worried about him."

"Jail's not going to help him," Lexie insisted.

"And being allowed to roam free starting fights is?" Jag asked.

Lexie pressed her lips together in frustration. "No, but he needs medical help. And maybe a friend more than he needs to be locked up and the key thrown away."

"Lexie! Are you sure you're all right?" Ashlyn exclaimed, trying to push her way through Slate and Pid to get closer. But Slate didn't budge. "Hey, can you move it?" Ash complained, pushing harder.

Slate looked more amused than anything as he finally stepped to the side. Making it obvious that the only reason she was getting through was because he was letting her.

"I'm fine. I wasn't ever in any danger," Lexie said. "How's Natalie? I can't believe she stepped in with her shotgun like that."

"She doesn't take shit from anyone. It's why she's such a good manager. I'm assuming this is Midas?" Ash asked, nodding at the man holding her.

"Oh, sorry! Yeah, guys, this is Ashlyn, one of the other full-time employees at Food For All, and, Ash, this is Midas, and these are his friends. Aleck, Pid, Jag, Slate, and Mustang."

"Dang, girl. You didn't tell me you'd hooked up with a Hotty McHotterson...or that his friends were so easy on the eyes."

Pid stood a little straighter and puffed out his chest a bit. Everyone laughed. Except Slate.

"Cut it out, asshole," he muttered, lightly punching Pid in the arm.

Ashlyn frowned. "Look who's calling who an asshole," she muttered back, taking a step away from Slate so she wasn't within arm's reach.

Which bothered Lexie. Even if she and Slate were getting

off on the wrong foot, he wouldn't hurt her. But apparently Ashlyn wasn't convinced. Lexie quickly tried to deflect the tension. "Natalie was amazing. She won't get in trouble, will she?"

"Naw, she's good," Ashlyn said. "I think things here are about as settled down as they *can* be. Why don't you go ahead and head out."

"Oh, but don't you guys need help cleaning up and reassuring everyone when they come back that things are okay?"

"We'll be fine. Have a great weekend. By the time you come in Monday morning, things will be back to the same old boring routine."

"If you're sure..."

"I am. I already got the go-ahead from Natalie. And she told me she's gonna look into hiring some extra security maybe. You know, some big hulks to hang around in our busy times, like Friday afternoons, just in case."

"Oh, that's good. I'm sure that will help make people feel better too."

Ash turned to Slate. "You need some extra cash? You're mean-looking enough...you'll scare any bad guys away."

Slate narrowed his eyes and glared at her.

She laughed, but it wasn't a relaxed and carefree sound. "Chill. I was just kidding. If you keep frowning, your face will freeze like that." Then she smiled at Lexie before heading into the back room.

"I like her," Jag declared.

Slate turned his glare onto his friend.

Jag held up his hands in surrender. "If looks could kill," he muttered.

"She's got a point," Aleck added. "You're extra surly today."

"Whatever," Slate said. "We gonna get out of here or what?"

"Right. Now that the excitement is over, Slate's impatient to get going. No surprise there," Pid said with a chuckle.

Lexie couldn't help but grin. She was already getting used to these guys. The way they kidded around and were almost brutal about it. "Thank you all for rushing to my rescue," she told them.

"We're a little jumpy," Mustang said. "After Elodie's incident, we're a bit faster to react...or overreact, as the case may be."

"Well, I appreciate it. I've never had anyone really care much about me before."

"We care," Aleck said seriously.

Lexie smiled at him.

"I'll walk you to your apartment," Midas said.

Lexie frowned as his teammates headed for the door. "Oh, but you came with them."

"I'm not leaving you," he told her.

Right. It seemed he was still a bit on edge. Lexie couldn't blame him. "Okay."

"We can take a taxi to my place."

"The bus goes out that way," Lexie said.

"No. That'll take too long. Taxi or Uber," Midas said.

Lexie shrugged. "All right. That works."

"Come on, we're leaving."

Lexie let Midas grab her hand, and she waved to her coworkers as he shuttled her out the door and toward her apartment.

CHAPTER TWELVE

Midas knew he was being a bit overbearing and heavy-handed, but he couldn't help it. Lexie had scared the hell out of him. He couldn't remember the last time he'd been that fucking terrified. He'd heard people screaming and yelling through the phone line and had no idea what was happening. Then Lexie had dropped that bomb about there being weapons on the premises before hanging up on him.

The half hour it took for him to get to her were the longest minutes of his life. He couldn't bear to take his hands off her or let her out of his sight.

He did his best to get his emotions under control as he escorted Lexie to her building. He stood right by her side in the elevator and the second she'd unlocked her door and they were inside her apartment, he took her in his arms once more.

"I'm okay," she reassured him for what seemed like the hundredth time. "I'm sorry. I wasn't thinking. I'm so used to fending for myself, it didn't even dawn on me that you'd be worried."

"Worried?" Midas asked. "Shit, Lex. I was way past

worried." Her lip wobbled, and he pressed her face against his shoulder. "Shhhh, I'm sorry. Don't cry."

"I just feel horrible about it all."

"I know."

"I promise, I'll never do anything like that again."

"I know you won't."

"Does this..." Her voice trailed off.

"Does this what?" Midas asked, putting his finger under her chin and tilting it up so she had no choice but to look at him. "Talk to me, Lex."

"Does this make you feel differently about me?"

Midas blinked in confusion. "Feel differently how?" he asked.

"I don't know. Are you upset enough to want to take a break? We don't have to spend the weekend together."

Midas's stomach clenched. "No!" he exclaimed. "Why would you even ask that?"

"I just... I know I disappointed you, and because I've been on my own for so long and haven't had anyone who's given a damn about me, I tend to not think about others as much as I should. That might not be something you want to deal with."

"Do you want to be with *me*?" Midas asked.

She frowned. "Yes. Of course I do, but—"

"Pack a bag," Midas said, interrupting her.

"What?"

"Pack a bag. With enough to last you for two nights. We're going to my house and spending the weekend together. All weekend. Days and nights. I'll bring you back here Sunday night, so you can get to work bright and early Monday morning."

Her eyes widened. "Really?"

"Yes. I don't think I can let you out of my sight for at least forty-eight hours. That should be enough to get my adrenaline to subside. Maybe. Lexie, in case it's missed your notice, I give a damn about you. I have since the moment we snuck out of that hospital room together. Probably even before then. And I'll teach you that you don't have to make every decision on your own anymore. I want to be your partner. Your sounding board. The person you turn to when you're happy, or scared, or sad. I'll celebrate with you, hold you tight when you cry, and comfort you when you need it. I want to be *everything* to you, just as you're quickly becoming everything to me."

"Midas," she whispered.

"And even though a lot has happened in the last couple of hours, I haven't forgotten what you said before the shit hit the fan. You want me to take you to bed? Done. Now, go pack. I'll just be standing here guarding the door so no one bursts in and interrupts us before we can get to my place."

She smiled and it lit up her face. "I have a bed," she said, looking back at the double mattress in the middle of her studio apartment.

"I see that. And believe me, I'll be making love to you in it sooner rather than later. But not now. And not this weekend. This weekend, you're all mine. And I want you in my space. It's a little caveman-ish of me, I admit. But I want to take you for the first time in my bed."

"Okay," she said.

"Okay," he echoed. "You gonna pack or what?"

"You gonna let go of me or what?" she countered.

"Not sure I can," Midas admitted.

Lexie wrapped her arms around his neck and went up on her tiptoes, getting even more in his space than she already was. "You know what I can't wait for?" she asked in a sultry, sexy tone.

"What?" he asked, thinking she'd say "seeing you naked" or something equally hot.

"A frozen Dole whip bar," she whispered into his ear.

Her response was so unexpected, Midas burst out laughing. "Brat," he accused.

She was grinning from ear to ear, obviously pleased with herself.

But her teasing did the trick, made him relax enough to be able to drop his hands from her waist. She backed away from him, still smiling. And when she got to the door to her bathroom, she said, "Oh...and feeling you so deep inside me, I don't know where I stop and you start."

Then she spun and disappeared into the bathroom. Her giggle echoing in the space around him.

Midas groaned at the image her words evoked and collapsed against the bar separating her kitchen from the rest of the room. He eyed her bed, then closed his eyes.

No. He wanted to pamper her. Wanted to show her how good it could be between them. And not only in bed. He had no doubt living with her twenty-four-seven would be amazing. How could it not?

As eager as he was to take her to bed, he wanted to make sure she was comfortable with the change in their relationship even more. He'd go as slow as needed to make certain she was one hundred percent sure of him. He couldn't imagine a life without her in it, and wanted her to get to the same place before they took their relationship further.

Midas readjusted his hard cock and took a deep breath. Life with Lexie wouldn't be boring, that was one thing he was absolutely sure of.

* * *

Within twenty minutes, Midas and Lexie were in an Uber on the way to his house. They held hands in the back seat and Midas did his best to control his libido. Many people thought that after a hard mission, military guys only wanted to fuck or fight. And they weren't exactly wrong. Midas and the rest of his team had learned to control their adrenaline spikes while deployed, but at the moment, he felt as if he was a green SEAL who had just finished his first successful mission.

He couldn't even look at Lexie, because he felt as if he were a hairsbreadth away from jumping her. She'd changed from the jeans and blouse she'd worn at work, to a pair of short shorts that showed off her tan and toned legs, and a tank top. He could see her bra strap peeking out on her shoulder when she moved and it made him hungry to see her bare tits.

They'd made out on more than one occasion, and he'd felt her up, but they'd never actually gotten naked together.

Shit, he had to stop thinking about Lexie naked. He was too on edge. He needed to get her home, make her comfortable. Maybe he'd order something in for dinner so he wouldn't have to cook; being around a hot stove wasn't exactly the best idea right now. He'd pour her a glass of wine or make her a mixed drink and they could sit out on his deck and enjoy the Hawaiian evening. If she was too tired—because she'd had a hell of a day, just as he did—he'd take her in his arms and hold her all night, like he'd done when they'd had to hide out in that hole.

He could do that.

Maybe.

Then Lexie took his hand and placed it on her thigh. Her bare thigh.

Fuck. All thoughts of relaxing and making small talk on his deck evaporated in a puff of smoke.

She grinned mischievously at him and slowly moved his hand upward, until his fingers were under the hem of her shorts. Midas swore he could feel the heat of her pussy. All he'd have to do is move his hand a few inches higher, and he'd be touching her.

Lexie spread her legs a fraction, as if she could read his mind.

Midas felt his heart beating out of control in his chest. He wanted to shove her backward and take her right then and there.

"It's supposed to be a nice day tomorrow," their driver said, jerking Midas back to where he was. And more importantly, to the fact that he wasn't alone with Lexie.

He heard her chuckle under her breath.

Midas wanted to respond, but his teeth were clenched together too hard.

"I think we're gonna go to the Dole Plantation tomorrow. You ever been?" Lexie asked.

Midas tuned the man out, his gaze riveted on his large fingers resting on Lexie's inner thigh. He brushed his thumb back and forth over the sensitive skin, and smiled when he heard her inhale sharply. She might have started out teasing him, but two could play that game.

He moved his gaze from her thigh to her chest, and was pleased to see her nipples poking through her tank top. She was obviously enjoying this as much as he was.

A car nearby honked its horn, making Midas look up—and he caught their driver checking Lexie out in the rearview mirror. He glared at the man and growled, "Watch it."

"Oh, they weren't honking at us," Lexie said, patting his arm.

Midas hadn't been talking about the other vehicles, and both he and the driver knew it.

The ride was fairly quiet after that, and Midas made it a point to keep his hand in safe territory on Lexie's leg. As much as he enjoyed turning her on, he wasn't about to put on a show for the asshole driving.

They arrived at his house without further incident, and Midas was feeling pretty proud of himself for not devouring Lexie in the back seat. He led her into his house with a hand on the small of her back. He unlocked the door and sighed in relief when it clicked closed behind them.

They were finally alone. But then he reminded himself that he was trying to go slow. He absolutely didn't want to rush Lexie.

He started to hand her the bag she'd packed and tell her to make herself at home, but when he turned away from the door, he grunted abruptly as Lexie threw herself into his arms.

Dropping the bag so he could catch her, Midas groaned as she twined her fingers in his hair and brought his head down to hers.

She kissed him as if she wanted to devour him. Hard, fast, and so fucking deep. Midas's cock hardened again. He wrapped an arm around her waist and yanked her against him. Lexie immediately began to undulate her hips, raising one leg as if trying to get as close as possible.

When her hands slipped under his shirt and roughly pushed it up his chest, Midas took a deep breath. He needed to find his legendary control, because he was about to fuck her right here in the entryway of his house.

"Lex," he said, pulling his lips from hers.

But she shook her head and actually managed to get his shirt up and over his head. Midas groaned when she leaned forward and wrapped her lips around one of his nipples and sucked hard.

"Damn," he swore, even as he palmed the back of her head to hold her to him. Her mouth felt so fucking good, and he was about two seconds from losing it.

It was that knowledge that had Midas tightening his fingers in her hair and using his hold to pull her head back a fraction. She looked up at him, her pupils dilated, and she was breathing hard. She licked her lips as she stared at him.

She was so damn beautiful like this. Almost lost in lust. For *him*. But as much as he wanted her, Midas didn't want her to do anything that she might regret later.

"Lex?" he said. "Be sure."

"I'm sure," she said immediately.

But for some reason, Midas still hesitated.

Then Lexie ran her hands up his bare chest, and it took everything in him not to arch into her touch.

"I want you," she said succinctly. "I haven't been able to stop thinking about you. I'm really sorry about today, about making you worry about me. No one has ever done what you did. You dropped everything and got to me as soon as you could because you thought I might be in trouble. You might get tired of me, might decide I'm too dorky, work too hard, befriend too many random strangers, or a million other things that make me weird. But as long as I live, I'll never forget the sight of you and your friends busting into that building today for *me*. You have no idea what that felt like. How amazing it was to know you cared that much. Please, Midas. Fuck me. I need you!"

That was it. He was done protesting. All thoughts of taking things slow and seducing this woman were blown to bits by her words. He'd never get tired of her, and she definitely wasn't too dorky. He might need to have a talk with her about befriending strangers, but she was his. Period.

He tightened his hand in her hair a bit more and heard her inhale sharply. "This is gonna be hard and fast. Can you take it?" he asked. That would be her only warning.

"Bring it," she said with a sexy grin.

So he did. Midas walked her backward until she hit the wall behind her with a thump. Then he lowered his head once more and brutally kissed her. She gave as good as she got, not protesting his sexual aggression, but meeting it head on. She moaned in her throat, and he felt her hands frantically begin to work on the fastening of his pants.

For a fleeting moment, he wished she was wearing a skirt so he could just shove it up to get access to her pussy, but her shorts wouldn't keep him from what he so desperately needed.

He wanted to be deep inside her, fucking her hard and fast here in his entryway, but he also didn't want to hurt her.

Midas felt her fingers brush against his cock as she tried to push his boxer briefs out of the way, and he made a split-second decision.

He dropped to his knees and yanked her shorts and underwear over her hips. Then he palmed her bare ass and pulled her to his mouth.

"Midas!" she exclaimed. Her hands clenched around his head, holding on for dear life as he feasted on her pussy.

He knew the second he tasted her, he'd be doing this a lot.

Midas *loved* oral sex. There was nothing more personal and intimate than this, and it seemed as if Lexie was a fan as well. Her hips immediately began to move against him, her excitement coating her inner thighs as he did his best to please her.

Narrowing in on her clit, Midas latched onto it and sucked. Much as she'd done to his nipple earlier. He needed her to come. Needed to get her soaking wet so she could take him without pain. He never wanted to hurt this woman. Midas knew he was more generously endowed than some men, and he wanted Lexie to be dripping when he fucked her.

"Oh my God, Midas," she breathed as she squirmed against him.

Holding her tightly with one hand, Midas moved his other between her legs and eased two fingers deep inside her body. Her inner muscles immediately clenched tightly on them, and he couldn't help but groan, thinking about how she'd feel doing the same thing on his cock.

He continued his rhythmic sucking of her clit as he began to fuck her with his fingers. The wet squelching noise coming from between her legs was sexy as hell. Turning his hand, he added a third finger and began to thrust even harder.

"Yes, please...right there. Shit!"

Midas would've laughed at Lexie's almost incoherent

mutterings, but he was concentrating too hard on keeping his mouth on her clit as she bucked against him. When she finally flew over the edge, it was one of the most beautiful things Midas had ever experienced. Her stomach muscles tightened and she trembled uncontrollably as she came.

His fingers were soaked with her juices, and he knew his face was covered as well. Licking his lips, he reached for his back pocket. It was so cliché to carry a condom in his wallet, but he'd wanted to be ready to protect Lexie no matter when the time came for them to make love. He had a new box of condoms in his nightstand, in his bathroom, a few packets in the glove box of his car, and he'd put one in his wallet. Just in case. He hadn't known this would be how things played out, but he wasn't sorry. And he was so fucking glad he'd had the foresight to be prepared, because there was no way he'd make it to his bedroom.

He had to be inside this woman. Now.

He stood and ripped open the small packet with his teeth, then shoved his pants over his hips. It almost hurt to touch his dick, but he quickly rolled the condom over his erection. He stepped on Lexie's shorts, which were around her ankles at this point, freeing one of her legs. He palmed her ass once more and lifted her, propping her back against the wall.

"I'm gonna fuck you, Lex. Right here. If you don't want it, want *me*, now's your chance to tell me," he said, giving her one more opportunity to slow this down, stop it...something.

But his Lexie merely smiled and draped her arms around his shoulders. "Inside. Now," she ordered.

Using one arm to easily hold her up, Midas reached down and grabbed ahold of his cock. He could feel it throbbing under his palm. He brushed the head against her soaking-wet folds, then pushed inside her body with one long, forceful thrust.

* * *

Lexie moaned as Midas filled her. He was bigger than anyone she'd ever been with, but she was so wet, his entry pinched but didn't actually hurt. He held still when he was deep inside her, as if to give her a second to acclimate to his size.

She'd never had someone go down on her so eagerly before. Men she'd been with in the past—and it wasn't that big of a number—had halfheartedly licked her a few minutes before commencing with the fucking.

But Midas had obviously loved it. He'd made her come so damn fast, she would've been embarrassed if she hadn't been so turned on. It was a completely different experience orgasming while standing up. That was a first for her as well.

And she appreciated him being prepared with a condom. She had a box in her bag, but it would've taken too long to get them. And the fact that they were standing just inside his door, his pants around his ankles and her still wearing her tank top, was hot as hell too.

"I'm not gonna last," Midas gasped. "You feel too damn good."

She tightened her Kegel muscles, and he finally moved. He pulled out, then slammed inside her once more. He did it again. And again.

Lexie closed her eyes and let her head thump back against the wall behind her.

Midas grunted with every thrust, which made the moment all the more carnal. She wanted to move, wanted to widen her legs, to push back against him, but all she could do was take what he gave her.

And while Midas was being rough, he was still being very careful not to hurt her. He wasn't slamming her against the wall, wasn't holding her tight enough to leave bruises. And suddenly it wasn't enough. She needed more.

Knowing he wouldn't drop her, Lexie wiggled her hands between them until she could grab the hem of her tank top. She pulled it up and over her head, feeling her hair fall in waves against her shoulders once more when it was freed. She couldn't reach the clasp of her bra at her back, so she pulled the straps down roughly until her breasts bounced free.

Lexie leaned back as far as she could and said, "Suck me."

She'd never been so forward during sex. But something about Midas made her feel uninhibited. She felt sexier than she ever had before.

Without a word, Midas bent his head and took a nipple into his mouth. The position was awkward, and he stopped fucking her as he sucked. Lexie groaned. God, he was sucking on her nipple just as he'd done to her clit. Hard and with no hesitation. Electricity shot from her breast down to her pussy, and she writhed against him.

He let go of her nipple with a pop and grinned. "Problem?" he asked.

"Move," Lexie ordered.

"Like this?" he asked, lazily pulling out a little, then slowly pushing back inside her body.

"No!" she complained.

"Hey, I was interrupted," Midas said with a gleam in his eye.

"You complaining?" Lexie asked, grasping one of her breasts, teasing the hard nipple with her own fingers.

"Damn, your tits are magnificent," Midas breathed.

She could barely see the blue color in his irises because his pupils were so dilated. She felt beautiful. And powerful. But she still needed more.

"Please," she begged. She'd never begged a man to fuck her, but she'd do whatever it took for him to make her come again.

She didn't need to ask twice. Midas began pounding into her, his eyes fixated on her boobs as they bounced with each and every thrust.

"Touch yourself," he ordered. "I want to feel you come all over my cock."

Lexie didn't hesitate. She grabbed his shoulder with her left hand, while her right snaked down between them. It wasn't easy, as their stomachs smacked together with every one of his thrusts, but she managed to flick her clit as he continued to fuck her hard against the wall.

Using two fingers, she frantically fondled herself, stroking his cock with her pinky every time he pulled out.

They were both grunting now, lost in the pleasure. For just a moment, Lexie hung on the precipice, caught between a monster orgasm and the fear that she'd fly apart if she came. But then Midas bent and caught her earlobe between his teeth. He bit down, not hard enough to hurt, but enough to send tingles straight to her clit.

She cried out as she came for the second time that evening, every muscle seizing as she trembled and shook with pleasure.

"Oh, yeah, fuck... Lex!" Midas panted as he shoved himself as far inside her as he could get and exploded.

She could feel his muscles shaking as he came, and she prayed he wouldn't drop her. But she shouldn't have worried. Midas would no more hurt her than cut off his own arm. He gathered her to him tightly, taking a deep breath as he pulled away from the wall. She felt him lean over and, with one hand, he somehow managed to get his boots and socks off before stepping out of his pants, leaving them in the foyer as he headed through the living area toward his bedroom.

Lexie couldn't help but giggle. They were sweaty, she could feel how wet she was between her legs, her bra was wrapped around her belly, and Midas was completely naked. They had to look ridiculous, but she could feel his cock still inside her as he walked. Even though he'd come, he felt like he was still half hard.

And just like that, she was turned on again.

Instead of bringing her to his bed, Midas headed for the large bathroom. She'd oohed and aahed over it when she'd first seen it, but now she barely glanced at her surroundings. She had eyes only for Midas.

He gently placed her butt on the counter and she winced at the chill that immediately met her skin.

"Sorry," he muttered as he slowly pulled out of her body.

Looking down, Lexie saw the condom on his cock was shiny with her juices. Without hesitation, Midas pulled it off and threw it away. Then he wrapped his arms around her and unclasped her bra, throwing it on the floor behind him.

She did her best to suck in her belly, as she wasn't in the most flattering position, but she needn't have bothered. The look in his eyes was one of complete awe. He braced his palms on either side of her hips and leaned in.

"You are so fucking beautiful," he said. "And you're mine."

Lexie had no problem with him claiming her. She ran her hands up and down his biceps. She felt the tip of his cock brush against her inner thigh and smiled. "Only if you're mine."

"Yours," he agreed, then dipped his head.

She expected him to kiss her hard and deep, but instead, he sipped at her lips, taking his time and licking and nipping at her. It was...sweet. And after what they'd just done, it was the last thing she'd expected from him.

"Are you sore?" he asked against her lips.

Blushing, Lexie shook her head. Right this second, she was anything but sore. Tomorrow? Yeah, she had no doubt she'd definitely feel their workout, but right now she just felt...horny.

Midas shifted and pushed her legs even farther apart. Lexie leaned back, letting him look his fill. It should've been embarrassing, but it wasn't. This man had moved heaven and earth to get to her when he thought she was in trouble. She still couldn't get that out of her head. He wasn't a manwhore. Wasn't with her just for sex. He actually liked her, which was pretty damn amazing for a kid who'd been called stupid, and who'd felt as if she'd been in the shadows her whole life.

She liked being the center of Midas's attention. Lexie arched her back a bit, and his eyes move to her chest.

"You're gonna come again, then I'm gonna take you nice and slow," Midas informed her.

"You think you can go slow?" she asked, genuinely curious.

He winced. "I don't know. But I'm gonna try," he said. Then his hand went between her legs once more, and Lexie groaned. He didn't fumble around, wasn't hesitant in his movements. Just like when he went down on her, he knew exactly what he was doing.

"You ever had a G-spot orgasm?" he asked.

Lexie couldn't speak, all she could do was shake her head.

"Excellent," he said. "I've never done this, but I've watched videos."

"Porn?" she breathed as she squirmed on his counter.

"No. Not really. Instructional videos," he said. "This could get messy, which is why we're in here."

"You planned this?" she asked.

"From the second you came on my tongue," he told her. "Now, relax and let it happen. I promise this will blow your mind."

Lexie had no doubt of that. Everything he'd done so far had blown her expectations to smithereens.

Midas began to piston his fingers in and out of her body, rubbing against what she knew was her G-spot deep inside her body. His other hand held her down, even as he used the thumb to flick her clit hard and fast.

Erotic pain bloomed in her body at his actions. "Midas!" she cried out.

"That's it, let it come."

She wanted to pull away. *Tried* to pull away, but she couldn't escape his hands and fingers. The room began to spin as Lexie both reached for the orgasm that was building and at the same time, shied away from it.

"Don't resist. You're so damn beautiful, Lex. This is so amazing. You're *soaked*. You got this. Come all over me. That's it. Fuck yeah..."

Lexie had no idea how much time had passed, all she knew was that this man owned her. She was putty in his hands, and if he left her, she'd never recover.

One second it felt like she had to pee worse than she ever had in her life, and the next, she almost blacked out from pleasure. The orgasm that shot through her body was nothing like anything she'd experienced before. It was all-consuming. As if every molecule in her body was turning inside out. Her legs trembled and she couldn't think straight.

"Oh my God, that was fucking amazing," Midas said reverently as his fingers gently pushed in and out of her body now.

"I think that's my line," Lexie whispered.

He chuckled, then gathered her against him once more and picked her up. He carried her into his bedroom, using one hand to pull the covers down before gently placing her on her back.

Lexie's entire body tingled, and she could feel how wet she was, could even smell her own passion. She heard a wrapper crinkle, then Midas was back between her legs. Without a word, he pushed inside her body once more.

Lexie saw him close his eyes for a moment as he stayed completely still. He looked down at her, and she inhaled sharply at the look in his eyes. It was...

Devotion.

She couldn't use the word love, because that was crazy, wasn't it?

Then he moved, and she couldn't do anything but feel. There was no pain this time, not even a small pinch. All she felt was pleasure as Midas slowly made love to her. There was no other word for it. Earlier, he'd fucked her; now they were making love.

He leaned down and worshiped her breasts as he continued to move in and out of her body. Strong pulls, followed by gentle licking and sucking. Then pulling back and using his hands to knead and play with her nipples. Everywhere he touched, it felt as if electric sparks shot from each contact point, straight to her sex.

Tears fell from her eyes as she looked up at him. She had no idea why she was crying. Overload of feelings and emotions, probably. But Midas didn't freak out. He smiled gently.

"I know," he whispered. "It's overwhelming, but in a good way, isn't it?"

Lexie swallowed hard and nodded.

"This is how it's gonna be from here on out. Maybe not this intense every night, but this is our new normal."

She couldn't help but be turned on by his complete confidence that they would make it. Lexie wanted that. More than anything she'd ever wanted in her life.

Midas continued to make love to her slow and easy, until he couldn't take it anymore. Then his loving thrusts turned hard. Fast. Lexie enjoyed his lovemaking, but absolutely *loved* his fucking. There was a distinct difference.

She felt a small orgasm well up, then settle over her like a comfortable blanket, instead of the tsunami she'd felt earlier. Midas grunted and slammed into her once more, throwing his head back as he came.

He immediately fell down on her, careful not to squish her, then turned, tucking her against him as he did. He held her to him as he'd done in Somalia, and Lexie began to play with his nipple as she lay boneless against him.

"Would you think less of me if I admitted that I'd thought about you being naked against me, just like this, down in that hole?" Midas asked.

Lexie chuckled. "No. Because I had the same thoughts."

Several quiet minutes went by, then he said, "I need to get up."

Sighing, Lexie nodded and rolled away. As he walked to his bathroom, she couldn't help but admire his ass. Midas was a fine specimen of a man, and he was all hers.

She was still smiling when he returned. "What's that grin for?" he asked.

"Nothing," she said.

Midas was holding a washcloth. "Spread," he ordered.

This time, Lexie blushed. It was one thing to expose herself to him on his counter when she was lost in a haze of lust, but it was another thing altogether after the fact.

"I need to clean you," he said gently. "Don't be embarrassed."

"I can do it."

"I know you can," Midas said. "You're a grown-ass adult. But I want to. I want to make sure you're all right. I took you hard. Pushed you."

"I'm fine," she told him.

Midas simply stared at her.

Sighing, she pushed the sheet back and spread her legs slightly.

Midas sat on the side of the mattress and put one hand on her belly, reminding her of how he'd held her down while he'd fingered her in the bathroom.

"You're swollen," he said as he gently ran the washcloth between her legs. "And your clit is still sticking out from its hood."

Lexie wasn't sure what to say. She'd never had this kind of conversation with a man before. So she kept quiet.

Midas smiled, but seemed to know how hard this was for her and didn't say anything else. After cleaning her, he leaned down and pressed a light kiss right on top of her clit. Her inner muscles spasmed, and Lexie groaned.

"Don't worry, I'm done. For now," he told her, throwing the washcloth across the room. It landed with a splat on the tile floor in the bathroom. "I'll get that in the morning," he told her, then lay back down and gathered her against him once more. He pulled the sheet and comforter back up, and Lexie sighed in contentment.

"Earlier?" he said after a minute or two. "That was the most beautiful thing I've ever seen. You trusting me to bring you to pleasure in a way neither of us had done before."

"It was overwhelming," Lexie admitted.

He kissed her forehead. "I know," he said simply.

She supposed he did. But he'd pushed her to do it anyway. She realized that this man would always push her. He wanted her to experience the most out of life. Whether that was emotionally, professionally, or while in bed, simply having fun.

And she loved him. Down to the very marrow of her bones.

It was scary as hell to admit that, but then again, being around Midas made her feel brave. She wasn't ready to tell him how she felt yet, but she would when the time was right.

She yawned and felt her muscles growing lax. "Midas?"

"Yeah, Lex?"

"You still taking me to get a Dole whip tomorrow? I want to get lost in that maze as well."

She felt him chuckle under her cheek. "Yes, I'll take you to the Dole Pineapple Plantation."

"Thanks."

"Then we'll come back here and spend the rest of the day in bed."

She smiled against his chest. "Okay. If you insist."

He ran his hand over her hair, and she sighed in contentment. It felt wrong to admit that being kidnapped had been the best thing that ever happened to her, but it had brought her Midas. For that, she'd always be thankful.

CHAPTER THIRTEEN

Lexie waved to Midas as he pulled away from the curb outside Food For All. The last week had been amazing. She had to pinch herself to make sure this really was her life. For so long, she'd been completely alone, and now, she not only had a *very* attentive boyfriend, but she was quickly making close friends.

If she wasn't working, she was with Midas. If she wasn't with Midas, she was chatting on the phone with Elodie. And she'd also become closer with Ashlyn from work. Since she spent so much time with her during the day, it was only natural that they get to know each other. They'd been out to lunch a few times and even texted fairly regular.

It was safe to say Lexie was thrilled with her job in Hawaii, and she couldn't imagine being anywhere else. For the first time in her life, she felt as if she'd found her "tribe."

She'd spent every night with Midas since they'd moved their relationship to the next level. Some nights he picked her up after work and brought her back to his house. They talked about their day, laughed, made dinner together, then spent the evenings learning more about each other...in bed and out.

Other times he met her at her apartment, where they did

the same. Lexie had to admit that she much preferred to stay over at his house, as it was bigger and just had a more relaxed vibe than her place. But the fact that Midas was willing to go out of his way to come into town to see her meant the world.

And every morning, he dropped her off at Food For All bright and early, so she could start getting things ready for the day. A few of the part-time employees joined her soon after, but that thirty minutes or so when she was alone was a great time for her to reflect on how lucky she was.

Theo was usually waiting near the building when she arrived, but he never tried to come in when she did. Most of the time he ignored her...knowing that he wouldn't be allowed inside until other employees arrived.

The last few days, Midas had come back to the building after he'd dropped her off, bringing her a large coffee from a chain place, made exactly how she liked it. He didn't have to do that, and Lexie told him each time; the coffee she made at work was fine. But he insisted that he enjoyed spoiling her.

Lexie wanted to do the same for him. Midas worked hard. He and his team were constantly training for whatever evils the world might throw at them. After he dropped her off at work, he went straight to the base to meet up with the rest of the guys and work out. Then he had meetings during the day, and of course training.

He'd admitted there was a possibility he and the team might be deployed soon, which scared Lexie to death, but she knew better than most how important his job was. So while she'd worry about him when he was gone, she had to believe that he'd be back safe and sound after the mission was completed.

Lexie moved through the main room of the building, turning on lights, picking up the odd piece of trash left behind from the night before and straightening chairs. She headed into the kitchen to plug in the coffee machines and get out the finger foods for breakfast. They didn't have a lot of people coming by so early, other than Theo, but they always made sure they had toast, fruit, and coffee for those who did.

Ten minutes after she'd arrived, Lexie heard the front door open and headed down the short hallway to make sure it was one of the other employees. It was. She greeted Stephen, then said hello to Theo, who entered behind him, but he didn't return her greeting, simply went to his chair and sat down.

Five minutes after that, Lexie heard the front door open once more. Smiling, she turned toward the door that led into the kitchen and waited for Midas to appear.

He came in with a cup of sweet coffee in his hand, and she caught her breath at the sight of him. Yes, she'd already seen him this morning, and he'd taken her hard and fast from behind while she'd been standing at the sink in his bathroom, but it took her breath away *every* time she saw him.

He wore a pair of black shorts and a navy-blue T-shirt with a gold eagle on the left chest. It was the official "uniform" the Navy used for physical training. His thighs rippled as he walked toward her, and it was all Lexie could do to get her mind out of the gutter.

"Thanks," she said as he got close. "Seriously, you don't have to keep getting me coffee. I know it's expensive. And a pain in the ass to drop me off, go pick it up, then come back."

"It's fine," Midas said. "I don't mind in the least. It gives me an excuse to come back and see you once more before I start my day."

Gah. He was amazing.

"Well, it's appreciated. Maybe I'll show you how much tonight."

"Maybe I'll let you," Midas drawled.

He pulled her close and they stood together in an embrace for a long moment.

"You coming to my place tonight or am I coming to you?" Midas asked.

Lexie looked up at him. "I know my living here is way out of your way," she told him. The fact that she didn't have a car, and he didn't really like her taking the bus all the way out to where he lived, meant he was always driving back and forth.

"It wouldn't matter if you lived up on the North Shore, I'd still find a way to spend as much time as possible with you."

"You're too good to me," she said.

"Nope. It's called being in a relationship. And it's really not a hardship," Midas told her. "There will be plenty of times when we can't be together, and I want to take advantage of the time we've got, when we've got it."

Lexie knew he was talking about when he was sent on a mission. They'd talked about it a little, and she'd done her best to reassure him that she was all right with what he did for a living. In fact, she was extremely proud of him, despite knowing he put himself in harm's way to help others.

"Your place?" she asked with a scrunch of her nose.

He smiled. "You got it. I think we're working later tonight, so I won't be able to pick you up here."

"It's okay," Lexie said. "I'll walk home. You can call when you get close, and I'll come down and meet you so you don't have to worry about parking in the garage and coming up."

"Be careful," Midas warned.

"I will. Pika or Jack will walk me home if I ask them to. Or one of the part-time guys can do it."

"Don't want anything happening to my girl," Midas said.

"I've been on my own for a long time and lived in much more dangerous places than here," Lexie reminded him.

"But I didn't know you then," Midas returned. He leaned down and kissed her briefly, running a hand over her head gently. "Have a good day," he said.

"You too," Lexie replied.

"See you tonight."

218

"See you."

Lexie sipped her coffee as she watched Midas walk out of the kitchen. She listened as the door shut at the front of the building, sighing with contentment. Then she turned and got to work.

* * *

"Looks like someone had a good night," Aleck commented as the team stretched before heading out on a long run.

Midas merely grinned.

"Seriously, between you and Mustang, you're giving the rest of us a complex," Slate grumbled.

"Hey, all you gotta do is find yourself a woman," Mustang said.

"Right, easier said than done," Jag complained. "It's crazy that after all the missions we've been on, the two of you hooked up with chicks you *met* while on missions," Pid threw in.

"First, I'm not sure you can call it hooking up," Mustang said. "A hookup is more of a one-night stand kind of thing. And Elodie was never that, not even from the start."

"Same with Lex," Midas threw in.

"Not sure how you knew the difference. I mean, what made them different from all the other women we've rescued over the years?" Aleck asked seriously.

Midas shared a look with Mustang. Then he said, "I'm not sure I can explain it. For me, maybe it's because I knew her when we were in high school. Though, I don't want to have a relationship with any other girls I knew back then. I think it was a combination between her bravery and her strength that first drew me to her. And of course, spending hours getting to know her when we were in hiding didn't hurt either."

Mustang nodded. "It was similar for me and Elodie. And I can't deny the mystery behind why she was using a fake name was a draw. I wanted to know why, wanted to fix whatever her problem was."

"So it's a damsel-in-distress thing?" Jag asked.

"No," Midas and Mustang said at the same time.

Midas smiled at his friend. "We've saved women in the past, and I hadn't felt a draw toward any of them. Not like I do toward Lexie. Maybe it's chemistry. Maybe it's a higher power intervening. I don't know. But I'm not questioning it. All I know is when I'm with her, I don't constantly think about work, or some of the shit we've seen. She makes me believe for the first time that maybe I can have a relationship like my parents have."

"Same," Mustang said. "My mom and dad don't have the most conventional marriage, they fought a lot when I was growing up. But they never went to bed mad and I always knew their love was unbreakable. When I met Elodie, something told me she'd be worth fighting for. I can see us being together for the next fifty years. And instead of freaking out at the idea, it calms me."

Slate scoffed.

"What? You don't want to find someone to be with for the rest of your life?" Mustang asked.

"It's not that. I mean, I love Elodie, and Lexie seems cool. It's just not that easy to find someone who can put up with what we do," Slate said.

"Not to mention, someone who isn't annoying," Pid added.

Mustang picked up a stick and threw it at their teammate.

"Kidding!" Pid said, holding up his hands.

Midas grinned. He knew what his friends meant. He'd felt much the same way before he'd met Lexie. He liked living alone and couldn't imagine having someone in his space all the time, for the rest of his life. But now he looked forward to the end of the day because it meant he'd get to see Lex. Yes, the sex was amazing. The best he'd ever had. And yes, sexual compatibility was important in a healthy relationship. But he looked forward to sitting on his back porch and talking about their day. To laughing in the kitchen. To holding her hand when they drove.

Like Mustang, he could picture himself with her when they were old and gray, still laughing and enjoying each other's company.

"Oh shit, now he's gone quiet," Aleck muttered.

"Probably thinking about all the sex he's gonna get that we aren't," Jag added.

He hadn't been, but now that they mentioned it... Midas couldn't help but recall how amazing Lexie had felt that morning. Yes, he was a lucky man, and he knew it.

"Enough sex talk," Slate said. "Some of us aren't getting any, and these ten miles aren't going to run themselves."

"Why are you so damn impatient, man?" Jag bitched with a shake of his head. "Seriously, haven't you heard the best things in life come to those who wait?"

"Not for me. If I have to wait too long for something, it's usually disappointing," Slate retorted. "Come on, slackers. Let's get this done." Then he took off running at a fast clip.

Because they were all super competitive, the rest of the team took off after him in a flash.

* * *

Later that day, Midas pulled up in front of Lexie's apartment. The afternoon had been long and stressful, and he couldn't think of anything better than seeing and spending time with his woman. She always made him feel better.

He'd called her when he'd gotten close to her building, and she said she'd be waiting for him. The moment he pulled up, she exited the doors and headed for his car. He started to get out to open her door, but she beat him to it. She sat, and the smile on her face made him feel one hundred percent better.

"Hi!" she said cheerfully as she leaned toward him.

Kissing her was second nature now, and Midas eagerly accepted her invitation. He shoved his hand into her hair and pulled her across the console, kissing her almost desperately. When he pulled back, some of the brightness had bled from her eyes.

"Are you all right?"

Shit. He hadn't meant to worry her. "I'm good. Long day," he said. "But seeing you makes it much better."

"Same," she agreed. "Not that I had a bad day, but seeing you..."

He smiled, ran his thumb across her bottom lip, then reluctantly let her go. "I thought we could pick something up on the way home. Are you hungry?"

"I could eat," she said.

"Good."

The trip back to his house went by relatively quick, as they lucked out and there weren't any traffic jams on the interstate. Lexie called ahead to Dixie Grill and ordered some barbeque to go. Midas's stomach growled as the delicious smell of the food filled the car as they headed home.

They worked in his kitchen as if they'd been together for years. Lexie got plates and cutlery while Midas grabbed some drinks for them both. Without having to discuss it, they walked out to his deck with their food. They made small talk while they ate and, after they were finished, Lexie put their plates on a small table to bring inside later, before straddling his lap.

They'd made love this way once, and Midas knew he'd never be able to sit out here and not think about how sexy she'd looked as she rode him, but for the moment, she was obviously feeling more cuddly than sexy. She put her head on his chest and he wrapped his arms around her, holding her securely against him.

"Wanna talk about it?" she asked quietly.

Yeah, she knew he wasn't his usual self, even though he'd done his best to keep his worries hidden. Midas didn't even consider not talking to her.

"Looks like we'll be heading out in a couple days. I can't say where we're going or how long we'll be gone."

"Okay."

Midas blinked at her simple response. "Okay?" he asked.

Lexie lifted her head. "Yes."

He frowned. "I thought you'd have questions. Or that you'd have more of a response than merely 'okay.'"

"I have questions," Lexie said. "But I know you can't answer them. So there's no point in asking and stressing us both out. Midas, I know what you do. Do I like not knowing where you'll be or when you'll be back? No. Can I do anything about it? Also no. I have to believe that you'll be careful, and that you'll come back to me safe and sound. You've got your friends with you, and I've seen you all in action firsthand. So instead of peppering you with pointless questions and stressing us both out, I'm choosing to be chill about this."

"*Are* you chill about this?" Midas asked.

Lexie lay back down against him. "No," she said quietly.

Midas ran his hand over the back of her head gently. "And that's why I'm in the mood I'm in," he admitted. "I never thought twice about leaving before. It was my job. It was just what I did. In fact, I looked forward to missions. But now it feels different. As if there's more at stake. I guess that's what happens when you love someone."

The words had escaped without thought.

Midas tensed. Shit. Had he fucked up?

Lexie sat up again. She stared at him for a long moment. Just when he began to panic and was trying to think of a way he could backpedal and keep her from freaking out, she smiled.

"I love you too," she admitted softly.

Midas let his breath out with a long whoosh. "Thank fuck," he muttered.

Lexie chuckled and lay back down.

"Were you seriously worried?" she asked.

Midas shrugged. "I mean, if you weren't ready to hear that from me, it might not have been good. Especially since I'm about to leave for a while."

"I'd be stupid not to love you," Lexie said. "And seriously, what's not to love? You're amazing in bed, you make sure I orgasm every time, you have a kick-ass body, you bring me my sweet coffee, you drive me everywhere, and you've been to all the tourist traps this island has to offer simply because I wanted to go."

"Don't forget that I put that hula dancer thing on my dashboard," Midas teased.

"Yup. That too. But seriously, I've been on my own for a long time. I've dated in the past. I've seen examples of relationships that I don't want to be in, and I've seen other couples who've been together for years and years. I know when I've got something good, and you, Pierce Cagle, are the best of the best."

"I'm just a man," he countered.

"Yes, you are," she agreed. "My man."

He grinned. "Yup."

The angst that Midas had felt all day since learning they would be deployed soon drained out of him as he lay there with Lexie in his arms. After a while, he said, "You'll be careful while I'm gone, right?"

"Yes," she said immediately.

"I'll leave my car for you to use while I'm away."

She shook her head. "No need. Ashlyn said she'd take me anywhere I needed to go."

"You talked about this with Ashlyn?"

"Well, not specifically. I mean, I didn't know you'd be leaving so soon, but we talked about the fact that you'd be deployed at some point, and she offered. Of course, she assumes you'll be gone for six months or more, since she doesn't know you're a SEAL."

"You didn't tell her?"

"Am I allowed to?" she countered.

"It's not something we advertise, but it's also not top secret either," Midas said. "If you trust her, and it's obvious you do, then you can tell her."

"Okay."

"But still, I can leave you my car."

"Nope. With my luck, I'll crash it. Besides, I don't have that big of an interest in doing anything touristy if you aren't here to go with me."

"I'm sure Elodie will want to hang out when we leave."

"I'd already planned to call her. I'm thinking maybe I need a girls' night with her and Ashlyn."

"El would like that, I'm sure."

"Midas?"

"Yeah, love?"

She didn't say anything for a long moment.

"Lexie? You wanted to ask me something."

"Sorry, yeah. I was just enjoying you calling me 'love' for a second."

Midas grinned, knowing he'd call her that as often as possible now.

"I just wanted you to know I'm happy. For so long, I was just going through the motions of life. Traveling from one country to another, searching for something that would truly fulfill me. I'm not saying that I *need* a man to feel as if my life is complete, but I sure am glad I met you."

Her words meant the world to him. He liked that Lexie

was independent. That she wasn't afraid to try new things. But he was fucking thrilled that he was important to her.

"Same," he said, kissing the top of her head.

They sat on his deck for a long while after that. Talking about how work had been at Food For All and what she had coming up. He told her about his day, how Pid had tripped over his own feet on their run that morning and scraped the shit out of his knees. The man was a deadly SEAL, but clumsy as hell, which was fucking hilarious.

Eventually, as it always seemed to, their platonic embrace began to change. Lexie's hands began to roam, sliding under his shirt and stroking his abs. She played with the hair at his nape, as he did the same to her. When she sat up and repositioned herself so she was right over his cock, he grinned.

"You trying to tell me something, love?"

She shrugged, but was grinning as she said, "I just think that since this is such a momentous occasion and all, you know, saying the L word to each other for the first time, that maybe we could celebrate."

"What'd you have in mind? I might have a bottle of champagne in the back of my pantry."

"Hmmm, I was thinking that we both need a shower after our long, hard days of work."

"Yeah?" Midas asked, his cock growing at the thought of a naked and soapy Lexie in his shower.

"Yup. I mean, obviously we don't smell like we did when we were in Somalia in that hole, but you know...we're not exactly clean right now."

"You're right. I know how much you like being clean." And he did. That wasn't an exaggeration. Ever since she'd spent three months in the desert without a shower, she liked to shower both in the morning and the evenings. Which he had absolutely no problem with because he got to see her naked and wet twice each day, rather than just once.

"I do," she agreed. "So?"

Midas was more than ready to do whatever his woman wanted when it came to sex, but first he needed to say something. He sat up, putting one hand on the small of Lexie's back to make sure she didn't fall backward. With the other, he palmed her cheek, gazing into her beautiful hazel eyes, which seemed more green than usual.

"I love you, Lexie Greene. I admire your strength and your bravery. I love how you don't hesitate to help others without a thought to your own safety. That also freaks me out, but I still love that about you. You are literally the nicest person I've ever met, and yes, that's a compliment. I have no idea why you're with me, but I will never take you for granted."

Her eyes filled with tears as she said, "Midas."

"Don't cry. You shouldn't ever cry when someone is complimenting you. Say thank you."

"Thank you," she whispered.

"Good. Now, you wanna fuck or what?"

Lexie laughed, which was his goal. He didn't like it when she cried, even when they were happy tears.

"I love you," she told him.

And damn if those words didn't feel good. Midas vowed to tell her he loved her every day. He didn't want her to ever doubt his feelings.

He stood then, holding his woman to his chest as he did. She giggled as he headed for the door.

"The dishes," she reminded him.

"We'll get them in the morning," he said. They had more important things to do. Like she said, they needed to celebrate the first day of the rest of their lives.

CHAPTER FOURTEEN

Lexie missed Midas horribly. She'd known his being on a mission would be hard, but she hadn't understood exactly *how* difficult it would really be. Especially after seeing or talking to him every day for the last month or so. Going cold turkey and having no idea how he was doing was torture.

She'd been working a lot in the last week, trying to keep her mind off how much she missed him. Natalie was appreciative of the amount of time she'd been spending at Food For All, and she'd gotten to know all of the part-time employees—Courtney, Christine, Stephen, Richard, Aolani, Lopaka, Mandi, Tabitha, Josie, Ramon, and Beth—fairly well. She was also becoming more familiar with the volunteers.

For the most part, her days had been uneventful. She'd begun helping Natalie with some of the paperwork, determining which families they'd assist and talking to businesses on the phone to try to drum up donations.

Theo still came by frequently, and Lexie was keeping a cautious eye on him. He was definitely watching her too, which was a little disconcerting, because she didn't know his motives. Ashlyn had noticed, and even Jack had said something about it, about how she had an admirer. Lexie wasn't sure about that, and for her own peace of mind, other than saying hello to him in the mornings, she didn't talk to him much.

They hadn't seen any of the four men who had caused the ruckus two weeks ago, though every now and then, there were other visitors who seemed determined to disrupt the peace for whatever reason.

But generally, work was work. Lexie supposed that wasn't a bad thing. She didn't need excitement in her life, not like the fight that had broken out when she'd been on the phone with Midas. And he wouldn't be happy if something else happened while he wasn't in town. Lexie could take care of herself, but if the shoe was on the other foot, she'd be extremely worried about him, so she understood.

Despite missing Midas, she was looking forward to tonight, which was going to be more fun than her usual evening plans. Instead of going home and listening to an audiobook and going to bed early, she'd invited Elodie and Ashlyn over for dinner. Of course, knowing Elodie was a chef, and anything Lexie made could certainly fall short, she had the idea to have an hors d'oeuvre dinner, where everyone would bring an appetizer. That seemed like a lot less pressure than making some big main dish, especially in her small kitchen.

Lexie had made another batch of pumpkin spice cookies, since she knew Elodie had liked those when she'd had them at the barbeque a while back, and she'd also made some deviled eggs, put together a charcuterie board with meat, cheese, and crackers, and baked some crispy cheese twists. They looked super fancy, but were actually just puff pastries twisted into a rope with shredded cheese.

She'd also gone a little overboard with the drinks, not sure what the other women liked. She'd gotten some bottled water, White Claw, some Smirnoff Ice mimosas, a bottle of red wine a nice lady in the grocery store had suggested when she saw Lexie looking lost standing in the wine section, and some light beer, just in case. Anything she had left over she'd bring to work and let her fellow employees have their pick.

Lexie wasn't much of a drinker, but she enjoyed the occasional alcoholic beverage. She was more excited about getting to know Elodie and Ashlyn better. Tomorrow was Saturday, so she had two whole days off to recover if she binged. Of course, the weekends weren't quite as exciting without Midas.

A knock on her door sent Lexie scurrying to look through the peephole, and she saw both of her guests standing on the other side. She quickly opened the door and invited them in.

As they entered, Lexie said, "Welcome! I know it's not much, but—"

"It's fine," Elodie interrupted before Lexie could finish her words. "It reminds me of the room I was renting when I first got here," she said. "I loved my landlady, Kalani, and my room was just as tiny."

"My place is a lot like this," Ashlyn said. "No worries."

"I should probably introduce you two," Lexie said.

"No need! We chatted on our way up here. We arrived at the same time. We're practically besties now."

Ashlyn smiled at Elodie and nodded.

"Right, great. You can bring your stuff in here and we'll see what needs to be thrown in the oven for a while to be heated or cooked, then start on the food that doesn't need to be hot."

The two women put their bags down on the counter and began to unpack.

"This was such a good idea to have an appetizer dinner," Elodie said. "Mostly because I freaking love hors d'oeuvres!"

"Right?" Ashlyn said. "My favorite part of going out is all the appetizers."

"Don't get me started on the chips and salsa at Mexican restaurants," Elodie warned with a chuckle.

Lexie smiled. She loved that the other two women were

so excited.

"What did you guys make?" Ashlyn asked.

"Bacon-wrapped water chestnuts, garbanzo-stuffed mini peppers, and sausage wonton stars," Elodie said absently, still unpacking.

Ashlyn and Lexie stared at each other for a moment, before they both burst out laughing.

Elodie glanced up. "What?" she asked, obviously wondering what was so funny.

When Lexie got herself under control, she said, "Oh my God, you're so fancy!"

"No, I'm not! I wanted to bring things that were easy to eat, but also delicious."

"All that sounds great," Ashlyn said. "How long did it take to make?"

"Not long at all. I started this morning, prepping, then put it all together around lunchtime. I timed it so I'd be done right before I came over here, so everything would still be warm. It could all probably use a bit of a zap in the oven, but it'll be good regardless. Why?" The last question was a bit of an afterthought, when she saw both Lexie and Ashlyn trying not to laugh again.

But it was no use trying to hold in their amusement, and both women started to giggle.

"Seriously, what's up with you guys?"

"Sorry," Lexie said when she'd composed herself. "It's just that the stuff I made took like twenty minutes and is nowhere near as complicated or fancy as yours. A cheese and cracker plate, deviled eggs, and bread twists."

"And I brought Fritos and cheesy sausage dip and Jell-O shots," Ashlyn added, still giggling.

"Oh shit. I went overboard, didn't I?" Elodie asked, frowning.

"No!" both Lexie and Ashlyn insisted at the same time.

"Your stuff is probably the most healthy out of everything.

And I for one can't wait to taste it all," Lexie reassured her.

"I don't tend to eat all that well because I don't know the first thing about cooking, not to mention I'm usually too tired and hungry when I get home from work to think about making anything more complicated than a sandwich. I'm super stoked to try those bacon water chestnut things. My mouth is watering just thinking about it," Ashlyn said.

"I guess I should've asked a few more questions about what to bring..." Elodie fretted.

"Nope. And from here on out, I'm always gonna be super vague about things like this, in the hopes that you continue to use your amazing super-chef skills to bring some class to our get-togethers," Lexie said, reaching out and squeezing her forearm gently.

"What? Jell-O shots aren't classy?" Ashlyn asked.

This time they all laughed.

"I've got the oven set at two hundred, which I know is low, but I figured that should be enough to warm some food?" Lexie asked more than stated.

"It's perfect," Elodie said.

"Great. I nominate you to be in charge of the food," Lexie said. "I've got the drinks handled."

"And I'll be in charge of ambiance. This place is dark!" Ashlyn said as she headed across the room toward the window.

"No, don't!" Lexie warned, but she was too late. Ashlyn had already thrown back the curtains. She was obviously expecting some sort of amazing view, but when all she saw was her elderly neighbor sitting on his couch, eating some sort of chips straight from the bag, wearing nothing but a pair of tighty-whities—*again*—she screeched as if she'd been prodded with an electric probe.

She frantically tried to grab the curtain to pull it shut again, but it took a few long seconds for her to untangle the material before she could get them closed.

By this time, both Lexie and Elodie were bent over double. They were crying, they were laughing so hard, and within moments, Ashlyn had joined them. It took several minutes for the three women to get control over themselves.

"Oh my God, I know you said he kind of looked like Homer Simpson, and you were so right!" Elodie said with a huge smile.

"I can't believe you didn't warn me!" Ashlyn gave an exaggerated shudder. "Seriously, I could've had a heart attack or something!"

"Hey, I tried, you were just too fast," Lexie told her, grinning.

"Right. You said something about drinks? I think I need one," Ashlyn said.

Within minutes, Ashlyn was drinking one of the bottled mimosas, Elodie had a glass of wine, and Lexie chose a White Claw. They chatted about nothing in particular as Elodie got her appetizers sorted. Twenty minutes later, the countertop was full of plates of food.

The three girls sat on barstools around the bar and dug in.

"These bacon things are so good," Ashlyn praised with her mouth full, having just eaten another.

"I'm gonna need the recipe for this cheesy dip," Elodie replied, as she licked some off her lips.

"And this deviled egg is delicious! And I'm kind of a deviled egg connoisseur, so I would know," Ashlyn told Lexie with a wink.

After they'd stuffed themselves to the point of pain, and made quite a dent in the food, Lexie hopped off her barstool and grabbed the plate that she'd put in the corner, out of the way. She took off the aluminum foil and said, "Ta-da! Dessert!"

"Tell me those are your pumpkin spice cookies with the cinnamon cream cheese frosting," Elodie said.

"Yup," Lexie told her.

"Wait until you try these," Elodie told Ashlyn. "You'll be ruined for all other cookies for the rest of your life."

"I couldn't eat another bite," Ashlyn said on a moan.

"How about a wafer-thin mint?" Lexie asked, quoting one of the funniest movies of all time.

"I'm absolutely stuffed," Ashlyn answered without hesitation. "Bugger off!"

Lexie grabbed a paper towel and draped it over her arm as if it were a cloth napkin. Then she grabbed another and put a cookie on it before holding it out to Ashlyn like a waiter at a fancy restaurant. "Oh, but, madam, just one."

"Fine. Just one," Ashlyn said, grinning.

"Just one," Lexie echoed as she bowed a little.

"What in the world are you guys going on about?" Elodie asked.

Lexie and Ashlyn merely grinned. When Ashlyn took the cookie from her hand, Lexie ran across the room to the window and hid behind the curtains, peeking out as if waiting for something exciting to happen.

"Seriously, what the hell, you guys?" Elodie asked.

Both Lexie and Ashlyn burst into laughter.

Lexie couldn't remember laughing this much in a very long time, if ever. She came out from behind the curtains, explaining as she walked back toward the small kitchen. "It's from Monty Python's *The Meaning of Life* movie. Haven't you ever seen it?"

"No," Elodie said, shaking her head.

"Oh, man, you're missing out!" Ashlyn said as she took a small bite of the cookie, then moaned. "Holy shit, this is orgasmic!"

"Well, I'm not sure I'd go *that* far," Elodie said, smirking.

"Yeah, it's good, but orgasmic?" Lexie added. "I'd have to disagree with you on that one."

"That's because you've got a hot-as-hell boyfriend," Ashlyn said.

"True," Lexie said with a small smile. "And Elodie's husband isn't too shabby either."

Elodie playfully smacked Lexie's arm. "He's more than not too shabby," she said, defending her husband.

Ashlyn sighed. "I have to say, I miss sex."

Lexie almost choked on the sip of drink she'd just taken. She'd consumed more alcohol than she had in ages. The buzz she had was just enough to lower her inhibitions and give her the courage to be more forthcoming than she might've been otherwise. Ashlyn's cheeks were flushed, and she figured her new friend was probably also feeling the effects of the alcohol.

Elodie grabbed the bottle of wine and poured herself another glass, and Lexie noted that she'd drank three-fourths of the bottle already. Yeah, it was safe to say they were all a bit tipsy. But since they were safe and sound inside her apartment, Lexie wasn't concerned in the least. The women would definitely be taking taxis home.

"You're single and beautiful," Elodie said, as she leaned her elbows on the counter. "That brown curly hair of yours, those hazel eyes, pretty smile...why aren't you out there finding some hot Hawaiian men to get it on with?"

Ashlyn shook her head. "I came to Hawaii with a guy," she admitted. "Things didn't work out."

Lexie tilted her head in surprise. Before tonight, she hadn't known Ashlyn had moved here with anyone, and while she hated that things didn't work out, she was pleased the woman was still here. "What happened?" she asked.

"I was living and working near San Diego. I'd graduated from college and wasn't ready to start a career, so I got a job at a place called Aces Bar and Grill. It was awesome. The owner is a super-cool chick who's married to a former SEAL."

"No way!" Elodie chirped. "I wonder if Scott knows him?"

"Stop interrupting," Lexie told her friend.

"Oh, sorry," Elodie apologized, not sounding too sorry

at all.

"Anyway, the pay was awesome, the guys who came in tipped really well, and I even had benefits. A man started coming in every night, and he flirted with me *hard*. He was hot and a little older than me—"

"Wait, how old are you?" Elodie asked.

"She's never gonna get through this story if you keep interrupting," Lexie scolded. She never would've been so bold if she hadn't been drinking, but Elodie didn't get offended, she just shrugged sheepishly and pantomimed zipping her lips shut.

"I'm twenty-eight," Ashlyn said, and held up a hand. "I know, I know, just a baby. But anyway, he was in his early thirties. He was respectful and attentive. We started seeing each other outside the bar, and I fell for him. He said he lived here on Oahu, and that he was planning on coming back soon to help out with his family. I hated the thought of never seeing him again, so when he said he could see himself spending the rest of his life with me...I agreed to come to Hawaii with him."

"What was he doing in Southern California?" Elodie asked.

Ashlyn sighed and took another long sip of her drink. "Yeah, that's one of about a hundred questions I really should've tried harder to find the answer to before I upended my entire life to fly thousands of miles to come here."

Lexie covered her friend's hand with her own, and Ashlyn gave her a small sad smile.

"Suffice it to say, things weren't all sunshine and roses when we got here. The job he said he had didn't exist, and the connection he claimed to have to help me find a half-decent apartment turned out to be a lie too."

"That sucks!" Lexie said.

"Yeah. Anyway, Franklin said it wasn't a big deal, that I could live with him."

"Franklin?" Elodie said with a grin. "His name is Franklin?"

Lexie smothered a chuckle.

"Do you want to hear the rest of my sad tale of woe and no sex or what?" Ashlyn asked with a huff.

"Sorry, yes. Go on," Elodie said.

"Right, so even though I moved to Hawaii because this is where he lived, I wasn't ready to live with him full time. Especially not in the studio apartment he had. I started to get the feeling he'd convinced me to come to Hawaii simply so he could mooch off me. Needless to say, the relationship didn't last very long after the move at all."

"Yeah, I can't blame you," Elodie said.

"I mean, I'm not opposed to a woman making more money than a guy in a relationship, or having the man stay home with the kids while the woman works, but I thought I was moving to Hawaii to be with a man who had a stable job, and who would be fun to hang out with and take me sightseeing...but in reality, I got a lazy asshole who was really good at selling a lie."

Ashlyn gave the other two women a small smile. "But it's been almost a year since all that, and I got the job with Food For All, and I'm happy. So to bring this depressing conversation full circle...that's why I miss sex. Because I haven't had it in so long, I think I'm a born-again virgin."

"That sucks, Ash," Lexie said. "Did you call the police?"

"Because I haven't gotten laid in months? I think that's a little drastic, don't you?" Ashlyn quipped.

Lexie chuckled and rolled her eyes. "No, because he's a predator who's obviously preying on women."

"He's not technically a predator. An asshole and a liar for sure. And I should've asked more questions and not moved so fast with him. I shouldn't have been so eager to upend my entire life to move out here," Ashlyn said. "I've learned my lesson. I'm not nearly as willing to jump into a serious relationship now than I was back then. I mean, I'm not opposed to dating, or having sex, but I'm going to be very cautious before I agree to move in with someone or marry them."

"That's kind of sad," Lexie said.

"It's fine," Ashlyn insisted. "It's just me being smart. Besides, things have worked out not so bad for me here in Hawaii. I've only been working for Food For All for a few months now, but I really enjoy it. It's not like working in a bar, and that's not a bad thing. Like you, they're paying for an apartment for me to live in. It was furnished too, which was a blessing. I've got a better view than you though," she said with a smile. "I get to see the top floor of a parking garage next to my building."

"Well, I'm glad you're my coworker," Lexie told her.

"And I'm glad to now be your friend," Elodie chimed in. "And if you ever get curious about what the hell is going on with Franklin, just say the word. There's a guy who Scott and the rest of the guys know named Baker, who I am *sure* would love to look him up."

"Yes!" Lexie exclaimed. "Midas told me about him. He lives up on the North Shore, right? He's like a surfer dude?"

"He surfs, but..." Elodie lowered her voice until she was whispering, as if she were afraid someone would be listening to their conversation. "He's also some sort of super spy or something."

"I don't think he's a spy," Lexie said with a frown.

"Okay, he's not a spy, but he can get things done. He actually went to New York and had lunch with the head of the mob family that caused me so much trouble."

"He did?" Lexie asked.

"Holy shit! Mobsters?" Ashlyn breathed.

"Yes. And he promised that I was safe. And for some reason, I believe him. It helped that Scott and the rest of the guys visibly relaxed when he told me that."

"I'll tell you the whole story about the mobsters later,"

Lexie told Ashlyn in a stage whisper. Then louder, "Baker was able to get Shermake and his brother and sister scholarships to Somali universities," Lexie said. "They won't cover the entire cost of attending, but a lot of it."

Elodie nodded. "I'm not surprised. Anyway, I'm sure he could find out what Franklin's deal is."

"Baker sounds kinda scary," Ashlyn hedged.

"I haven't met him," Lexie said. "But he's apparently got some pretty impressive connections."

"I've met him. And he's more mysterious than scary," Elodie said. "But he's totally got the surfer thing going. He's tan, has tattoos all over, and he's got longish hair. It's mostly gray, so he's like a silver fox surfer dude."

Both Ashlyn and Lexie sighed.

"Right?" Elodie said. "I have no idea what his whole story is, but he's definitely got demons. I mean, I owe the man everything for making sure no more hitmen would come after me, and he *still* kind of scares me. There's something in his eyes that makes me want to keep my distance, while wanting to hug him at the same time."

"Why is that such a lethal combination?" Ashlyn asked. "I mean, women in general should run from men like that, but instead we're drawn to them like moths to a flame."

"You interested?" Elodie asked.

"In this old surfer guy? No," Ashlyn said firmly.

"I don't think he's old," Lexie mused.

"So who *are* you interested in?" Elodie pushed.

"No one," Ashlyn said, staring into her drink.

"Wait...so there *is* someone," Elodie said cheerfully. "Who?"

"No one. I'm done with guys," Ashlyn mumbled.

"But you said you missed sex," Lexie teased. "We all know sex is possible with a vibrator, but it's not nearly as good. Trust me, I know. When did you meet him? Come on, tell us!"

"I've only seen him once..." Ashlyn admitted.

"Spill!" Elodie exclaimed.

"If you can't tell your best friends, who *can* you tell?" Lexie asked. The alcohol had loosened her tongue for sure. She felt extremely close to these women. Saying they were best friends was more wishful thinking than anything else.

"Slate."

Elodie and Lexie stared at Ashlyn with wide eyes—then began screeching in excitement.

"Yes!" Elodie crowed.

"That would be awesome!" Lexie agreed.

"But he's pretty grumpy," Elodie added.

"Guys, I don't even *know* him," Ashlyn said.

"Ashlyn would fit against him perfectly, since she's so tall," Lexie said. "He's what, only a few inches taller than her?"

"Something like that. But those muscles of his are so freaking huge," Elodie said.

"Maybe Ash can curb his impatience," Lexie teased.

"You guys—" Ashlyn started, but the other two women ignored her.

"I mean, there's something to be said for impatience," Elodie responded with a smirk.

Lexie nodded. "Oh, yeah," she agreed. "And they—"

"Enough!" Ashlyn shouted, making both Lexie and Elodie look at her in surprise. She sighed again. "Sorry. But seriously, I shouldn't even have said anything. I literally saw him *once*, and he was annoying. He was all hulk-like and arrogant when he came into Food For All. He also tried to keep me from approaching you," Ashlyn continued.

Lexie nodded.

"And after Franklin, I'm done with older men. No, thank you."

"I think Midas told me he's our age, thirty-two," Lexie told her. "Which isn't much older than you. And you were the one who brought him up."

"Which I regret," Ashlyn muttered.

"Okay, okay, we'll shut up," Elodie said. "But real talk here. I was intimidated by Scott and his team when I met them, but there was just something about my husband that caught my attention the second I saw him. And I don't think it was just because I was scared out of my mind either. Yes, Slate is older than you. Yes, he's a bit grumpy and, from what Scott tells me, a lot impatient. But I don't think you'll find anyone who would be more respectful than Slate."

"Do *not* set me up," Ashlyn said firmly. "I mean it. I recently got out of a bad relationship, I don't need to jump into another one."

"Fine, but it doesn't sound like you had much of a relationship at all with that Franklin guy. And it's been almost a year," Elodie pointed out.

"Maybe you could see if he's interested in something casual," Lexie suggested. "Don't SEALs have a reputation for being ladies' men?"

Ashlyn shrugged, but not very convincingly. "I saw first-hand how many women threw themselves at the Navy SEALs at Aces, back in California. It was disgusting. I'm not like that."

"Of course you aren't," Lexie told her. "But that doesn't mean you can't date him."

"I just...is it too much to ask for a man who will support me, but not suffocate me? Who will love my outgoing personality, but understand that I want to sit at home and not be social every once in a while? Who actually knows where my clit is without me having to point the damn thing out?" Ashlyn asked.

Lexie and Elodie shared a smile at her last question.

"Oh, for God's sake, I don't want to hear about both of your awesome sex lives," Ashlyn said, balling up a napkin and throwing it at Lexie.

"Hey, guys talk. And since Scott has no problem finding

my clit, I'm guessing that Slate wouldn't have a problem either."

"Okay, I'm officially changing the subject," Lexie said. "I can't think about any of Midas's friends that way."

"Fine. Ashlyn, I have a question," Elodie said.

"Shoot."

"You said that you loved working at the bar, so how'd you know you'd enjoy what you do now?"

"What do you mean?" Ashlyn asked.

"Well... I used to love being a chef. But then my world kind of blew up in my face and I can't imagine doing that as a career again."

"You don't enjoy cooking anymore?" Lexie asked.

"It's not that. I do. I mean, I had a great time cooking for tonight, but it was for you guys. Not a bunch of strangers. And I love hanging out with Scott and the rest of the guys and grilling and stuff. But I've struggled to figure out what I want to do with my life. Obviously being a charter fishing guide is out...since being out on the ocean hasn't been that good to me," Elodie said.

"I've been thinking..." Ashlyn started.

"Oh, Lord," Lexie blurted.

"No, seriously. You know how many people we help at Food For All. But there is so much more food that gets wasted. Grocery stores throw away expired bread and wilted vegetables. And cans that are dented get tossed as well. Restaurants throw away tons of food. We try to get some of that stuff to give away, but we're only talking to the places close to where we are. And think about all the families who travel down from the North Shore or out east, to where we are, just to get food. It has to be expensive, not to mention how much time it takes to drive all the way downtown."

"What are you saying?" Elodie asked. "And what does it have to do with me?"

"I was thinking of talking to Natalie about starting up a

satellite location of Food For All, but with a slightly different focus," Ashlyn said. "And while it's not exactly cooking, many of the lunches we put together aren't that healthy. It's just chips and an apple thrown in with a not-very-appetizing sandwich. What if we could tap into more stores to get food they're going to throw away? Restaurants too. It would help if we had someone who could turn those donations into more appealing and nutritious meals."

"How old are you again?" Elodie asked.

"Twenty-eight. Why?" Ashlyn asked.

"Because you seem a lot older. And...that sounds like a huge challenge," Elodie said. "And a lot of hard work."

Ashlyn merely lifted an eyebrow. Then she turned to Lexie. "I was thinking there are probably a lot of military families who live here who could use some assistance. And elderly people. I'd considered maybe starting my own charitable organization, but I like working for Food For All, and there's some comfort in working for such a well-known and established organization. The Barbers Point area would be a good location to start with. To see if we can make this work. And if I could convince Natalie to talk to the Food For All people, and if they gave me the go-ahead, I'd need help. You know, with getting it up and running, talking to managers at stores and restaurants, getting the word out. And I know for a fact that it's a hell of a drive for your man every morning to bring you to work downtown."

Lexie felt excitement well up inside her. She loved helping people, and the idea of being able to bring assistance to more of those in need seriously appealed.

"Shit, she's good," Elodie whispered.

"So, you in?" Ashlyn pushed. "We could use a professionally trained chef to help us."

"I'm in," Elodie said with a smile.

"Lex?"

"You know I'm in too," Lexie promised.

"This calls for a toast!" Ashlyn said, lifting her bottle.

They all clinked their drinks together and took long sips.

Then Elodie asked, "So what's up with this Theo guy?"

"Jeez, you're taking lessons from Midas with the abrupt change of topic," Lexie said wryly.

"Not really. I was thinking about Food For All and the people we could help, which made me think about the homeless men and women around here, and how many are on the streets through no fault of their own. Which made me think about Theo. Scott told me about him after the altercation the other week. Is he still around?"

"He is," Ashlyn said. "And he watches Lexie like a hawk."

"No, he doesn't," Lexie protested, trying to downplay the issue.

"He does," Ashlyn insisted. "The only reason Jack and Pika haven't kicked him out is because that's *all* he does. He hasn't said anything derogatory about you or tried to talk to you. But he definitely has his eyes on you whenever you guys are there at the same time."

"Is he dangerous?" Elodie asked.

"No," Lexie said. At the same time, Ashlyn shrugged.

"He's just...different," Lexie said. "Sometimes he seems pretty lucid, and other times he just sits in a corner and talks to himself. He seems more on edge since those guys started shit though."

"He does," Ashlyn agreed.

"You need to be super careful," Elodie told her.

"I will. I am," Lexie reassured her.

"The guys have been walking us home," Ashlyn explained. "Setting up the second location for Food For All is also a good idea for safety reasons. I'm hoping to concentrate on getting meals to people who aren't necessarily homeless, but are struggling financially and could use some help. So we wouldn't necessarily be handing out food to the homeless."

Lexie nodded. She'd never mentioned to Midas how

uneasy she felt walking home. If she did, she knew without a doubt he'd do whatever it took to make sure he was there to pick her up, or one of his acquaintances. And she never wanted to be a burden like that. Besides, she was a grown adult, she could more than take care of herself. Had done so her entire life.

"Looks like you girls have some talking to do with your boss. And some pretty hefty convincing. But I know you can do it!" Elodie encouraged.

The three women smiled at each other. Tonight was not only fun, but the women had begun to forge a strong bond. Lexie had wanted girlfriends her entire life, and it seemed that she now had them.

"You guys want to take leftovers home?" she asked.

"Yes!" both Ashlyn and Elodie said at the same time.

"And I'm gonna eat all the cookies before Scott gets back!" Elodie exclaimed.

Deciding to let that go, as they had no idea if it would be one day or twelve or more until their men got home, Lexie headed into the small galley kitchen to start preparing the leftover food. The others helped, then each got another drink and headed over to the bed to hang out and continue chatting.

Five hours later, Lexie's stomach hurt from laughing and her face was sore from smiling so much.

She'd never had as good a time as she'd had tonight. She was exhausted by the time Ashlyn and Elodie left in a taxi, but happier than she'd been in years. The only thing that could've made this night perfect was snuggling up to Midas as she fell asleep.

She didn't know where he was or when he'd get home, but she had to believe that he'd come back to her safe and sound. The alternative was unthinkable. Midas was tough, and smart, and he had five of the best SEALs at his back. Six, if she included the mysterious Baker. Lexie was fairly sure if

Midas and his team needed him, Baker would somehow know, and would do whatever it took to send in the cavalry. She really needed to meet this guy. He sounded both scary and amazing at the same time. He was definitely a man she wanted on her side. Maybe she'd make him a plate of pumpkin spice cookies to butter him up.

The room was spinning when Lexie finally climbed under the covers, but she couldn't help but smile. She was excited about Ashlyn's idea for the extension of Food For All. It would make the commute longer for her...unless she stayed over at Midas's house. That made her grin even bigger.

Yes, it was safe to say that Lexie was more than happy with how things were going in her life. She had an amazing boyfriend, great friends, and a good job. A few months ago, when she was staring up at the stars from an African desert, she never could've imagined she'd be this content right now.

Reflecting on being a hostage made her smile dim as she thought about Dagmar. He hadn't been as lucky. She hated that he hadn't made it out alive.

Closing her eyes, she sent up a short prayer to the other man. "Rest in peace, Dagmar. And please help your brother heal. He misses you terribly."

She knew Magnus was struggling by the way he talked about Dagmar in his emails and when they spoke on the phone. Maybe seeing how well she was doing would help him. Would bring some closure to what had happened. That, and getting involved in the organization that Dagmar loved so much.

Turning onto her side, Lexie put Dagmar, Magnus, even Elodie and Ashlyn out of her mind. Her thoughts were on Midas, the boy she used to know who had grown into one hell of a man. And he was hers. "Come home soon," she whispered before falling into a deep sleep, aided by the alcohol she'd consumed.

CHAPTER FIFTEEN

Magnus Brander scowled when he walked out of the Honolulu International Airport, just over a month after he'd first told Lexie he'd be visiting the island. He'd wanted to get here sooner, but there had a been a lot of red tape and paperwork to struggle through. He'd begun to think Food For All wouldn't allow him to travel to Hawaii at all, but after they'd received a very generous "donation" from the Brander family, the board had finally signed off on his visit.

He could have come at any time, of course. But he needed an official reason for being here to deflect suspicion when poor Lexie was found dead.

He wasn't one hundred percent sure as to his plan, other than not leaving Hawaii before killing the bitch who was responsible for his brother's death. There were too many unknowns to effectively plan from afar, but the fact that Lexie worked with the homeless population in downtown Honolulu should give him plenty of opportunities for a solid strategy. He'd always been good at thinking on his feet. He'd play things by ear once he'd observed Lexie and Food For All.

In less than a week, his brother's death would be avenged. That was all that mattered.

Magnus took a deep breath. Honolulu was way too fucking hot. And humid. He already missed Denmark. But with every day that passed after his brother had died, he'd felt more and more empty. The hole inside him was growing, festering, taking over his body little by little. Soon, he'd be nothing but an empty shell, and he needed the person responsible to pay.

Every time he got an email or message from the little bitch, the urge to kill her grew stronger. She sounded so *happy*. So content. She went on and on about her boyfriend and how much she loved Hawaii. Fuck that shit. She didn't even care that because of *her*, one of the greatest men he'd ever known was dead!

And worse, she'd used her feminine wiles to escape the hospital when the kidnappers came to take back what had been stolen from them. He'd read the report from the Jaeger Corps. Knew *exactly* what happened. He wasn't surprised she was fucking the SEAL who'd rescued her. She'd probably had her legs spread for him even as the kidnappers closed in on the hospital. What a whore. It should've been *her* who'd died in that fucking cesspool of a town in Somalia. Not his brother. Not Dagmar!

Magnus climbed into a taxi and gave the driver the address of the Food For All headquarters downtown. He needed to get the lay of the land before heading to his hotel. Lexie had told him about an incident with some men who'd had outstanding warrants, who'd caused trouble at Food For All. She'd also mentioned someone named Theo, who apparently was out of his fucking mind and had scared her a time or two.

He hoped to exploit her fear as best he could.

He'd spend a few days solidifying a plan, while messing with Lexie at the same time. He didn't give a shit about the audit he'd been sent to complete. As far as he was concerned, the entire organization could go down in flames. It was his next target, after he took down Lexie Greene. Food For All was just as much to blame. If it hadn't been for that company, Dagmar wouldn't have been in Somalia, wouldn't have been taken hostage, and wouldn't be dead.

Yes, he had a lot of work to do before he could go back to his beloved homeland. He wouldn't rest until everyone and everything with a hand in Dagmar's death burned to the ground. It wouldn't bring his brother back, but maybe it would make the giant hole in his soul begin to shrink.

* * *

Lexie shifted impatiently next to Ashlyn, Jack, and Pika. Natalie was waiting outside to greet Magnus, who was on his way straight from the airport. She'd give him a tour of the building and show him their processes. It was a Wednesday afternoon, and there weren't a lot of people there for food at the moment, which was probably better as far as an audit was concerned.

Theo continued to come by, and Lexie was trying give him a wide berth. She felt guilty about it, but after Midas had told her how concerned he was about the man, she was doing her best to try to mitigate his fears. But that didn't mean she wasn't still keeping watch over Theo and hadn't asked Ashlyn to make sure he was eating properly.

The four men who'd fought with Theo still hadn't been back, but there had been other men, and even a few women, who'd made Lexie nervous. It seemed that her experience being kidnapped had made her more wary. Midas said it wasn't a bad thing, but it still bothered her. She wasn't quite as naïve or clueless as she'd been in the past.

She was thrilled when Midas returned from his mission without a scratch on him, just a couple days after her girls' night. Lexie was well aware that wouldn't always be the case, but she was relieved things had gone well this time.

She was also very satisfied with how their relationship was progressing. He'd been back for a week and a half, and they'd spent every night together. Usually at his place, but sometimes when he worked extra late, he stayed at her apartment. He'd been working long hours, but reassured her that was normal after a mission. The Navy had also ramped up their training because of a few incidents that happened with other teams, so that meant he hadn't been able to pick her up in the afternoons.

Lexie was all right with that, because she still got to see him every evening when he got off work. Even though Midas was usually tired, he still asked about her day, about her conversations with Magnus, about Theo, and about her blossoming relationships with Ashlyn and Elodie.

All in all, Lexie was unbelievably satisfied with her life at the moment. She knew she and Midas would eventually have disagreements and would both have their bad days, but she was becoming more and more confident that they'd be able to work through the tough times and stay as close as they were now.

Today, she was excited to see and talk to Magnus. The communication between them had become more regular and it felt as if they were friends now. As much as two people who'd never met *could* be friends. He was only scheduled to be in town four days, so he'd be very busy, but she hoped he'd be able to find some time to go to the beach or do something fun while he was here.

The second Magnus stepped through the door, Lexie felt as if a ten-pound weight was pressing on her chest. He looked *exactly* like Dagmar.

Of course he did. The men were twins, after all...but for some reason, it still surprised her. Magnus had the same blondish hair, same height—around five-ten or so—same blue eyes. And even though Magnus was in his fifties, his body was still quite fit.

"You okay?" Ashlyn asked quietly.

Lexie nodded. Seeing Magnus looking so healthy was painful. She remembered when Dagmar had looked that way, but months in the desert, and his stroke, had made him deteriorate quickly.

Magnus looked around the room and when his gaze landed on her, he stopped in his tracks. Lexie had told him what she looked like, and he'd probably seen the photo Food For All had on file. It was a little unnerving to be the sole focus of his attention.

He walked toward her, Natalie following behind him a little uncertainly. Magnus stopped in front of her.

"You must be Lexie."

"That's me. Hello, Magnus. I hope you had a good trip."

"It was fine."

He stared at her with a look Lexie couldn't interpret. After all their emails and calls, she'd expected something... different. A hug. A smile. *Something.* But instead, he just stared with a completely blank expression on his face.

"Yes, this is Lexie. And Ashlyn, Pika, and Jack. They are our full-time employees," Natalie said, filling in the awkward silence.

As if coming out of a trance, Magnus shook his head and smiled. He shook the others' hands and turned back to Lexie. "Forgive me for being so awkward. It's been a long day and I'm a little overwhelmed meeting you."

"No need to apologize. I have to admit that it's overwhelming to see you too. I really am sorry about Dagmar. I know I already expressed my sympathy, but he was a good man."

"Yes, he was," Magnus agreed. Then he turned back to Natalie. "I've got a lot of work to do in the next few days. How about we get this tour done, then you can show me to your office, where I can start looking over the accounts?"

His tone was all business, and Lexie frowned a little. She knew he was here to audit their branch, but still.

"Of course. I'll pull up the files so you can start today," Natalie said.

"Thank you. I'd appreciate that," Magnus said. "It was nice meeting you," he added, nodding at Lexie and the others before turning and following Natalie down a hallway to her office.

"Wow, he's kind of got a stick up his ass, doesn't he?" Pika asked.

"Shhhh," Ashlyn scolded. "The last thing we need is him hearing you."

"I thought you said he was cool," Jack asked Lexie.

She shrugged. "He's always seemed that way in our conversations. Maybe he's just tired from the long flight or something."

"He could be upset by meeting you," Ashley suggested. "Not that you aren't super nice and all, but you're a connection to his brother. And you said they were very close."

"They were," Lexie said with a nod. "I'm sure you're right."

The three other employees headed off to get some work done, but Lexie stood where she was for a long moment. That meeting hadn't gone at all like she'd thought. She didn't think Magnus would jump up and down with excitement, but she'd expected more than a weird stare and grumpiness.

Finally, she shook her head. The man was tired, just as she'd said. She remembered how exhausted she'd been when she'd first arrived. She needed to cut him some slack. He'd be more rested tomorrow and they could have a talk.

Nodding to herself, Lexie turned—and almost ran into Theo, who was standing right behind her. She hadn't heard him approach. "Oh, I'm sorry, Theo. I should've been watching where I was going. Are you okay? Can I get you anything?"

"You should be careful. Very careful," Theo mumbled. "You're nice. Nice people can be hurt."

Lexie studied him. "You're nice too," she said gently.

Theo shook his head. "No. I'm strange. My head is messed up," he said, pointing to his temple. "But I see people. Bad people. You should be careful."

"Okay," Lexie said, trying to soothe him. "Have you eaten today? If you go sit, I'll bring you a sandwich."

"No cheese," Theo said, rocking a bit where he stood. "And no crusts."

"I remember," Lexie said with a smile. "I'll make sure to only put on ham and take your crusts off."

"Good...that's good," Theo said as he started to head back to where he'd left his stuff at one of the tables. Then he turned and pinned her in place with a look so lucid, so intense, Lexie froze in place. "He's not a good man."

"What? Who?" she asked, but Theo had already turned again and was moving toward his table.

Feeling frustrated with how her afternoon was going, Lexie sighed and went to the kitchen to make Theo's sandwich.

* * *

A few hours later, Lexie's day hadn't improved. It seemed as if everyone was on edge. It could've been the weather, it had been unusually rainy and cloudy all day. It might've been the fact that Magnus was here, and had come out of the office and was sitting on one side of the room, watching and observing their everyday operations. It could've been because Theo was not having a good day, and he'd started two fights with other people who'd come in for meals and information on long-term assistance.

But Lexie knew she was out of sorts because of Magnus. He'd watched her all day, though he hadn't approached. She could admit that she was disappointed. She'd had pretty high hopes for meeting him and so far, her expectations had proven to be way *too* high.

When her phone vibrated with a text, she eagerly took it out of her pocket. Seeing Midas had sent her a message, she smiled.

Midas: I'm so sorry, I'm not going to be able to pick you up this afternoon. Our commander promised that we'd get to go home early, but there was a huge explosion at a military base overseas and we need to discuss the situation.

Midas: I promise I'll make it up to you.

Lexie sighed. With how her day was going, she'd been looking forward to having a long evening with Midas. She brought the phone up to her lips and dictated a response.

Lexie: It's okay.

Three dots immediately showed up, indicating he was responding. Lexie waited to see what else he had to say.

Midas: People have been extra grumpy today. It must be a full moon. Be careful walking home and text me when you get there. I'll let you know when I'm on my way.

Lexie: You've noticed too? I hope the sun comes out soon because I can't handle people's weirdness. I'll be fine. Love you.

Midas: I love you too, Lex. Thank you for being so understanding.

Lexie: Would me pitching a fit make you get off earlier?

Midas: lol. No, but I wish.

Lexie: Right. So I'll see you when you get off work. Drive safely.

Midas: Always.

Lexie put her phone back in her pocket and contemplated what to do. There was really no reason to leave at her usual time because all she'd do was sit around her apartment being grumpy. Maybe she could go shopping on her way home and pick up some groceries to make Midas a nice dinner. But then again, she had no idea what time he'd get off work, and he might eat before he left the base.

Her musings were cut short by a shout from the kitchen. She rushed toward the back room and grimaced when she saw Jack lying on his back under the sink. It had obviously sprung another leak because water was spraying everywhere. This wasn't exactly the best impression for Magnus, but at least Lexie knew what she'd be doing the rest of the afternoon.

She ran toward the water shut-off valve. When she'd cut it off, she looked around and wrinkled her nose. There was water everywhere. It would definitely take all afternoon to clean up the mess. Rolling up her sleeves, Lexie got to work.

* * *

Magnus knew he should be tired, but he was running on pure adrenaline. The second he saw Lexie Greene, a red mist descended across his vision. He pictured himself reaching out right then and there and wrapping his hands around her throat, choking the life out of her.

She looked so damn healthy. And happy. And it wasn't fair!

She should be feeling guilty. Shouldn't be able to eat, to sleep. But instead, she glowed with vitality.

Bitch.

He'd sat in the director's office for an hour or two pretending to look at files on her computer, but he didn't give a shit about any of it. The organization could run itself into the ground. In fact, he'd do everything in his power to make sure it did.

When he couldn't stand not knowing what *she* was doing any longer, he left the office and lurked in the main room, watching Lexie as she flitted from one person to the next. Always smiling, always positive. He wanted to smack that damn smile off her face, and he would. Soon.

Magnus had already noted that the Food For All building seemed to be in a somewhat rough neighborhood. And he also knew that Lexie had been given an apartment in a building nearby. She'd told him she walked home sometimes, when her boyfriend wasn't able to pick her up. He didn't know the asshole's schedule, but he was counting on the fact that at least once in the next three days, he wouldn't be able to come get her.

When a water pipe broke in the kitchen, it gave Magnus a convenient distraction. He slipped out the front door. His eyes scanned the area as he walked, until he saw what he needed.

As he looked down a dark, narrow alleyway between two buildings, he saw a large man sitting against the wall with a shopping cart parked next to him. He stared at the opposite wall as he drank from a bottle wrapped in a paper bag.

Glancing around and seeing no one, Magnus slipped into the alley.

He could smell the homeless man's body odor as he approached. It was offensive, but that didn't matter. His face was covered in a scruffy beard, with what looked like pieces of food stuck in the coarse strands. He had on a pair of torn and dirty tan pants and a T-shirt with holes of varying sizes. He had no shoes on his feet, but a pair of worn-out flip-flops were on the ground next to him.

"What d'ya want?" the man growled as Magnus approached.

"A moment of your time," Magnus said.

"Damn foreigners," the man said. "How about some money? You look like you got plenty."

"I do," Magnus said, ignoring the deepening of the man's frown. Clearly, his answer wasn't what the man expected to hear. "And I'd be happy to give you some. But I need a favor first."

The homeless man looked disgusted. "I ain't no homo," he said belligerently.

Magnus sneered. "I do not want sex." Then he went on to explain what he wanted from the man.

The skeptical look hadn't faded from the guy's face. "That's it?"

"That's it," Magnus told him. "And to show you how serious I am, I'll give you twenty bucks right now, and the other four hundred and eighty after you do what I want." He pulled a wad of cash out of his pocket and peeled a twenty dollar bill off the top, holding it toward the man.

"Half. I want *half* now," the man bargained.

Magnus shrugged and put the money back in his pocket and turned to walk away.

"Wait!"

Magnus smirked and waited.

"Fine. Gimmie the money."

Magnus took the bill back out of his pocket and turned to face him. The homeless man snatched it out of his hand and crumpled it up in his fist.

Leaning down, Magnus did his best not to inhale as he spoke. "If you fuck me over, you're a dead man. I know twenty ways to kill you and make it look like suicide."

"Whatever," the man said, not impressed. "How'll I get the rest of my money?" he asked.

Magnus stood and straightened his tie. The slacks and long-sleeve shirt were too hot for this climate, but he had a reputation to maintain. "*If* you do a good job, I'll find you afterward."

"You better," the man mumbled.

Magnus's leg shot out. He kicked the guy in the side with all his strength.

The homeless man flew sideways with a cry. Magnus quickly crouched and wrapped a hand around his throat...and squeezed.

The man immediately tried to pry the hand off his neck so he could breathe, but Magnus was too strong. "Don't *fuck* with me," Magnus warned. "Understand?"

The man nodded frantically, his eyes widening with panic as more and more seconds raced by without him being able to get air into his lungs.

Magnus had no idea he'd get such a rush out of this! Seeing the desperate fear in the man's eyes was a game changer. Made Magnus feel powerful for the first time since Dagmar had died. He'd been powerless for so long, and now he held this man's life in his hands.

He fucking loved it.

But he also knew he couldn't kill him. Not now, in the middle of the day. And he still needed him. A healthy dose of fear would make sure he did exactly as he was told.

Magnus let him go with a shove, then stood. He watched with a smirk as the lowlife gasped for air. He turned and headed back down the alley toward the street. Peering out, he once again saw no one looking in his direction.

The way Americans pretended not to see those on the fringes of society would definitely work in his favor. Smiling, and feeling much better than he had even twenty minutes ago, Magnus headed back toward Food For All. He looked down at his hands and flexed them. He could still feel the man's throat in his palm. It had felt amazing.

But having Lexie fucking Greene under his hands would feel even better.

He had to be patient. Had to set things up so when he left Hawaii, no one would find him the least bit suspicious.

CHAPTER SIXTEEN

Lexie was more than ready to head home by the time the mess in the kitchen had been cleaned up. She just wanted to see Midas and not think about anything for a few hours. She slung her purse over her head and walked toward the door.

Angry shouts from outside made her stop in her tracks.

Looking over her shoulder, she saw Jack was nowhere in sight, and Pika had left fifteen minutes ago. There were a few part-time employees around, but they all seemed busy with other people.

"I'll walk you home," Magnus said from her right, making Lexie jump in fright.

She chuckled nervously. "I didn't see you," she told him.

"I noticed. I would like some time to talk to you anyway. I am sorry I haven't been able to talk to you much today."

"It's okay," Lexie said. "You've been busy. Besides, you aren't here to hang out with me, you're here to work. I hope the audit is going okay?"

"It is fine. Come on, it sounds like someone isn't happy out there. You should get home."

"Thank you," Lexie said. She was beyond relieved she

wouldn't have to walk home by herself. Especially with whatever was going on outside.

"Wait here a moment," Magnus said as he headed for the door. He disappeared out onto the sidewalk, and Lexie shifted nervously where she stood. He was back within two minutes and held out his arm to her.

Lexie hooked her arm with his and they headed out into the humid Honolulu evening. Looking around, she didn't see anyone who might've been making the ruckus she'd heard. Relieved, she glanced up at Magnus. He looked just as prim and proper as he had when he'd arrived earlier. His white shirt was still crisp and his tie was still perfectly knotted. His back was straight as he walked, his gait somewhat stiff.

"What do you think of Hawaii so far?" she asked as they walked.

"It's hot. And humid," Magnus said.

Lexie laughed. "Yes, it is. But today was very unusual. It storms in the afternoons a lot, but most of the time they don't last very long and the sun comes out again. Are you going to get some time to go to the beach or sightsee?" she asked.

"I doubt it. There's a lot of work to be done for the audit and my plane leaves in three days."

"Yeah," Lexie said. She knew his schedule. She wasn't sure why he hadn't planned more time. But he seemed much more uptight and...proper than his brother had been. Dagmar had also been businesslike, but Magnus seemed constantly on edge for some reason.

"Do you want to go out to dinner one night with me and Midas?" she asked. "There are a few amazing Hawaiian restaurants we could take you to."

"We will see," Magnus said with a nod.

Hmmm. She'd hoped for a more enthusiastic response. But maybe he was just tired. Wracking her brain to try to think of something else to say as they walked, Lexie jerked in surprise when a man yelled from what seemed like right behind her.

"Hey, bitch!"

She turned to see a large man with a scruffy beard standing way too close.

"Yeah, you," he said when he caught her eye. "You got any money? I need money."

"I'm sorry, I don't," she said honestly. She never carried cash, it just wasn't safe in this part of town.

"Liar!" the man exclaimed. He reached for her, but Magnus pulled her out of the man's reach.

"It's time to go," he told the man.

But the scruffy man just sneered. "Ooooh. The big bad protector. What about you? You got any money?"

"Ignore him," Magnus said, turning his back on the man and heading back down the sidewalk.

Lexie wasn't sure it was a good idea to let the man out of their line of sight, but she followed Magnus's lead.

The guy followed behind them, verbally harassing them as they walked.

"Nice ass. I bet you've got a pretty pussy too. You can't like that stick in the mud. I bet he's got a tiny dick. My cock is huge. I'll fill you right up."

Lexie winced. She wasn't comfortable at all. She'd never experienced anything like this kind of sexual harassment here before, and it seemed so out of place. Not to mention, it was very scary.

"Back off," Magnus told him, but kept walking.

"I've seen you," the man said. "All that pretty hair. Walking home alone. I can be your boyfriend. I'll take care of you."

Shivering, Lexie didn't like the fact that he'd watched her. She felt vulnerable, and she hated it.

Without a word, Magnus turned and stepped toward the man. Lexie let go of him and watched in disbelief as he punched the guy in the face.

He went down with a thud, laughing as he looked up at them. Blood dripped from his nose as he said, "That all?"

"That's all," Magnus growled.

"Bitch is probably frigid," the man retorted, then staggered to his feet and went back the way he'd come, toward Food For All.

"Holy shit," Lexie exclaimed softly. "Are you all right?"

"Yes," Magnus said. "Come on, let's get you home before anything else happens. This is not a good part of the city."

"It's not usually this bad," she said.

"I have been here one day and there has been much... excitement," Magnus countered.

"I know, but seriously. I've been here for a while and no one's ever come up to me like that."

"You can't trust people," Magnus told her as they walked a little faster toward her apartment building. "I would think you would have learned that after what happened."

"I prefer seeing the good in people," she said.

"Sometimes there is none," Magnus countered.

Lexie frowned. She didn't like that anyone thought that way, but especially someone who worked for Food For All. Too often the people they met had been discriminated against and had many strikes against them. Some had been in prison and were trying to get back on their feet, others were alcoholics or addicted to drugs. And while Lexie was aware that not everyone had good intentions, she still preferred to give people the benefit of the doubt.

They reached the doors to her building and Magnus turned to her. She saw he had some blood on his knuckles. "You should get that cleaned up." For some reason, she didn't offer to let him come up to her apartment to do it.

"I will," he said. "Look. I am sorry about that man scaring you. But there are many like him who would want to hurt a pretty woman like yourself."

"He was an anomaly," she insisted stubbornly.

"Like him?" Magnus asked, turning and using his head to gesture across the street.

Lexie looked where he'd indicated and saw an alleyway. She was about to ask what he was talking about when she saw movement. A man stood up and stared at her.

"I believe that is...Theo?" Magnus said. "You told me about him in our correspondence. You said he scared you."

"It was just that once. Things got intense in the fight," Lexie said a little nervously.

"Then why is he watching your apartment complex? Lurking in the dark, following you?"

Lexie didn't have an answer to that. She wanted to protest, saying Theo was probably just staying in the alley for the night. That it was a coincidence he was there. But the truth was, she didn't know that for a fact. He had a tendency to leave before her in the afternoons, and she had no idea where he went or what he did at night. He was usually one of the first people there in the mornings for breakfast. Sometimes he stayed all day and other times he left right after he ate.

"He is not right mentally," Magnus said gently. "It is not good that he is here. He watches you. I saw it today. And you told me earlier that he's always waiting in the morning for Food For All to open, right?"

"Yeah."

"And you're usually the first one to enter the building. He could overpower you when you get there. You need to be careful, Lexie."

Lexie nodded and pressed her lips together in agitation. For the first time in months, she didn't feel safe. She'd had no problems walking around Galkayo by herself. She'd roamed the streets of Berlin and New York on her own. She'd even lived in East Saint Louis for a time and had made friends with the people she'd interacted with on a daily basis.

And not once had she ever felt as nervous as she was right now. She *hated* the feeling. She needed to get inside. "I will. Thanks for walking me home," she told Magnus.

"It was my pleasure. You will be there in the morning, like usual?" he asked.

"Yes. Why?"

"Natalie has given me a key, so I can come and go as needed to make sure I have enough time to finish the audit. I'll think I'll also go in early, to keep an eye on you."

Lexie nodded, feeling only slightly relieved. "Okay. I'll see you then."

"Goodbye. Until tomorrow."

Lexie let out a relieved breath when the doors closed behind her. She reassured herself that Theo didn't know what apartment she lived in. Besides, Midas would be there soon. She was fine. Safe.

But the goose bumps that rose on the back of her neck belied her positive thoughts.

* * *

Midas tapped his foot impatiently as the elevator rose to Lexie's floor. He'd hated not being able to pick her up earlier. The meeting with the commander was important, but he'd wanted to be there to see how her meeting with Magnus had gone. She'd been looking forward to it for weeks now.

The elevator opened and he strode down the hall toward her door. He'd texted Lexie to let her know he was on his way up. Most of the time she met him at the door and had it open before he even got there. But for some reason that wasn't the case today. Midas knocked, concerned about the change in their routine.

He was even less happy when he got his first look at Lex, when she finally opened the door.

There were dark circles under her eyes and she looked stressed way the fuck out. He didn't get much time to examine her before she threw herself into his arms.

Midas walked them into her apartment and locked the door behind him before he took her shoulders in his hands and backed her up so he could look into her eyes.

"What happened?"

"Nothing. I'm just glad to see you."

"Don't bullshit me, Lex. Something's wrong."

She sighed and sagged. "It's been a long day."

Deciding to change tactics, Midas grabbed her hand and led her to the bed. It was too early to go to sleep, but since she didn't have a couch, the bed would have to do.

He set her down, and she smiled up at him. "You that eager for some lovin'?" she teased.

Ignoring her, Midas leaned down and took off his boots. "Scoot over," he told her.

She did so without a word, and Midas sat next to her. He plumped the pillows behind him, stretched his legs out, and pulled her toward him.

Lexie came willingly, melting against him with a long sigh.

For several minutes, neither spoke. Midas just stroked her hair and held her tight.

"How was your meeting?" she asked after a while.

"Long," he said. "Talk to me, love."

"I'm okay," she said. "It's just been a stressful day."

Fine. So he'd have to pull what was wrong out of her. He could do that. "Did Magnus make it here okay?"

"Yeah."

"Did you get a chance to talk to him much?"

"Not really. He went right to work on the audit."

"How's Ashlyn?"

"Fine. Why?"

"Just wondering. What time did you get home?"

He felt her stiffen a bit against him and knew he was getting closer to finding out what the hell was wrong. He hated not being able to immediately fix whatever had happened.

"I stayed a bit later since I knew you were in that meeting. That pipe in the kitchen finally burst, and we had a lot of water to clean up."

"That sucks," Midas said.

She shrugged.

"So you left later...did you eat something?"

Lexie nodded.

Right, so he obviously sucked at figuring out what was bothering her. Midas decided to quit beating around the bush. "You need to talk to me, Lex. What happened? And don't say nothing. You're not yourself, and it's freaking me out."

"I'm sorry. It's just been a lot of things today. Magnus was... I don't know how to explain it. Just different from the man I'd gotten to know through emails and our few phone conversations."

"How so?"

"More formal, I guess. I mean, I didn't expect him to dance a jig when he met me, but I wouldn't have minded a hug or something."

"He might've felt weird doing that in front of others."

"I know."

When she didn't say anything else, Midas kept probing. "You said it was a lot of things. So what else?"

"The sink. Magnus. Not seeing you before now. Theo. Walking home..." Her voice trailed off.

"Walking home?" he asked, not liking how she'd stiffened when she'd said that.

"I'm fine," she said.

"What happened?"

"Magnus walked me home because there was some sort of ruckus outside right before I left. A guy followed us for a while. He said some mean things. Magnus hit him and that was that."

Midas felt helpless, and he hated the feeling. Knowing Lexie was downplaying what happened wasn't helping. "And Theo?" he asked.

"He was in the alley across the street. Magnus said he'd seen him staring at me throughout the day. I don't know why he was there, but what if he's been following me home for a while now? I just... I hate feeling afraid of anyone we help at Food For All. It's not like me, and it's unfair to them."

"It's not unfair if someone is an actual danger to you," Midas said.

Lexie didn't say anything, just stared up at him.

He could see the frustration in her eyes. One of the things he liked best about Lexie was her positivity. Her sunny outlook on life. What he'd seen as naivety at first, something that had concerned him, he now recognized as her innate kindness, a natural part of who she was. She balanced out his overly cautious, cynical self. He also knew she wanted to trust Theo...but that didn't mean *he* had to.

He wasn't all that surprised that Theo had been lurking around in a dark alley, watching her. And he definitely wasn't happy about it either. "I'll pick you up from here on out," he told her.

She shook her head against him. "We both know that won't always be possible. Look at what happened today. You've got work and stuff you can't get out of."

She was right. "Fine. But if I can't pick you up, I'll arrange for someone else to."

Lexie picked her head up and put her hand on his cheek. "I appreciate that. More than I can say. But I've never relied on a guy for anything before in my life, and I don't want to start now."

"I'm not just some 'guy,'" Midas retorted. "And there's no fucking way I'm gonna let you keep walking home by yourself when men are harassing you, or if Theo is out there watching you."

"I usually have Jack or Pika walk me home if they're available," Lexie told him. "And Magnus was really a great help today. He hit that guy and didn't act like it even hurt him at all. I know it had to, because that guy was huge and Magnus's knuckles were bleeding. I love that you want to protect me, but you can't always be with me. I need to figure out how to keep *myself* safe. Today was just...a lot. I'll be my usual positive self tomorrow. Promise."

Midas picked up the hand on his cheek and kissed her palm before resting it on his chest. Lexie put her cheek against his shoulder and snuggled into him.

He'd heard what she said, but he was still going to do whatever he could to take better care of her. She was right, he couldn't always drive all the way downtown from the base to pick her up when he was working, but he knew a lot of people, he could call in some favors.

Hell, he bet if he told Baker what was going on, the man would drive down from the North Shore every day to pick her up and take her home.

"What are you smiling about?" Lexie asked suspiciously.

"I was just thinking about asking Baker to pick you up when I can't."

"*The* Baker? Yes! Do it!"

Midas blinked in surprise. "I thought you'd put your foot down and tell me I'm being ridiculous," he admitted.

"Okay, it *is* ridiculous. But I've heard a lot about him from Elodie, and I'm curious." She shrugged a little sheepishly.

"You want to meet him?"

"Well, yeah. Of course."

"Then I'll make sure that happens," Midas said. The more he thought about it, the better the idea seemed. Baker wasn't a man who suffered fools easily, and he'd be more than happy to keep his ear to the ground for any threats against Lexie. He hated violence against women, and Midas knew once he found out what Lexie had been through, she'd have another champion.

"Why do I suddenly feel uneasy about this?" Lexie asked, giving him the side eye.

"I don't know. Baker's cool."

"Midas?"

"Yeah, love?"

"You make everything better just by being here."

Fuck, he loved her. "I feel the same. No matter how long my day's been or how hard a mission is, knowing you're here waiting for me gets me through."

"You hungry?" she asked softly. "I can make you something."

"No. I'm fine just as I am," Midas said. His mind was racing with what he needed to do the next day. He needed to talk to Natalie about Theo. And definitely Baker. If anyone could find out what the hell Theo's deal was, it was that man. He could probably even find the guy Magnus had punched as well.

Midas also wanted to meet Magnus. He would've been there today if the emergency meeting hadn't come up.

"You're thinking really hard," Lexie accused after a moment.

He chuckled. "Sorry."

"It's okay. You just go ahead and think. I'll just do my own thing here."

Her hand slowly moved down his chest and played with the buttons on his uniform pants. Looking down, Midas saw her grinning as she continued to lie against him.

He grabbed her hand in his and said, "Are you okay now?"

Lexie looked up and nodded. "Promise."

"I'm sorry you had a hard day and that I wasn't there for you."

"You're here now," she said.

"I am," Midas agreed, then scooted down until he was on his back. Lexie laughed when he rolled them until she was under him. He lowered his mouth and loved that he could feel her smile against his lips.

When he lifted his head, they were both breathing hard. "I love you, Lexie. I hate that you were scared today. I'd kill anyone who dared fuck with you like that asshole who followed you today. And if Theo lays a hand on you, he'll wish he hadn't."

She shivered, and Midas regretted his words for a second, until she spoke.

"Why is you being all alpha such a turn-on?" she asked.

"Because it means I love you."

"And I love you," she returned as her hands slipped between them to tug at the button at his waist once more.

"Something you want?" he teased.

"Yes. You," she said, completely serious now.

His head dipped again as he went to work making his woman forget her shitty day.

* * *

Magnus settled into the king-size bed in his ridiculously expensive hotel room. He didn't ask the Food For All board if his choice was all right. Lodging was included in the expenses for auditors, and no one had specified where he had to stay or what the budget was.

Today had gone better than he could've hoped. The asshole he'd hired to harass Lexie on her way home had done exactly as he'd told him to do. Magnus had felt Lexie's tension, and he knew she was scared. He'd gotten to play her hero and gain her trust.

The fact that he'd spied the bat-shit crazy Theo in the alley across from her building had been icing on the cake. He'd planted the seed that he was following her...so it would be no surprise in a day or so when the mentally ill man attacked her.

The only loose end was her boyfriend. The Navy SEAL. But he knew from talking with Lexie that he dropped her off in the mornings, then headed for the Naval base.

He hadn't come to town with a definitive plan in mind, but things were working out better than expected so far. Food For All was in a shitty part of town, and Lexie was stupidly oblivious to the dangers around her. Perfect. He hoped to get Theo in the right place at the right time. Magnus would arrive at the building first thing in the morning, observe the man's routine, then make his final plan.

His palms itched, and Magnus inspected them. They didn't look any different than they had this morning, but he could literally still feel that homeless man's dirty flesh on the skin of his palm. Could feel the struggle as he'd tried to suck in air and couldn't.

Except when he thought of what had happened, it wasn't a bearded man's face he saw in his mind. It was that bitch's.

She was too naïve. Too perky. Too fucking *happy*.

How she could be happy when he'd been left with an empty void inside him, Magnus didn't know. Out of everyone in the world, Lexie Greene was the very last person who should feel happiness. She should *always* be as terrified as she'd been tonight. Should feel fear and dread every damn second of her pointless life.

The only consolation Magnus had was the fact that the last thing she'd *ever* experience was terror. Just as Dagmar had.

Satisfied that things would work out just as he hoped,

Magnus closed his eyes. He really was tired from traveling, then working all day. His internal clock was all fucked up. But soon he'd be back home, and maybe, just maybe, Dagmar would be able to rest in peace. And in return, the gaping cavity inside Magnus would begin to heal.

CHAPTER SEVENTEEN

The day after Magnus had arrived was relatively uneventful, for which Lexie was grateful. Midas had dropped her off at Food For All early as usual, and she'd gotten a head start on the day. Magnus showed up not too much later than she had and went straight to the office to get to work. After Stephen arrived and unlocked the doors, Theo had appeared, as was his custom. She'd been worried at first, but he'd taken a seat on the far side of the room while she'd been in the kitchen and hadn't said anything to her. He rocked back and forth, and even when she put a piece of toast in front of him, with the crusts cut off, he didn't look up.

Deciding not to confront him about why he was in the alley across from her building, especially when she wasn't sure how he'd react to an interrogation, Lexie went back to work. She'd never seen Theo in that alleyway before, so she couldn't really accuse him of watching her when she had no proof.

Midas called around two and said he had the rest of the day off and was coming to pick her up. Lexie headed to Natalie's office to let her know.

"I'm sorry to interrupt, but I wanted to let you know that Midas is coming to pick me up now," Lexie said.

"That's fine. You've been working really long hours lately."

"Will I get to meet him?" Magnus asked from behind the large desk, where he was sitting and looking at computer files.

"If you want to."

"Oh, yes. I've heard a lot about him. And maybe he can tell me more about my brother."

Lexie mentally winced. She wasn't sure this was the time or place to talk about what had happened in Africa, but since Magnus hadn't accepted her offer of dinner, and Midas couldn't just take time off work whenever he wanted, she supposed there wouldn't really be another good time.

"I'll let you know when he gets here," she told them.

Natalie nodded, while Magnus just stared at her with that penetrating gaze of his.

Closing the door, Lexie took a deep breath. Man, Magnus had turned out to be very different from what she'd thought, based on his messages and from talking to him on the phone. She assumed he was still in mourning, maybe even a little stressed because of this being his first audit.

Lexie headed back down the hall and visited with the men and women who were in the main room until Midas arrived. Luckily, Theo had left by the time he got there. She had a feeling Midas would've wanted to have a "chat" with the poor man.

"Hey," Midas said, coming straight for her.

"Hi," Lexie said with a huge smile. It was almost embarrassing how happy she was to see him. Midas never failed to make her feel good.

"How's your day been?" he asked.

"Good."

He crooked an eyebrow at her.

"Seriously. Good," she insisted. "Except... I think Magnus wants to have a talk with you about his brother."

"I'm okay with that," Midas said.

"Really? I mean, I just figured it would be awkward."

"It's not. But I'm afraid he's not going to be all that impressed with what I have to say. I was with you, not Dagmar, when the attack on the hospital happened, and even before that the Danish special forces took over his care in the field and on the way to Galkayo."

"True," Lexie said.

"Come on. Let's get this done so we can head out. I have a surprise for you."

"You do? What is it?"

"It wouldn't be a surprise if I told you what it was," Midas replied with a grin.

They walked back down the hall toward Natalie's office, and Lexie knocked once more before sticking her head in. "Midas is here," she said.

They walked into the office and Midas nodded at Natalie. "Good to see you again," he told her.

"Same. I hope you're well?" Natalie said.

"I am, thanks."

"And this is Magnus. I've told you guys a lot about each other," Lexie said a little nervously.

As Magnus stood, Midas took a step forward and held out his hand. Magnus looked at it for a beat too long before he shook it.

"It's good to finally meet you. Lexie *has* told me a lot about you," Magnus said.

"Same. I'm sorry about your brother," Midas said.

Magnus nodded his head in acknowledgement of the sympathy.

"I'm going to slip out and check on things," Natalie said, heading for the door.

The second she was gone, Magnus said, "I would like to hear about Dagmar and what happened."

It wasn't a question, and it wasn't said in the most friendly tone either. Lexie tensed, but Midas put his hand on the small of her back as if to let her know he had this conversation under control.

"I wish I could tell you something you wanted to hear. But my team and I weren't involved much in his transport or his care once we got back to the hospital. We were surprised that we were even headed back to Galkayo in the first place. We didn't learn of the unexpected stop until we were in the helicopter on the way to the LZ in the desert."

Magnus visibly stiffened. "My brother was ill. He needed a doctor. Immediately. The flight to the US ship could've killed him."

Midas nodded in acknowledgement, but didn't respond.

"So you know nothing?" Magnus asked.

"I'm sorry, no. I was with Lexie when the hospital was attacked. I didn't learn of your brother's death until much later, after we were able to meet up with my team. I didn't even know the Jaeger Corps had left the country."

Magnus made a snorting noise in his throat and turned back to his chair. He sat and concentrated on the computer screen in front of him. "It was nice meeting you," he said absently. "I have much work to do in the short amount of time I have here in Hawaii."

"Right. My deepest condolences for your loss," Midas said, then pressed on Lexie's back as he turned her toward the door.

"I'll see you tomorrow," Lexie said over her shoulder. "Maybe we can go out to lunch?"

"That would be nice," Magnus said.

When the office door shut behind them, Lexie scrunched her nose and looked up at Midas. "Wow. He was kinda rude. I'm sorry."

"Don't be," Midas said. "It reflects on him, not you."

"But I've been talking him up for weeks," she fretted.

"Doesn't matter. People aren't always how they seem. You

mostly knew him through email, Lex. And a few phone conversations don't always show someone's true colors."

"I know, but still. And I appreciate you not getting into it about whether or not his brother should've gone back to Galkayo or straight to the ship."

"I still believe he was wrong. He used his money and influence and got the government to approve taking Dagmar to the hospital, but it was the wrong decision. I'm not saying he wouldn't have still died, because from what I understand, he was in bad shape, but I wasn't about to tell a grieving brother that. What we know for certain is that if we'd gone straight to the ship, the kidnappers wouldn't have had a second chance to try to get their hands on either of you."

Lexie nodded. Midas's response just proved what a good man he was. He could've defended his actions that day, made it clear that it was Magnus's insistence on his brother being seen by his doctor that had most likely resulted in his death. But he hadn't.

"Come on. Enough work talk for both of us. I have plans."

"What kind of plans?"

"You'll see."

"Gah. I'm dying of curiosity," Lexie complained.

"All will be revealed soon," Midas said mysteriously.

Lexie said goodbye to Natalie and the other employees who were there, then she and Midas headed out the door. As they walked toward the parking garage, Lexie almost stopped when she saw Theo out of the corner of her eye. He was sitting on a bench across the street from the entrance to Food For All.

"Ignore him," Midas said mildly.

Lexie nodded. She'd planned to. Theo wasn't doing anything threatening. He was just sitting there. But she couldn't help the shiver as she walked with Midas to his car.

* * *

Lexie grinned as she watched Midas devour the shrimp taco he'd bought from a truck parked along the side of the road. She'd already eaten one and was about to dig into her second. Midas had said that the North Shore had the best food trucks, and nothing beat Giovanni's. He was right as far as she was concerned.

He'd already promised they'd stop at the Dole Plantation so she could get a dole whip on the way back to his place, but first he had another surprise for her. They were at Waimea Bay, one of the most famous and popular surf spots on the North Shore. At the moment it wasn't crowded, which Midas said was the only reason they were there. During competitions, even getting to the North Shore was almost impossible. Apparently, the traffic was horrendous, bumper to bumper on the two-lane road as people came to watch the athletes take on the huge waves.

Today, the sea was relatively calm and only a few diehard surfers were out in the bay. But that didn't matter to Lexie. She was thrilled to be there.

Out of the corner of her eye, she saw a man approaching from their right.

Midas turned to her. "Baker didn't promise he'd be here, but I hoped he'd be intrigued enough to meet you that he'd show."

"Holy crap," she breathed as she stared at the man coming toward them. He'd just come from the ocean and was wearing a wet suit that didn't hide any of his muscles. He was exactly as Elodie had described. Tall. Black hair—liberally speckled with gray—that fell over his forehead, jade green eyes that seemed to be able to see right through her. Definitely a silver fox...one with an incredibly dangerous aura around him.

Midas stood and held out his hand as he nodded at the older man. "Baker. Good to see you."

"Same," Baker said, then turned toward her. "And you're Lexie."

"I am," she said as she stood. She wiped her hand nervously on her shirt, then held it out. "It's good to meet you. Elodie has nothing but good things to say about you."

Baker took her hand and shook it, but didn't let go right away. He just stared at her for a long moment.

"Baker," Midas warned.

He grinned and let go of her hand. "Sorry. I'm just amazed at all that hair."

Lexie blushed, glaring at Midas. "I *told* you I needed a hair tie." Then she turned back to Baker. "We came up here straight from my work. Midas didn't tell me where we were going, and if I knew we'd be coming this far in his convertible, I would've insisted he stop so I could find something to tie my hair back. It's not usually this crazy."

"Yes, it is," Midas said with a laugh.

"Shut up," Lexie hissed quietly.

"Oh, hey," Baker said, turning to Midas. "I brought Elodie's dish for you to bring back to her. That apple crumble she made was amazing. Want to run and grab it from my car?"

"You just want to talk to Lexie without me around, don't you?" Midas asked.

Baker shrugged.

"Fine. But don't be an asshole," Midas said.

Baker unzipped a tiny pocket on his wet suit and pulled out a single key on a keyring and lobbed it to Midas. He caught it, then leaned over and kissed Lexie briefly before heading for the parking lot.

"I'm at the end," Baker called out.

"Figures!" Midas yelled back.

Lexie didn't know what this man could possibly want to talk to her about, but she had to admit she was curious.

Baker straddled the bench of the picnic table where she and Midas had been sitting. Taking his lead, she sat back down as well.

Baker rested an elbow on the table and stared at her for a

moment before saying, "You look different than what I expected."

It was an odd way to start a conversation, but Lexie went with it. "How did you think I'd look?"

"I'm not sure. I mean, after watching the videos, I figured you'd clean up well, but you're not quite as...sturdy as I'd expected."

Lexie had no idea what that meant, so she merely shrugged.

"So, you and Midas are dating," he said.

Lexie nodded.

"And you knew each other in high school."

"Yeah. I moved to Portland my senior year," Lexie confirmed.

"It shouldn't come as any big surprise that I looked into you and your situation," Baker said.

Lexie stared at him, again not sure what to say.

"You were a shitty student, but I suppose undiagnosed dyslexia would do that to anyone."

"Wow, how did you know that?" Lexie asked, not ashamed of her disability in the least. She'd actually been relieved when she'd finally been diagnosed.

"It was pretty damn obvious, looking at your record," Baker explained. "You must've had some terrible teachers for none of them to even suggest it was a possibility. Anyway, so... now you're with Midas...I guess you feel pretty lucky."

Lexie nodded. She did feel that way.

"Big bad Navy SEAL rescued you from the desert, you came here to Hawaii, and he dotes on you now. You probably thought you were worthless, like your dad always claimed, huh? So someone as good-looking and tough as Midas taking a shine to you had to have been pretty heady."

Lexie's brow furrowed and she shook her head. "No. I mean, I'm thrilled to be with Midas, but that's not—"

"He's paid well, has a good job, but it's not all sunshine

and roses. There's plenty of shit to go with his poster-boy good looks."

Okay, Lexie was really getting irritated now. She thought this guy was supposed to be Midas's friend. And the second he'd left, the guy turned on her.

"You feel as if all your dreams have come true, Lex? What're you gonna do if he comes back from a mission that went south? And trust me, eventually, one will turn bad. What if he comes home with a leg missing? Or an arm? Or *all* his limbs? You gonna think you're lucky then? He could get a TBI...a traumatic brain injury...and not be the same man you know today. It's hard work being with a SEAL. He might've rescued you, and you might be proud to have him on your arm now, but will you feel so lucky if he's been burned over ninety percent of his body?"

"Why are you being so cruel?" she asked.

"You think this is cruel?" Baker asked. "It's not. It's called real life. I'm trying to find out how tough you are. If you can hack being with him."

"I can," Lexie said between clenched teeth.

Baker raised a brow, clearly showing his skepticism.

That was it, Lexie was done. Elodie might like this asshole, but she definitely did *not*. "You're a real jerk," she said quietly. "Yes, I was amazed that Midas was interested in me, but that didn't last long. I'm also stronger than you think. If Midas was hurt, I'd one hundred percent stick by him. That's what love is. And I love him, and he loves me.

"The question isn't whether I'm good enough for him. I am. I have no doubt about that. I've come a long way from the outcast teenager you obviously still think I am. I lasted three months in the desert after being kidnapped without losing my mind, I've lived in more dangerous places in my lifetime than you probably have, and I'm a damn good person. Maybe you should be asking Midas if he's good enough for *me*," Lexie bit out.

Surprisingly, Baker smiled. It transformed his face from almost scary to...almost friendly.

"Exactly," he said with a nod. "And for the record, I seriously doubt that he is. As I said, being with a SEAL, with any soldier or sailor, isn't easy. Their partners need to be independent, not the type who freak out if the smallest thing—hell, the *biggest* thing—goes wrong while they're deployed. And most of all, Midas needs someone who he knows without a doubt will be there when he gets home, and who will stick by his side no matter what."

Lexie frowned. "So you were...what...testing me?"

"Yup," Baker said without embarrassment or remorse.

"So if I'd burst into tears or something, I would've failed your test?"

Baker shrugged.

"You're kind of an asshole," Lexie commented.

"Yup."

"But... I can't fault you for wanting to look out for Midas."

"Which is something a woman with high self-esteem would say," Baker said with a laugh. "And so you know... I'm impressed with your work at Food For All. You *have* lived in some shitty places, but you seem to make friends everywhere you go. And by the way, Astur and Yuusuf cried when they learned about the scholarships their children were receiving from you and Midas."

Lexie's eyes widened. "You *talked* to them?"

"Well, not directly, but I have it on good authority that Shermake will definitely be taking you guys up on your generous offer. As will the younger kids."

Lexie wasn't sure how she'd gone from being so irritated to wanting to cry, but she blinked back her tears. She studied the man sitting next to her.

"What?" he asked.

"You're kind of scary."

He smiled.

"That wasn't a compliment." She felt compelled to inform him.

His grin widened.

"I'm back," Midas said. "I put the dish in my car."

Lexie jumped in surprise. She hadn't seen or heard him approach.

"Sorry, didn't mean to scare you."

Lexie noted that Baker didn't seem startled in the least. The man was definitely spooky. But damned if she didn't like him.

"You good?" Midas asked Lexie.

"Of course, why wouldn't I be?" she said a little too enthusiastically.

Midas narrowed his eyes and turned to glare at Baker.

"We had a nice chat," Baker said as he stood. "She's feisty. Kind of like that hair of hers."

Lexie also stood, pleased when Midas immediately draped his arm around her shoulders. "Would you stop commenting on my out-of-control hair," she grumbled. "You're gonna give me a complex."

"Naw. You've got too much confidence for that," Baker said.

It was true. Lexie didn't give a shit if others didn't like her hair. Or her. She'd grown out of the need to be liked by everyone she met. And Baker made her realize that yes, Midas *was* lucky to have her as a girlfriend. She was loyal, would never cheat on him, would stick by his side no matter what, and she might not be that good of a cook, would never make a ton of money, but she was a damn good person. She smiled at Baker.

He nodded at her in return. Even though he'd been a jerk, Lexie knew he'd done it for his friend's benefit.

"You headed out to surf again?" Midas asked.

Baker looked out at the sea for a moment, then shrugged. "Haven't decided."

"Be careful if you do," Lexie said.

Baker looked amused. "You worried about me?" he asked.

"I'm worried about everyone. You know, because of sharks, rip currents, rogue waves..."

"Sounds like someone else I know," Baker muttered.

Lexie had no idea who he was talking about, but she let it go when he turned to Midas and they began talking about people she didn't know. She assumed they were other SEALs, or at least people Midas worked with on the Naval base.

Several minutes went by before Midas said, "Thanks for coming to meet us today."

"Wouldn't have missed it," Baker said. "Be careful out there," he warned.

"Always."

"Talk to you soon," Baker said with a chin lift as he headed for the parking lot. A brightly colored VW van had just pulled in, and he walked right toward it. A petite dark haired woman was behind the wheel.

"What did he say?" Midas asked, pulling her attention from Baker and the woman in the stereotypical Hawaiian surfer van.

"Nothing."

Midas cocked an eyebrow at her.

"Fine. He let me know he'd looked into my background and wanted to make sure I was good enough for you."

"Seriously? Fucker," Midas said, looking like he was going to go after Baker.

Lexie caught his arm and tugged. She snuggled into his chest and looked up at him. "You didn't ask me what *I* said in return," she said.

"What did you say?" Midas dutifully asked.

"I told him I was more than good enough for you."

"Yes, you are," Midas agreed. "Too good."

Lexie grinned. "How about we say we're perfect for each other?"

"I can live with that. You done with your tacos?"

"Hands off my food," she warned. "I love you, but not enough to give up my tacos."

He chuckled. "How about you bring it with you and finish in the car? If we're gonna stop at the Dole Plantation and get you an ice cream, we had better get going. Besides, I have a hankering to sit on the deck and just relax tonight."

"That sounds perfect," Lexie said.

They packed up their food and headed for his convertible. Lexie smiled and waved at Baker and the woman he was talking to. The woman waved back with a friendly smile, and yelled, "Aloha!"

"Aloha!" Lexie called back.

"Come on," Midas said, urging her on.

"What?" Lexie asked.

"You're thinking about going over there, finding out her name, how she knows Baker, and what's going on between them."

She grinned. "Okay, I *was* thinking about doing that. I mean, did you see the way Baker's expression changed when he saw her pull up?"

"Yup. But I'm not going there. And neither are you."

"But he was all fired up about making sure I was a good match for *you*, seems only fair I have that woman's back when it comes to *him*."

"Nope," Midas said, putting a hand in the back of her hair and holding on tightly, making sure she met his eyes. He wrapped his other arm around her back and pulled her against him. "He can take care of himself."

"But can she?"

"Baker wouldn't be with a woman who couldn't," Midas said.

And he sounded one hundred percent sure of that. Then

he palmed her ass and tucked her into the vee of his legs, and the feel of his cock against her stomach made Lexie forget all about Baker, the woman, the van, tacos, and even Dole whips. She wanted this man with every fiber of her being. Even the hold on her hair took on new meaning, making her nipples tighten under her shirt.

"Maybe we can skip the ice cream," she said breathlessly.

She watched as Midas's eyes dilated.

"It'll mean we can get home faster."

"I'm all for that," Midas said. Then he dipped his head and kissed her. Long, slowly, and so damn passionately, Lexie was a pile of mush when he finally pulled back.

He opened the door for her and got her settled in the seat before jogging around to the driver's side. Turning to her, he smiled, bringing up a hand to smooth a lock of her hair behind her ear. "I fucking love your hair. And you."

"I love you too. Now drive."

"Yes, ma'am," Midas said with a smile as he backed the car out of the parking spot and headed for his house.

CHAPTER EIGHTEEN

Lexie leaned over and kissed Midas before she climbed out of the car the next morning. She was a bit sore from his overexuberant lovemaking the night before, but she wasn't going to complain. Nope. She'd been a bit rough herself. There was something about Midas that made all her inhibitions disappear.

"Have a good day," he told her.

Lexie rolled her eyes. "You know I'm gonna see you in a bit when you bring me my coffee," she told him. It had become their routine. He dropped her off at Food For All so she could open the building and get coffee started. Then he'd go and pick up her sugary brew and bring it back, giving them both an excuse to see each other once more before they started their days.

Midas simply smirked.

Truth be told, Lexie loved their teasing banter. "Right. Have a good day, honey. I'll talk to you later."

He smiled as she headed for the front doors of Food For All. They'd talked about her being there so early, and by herself, yesterday on the way home from the North Shore. After what had happened two days ago, when she'd walked home with Magnus, and after seeing Theo lurking in the shadows near her building, she'd agreed that she would talk to Natalie about having one of the part-timers come in half an hour earlier so she'd never be in the building by herself. Safety in numbers and all that.

Looking up and down the street, Lexie didn't spot anyone. It was still fairly early, so that wasn't surprising. She turned and waved at Midas, knowing she'd see him soon. He waited until she was inside before pulling away from the curb.

Lexie turned on the lights and headed for the kitchen toward the back of the building. A few minutes later, she was filling one of the coffee carafes with water when she heard the front door open. She figured it was Stephen. It was a bit early for him to be there yet, but it couldn't be anyone looking for food, since she'd locked the door behind her when she'd entered.

Despite that...after everything that had happened lately, she reached for a knife from the block near her and placed it within easy reach on the counter. She felt stupid being so paranoid, but better safe than sorry.

A second later, a noise at the door to the kitchen caught her attention. She looked up expecting to see Stephen, and instead saw Magnus standing there. He was once again wearing a long-sleeve white shirt, which looked like it had just been ironed, and a neck tie. His brown pants also had creases down the front. She'd tried to get him to loosen up in the last couple days, but he was obviously comfortable in his formal attire.

She turned back to the sink to fill a second carafe, mentally berating herself for being paranoid. "Morning, Magnus. You're here early," Lexie said easily.

"Wanted to get a head start on the audit today. Thought I would take your advice and head to the beach later."

"That's great!" Lexie said enthusiastically. "If you want suggestions, I'm happy to ask Midas for you. I'm not really a beach person, but I bet he knows all the good spots that won't be too crowded."

Magnus walked closer until he was standing right next to her. "You okay?" he asked, nodding toward the knife.

Lexie smiled self-consciously. "Yeah. Just being cautious, I guess." She turned her attention back to the water.

She was concentrating on not overfilling the carafe when the first blow hit her face.

She dropped the glass container with a grunt, hearing it shatter as it fell into the sink. Before she could get her bearings and figure out what the hell happened, Magnus had spun her around to face him—and had his hands around her throat.

Lexie was shocked beyond belief.

More than that, she immediately knew she was in deep trouble. Magnus wasn't fooling around. He was squeezing her throat so tightly, she couldn't get even the smallest breath of air.

Immediately, her hands flew up, clawing at the fingers around her throat.

And she realized with horror that he was wearing gloves.

He hadn't been wearing them when he'd walked into the kitchen. She would've noticed. He must've put them on while her attention was on the coffee pot.

He'd *planned* this.

"You fucking bitch," Magnus growled in a guttural tone she'd never heard from him before. "It should've been you. *You* should've died out there in that desert. Not my brother! Dagmar was worth ten of you. A hundred!"

Lexie opened her mouth to beg him to stop, but nothing came out.

"That's right," he said, his eyes narrowed. "From the second I heard those assholes had doubled their price and wouldn't let Dagmar go, I swore you'd pay. All your emails.

Those goddamn phone calls. Even this fucking job. All a means to an end. *Your* end."

For some reason, something she'd seen while watching one of those crime shows on TV suddenly popped into her mind. A father was mourning the murder of his daughter... and the fact that it took seven and a half minutes for her to die by strangulation. He'd said he couldn't believe how long seven and a half minutes actually were.

For Lexie, right this moment? It seemed too short. Way too short.

Her mind instantly switched to Midas. How happy they'd been...

She wasn't ready to die.

She fought for her life, clawing her fingernails down his face. When that didn't make him loosen his hands, Lexie jerked her knee as hard as she could into his groin.

She didn't get a direct hit on his balls, but she must've at least glanced off them because Magnus grunted and his hands loosened for a fraction of a second. It was enough for Lexie to get a bit of oxygen into her lungs—but not enough for him to let go of her throat.

Magnus shifted and practically threw Lexie to the floor, tightening his hold around her neck as he followed her down.

She felt her head bounce off the floor, but it didn't hurt. Nothing did.

"*Bitch*," he snarled as he straddled her chest, putting all his weight on her.

Lexie's feet scrambled against the tile floor, trying to get some traction, without luck. She tried to buck Magnus off but he was too heavy. Too strong.

She tried to move a hand between them to grab and twist his dick, but she couldn't quite reach. She was quickly running out of options.

"Just fucking *die* already!" Magnus shouted, panting now as he squeezed her throat. "It's all planned. Theo's dead already. I invited him in when I arrived and stabbed him in the back. And when *you* die, I'm gonna drag your body out and put you under him. I'll tell the authorities I found him strangling you. I had to stab him to get him to stop...but it was too late. I'll tell them all about him following you...about the fact he's fucking batshit crazy. Everyone will back me up! And I'll be free to head home, knowing I've avenged Dagmar."

Blackness began to creep in from the sides of Lexie's eyes. The shit thing was, his plan had a pretty damn good chance of succeeding.

And she'd had no inkling he'd hated her so much.

"Die, bitch!" growled the man she'd come to think of as a friend, even as he leaned forward, putting yet more pressure on her neck.

Lexie had no idea how much time had passed. Three minutes? Four? She desperately tried one more time to kick her legs, to dislodge him, but it was no use. He was bigger and heavier, and he had rage on his side.

Her thoughts once again turned to Midas. How upset he was going to be that he hadn't protected her. And the thought of Magnus playing the part of the grieving coworker, and everyone believing he was a hero, was absolutely repulsive.

The last thing Lexie saw before she lost consciousness was a pair of evil blue eyes glaring down at her.

* * *

Midas was irritated. When he pulled into the coffee shop parking lot, the line at the drive-through was eight cars deep. It would take forever to get Lex's coffee, return to Food For All, and then get back on the road. At this time of the morning, there were usually only one or two cars ahead of him. He hated not to get Lexie her treat, but he didn't want to be late for PT.

So he turned around without the coffee, already thinking of ways to make it up to her as he headed back downtown.

There was a parking space not too far from the front of Food For All, which he took as a sign to stop, coffee or no coffee. It was silly to come back so soon after dropping her off, but it had become a small tradition between them, and besides, he loved being around her. Even if it was only for an additional five minutes each morning.

Midas strode toward the building, his thoughts going to the night before. He and Lexie were extremely well-matched, in bed and out. He'd never enjoyed sex as much as he did with Lex, but more than that, he loved *sleeping* with her. Loved how she draped herself over him and used his shoulder as a pillow. It reminded him of when they'd done just that for hours in Galkayo. Of course, now they were much more comfortable, and no one was trying to hunt them down.

Smiling at the memory of her grumbling as he shifted too much under her this morning, Midas reached for the door to Food For All, preparing to knock...

But the knob moved easily under his hand. The door was unlocked.

Frowning, he entered—and immediately, all loving thoughts fled from his mind.

A bloody trail led from the middle of the floor toward the small hallway leading to the kitchen.

Midas reached for his KBAR knife, and swore when he remembered he was in his PT uniform of a T-shirt and shorts. He had no weapons other than his hands.

He didn't immediately see the source of the bloody trail on the floor, and he moved silently toward the hall, praying harder than he'd ever prayed in his life that it wasn't Lexie's blood.

As he turned a corner, Midas saw a man attempting to

drag himself toward the kitchen, and immediately recognized him. Theo.

Midas knew he had a habit of coming in first thing in the mornings. Even though it made him leery, Lexie had reassured him that she was never alone with him, that if something did happen, one of her coworkers would be there to help her.

But something had definitely happened, and clearly Theo wasn't the aggressor. The man hadn't stabbed *himself* in the back, and Midas was one hundred percent sure that Lexie hadn't done it. She didn't have it in her.

That meant someone else was there.

Midas stopped long enough to put a hand on Theo's shoulder. "Easy," he said in a toneless whisper. But Theo heard it. He looked up, and Midas could see blood coming from his mouth. Whoever had stabbed him had most likely hit a lung. He was lucky they hadn't hit his heart, which Midas guessed had been the plan.

"Lexie!" Theo whispered in a tortured tone.

"I'm gonna get her. Hang on."

Theo didn't respond, just collapsed on the floor with a long sigh.

Midas crept on the balls of his feet toward the kitchen and peered around the door. He didn't immediately see anyone, but he heard a deep voice, indicating someone was inside.

Knowing the element of surprise would definitely work in his favor, Midas moved quickly. He stalked around the edge of the counter—and even before his brain could process what he was seeing, he was moving.

His training kicked in and Midas leapt toward the man straddling Lexie.

He wrapped his arm around the man's throat and wrenched him away from his woman. He had surprise on his side, and the man let out a startled cry as Midas hauled him backward.

He had a single moment to register the fact that bruises were already forming around Lexie's throat, and she was utterly still, before the man in his arms began to struggle.

"I was trying to help her!" he yelled. "Let me go!"

Magnus.

Midas might not know what was going on, but he knew with one hundred percent certainty Magnus had *not* been trying to help Lexie.

The two men wrestled, but Midas had fear for the love of his life on his side. Both men struggled to their feet, though Midas hadn't loosened his grip. Magnus flailed and tried to buck Midas off his back.

Midas could barely contain him. The man might be in his fifties, but he possessed the kind of strength only a fucking insane person could have. He fought hard, not making it easy for Midas to subdue him or knock him out, so he could get to Lexie.

The fight was strangely quiet, both men concentrating on trying to get the upper hand. Magnus grunted and growled while Midas fought in silence as he'd been trained. After what seemed like ages but was likely just a few minutes, Midas's military hand-to-hand combat training began to win out over the other man's desperate struggles.

Then Magnus suddenly sagged, making Midas stumble backward as he instinctively tried to hold up the man's dead weight.

Magnus used the opportunity to grab a knife that was sitting on the counter by the sink. He wildly threw his arm back, aiming for any part of Midas's body he could reach. He swiveled, and Magnus missed, immediately swinging blindly once more.

Knowing it was only a matter of time before the man got

in a lucky strike, Midas struggled to keep hold of Magnus while trying to disarm him at the same time.

Magnus suddenly found his voice. "Fucking bitch should've died in that desert! They should've let my brother go and kept her! Let me go so I can fucking finish this! *Dagmar deserves justice!*"

Midas couldn't even guess why Magnus had suddenly snapped and tried to kill Lexie, but with the man's frantic, impassioned words, it all made sense.

Everything had been a ruse. The messages, the phone calls...befriending Lexie. The decision to take up where his brother had left off with Food For All.

He'd done it all to get to Lexie.

And if this wasn't finished here and now, he'd try again. Midas could hear it in the other man's voice. He wasn't going to stop.

Theo hadn't been the threat. All along, it had been Magnus.

"Put down the knife," he ordered in a low, harsh tone, trying to get through to Magnus.

"Fuck you!"

Midas's eyes went to Lexie. She hadn't moved since he'd pulled Magnus off her. Every second he spent trying to subdue Magnus was one second she might not have. He needed to end this and get to his woman...

So Midas did what he'd been trained to do. He eliminated the threat.

It wasn't easy to kill someone by snapping their neck. In fact, it was damn near impossible. But that didn't mean Midas couldn't do a hell of a lot of damage. Taking a deep breath, tuning out Magnus's shouts, Midas forced the man's chin up, then jerked his neck as hard as he could to one side, letting go of his body at the same time.

Predictably, Magnus's body flew sideways, landing face first on the floor.

Midas staggered toward him. He'd pound the other man's head on the floor to knock him out, or get an arm around his neck and cut off his air, making him lose consciousness. If he'd already paralyzed Magnus in the process of wrenching his neck, so be it. At least then he wouldn't be able to hurt Lexie.

But Midas had forgotten about the knife the other man had been swinging wildly. When Magnus fell, he'd landed on his own hand.

And the knife.

Blood immediately began to pool under his body. Magnus twitched a few times, and gurgled, but he didn't get up or come after Midas again.

Sparing two more precious seconds to make sure the man was no longer a threat, Midas rolled Magnus. The knife was sticking out of his chest. It was obvious from the vacant stare on his face that the threat was eliminated.

Midas didn't spare another thought for the man. All his concentration shifted to Lexie.

He dropped to his knees beside her and felt for a pulse. "Come on," he pleaded as he tried to control his shaking hands enough to see if she needed CPR.

Just when he was about to bend over to administer rescue breaths, her eyes popped open and her hands flew up. She fought. Fought for her life.

Midas tried to catch her wrists, but she was too frantic, clawing at his face, his arms, anything she could reach.

"It's me, Lex! You're okay. You're okay!" he shouted, trying to break through the terror blanketing her features.

It took several moments, but finally her gaze cleared a fraction.

"It's me, Midas. You're okay. Take a deep breath, love."

Her mouth opened, and she took the longest, most heart-breaking breath he'd ever heard someone take in his life.

Then she did it again, and again. Until she was almost hyperventilating.

"Slow it down. You're okay. You can breathe now. All the air you want. Easy, Lexie."

"Magnus," she croaked.

"I know. He won't hurt you anymore."

She frantically looked around, then picked up her head, wincing as the muscles in her throat protested the movement.

"No, lay back down," Midas ordered, easing her head back to the floor.

But it was too late. She'd seen Magnus lying near their feet. "Dead?" she asked.

"I'm pretty sure. And I hope like hell he is," Midas told her honestly. "I need to call for help," he said. And for just a second, her fingers tightened around his biceps, but then she took another deep breath and gave him an almost imperceptible nod.

Fuck, this woman slayed him.

"I'll be right back."

"Theo?" she asked.

"He's hurt," Midas told her, not wanting to tell her the truth, that it would be a miracle if the man lived, but respecting her enough to not completely lie.

She pushed at him then, as if urging him to hurry up and call the police.

Midas wanted to smile, but he didn't have it in him. Of course she'd be more worried about Theo than herself.

He found her cell phone lying on the counter next to a coffee machine and immediately dialed 9-1-1. He informed the dispatcher of what had happened and made sure she knew the urgency of the situation. Midas knew he was supposed to stay on the line, but he couldn't. He clicked off the connection, put the phone back on the counter, nudged Magnus with his foot—satisfied when the man didn't move—and knelt on the floor next to Lexie once again.

"They're comin'," he told her. He picked up one of her hands and held it tightly within his own. He wanted to lie down next to her. Wanted to make sure she truly was still breathing and her heart was still beating. But all he could do was hold on for dear life.

* * *

Three hours later, it was all Midas could do to keep Lexie in her hospital bed.

"I'm fine, Midas," she insisted.

The huskiness of her voice belied her words. As did the marks on her throat. He couldn't stop thinking about the fact that if he'd stayed in line to get her a coffee, he would've been too late. Magnus would've choked the life out of her.

"Humor me," he pleaded.

"I want to see Theo," she said with a pout.

"I know you do, but he just got out of surgery," Midas told her.

"He was trying to crawl to the kitchen to help me," she whispered.

Midas pressed his lips together and nodded. He had. He absolutely had. And in doing so, had fucked up Magnus's plan. If he'd succeeded in killing Lexie, dragging her body back into the other room, it would've been hard for Magnus to explain the smear of blood across the floor. But luckily, the asshole hadn't succeeded. He'd missed hitting Theo's heart when he'd stabbed him, and Midas had arrived in time to stop him from strangling Lexie.

A commotion outside the door had Midas standing and spinning, ready to defend Lexie from whatever threat was coming. But it wasn't a threat. It was Elodie. And Ashlyn. And Slate and Mustang. The rest of the guys were in the waiting room. They'd refused to leave as long as Midas was there.

"Lex!" Elodie exclaimed as she rushed toward the bed.

Midas tried to step out of the way, but Lexie refused to let go of his hand. So he moved to stand by her hip as she greeted her friends.

"I'm okay," she croaked.

Ashlyn sniffed behind Elodie.

"Don't cry," Lexie ordered. "If you do, you'll get me started."

"S-sorry," Ashlyn said—then she burst into tears.

The next thing Midas knew, he was surrounded by three sobbing women. But he didn't say a word, nor did Mustang or Slate. The best thing they could do was release their fears and stress. He ran his thumb over the back of Lexie's hand as she attempted to get herself under control.

Finally, Ashlyn turned to him and said, "He's dead. Right?"

Midas nodded. He wasn't sorry in the least that Magnus was dead, he was just sorry he hadn't been the one to end his life. If the jerk to the neck hadn't stopped his attack, Midas had every intention of bashing his head into the floor, but the knife he'd fallen on had punctured his aorta, making him bleed out in seconds, doing the job for him.

"Good," Ashlyn said vehemently.

"I can't believe he planned the entire thing," Elodie said.

"The cops found the guy who harassed you the other evening," Slate told them. "He claimed Magnus paid him to do it."

"Which is good," Ashlyn said.

"Good?" Elodie asked with a frown.

"Yes, it means that he never would've done it if he hadn't been paid."

"True," Elodie agreed. "And Theo was never a threat to you either. Magnus was going to blame him for everything."

Lexie nodded, and Midas saw the guilt in her eyes return.

"We appreciate you coming, but maybe we can all talk about this later?" he suggested.

Elodie and Ashlyn immediately nodded.

"Come by my place tomorrow afternoon. You can stay as long as you want," Midas told them.

"Okay. Don't think I won't take you up on that," Elodie warned.

"You'll probably get sick of us hanging around," Ashlyn added.

"Never," Midas assured them.

"Thanks for coming, guys. I promise I'm good. I'll be back at work soon."

"No, you won't. Natalie told me to tell you she's giving you two weeks off. And if she sees your butt back before then, she's gonna be pissed," Ashlyn informed her.

"But—"

"No buts," Ashlyn told her. "And... I didn't get to tell you before, was planning on breaking the news this afternoon, but we got the green light to set up a Food For All location in Barbers Point."

Lexie beamed. "We did?"

"Yup." Ashlyn smiled, then glanced at Elodie. "You still interested?"

"Yes!" the other woman said immediately.

"Awesome. By the time you come back, we'll have more info," Ashlyn told Lexie.

"That's great."

"Okay, it's time to go," Slate said, stepping toward Ashlyn and taking her elbow in his hand.

Midas was somewhat surprised that Ashlyn didn't immediately yank her arm out of his grip. Instead, she simply nodded. "We'll see you tomorrow, Lex," she called as she let Slate usher her toward the door.

"I'm really glad you're all right," Elodie said. "I'll bring by some of the four hundred and twenty-two magazines Scott bought me while I was healing."

"Thanks," Lexie said.

Midas gave his friends a chin lift. "Tell the guys they can head home. Lex should be discharged tomorrow morning."

"Will do," Mustang said. "Expect to see us all there."

Midas nodded. He didn't need his friends to help him get Lexie settled in his home, but he sure did appreciate them being there all the same.

When it was just the two of them alone once more, Midas sat on the edge of the bed and smoothed his hand over her hair. He tried to ignore the ugly marks on her neck. They'd fade, as would hopefully the memory of seeing her lying unconscious on the floor with Magnus hovering over her.

"Are you all right?" she asked.

Midas smiled. He wasn't surprised she was worried about him. "Yeah. How about *you*?"

"I'm sad," she said. "I thought Magnus was my friend."

"I know," Midas said. And he did. She'd obsess over what had happened for a long time to come. He knew *he* would. He'd think about the signs he may have missed. What he could've done differently.

"The thing is, I kind of understand why."

"Why he tried to kill you?" Midas asked in disbelief.

"No, not that. That was fucked up. I mean how he went crazy. He and Dagmar were twins. They were connected in a way that not many people can understand. Did you know that some people can actually feel it when their twin is hurt? Even if they live thousands of miles apart? I imagine that Dagmar's death probably left a huge hole inside Magnus. I'm not condoning what he did. But the pain he must've been in had to have been overwhelming."

Midas pressed his lips together. He didn't understand it. Not at all. He'd lost men who were close to him. As close as brothers. No, none had been his twin, but the pain had been intense.

Magnus should've embraced Lexie's friendship. He would've gotten so much out of it. But instead, he was full of hate and misplaced anger toward her. She didn't kill Dagmar. She didn't ask the kidnappers to raise the ransom amount. From what she'd told him, she'd begged them to let Dagmar go. But of course that hadn't happened. And Dagmar had died. It was a tragedy all around. He was just so damn glad things hadn't ended differently today.

"You don't agree," Lexie said after a minute.

"No," Midas said with a shake of his head. "But I love your tender heart. I love your kindness and ability to forgive."

"I don't forgive him," Lexie told him. "I'll never forget how he crouched over me and spewed hatred while his hands tightened on my throat. But he's gone. And I'm still here. He failed. Fuck him. I have you. And Elodie and Ashlyn. And your team. Even Baker. And Theo."

Midas sighed. "He's gonna be your new project, isn't he?"

She gave him a small smile. "Yup. He needs someone to look out for him, like he tried to do for me."

"And that's us, huh?"

"Yup."

"I can live with that," Midas said. And he could. The man had desperately tried to get to Lexie when she'd needed him the most. He had a feeling those times he'd been seen watching Lex, he'd actually been watching *over* her, not stalking her with the intent to do her harm. Time would tell, but for now, he'd do what he could to help the man.

"Do you think he'll be out of recovery and awake enough to have visitors before we leave?" Lexie asked.

Midas couldn't help but smile.

"What?"

"You. I don't know. But we'll find out."

"Thanks. Midas?"

"Yeah, love?"

"I never did get my coffee this morning," she said with a pout.

With that, Midas burst out laughing. "I love you," he told her.

"And I love you," she returned.

Her eyes drooped, and Midas knew she had to be exhausted.

"Sleep."

"You won't leave?"

"Nothing could tear me from your side." He picked up her hand and kissed the back.

"Okay, maybe for an hour or so. But then I want you to check on Theo."

"I will."

Midas sat at her side as she slipped off into sleep. He couldn't take his eyes from her.

Life was fleeting, he knew that more than most men, but he wanted as many minutes, hours, days, years with this woman as he could get.

He didn't know how he'd gotten lucky enough to have caught her eye, but he'd do whatever it took to make sure she never regretted choosing him.

EPILOGUE

Dear Lexie,

Thank you seems light compared to what you have done for me and my family. I did not assist you for money. You saved my family when we needed it, and I never forgot. The scholarship to the university will allow me to get an education so I can get a job and help my family. And my brother and sister will also be able to go. My mom cry when she found out. It is like I told you, I want to learn how to do for myself so I can help my country. I am sorry my English is not so good, but I will be better.

Sincerely,
Shermake

Lexie wiped a tear off her cheek and put down the letter she'd received in the mail. She went looking for Midas and knew exactly where to find him. He was in the backyard, picking some mangos for dessert.

She walked up behind him and wrapped her arms around his waist, laying her cheek on his back.

"You okay?" Midas asked.

"Perfect," she said with a sigh.

Midas turned in her grasp and put his finger under her chin, tilting her face up so he could see her eyes. Ever since he'd walked in on Magnus trying to kill her, he'd been over-protective. But Lexie couldn't blame him.

"You've been crying," he said.

"Shermake sent me a letter," she told him.

"He all right?"

"He's great. He was just thanking me. Although he really should be thanking you and Baker," Lexie said.

Midas shrugged.

It had been a month since the incident at Food For All. Sometimes it was hard to believe so much time had passed, and in other ways it felt like yesterday. Plans were progressing for the new location, and hopefully within another month or two, it would be open. Ashlyn and Lexie had been working nonstop to meet the local business owners in Barbers Point and to let them know the plans for the organization. So far, they'd had nothing but positive reactions.

Elodie was also getting excited about helping out, and had started gathering recipes for the lunch boxes she'd be in charge of putting together. The new location wouldn't have hot meals, but it would provide nutritious take-away meals for those who needed them.

Midas reached for Lexie's hand and pulled her toward the chairs on the deck. He put down the mango he'd picked and sat, bringing Lexie with him. She sat without complaint, settling into Midas. He'd been more touchy-feely recently, which was perfectly all right with her.

"So, you gonna officially move in or what?" he asked.

Lexie blinked in surprise, though, she really shouldn't have been. She'd gotten used to Midas's abrupt topic changes.

And she'd been practically living with Midas ever since she'd come home from the hospital. He'd taken some time off work to stay with her and make sure she really was all right, and then he took her to work every day and picked her up as well. She was looking forward to the satellite branch opening so Midas didn't have to drive so much every day.

"I want to," she said, then hesitated.

"But?" Midas asked gently.

"I don't want to overstep. And I'm not ready to get married." The latter was something she'd been thinking about a lot. Elodie and Mustang had tied the knot fairly quickly after they'd met, but that was a big step for Lexie, and she wasn't sure she was ready yet.

"First, you aren't overstepping. I love you, and I love having you here. I never really thought much about living with a woman before, but now that you've been here, I can't imagine not waking up with you by my side every day or falling asleep with you in my arms. Second, I'm not ready for marriage either. I love you, and that's not going to change, but I like how things are going right now."

"Me too," Lexie said with a relieved sigh.

"I want you to meet my parents. And my brother and sister. I want to marry you on the beach in a laid-back, simple ceremony."

She grinned. "And if I want a huge formal shindig?"

Midas stared at her, as if trying to figure out if she was serious or not. She held the serious look as long as possible before grinning.

"That was mean," he said with a pout.

"I know, sorry. I don't want something huge," she reassured him. "The beach thing sounds amazing. If your folks don't like me, is that a deal breaker?" she asked nervously.

"You have nothing to worry about. They're gonna like you," Midas told her. "They already do. You know my mom's been bugging me to give her a time when she can come out and visit."

Lexie snuggled into his chest and sighed. "I'll move in," she told him. "I mean, the view is much better here than in my apartment."

Midas snorted. "I'm being used for my view," he said under his breath.

"Well, that, and I love you to distraction," Lexie told him. "You think Theo's gonna like living in Barbers Point?" Shit, now *she* was doing it, changing subjects on a whim. Midas was rubbing off on her.

He chuckled as if he knew what she was thinking. "I think he's gonna love it."

Midas had worked with Baker to find a tiny one-room apartment for Theo to live in He'd always have a roof over his head and wouldn't have to worry about rent. Lexie wasn't a millionaire, but she'd saved up a nice nest egg after years of free lodgings, thanks to Food For All. She wouldn't have a problem paying the rent for the small space for Theo. After learning he'd dragged himself across the floor to try to help her, even while the knife was still sticking out of his back, she'd do anything for the man.

She wished she could get him psychological help, but Theo had lived on his own on the streets for too long to be cooped up in a hospital. So she'd done what she could by providing him a safe place to sleep at night. The room wasn't far from where Food For All's new building was located, and Lexie would be able to see him every day.

"Love you, Lex."

"Love you back, Midas."

His hand shifted under her shirt and began to rub her bare back, and just like that, thoughts of Theo, Midas's parents, and even what she'd been planning to make for dinner flew out of her head.

She wanted Midas. Bad.

After she'd gotten out of the hospital, he'd been reluctant to initiate any sexy times, but Lexie hadn't had any problem convincing him that she was completely healed.

Sitting up and straddling his waist, Lexie scooted forward until she could feel his hard cock between his legs. Without a word, she reached for the hem of her shirt and pulled it over her head.

Midas smiled, palmed her ass, and leaned forward to nuzzle her breasts.

Yeah, it was safe to say she was one hundred percent happy.

* * *

Kenna Madigan did her best not to sound like an out-of-shape hippo as she ran near the Ala Moana Park, toward the Magic Island Lagoon. It was at the end of a piece of land across from the Ala Wai Boat Harbor. It was early, but there were other people out exercising like she was. Kenna didn't love running, but it was the best way to keep in shape, and to keep the Malasadas she loved so much from adding forty pounds to her average-sized frame.

This was a rare morning off for her, and she'd decided to get out into the Hawaiian sunshine and enjoy the day.

She was thinking about the errands she needed to get to before her waitressing shift at Duke's, not paying much attention to what was going on around her, when something to her right caught her eye. It was hard to figure out what she was looking at, but as she got closer, her eyes widened in horror.

A *body* was floating in the ocean, just on the other side of the lagoon!

It was a man. She knew that much from the size. He was wearing some sort of black wet suit and was face down, bobbing up and down.

Looking around, Kenna didn't see anyone else nearby. Certainly no one seemed concerned that someone was drowning.

Without thinking twice, Kenna sprinted around the edge of the lagoon. She peered down into the dark water and saw that the man hadn't moved. Immediately, she toed off her tennis shoes and whipped her tank top over her head. Wearing nothing but her socks, shorts, and sports bra, Kenna jumped into the ocean.

Unfortunately, but probably not surprisingly, she misjudged her leap into the water and instead of landing *near* the drowning man, she jumped right on top of him. Kenna wasn't known for being the most graceful person. Most of her coworkers teased her for being clumsy.

Thankful that she'd hit his legs and not his back, Kenna used her arms to bring herself back up to the surface before reaching for the drowning man.

But when her head broke the surface of the water, she found herself staring right into the confused and concerned eyes of the man she'd jumped in to save. He was very much neither dead *nor* drowning, and instead was looking at her as if she had a few screws loose.

He wore a black face mask, and she could now see the snorkel attached. As she treaded water and stared at him in shock, he pushed the mask onto the top of his head.

"Are you all right? Did you fall in?" he asked.

To complete her embarrassment, five more heads popped up in the water around them. Each had on the same black mask, but were also wearing scuba tanks on their backs.

"Oh shit," she said, knowing her cheeks were probably bright red. She had no idea why this group of men were scuba diving where they were, but she'd obviously screwed up. Bad.

"Ma'am?" the man she'd jumped on top of asked again.

"I'm fine," she said. "Um... I just..." Kenna looked around, trying to find the fastest way to climb up the rocks surrounding the lagoon so she could go home and die of mortification.

The man gripped her arm and easily held her above water. She was a good swimmer, but his grip definitely made it easier to float.

"What happened?" one of the other men asked.

"She fall in?"

"She hurt?"

"I'm trying to find out, if you'd shut up and give me a second," the man holding her said.

Kenna couldn't help but grin slightly.

"Right, so...you fell in?" the man asked once more.

Staring into his dark eyes, Kenna was embarrassed all over again. "Not exactly. See, I was running up there," she said, indicating the path next to the lagoon. "Minding my own business, and I saw you. You were face down. Floating."

The man's lips twitched, and Kenna spoke faster, just wanting this over with. "I thought you were drowning, okay?"

"So you jumped in to save me?"

"Yeah," Kenna said sheepishly. "But you obviously aren't drowning, and I'm an idiot. So I'll just be going now." She looked over at the rocks meaningfully.

"We're SEALs," one of the other men said, obviously trying hard not to burst out laughing.

Aaaaand...Now her humiliation was complete.

"Didn't you see the scuba flag?" her not-drowning victim asked.

Turning her head, Kenna saw the red and white flag bobbing in the water nearby.

"Obviously not," she said with a shrug. "I just thought you were drowning and acted."

"Well, I appreciate it. I'm in charge of safety for our training today, so my job is to hang out up here while my team does their thing under the water. Which is why it probably looked like I was a dead body. Anyway, I'm Marshall."

"Kenna," she said, feeling as if she were in the twilight zone. Treading in the ocean and meeting a hot guy, a Navy freaking SEAL at that, wasn't what she thought she'd be doing today.

"Be back, guys," he told his friends.

"Don't mind us, Aleck," one of them said.

"Yeah, training can wait," another added.

"Pretty girls come before scuba any day," a third called out.

"I thought you said your name was Marshall," Kenna said.

"It is. My nick name is Aleck, it's what most people call me," he said. "But you can call me Marshall."

He kept hold of her arm and began to swim with her toward some rocks a bit away from his buddies, where it looked like she could climb up and out of the water somewhat easily.

"I can swim," she told him.

"I know," he said, without letting her go.

When she reached the rocks, Kenna wanted to scurry up as fast as she could, but clearly the man had other ideas.

"Don't be embarrassed that you were trying to help me," Marshall said. "Seriously, if more people got involved when they saw something wrong, I think the world would be a better place."

"But nothing *was* wrong," she told him.

Marshall shrugged.

"Right. Okay, well then...have fun with your training and whatnot," she said lamely as she reached up to grab one of the rocks and pull herself out of the water. She'd come to terms with her body a while ago, and had a pretty healthy self-esteem, but exposing herself in her sports bra to this man who didn't have an extra ounce of fat on him—based on what she could see from that wet suit he was wearing—wasn't exactly high on her list of things to do.

And she couldn't hang out in the ocean all day. The sooner she got out, the sooner she could get back to her apartment to try to pretend this never happened.

"Can I see you again?" he asked suddenly.

Kenna froze. "What?"

"I mean, I'd like to thank you properly...for trying to save my life and all."

If she wasn't mistaken, Marshall sounded...unsure. Why this man would ever need to be unsure while asking someone out, she had no idea.

"Um...okay," she said without thinking. Then mentally winced.

"Great," he said with a smile. "When? Where?"

"Duke's? I'll be there tonight."

The second the words were out of her mouth, Kenna wanted to take them back.

"Sounds good. Is seven okay?"

Kenna nodded.

She could've sworn she felt Marshall's thumb brush against her upper arm before he swam away from her.

"See you later then. Be careful."

"I will." Kenna began to climb out of the water, refusing to look back to see if Marshall was watching her. When she got to the top, there were a few people running by, but no one really offered to help. Luckily, her shoes were still lying where she'd left them.

Not able to resist, she looked back down into the water and saw Marshall staring up at her.

She gave him a lame wave, then rushed to her belongings. She grabbed her shirt and shoes and headed back the way she came. Exercising was done for the day.

Why had she told him to come to Duke's? Yes, it was a super popular restaurant on Waikiki Beach, so she wouldn't have to worry about being in danger if he showed up. But she was working tonight, and as a waitress, it wasn't as if she could sit and hang out with him.

"Stupid," she muttered to herself.

But she couldn't help taking one last look behind her as she hurried down the sidewalk. Marshall was back with his friends now, and they were all smiling as he said something to them.

Shaking her head, Kenna turned back around and squished her way back toward her apartment.

* * *

How's that for a hilarious meet-cute? Jumping in the water to save a Navy SEAL?!? ha! Find out what how their first date goes and what trouble is in the horizon in *Finding Kenna!*

Want to talk to other Susan Stoker fans? Join my reader group, Susan Stoker's Stalkers, on Facebook!

Also by Susan Stoker

SEAL Team Hawaii Series

Finding Elodie
Finding Lexie (Aug 2021)
Finding Kenna (Oct 2021)
Finding Monica (TBA)
Finding Carly (TBA)
Finding Ashlyn (TBA)
Finding Jodelle (TBA)

SEAL of Protection Series

Protecting Caroline
Protecting Alabama
Protecting Fiona
Marrying Caroline (novella)
Protecting Summer
Protecting Cheyenne
Protecting Jessyka
Protecting Julie (novella)
Protecting Melody
Protecting the Future
Protecting Kiera (novella)
Protecting Alabama's Kids (novella)
Protecting Dakota

SEAL of Protection: Legacy Series

Securing Caite
Securing Brenae (novella)
Securing Sidney
Securing Piper
Securing Zoey
Securing Avery
Securing Kalee

Securing Jane

Delta Force Heroes Series

Rescuing Rayne
Rescuing Aimee (novella)
Rescuing Emily
Rescuing Harley
Marrying Emily (novella)
Rescuing Kassie
Rescuing Bryn
Rescuing Casey
Rescuing Sadie (novella)
Rescuing Wendy
Rescuing Mary
Rescuing Macie (novella)

Delta Team Two Series

Shielding Gillian
Shielding Kinley
Shielding Aspen
Shielding Jayme (novella)
Shielding Riley
Shielding Devyn
Shielding Ember (Sep 2021)
Shielding Sierra (Jan 2022)

Badge of Honor: Texas Heroes Series

Justice for Mackenzie
Justice for Mickie
Justice for Corrie
Justice for Laine (novella)
Shelter for Elizabeth
Justice for Boone
Shelter for Adeline
Shelter for Sophie

Justice for Erin
Justice for Milena
Shelter for Blythe
Justice for Hope
Shelter for Quinn
Shelter for Koren
Shelter for Penelope

Ace Security Series

Claiming Grace
Claiming Alexis
Claiming Bailey
Claiming Felicity
Claiming Sarah

Mountain Mercenaries Series

Defending Allye
Defending Chloe
Defending Morgan
Defending Harlow
Defending Everly
Defending Zara
Defending Raven

Silverstone Series

Trusting Skylar
Trusting Taylor
Trusting Molly
Trusting Cassidy (Dec 2021)

Stand Alone

The Guardian Mist
Nature's Rift
A Princess for Cale
A Moment in Time- A Collection of Short Stories

Another Moment in Time- A Collection of Short Stories
Lambert's Lady

Special Operations Fan Fiction
http://www.AcesPress.com

Beyond Reality Series
Outback Hearts
Flaming Hearts
Frozen Hearts

Writing as Annie George:
Stepbrother Virgin (erotic novella)

ABOUT THE AUTHOR

New York Times, USA Today and *Wall Street Journal* Bestselling Author Susan Stoker has a heart as big as the state of Tennessee where she lives, but this all American girl has also spent the last fourteen years living in Missouri, California, Colorado, Indiana, and Texas. She's married to a retired Army man who now gets to follow *her* around the country.

She debuted her first series in 2014 and quickly followed that up with the SEAL of Protection Series, which solidified her love of writing and creating stories readers can get lost in.

If you enjoyed this book, or any book, please consider leaving a review. It's appreciated by authors more than you'll know.

www.stokeraces.com
www.AcesPress.com
susan@stokeraces.com

facebook.com/authorsusanstoker
twitter.com/Susan_Stoker
instagram.com/authorsusanstoker
goodreads.com/SusanStoker
bookbub.com/authors/susan-stoker
amazon.com/author/susanstoker

Made in the USA
Las Vegas, NV
09 October 2021